C000069911

Tudor Warrior

Book 1 in the Tudor Warrior series
By
Griff Hosker

Tudor Warrior

Published by Sword Books Ltd 2022

Copyright ©Griff Hosker First Edition

Contents

Historical characters

King Henry VII-King of England
King Richard III
Jasper Tudor- Duke of Bedford and the uncle of King Henry VII
Edward Plantagenet- son of the Duke of Clarence and nephew of King Richard III, a prisoner in the tower
Margaret of York, the Dowager Duchess of Burgundy
Lord Thomas Stanley- Earl of Derby
Sir Henry Clifford- Lord of Craven
Sir Robert Clifford- A Yorkist
Sir Henry Percy-Earl of Northumberland
Lambert Simnel- pretender to the throne
Pierrekin Wezebeque aka Perkin Warbeck, pretender to the throne
Sir Richard Ratcliffe-*The Rat*
Sir William Catesby *The Cat*
Viscount Lovell- a Yorkist leader who escaped the slaughter at Bosworth Field -*The Dog*
John de la Pole- Earl of Lincoln and leader of the rebels
Gerald FitzGerald, 8th Earl of Kildare
Thomas FitzGerald of Laccagh, Lord Chancellor of Ireland
John Scrope, 5th Baron Scrope of Bolton
Thomas Scrope, 6th Baron Scrope of Masham
King James IV of Scotland

Prologue

1485 Bosworth Field

Viscount Francis Lovell could not believe that the day was going so badly for the Ricardians, the supporters of King Richard. King Richard was a better leader and knight than Henry Tudor and he had more men. Even the defection by Stanley could not explain the disaster that was unfolding before his eyes. The planning had been perfect and they had chosen a site that suited them. They had much better men and they even had some of the new cannons. Sir Francis, along with his two close friends, Sir William Catesby and Sir Richard Ratcliffe, had been sure that the opposition to King Richard would end here on Bosworth Field. The king was a better and braver warrior than Henry Tudor. The insulting anti-Ricardian squib, 'the Cat, the Rat and Lovell our dog' had merely made the three more determined to wipe out the anti-royalist faction. Even as Lovell looked for his next enemy to slay he saw that Henry Percy, the Earl of Northumberland was hanging back. He had been told to protect King Richard's flank. Too many men had failed to fight as hard as they could. King Richard had recklessly driven his horsemen towards the dismounted Henry Tudor, his bodyguard, men at arms and billmen.

Further to the right of the Viscount, Sir William Catesby was having exactly the same thoughts. He swung his poleaxe to chop through the leg of the Burgundian hand gunner whose weapon had killed two of Sir William's friends. He looked at the standard of King Richard, carried by Sir Percival Thirlwall, as King Richard led his two hundred armoured horsemen to the standard of Henry Tudor. The battle looked lost but if King Richard could end the life of Henry Tudor then defeat could turn into victory. Sir William wished that it was he and not his friend Sir Richard Ratcliffe that was close to the horse of King Richard, White Surrey. Sir William knew he was the better horseman but Sir Richard had been insistent. As Henry Tudor was on foot, despite being protected by a large number of men on foot, Sir William Catesby spied hope and believed that King Richard would win. When King Richard slew Sir William Brandon and the standard of Henry Tudor fell to the ground, then victory seemed to be in their grasp. It was at that critical moment that Lord Thomas Stanley showed his true colours, and the Earl of Derby led his own men, thus far unused, to charge into the flank of the rear of the men they had been supposed to support. Watching the act Sir William wondered if this had been prearranged. While King Richard was a better knight and warrior, Henry Tudor was a cunning man and was more than capable of such a deception. When Sir Richard Ratcliffe was hacked in the side by an English billman and then King Richard unhorsed, Catesby knew that all was lost. Sir Percival had both legs chopped off, but he refused to yield the standard. Those around King Richard were butchered where they stood. As Sir William looked around, he saw that King Richard's faltering army was now fleeing. Even his good friend Viscount Lovell was seeking an escape from this disaster. Sir William was made of sterner stuff and he swung his poleaxe even harder at a Swiss pikeman as he tried to get to the side of the king. The axe head split the pike and Catesby used the spike to drive it into the face of the mercenary. It was as he looked up that he saw King Richard had lost both his helmet and his crown. Welsh and English billmen and halberdiers were hacking at the King's head and, as Sir William Catesby was brought down by three Germans, the army of King Richard disintegrated. The Earl of Northumberland rode north having barely drawn his sword in the defence of the king. He was a pragmatic man and he had done all that was asked of him. He reconciled himself with the thought that it was the desertion of Stanley and the reckless charge of King Richard that had lost them the battle.

Viscount Francis was luckier than his two companions and even while the new king's name was ringing out across the battlefield, Viscount Francis removed his surcoat and used it to dress a corpse with a smashed-in face and found a wandering horse to make good his escape. There were simply too many of the defeated fleeing and too few horsemen in Henry Tudor's army to find a solitary warrior. Viscount Francis vowed vengeance upon Henry Tudor and all those who had killed what he believed to be the rightful King of England. He would rise like a phoenix. The cause of the Ricardians might be ended but the Yorkists could still rise. Edward Plantagenet was in the Tower and he would be a rallying point for those unhappy with the Welshman taking England's crown. Margaret of York was now Duchess of Burgundy and he would seek her help. He rode to Colchester and then disappeared. The disguised body was taken to be his and no-one sought the Viscount.

The king was dead and the new king reigned supreme but the threat from those who supported Richard was not over and with doubt over the deaths of those with a claim to the throne then Henry Tudor was not secure.

Chapter 1

1487 Ecclestone Lancashire

I am James son of Walter the Rat Slayer and when my father returned from the last battle of the civil war, it turned my head. I was the eldest child and when my father was away fighting for Henry Tudor it had been me who worked the land and it was hard work. It made for a broad back and strong arms. My two younger sisters helped but it was a hard life. I was my mother's favourite and had been named after her father, Jamie, a Scotsman who had settled after a wild and adventurous life in this part of southwest Lancashire. Until I was ten, I had been called Jamie, but then I had decided that James sounded more manly. I had seen just fourteen summers when he returned from the battle and I was a better person than I became. I was full of myself in those days. It was a combination of the gold my father brought back, the farm but, probably, my father's reputation that turned my head and I confess it now, I did not see it at the time. There was no mirror for me to see the monster I was about to become.

When my father returned from Bosworth and hung his billhook and falchion in the shed, I begged him to train me as a billman. They had formed a large part of the army brought by Henry Tudor to fight the Yorkists. Those and the archers had been the reason that they won. At least that was what my father said, and I believed him. With their helmets, padded brigandines called a jack, falchions and, most importantly, the bill hooks they used, they were a force to be feared and the fact that he had brought down a knight in plate armour riding a mailed horse, was a testament to that skill. He agreed to my request and while we worked the new land for six days a week, on Sunday when men were commanded by law to practise, he showed me his skills. At first, we used staves for it was less dangerous. As with all weapons, there is a skill to using a bill hook which men like my father make look easy. For the first six months, all was well and then my father took me, on the anniversary of the Battle of Bosworth Field, to the inn in the village, '*The Gryphon*'. There my head began to be turned. It did not happen overnight but when I heard all speaking of this hero of Bosworth, I began to take on the praise to my shoulders. It was as though they were complimenting me. I can see now that I was wrong, but I was young and foolish. I started to change. I began to resent the work around the farm. My sisters were able to stay in the house while my father and I worked in all weathers. He did not seem to mind but I thought it an insult for the hero of Bosworth Field.

The change in me coincided with the day that my father nodded and said, "Well done, James. You shall use a real billhook next time."

I almost felt myself swell with pride. My father had two. One was his and the other he had fetched back from the battle of Bosworth. I think it had belonged to a fallen comrade. The shaft had suffered a cut and he had replaced it. When I had been first shown the weapon and told that it would be mine, I treated it like a person. I kept the two blades as sharp as my father's shaving razor. I oiled them lovingly to stop the rust. I made sure that the hook, used for pulling horsemen from their saddles, was pointed and sharp as was the spike used to ram between metal plates. Warriors who had money were now well protected by metal plates on their bodies and legs. They thought that they were invulnerable but a spike could find a gap. My father told me all of this as we trained. All the practice with the stave had paid off although the first time I wielded the weapon the weight of the head came as a shock to me and my father had smiled when, after three or four practice strokes, the head had fallen from it.

"You need to tie a weight to your stave to help you become used to the weapon." I nodded and determined to become as good as he was.

There were only two other billmen in the village and the majority of those who practised were archers. My father was superior to the other two and as we trained each Sunday after church, I could see that, like my father, I had more natural skill than the other two. When I bested one, John Pendlebury, I felt I was ready to fight. That was when I had my first argument with my father. As we walked back to our home I boasted of my skill and he cuffed me about the head. I can see now that it was deserved for I, still a boy, had mocked a man grown and I had not shown him the respect he deserved.

"None of that, boy, for that is what you still are, a boy! John of Pendlebury is a good man and he was gentle with you for you are my son. I have stood shoulder to shoulder with him fighting our Yorkist enemies and I will not have you disparage him. As for being ready to fight then I will tell you that you are not. You will be ready when I say so."

I fell out with my father at that moment. How many times since have I regretted it? It was all my fault and I was a wild youth who thought he knew everything. I did not; few young men do. I began to resent him and look for ways to be disobedient. I became a bad son. It did not happen overnight but gradually I changed. The piglets of the wild boar are cute and adorable but the adult boar is a fearsome creature. I changed. What makes it all worse is that I was trying to be like my father when we fell out. I admired him and looked up to him more than anyone else. He was a hero. His name was Walter of Ecclestone and he was a Lancastrian billman. More than that he was the billman who had felled the Rat, Sir Richard Ratcliffe. King Henry himself had rewarded him with a bag of gold. It had enabled us to buy a smallholding in the village where we lived, and we went from being a family who worked for others to masters of our own destiny, producing our own food and owning our house. We had been happy then.

I took the cuff, but I brooded and the next Saturday after the evening meal I headed for the nearby village of Windle where there was another alehouse, *'The Raven's Head'*. It was a place where the younger men who wished to drink away from the eyes of their elders and betters could do so. The landlord was a disreputable man and my father had warned me to stay away from there. That, of course, made it even more attractive. My father paid me, and it was not a great deal but it was enough to drink the stronger ale there than I was used to. That first night I got into a fight and, sadly, I won. I was big, that came from my father, and the practice had given me skills. I say sadly for my victory over a youth whose name I cannot even remember added to my delusion that I was now a warrior. I saw myself on the battlefield slaying the king's enemies and not stuck on a small holding in Ecclestone where there was not even a cobbled road. I know not what caused the fight, it may have been the drink, I am not sure, but whatever the reason we left the alehouse and I knocked him to the ground so many times that he waved a hand in surrender. I was then applauded and received the accolades of the others. I was fooled by their false praise and my head grew. Others treated me to ale. When I returned home my father saw my bruised knuckles but said nothing. Perhaps he saw it as an inevitable event for young men. I wish he had said something, but he did not.

I could not afford to go to *'The Raven's Head'* often but when I had enough coins then I would go. The drink did something to me that made me become angry and belligerent. I got into fights on a regular basis. More often than not I won. On one occasion it was an honourable draw but that was the day my father said something. He had to for my face was battered and bruised and my mother was shocked.

"Son, I have tolerated this poor behaviour because I thought it was something that would pass and that you would grow out of. That has not happened. You are forbidden to leave this house and to go drinking."

The drink was still in me and I faced up to him, "You cannot do that for I am a man."

He gave me a sad smile and shook his head, "Not yet. You are almost the size but," he patted the side of his head, "in here you are still a child, and this is for your own good."

"You cannot stop me, and I will go."

He did not become angry, my father rarely did but he nodded, "And when you next leave then the door will be barred, and your belongings will be outside the house. You either obey me or you leave this home."

My mother had heard all, and I saw her hand go to her mouth. Despite my face and my behaviour, I was still her son and her favourite.

My father could have been vindictive and withheld pay from me but that was not his way. He continued to pay me for my labour. It was not much but it was money. He continued to practise with me each Sunday and even when I tried to hurt him in the combat, he both easily thwarted my efforts and yet did not use harsh words with me. When next I had money I chose not to go to the inn for at that moment I still thought he might relent and let me return to Windle. I did not know my father for he was a far better man than I knew. He was not just a great warrior and billman but he was also the best of fathers and a perfect husband. I did not see that. We had a few months of peace. We had Christmas and a sort of reconciliation and then we had snow and cold. There were no coins. It was only as January drifted into February that the fire of my anger was fuelled. It was when the pretender to the crown, Lambert Simnel, was raised as heir to the throne that things began to unravel. We only learned that his name was Lambert Simnel after the event. The news merely came that John de la Pole, the Earl of Lincoln was travelling to Burgundy to seek troops and have the boy, Edward, the Earl of Warwick crowned king of England. It was all a little vague and my father poured scorn on the idea, "Edward is the son of the Duke of Clarence, and he has a claim to the throne, but King Henry has him in the Tower. The one they parade in Burgundy is an imposter and this will come to nothing. There is but one Edward who has a claim to the throne and King Henry has him locked away. This is another Yorkist plot. We did not rid the land of all the rats at Bosworth, more's the pity."

"But if it does not, will you go to fight them?"

My father shook his head, "I am done fighting. The war that cost this country so much is over, and this is an attempt by the Yorkists and the Earl of Lincoln to resurrect a dead cause. I will not go."

I stared at him for what was the point of training every day if you did not get to fight? I was a good fighter; the inn in Windle had shown me that. "Then why do I train so hard if I am not to use my skills?"

He sighed, "Let me explain about how this works, James, for I ought to have done so when I began to train you. We train so that our lord, the Earl of Derby, can call upon us when he needs to and we will fight, for pay, for our lord and for our rightful king. That is how I always fought. The Earl of Derby has not asked for us and until he does we will stay. Men do not have to fight and I will not do so again. I lost brothers in arms at Bosworth and, when I was a young man, at Tewkesbury. I have no need to prove myself."

"But there are other ways to fight, are there not?"

He nodded, "Aye, there are captains, lords without land normally, who hire companies to fight for them. They are not like the companies that fought for the Black Prince for they are smaller. Nor are they like the White Company that fought in Italy. There are perhaps a hundred or two hundred men in each company and they fight for pay."

"I could join one of those."

He laughed and that made me become angry inside. He was not mocking me but laughing because the idea was ridiculous, "Son, you have a billhook and my old rondel dagger. You have neither jack nor helmet. None would hire you yet and, indeed, good as you are I do not think you are ready to go against men who would not be as forgiving as me. You are too young and although not a boy you are yet to become a man. John of Pendlebury did not fight you as hard as he might have, indeed as hard as he should. It has given you the idea that you are better than you are. Now enough of this. It is village gossip and nothing more. It will disappear like a morning fog."

Matters came to a head when we heard that a mercenary army had landed in Dublin and was led by the Earl of Lincoln, John de la Pole, and the man he said was the heir to the English throne, Edward Plantagenet. This time even my father took note as Dublin was but a short way across the sea from the coast close to where we lived. We were told to prepare for war should the Yorkists land close to our home. The beaches and dunes of Formby were a perfect place to land soldiers. When we had our practice on the next Sunday there was more purpose to it.

Sir Richard of Windle himself came to inspect us but his words were like a shower of cold water, "Lord Stanley has asked that the men of Ecclestone guard these manors under the command of that redoubtable hero of Bosworth, Walter of Ecclestone." The news was greeted with cheers as my father was popular. I began to wonder if I might get to fight despite my father's pessimism. "However, it is unlikely that you will be called upon to fight. The king has commanded the Earl of Northumberland and the Lord of Craven to raise an army and to be prepared to ride to meet these pretenders should they be foolish enough to land."

My moment of joy was crushed by the words. After the practice, I stood close enough to the knight and my father to hear their words.

"Is it a serious threat, my lord?"

"To here? No, but to England yes. The Irish have always supported King Richard and the Duke of Clarence was also very popular there. The Irish are always willing to fight the English and with the German and Swiss mercenaries then there is an army but the support for King Richard was ever in the lands around York and Middleham. That is where they shall make for and that is why it is the Earl of Northumberland who will lead the army. The Earl of Oxford, John de Vere, is also raising an army to protect London. All is well, Walter."

I was close enough to see the doubt on my father's face.

"Speak, Walter, for we both fought at Bosworth and there can be no hidden words or doubts between us."

My father nodded and I saw then the respect in which he was held for the knight meant what he had said, "The Earl of Northumberland was at Bosworth my lord and whilst he did not fight us his behaviour that day has made me doubt that he can be trusted. If he is the leader of the army to face his former comrades, then I am fearful."

Sir Richard said, "And King Henry along with the Earl of Oxford are ready to come north if Percy fails. The Earl of Northumberland is more handily placed. Do not fear, Walter, this will come to nothing, but we will be prepared in case they do not do as we expect."

I begged my father, after the knight had gone, for permission to seek a place with a company. I asked if I might march north to Skipton where the Lord of Craven would be. It was many miles to the north but it would be an adventure. I pictured myself with a helmet on my billhook leaving the village and all the girls crying at the brave warrior leaving Ecclestone. He would have none of it. Even when we heard, in May, that King Edward had been crowned in Dublin and that an invasion was imminent, he did not grant my request. It was when an old comrade in arms of my father called in and stayed for the night that matters came to a head. I had heard John's name mentioned and knew that he lived less than twenty miles from us, but I had never met him.

He was, like all archers, barrel-chested but unlike my father showed the ravages of time. My father always looked, despite the fact that he was middle-aged, to be fit. John of Warrington had the red face of a drinker and the belly to match. He was, however, an old comrade and my father greeted him warmly and offered him a bed for the night.

"Well, John, I can see from the longbow in its case and the sheath of arrows that you go to war."

The archer patted his gardyvyan and said, "Aye, I go north to seek employment with Sir Henry Clifford of Craven. He is raising a company to fight the rebels should they come."

As my father led his old comrade into the house he said, "Surely you are done with fighting? You and I are old men and have fought enough."

He shook his head and nodded to me, "I am not like you, Walter, I have no family. My wife left me after Tewksbury, and I tire of a life without war."

"What was it you did after Bosworth?"

He shook his head, "Became a ferryman across the river at Warrington. It kept my arms strong but that was all. I was made for war as are you, the Rat Slayer. Come, you and your boy join me."

My father's face clouded over, "I will not go, and I will not have my son go either. No more talk of war. I will give you a bed and we will feed you, but we will talk of other things."

Once more I saw that my father commanded respect and John of Warrington nodded, "You are right and I can see that you have a farm now. I understand and I will honour your request."

The two men did talk of war but it was a war that was in the past. They had been in many battles and they spoke not of the deaths and injuries but the humorous side of warlike knights falling from horses. They told of men becoming lost and arriving at battles the day after they had finished. They spoke of relieving the dead of their treasure. My mother frowned at that and made the sign of the cross; she saw it as robbing a corpse.

John the archer left before I was even up as he had a long walk if he was to make Skipton which I knew was where the Lords of Craven lived. I brooded all day, and it was that night as we went around the smallholding to check that the animals were all secure that the anger in me exploded. It was all in my head, of course. I exaggerated every insult my father had given to me. The cuff became a mighty blow. The order not to leave the farm became a deliberate torture in my mind and by the end of the day, I believed that he was afraid that I would become a better billman and achieve more than he ever had. Looking back I am ashamed of my thoughts and they make me squirm still but, at the time, all seemed reasonable. I was a man and I would go to war.

"I would follow John of Warrington, father."

"And I have said no. John of Warrington seeks either death in battle or great treasure. He has the chance of the former but not the latter. When his wife left him, she took his son and that broke his heart. He was a great archer but now he is a drunk. I doubt that he would be able to make a full draw. You stay here and become better at what you do. There will be other wars, the Scots have been quiet for some time and we are close enough that we would be the ones called upon to fight. Battling the enemies of your country is always better than fighting in a civil war, against brothers."

"No, I will go, and you cannot stop me."

"And I say that you will not go. I can bar the door and prevent you from taking your billhook. How is that?"

I saw red and pulling back my arm I hit him so hard on the jaw that he went down as though I had struck him with a poleaxe. He was not expecting it and that was why I succeeded. He had not thought his son would strike his father. I shocked myself and knelt to see that I had not killed him. It was at that moment that I made my decision. I would run; I had to for I had committed a great sin and struck my father. I could no longer stay. I went to the barn where we kept our weapons and I grabbed not only my billhook but my father's jack which I donned as well as his falchion and scabbard. There was a sack hanging there and I took it too putting in it a couple of lengths of bowstring and four fishhooks. I took the ale skin which hung there. It was empty but if I found a fresh stream, I could refill it. After putting on my rabbit skin hat I sneaked back to the house. I knew I would not have long until my father recovered his wits. Mother and my sisters were before the fire sewing where there was warmth from the fire. I slipped into the cool pantry and grabbed half a loaf of bread and I sliced off a large chunk of the salted ham which I deposited in my sack. That would have to do and after taking my oiled cloak, I closed the door silently and I slipped away before my father came to. I headed north towards Rivington. I stopped at the far end of the village where I rearranged my gear so that it was balanced. I hung the slightly curved falchion on my belt and slipped the helmet into the sack along with the arming cap. Those I hung from the billhook that I carried over my shoulder. I set off purposefully along the empty track that led first to Bleak Hill, through Windle and thence to Upholland. I would make as much time as I could but I planned on resting at Rivington before hurrying after John of Warrington. Hitting my father had been like burning my bridges. There could be no going back, and I was set on a course to be a warrior.

Chapter 2

I had travelled this road once before with my father but that had not been at night and then I had not been alone. It was a good start for my life alone as I learned as I trudged the road. I learned to smell the woodsmoke of houses so that I could avoid them before I reached them. Once I was twenty miles from home I would no longer need to be so secretive. I heard the sounds of animals on farms and I discovered that I was quite adept at hiding. Whenever I heard people moving on the road I moved out of sight choosing hedgerows and bushes to do so. It was nighttime and few moved around at night. Those that did might have sinister purposes. I also found that carrying my sack from my billhook's spike made my life much easier.

By dawn, I had almost reached Horwich, and I could see the watchtower at Rivington. I had chosen the tower as my destination as it was a clear marker for my route north to Skipton. I did not know if I was on the same route as John of Warrington, but the sight of Rivington told me I was heading in the right direction. I almost made it through the small village before I was seen. There was a charcoal burner at the edge of the village, close to the woods, and a woman came out. She saw me and put down her bundle of faggots. She did not seem surprised to see me and showed no sign of alarm at our meeting, "Now then young man, what are you doing out so early, armed and yet with barely enough fluff on your top lip for the cat to lick off?" I spied her cat then; it was seated on a rock and was washing itself but its eyes seemed to be fixed on me. I felt afraid. Cats were strange creatures. We had owned a dog and they were far easier to understand; you fed them and they were loyal but a cat was different. You could feed one every day and then suddenly it would leave. Men fear what they do not understand.

Although she was smiling as she said it, I found myself colouring. My father had said I was still young, and the woman's first comment had been about my age. I was defensive when I answered, "I am old enough to wield a bill hook and one day I shall have a full beard."

She nodded, "And how long have you walked for Wigan is a good walk from here and dawn has barely broken?"

"Long enough."

"Aye, well if you help me shift these faggots to the burner, I shall give you hot food and small beer."

I looked around, "Have you no man?"

Shaking her head she laughed and said, "And I need none. He left me ten years since and I say good riddance to him. I earn my own living without any useless apology for a man. Now will your stiff neck make you forego a breakfast, or will you help me?" I nodded and laid down my bundle. She said, as she handed me two bundles of faggots, "I am Mistress Gurton and what do I call you?"

I did not want to give her my real name, but I did not want to sound as though I was making it up, I said, "James the Billman."

She laughed, "And that sounds like a name you gave yourself. Still, I am guessing, from your eyes, that the James part is right. Come, James, this will not take long."

I was young in those days and a night without sleep followed by a good hour of hard work did not tire me but it made me ready to eat. It was repetitive work, carrying the faggots to the ovens where I stacked them. Mistress Gurton lit them and seemed satisfied. I felt my stomach rumble as we walked back to her humble home. As my father might have said, '*I could have eaten a horse with the skin on.*' While I washed and then drank the small beer she stirred the pot and cooked the food. The food was plain but filling. There was a bowl of porridge followed by yesterday's bread fried in salted ham fat. The thinly sliced ham was placed on the top. I was ravenous and devoured it all in a few bites.

Mistress Gurton shook her head, "It is good to see such a healthy appetite. I eat like a bird. Had you not come by I would have just eaten the porridge. Now then James, whatever your real name is, what brings you here?"

I fingered the hilt of my rondel dagger; it was as close to a cross as I had for I wondered if this woman who lived alone was a witch. She seemed to see into my head and know things about me that I wished hidden. The cat had entered the tiny dwelling with us and was before the fire staring at me with piercing green eyes. I decided to speak the truth although I would keep my true name a secret. "I am heading for Skipton. An archer, John of

Warrington, was heading there to join Sir Henry Clifford of Craven. If the Yorkists return, then I would fight them. Have you seen a large archer with a red face and nose?"

She cocked an eye as she began to clean the skillet pan she had used to fry the ham and bread, "And will they be grateful to have a boy who steals his father's jack and weapons?"

I started, she was a witch, "The billhook is my own!"

"Aye, but the jack is old and worn. I fancy it is as old as you and does not fit as well as it might." She tossed some of the fried ham scraps from the pan to the cat, "And this archer you seek, who is he?"

I shrugged, "Just an archer, pot-bellied, barrel-chested and with a red face."

She laughed, "That description could fit half of the men in the village, but I think I saw your archer. He passed through here the day before yesterday."

"And did you feed him too?"

She shook her head, "No, boy, I did not for he stank of ale having been in Gammer Parr's alehouse."

I was curious, "Then why did you feed me?"

Her face softened and she turned away to wipe the pan with a cloth, "Let us say that while my husband left, I kept the memory of the one child I had carried who died stillborn. He would have been your age and…" She waved an angry hand, "Does it matter? I fed you and there is an end to it." She turned and I saw that she was on the verge of tears, "Your mother, does she love you?"

It was not a question I expected but I nodded, the love of both of my parents was never in doubt, "Aye, she does. I am her favourite." I added lamely.

"Then when you have this foolishness scoured from your head by the clash of battle go home! There will be a hole in her heart that can only be filled by your return. Each day that hole will grow until it consumes her. Hear me?"

"Yes, Mistress."

She nodded firmly and I saw that the tears which had misted her eyes were now gone. They had been exorcised by her words. "I would suggest that you sleep awhile and then try to catch up with this drunkard, but I know you will not. Give me your empty ale skin." I handed it to her, and she filled it from her barrel. Pointing north she said, "You have forty miles to travel. Keep on this road and take the road to Burnley. It is a town that will have food and ale. It is twenty miles from here and you should make it by dark. I am thinking that the man you seek may have gone by the time you reach it, but you do not want to travel beyond it in the dark." She wagged a finger at me, "There is wild country up there and bandits. Travel in the day and, if you can find it, in company." She went back into her home and fetched out a small clay pot. "This is a salve I make myself. I usually sell it but as you look to have few coins, I shall make a gift of it. It has herbs and other ingredients that may ease bloody feet and can be used on cuts. That billhook looks sharp."

"Yes, Mistress." Why was this woman being so kind to me? "I thank you, Mistress Gurton, for your hospitality and wish there was something I could do for you in return."

She smiled, albeit sadly, "That is easy; return to your mother but I think you will not do that. Just promise me that when this madness has left your blood you will go to her, and your debt is paid."

"I will, I swear."

That was the first oath I ever swore and even though I knew that I would have to face my father if I kept it I knew that I would. I was just unsure when that would be. Hoisting my sack on my bill hook and slinging my bulging ale skin over my shoulder I bowed and then headed up the road. The strange woman with the terrifying cat would often wander through my dreams. I never saw her again, but I never forgot her either. I knew that I might meet many people on my journey, but I hoped they would all be as kind as her. I knew they would not, but young men always hope.

The road to Burnley and thence to Skipton was a busy one. The first part was not for I had to trek up along the ridge by Rivington and there I saw the hills that were the Pennines, rising ahead of me. I drank a little of the ale and then descended towards Darwen which I could see in the distance. It looked to be the size of Horwich. When I reached the knot of houses, I saw the sign for Burnley. The crossroads had a sign for Blackburn to the north but the road to Burnley looked to be busier. After washing at the horse trough and eating some of my now even staler bread I strode up the road that headed first west and then north.

Once more fortune favoured me as I met a carter and his son by Haslingden. The road was steep and the sumpter that pulled their laden cart was struggling. I took one of the traces and helped them to haul the wagon and the cart so that we were on the downhill section. "Thank you, young man. We are in your debt." He pointed to the horse, "Annie here is not as young as she was. I pray you, are you heading for Burnley?"

"I am."

"Then if you would stay with us," he looked around at the bleak landscape, "and help us with your strong arms and weapons then we will feed you and let you sleep under the wagon in Burnley. What say you?"

I was flattered that they saw me as someone who could defend them, and the offer appealed. The alternative would either be to risk punishment as a vagrant and sleep rough or use the two or three coins I still had in my purse. "I will aid you, sir. I am James."

"And I am William, and this is my son Will." Will was but ten and scrawny. I could see why William the Carter needed my arms. I discovered that they too were heading for Skipton, and they had a load of arrowheads and blades for poleaxes, halberds and bill hooks. I did not mind staying with them until Skipton, but I knew, from their words, that the road from Burnley to Skipton would be even steeper than this one and would add to the journey time. I said nothing but I would leave after a night under their wagon and sharing their food. They were good company, but we were moving slowly. Had I been alone then I would have travelled far quicker and we were overtaken by many travellers, even those on foot.

It was dark as we approached the small town and I was now suffering. A night without sleep followed by a day sometimes hauling on a wagon took its toll and I was looking forward to eating then collapsing beneath the wagon. There was a small square and green in the centre of the town and, as it was used by the market, William was able to unhitch his horse and allow it to graze. While young Will lit a fire I helped William to secure the wagon. The cover for the wagon was unfastened from the sides and by the use of four metal poles, we had a shelter for the night. We cleared the ground of animal dung while Will began to cook. William went to the nearest alehouse and bought us a jug, not of small beer but strong beer. I was ready for it.

Later that night after a meal of salted ham cooked with greens and beans and washed down with good beer, I simply rolled into my cloak and was asleep within a heartbeat. However, before I did so I slipped the dagger from its sheath and placed it where I could find it. This became my practice whenever I was on the road. It was not a dreamless sleep. My father's bloody face kept appearing and I heard my mother's wails although I did not see her. The result was that I woke before dawn. I needed to make water. After crawling from beneath the shelter I stood and headed for some oaks which grew in one corner of the green. It was a real relief. I was about to head back to the wagon when I heard a noise. It was not from the wagon but from a building just off the green. I was curious and headed there. As I neared the building, although I could not see what was happening, I could hear the words.

"You owe us money for the ale and we will either take it from your purse or, if that is empty, from your skin. An archer who loses two fingers is of no use to anyone is he?"

"I told you that when I reach Skipton, I shall pay you. It was just a few coins I owe. I swear you shall have them!"

I recognised the voice. It was John of Warrington. I did not draw my weapon, but I bunched my fists and used the sides of the buildings to approach the men. There were three. One was John of Warrington while the other two were smaller men and clearly not archers. John's gardyvyan lay on the ground and one of the men held John by his arms while the other searched John's purse. He held it upside down and shook it, "It is your face and your fingers then. Hold him, Ralph. You shall have your money's worth when I tire."

He pulled his arm back and swung at John's face. I heard the nose break and blood-spattered the attacker. John looked to have been willing to take the beating but suddenly he used the back of his head to butt into Ralph's face whilst bringing up his knee into the other's groin. He swung around the man he had butted, and his body clattered into the one clutching his groin. John had taken them by surprise, but things could change. I joined in. I ran to the one clutching his groin and using my right hand punched him as hard as I could in his ribs. I heard them break and I punched again and again until after hitting him in the side of the head, he collapsed. John glanced at me and then picked up the one called Ralph whose eyes were still streaming while blood poured from his nose and, swinging him around, smacked his head into the side of the building. He slumped to the ground.

I am not sure if John was a little drunk still, but he stared at me, "Thank you, young sir. Your help is appreciated although I could have taken these two gong scourers." He stopped and stared at me through eyes still streaming from the punch. "Do I know you?"

"Aye, but I think we can speak when we are away from these two before they awake."

"I can take them!"

Shaking my head I said, "If you owe them money then they can use the law. Hurry."

He nodded and picked up his gardyvyan, cloak, arrow bag and bow, still in its case. He kicked them both in the head and then took the purse of one of them, "If I am to be a fugitive let it be for something worth stealing."

That he was embroiling me in the crime did not occur then for I was just desperate to get away. When we reached the green others who had camped there for the night were just beginning to wake. We were the only wagon and the rest had packhorses. I pointed to the north side of the green. I had already ascertained that it was the road to Skipton, "Head up that road and I will join you." He peered at me as though he was finding it hard to focus. "Just walk and I will find you. I have food and ale."

That decided him and he set off. He would be disappointed when he discovered that it was just small beer. By the time I reached the wagon William was rising, "You are up early young James. As soon as we have eaten, we shall be on the road."

I did not want him to know I was fleeing and so I said, "I thank you for your food and shelter, but I must make Skipton sooner than you shall." I grasped his forearm. "May God watch over you."

"And you but what is the hurry?"

I smiled and said, "If I am to be a soldier then the sooner I begin the better. Say farewell to Will for me." I grabbed my gear and hurried across the green. I did not think I had been seen by the two men, but I could take no chances. They would be out for some time and I hoped that we might be a couple of miles along the road before they came round. The two men did not look as though they had horses.

Surprisingly enough, John of Warrington had managed to get half a mile north of Burnley and I was pleased. He turned and peered at me as I approached. The sun was just beginning to light the eastern sky and he said, "Who are you?"

He had to know who I was or else he might not aid me, "I am Walter of Ecclestone's lad, James. I am come with you to join the Lord of Craven."

He nodded and smiled as he recognised me, "It is the Lord of Skipton and the Guardian of Craven that you seek. Your father sent you?"

I lied. "Sort of."

"Good, you might be young but if you have half the skill of your father your fortune is made not to mention your reputation. You said you had ale?"

"Aye but let us step out first and husband what we have. Here," I handed him a large chunk of the stale bread. "Eat this and we will breakfast on the road."

He shook his head, "Ale is what I want but I thank you for your offer."

I began to chew on the hardening bread which was more like biscuit now than bread. I was learning about my companion. He liked drink more than food and that explained his ruddy face and his lack of coins. Once I had my introduction to the muster, I would let him find his own way. I saw him as trouble.

As we had left early in the day, we passed few on the road and none overtook us. We would be unlikely to meet people coming the other way for some time. We had the road to ourselves, but John appeared lost in his own thoughts. I had many questions, but I kept them in my head.

Six miles up the road we reached Colne which was a market town. It served all the farms and villages between it and Skipton.

Whilst smaller than Burnley it had more to offer travellers and John showed his dependence on drink when he used six pennies to buy a large sack of strong ale. I bought a mutton pie which cost me but a halfpenny. We ate and drank as we walked. The road between Colne and Skipton climbed through woodland and moorland. This explained why Mistress Gurton had been fearful. Had I tried this at night then I might have come to harm either through a fall from the road, that was little more than a track left over from the times of the Romans, or been attacked, for the woods through which we passed looked perfect for outlaws.

It was on the Lothersdale road which led to the east, that we were caught up by two men. The road was rising, and it was as I glanced back that I saw them. I was about to tell John to hurry when I saw that they were archers for they carried their bow cases. "We have company, John."

He nodded and happily stopped to take more of the ale. It was already less than half full. I took my sack from my billhook and took out some of the salted ham I had brought from home. We were close to Skipton now and I ate a little more of it. The hot pie from Colne had been filling but there had been little meat in it. My shoulder was aching from carrying the billhook and my sack. I wondered if my father had been right and I was not yet old enough to go to war. As one of my father's friends used to say, '*the carrot is out of the ground*'. There was no going back now.

"Hail friends. I can see that you seek employment too." The taller of the two archers gestured to his companion, "I am Sean of Flint and this Maredudd of Mold."

John of Warrington said, "Welshmen eh?"

Maredudd of Mold growled, "What of it?"

John laughed easily, "Nothing, friend, Welsh archers are good men and almost the equal of me. You may have heard of me. John of Warrington."

Maredudd just shook his head while Sean of Flint laughed and said, "I have lost count of the times I have heard that said, John of Warrington. It seems to me I heard of a John of Warrington who fought at Tewkesbury."

"That would be me." He burped, "I shall go and make water." He began unfastening his breeks as he headed to the ditch. I am not even sure he heard Sean's next words.

"Aye, many years since. I would have liked to see you in your prime, still if all we fight are half-naked Irishmen then none of us has aught to fear." His head whirled around, and he fixed me with his eyes. "And who is this who carries his father's billhook? Are you waiting for him, boy?"

I realised now the mistake I had made in wearing my father's jack. I coloured and said, "I am no boy and I seek to join Sir Henry Clifford of Skipton as a billman. My name is James the Billman."

That made Maredudd's face crack into a smile and Sean put his arm around my shoulder and said, "James, I would change your name to a more believable one. I like you for I can see spirit in you, but you are no more a billman than I am. You may have used one, but no one would give you the name of Billman."

Maredudd said, "Where do you hail from?"

I ran through all the places close by and picked the largest, "Prescot."

Sean said, "That is a better name; it may not be true but it has the ring of some truth in it. Now let us push on. There will be many seeking employment and I hope to be a vintenar!"

I said, quietly, as we moved along the ever-steepening road, "What is a vintenar?"

"An archer who commands twenty others and is paid more."

Sean nodded, "I am not sure how many more paydays there will be, and I wish to buy somewhere and raise a family."

Guilt rose like bile in my gorge, that was what my father had done and I had struck him. My guilt made me remain silent and I listened to the three archers as they spoke of battles in which they had fought. All three had been at Bosworth and I prayed that they would not mention my father for, if they did, then John of Warrington would say that Walter was my father. I was happy when we spied Skipton Castle ahead and the only talk had been of archers. I had never seen a castle and Skipton did not disappoint. The barbican was huge with two half-round towers while the castle which rose above it had six drum towers. It was a bastion, and I felt the excitement growing within me.

Thanks to my arrival with three much-needed archers, I was welcomed. The four of us marched up to the castle where Stephen spoke for us all. "We are three archers and a billman here to offer our bows and billhook to Sir Henry Clifford."

The sergeant at arms nodded and took a wax tablet from the table in the guardhouse of the barbican. He took out a wooden stylus and made three ticks in one column and one tick in another. "Go inside to the outer bailey. You can camp there until Sir Henry can find the time to see you."

We headed to the huge area filled with small homemade tents and the hovels made by archers and billmen alike. Sean said, "Until we find out if you have employment or not you had better stay with us."

I was grateful that he was taking me under his wing for John of Warrington, once he had ale, was a solitary man who did not speak to any. The two Welshmen I barely knew, but I felt safer with them. I was excited as I strode across the greensward. I did not think that my father would have thought I could get this far but here I was on the threshold of a life as a billman.

Chapter 3

The other three set about making us a camp. Without asking they took my oiled cloak and added it to theirs to make a tent supported by some hawthorn staves they had hacked as we had neared the castle and they stuck my billhook spike down in the ground so that the end made a point in the improvised tent to enable any water if it rained, to run down. They piled their gardyvyans and my sack around the sides to make it snug. I was amazed at how quickly they managed to make what amounted to a home. The two Welshmen then began to prepare a fire.

"James, fetch kindling."

John of Warrington said, "I will find us ale. There must be some!"

Maredudd said, dismissively, "He will use his nose as a divining stick!" As my father's former friend trudged off, he added, "If he is your friend I fear he will not survive this campaign. We may not be fighting the same men who died at Bosworth, but they will all have more skill than he has. The drink has addled his brain. He is a man who lives to drink."

I said, "He is just an archer I met on the road. I have known him but a little longer than you." That seemed to satisfy them and, after I had found the dead wood, they soon had a fire going. I gave them the ham I had left and the stale bread. The remains of the loaf were rock hard and using his hatchet Stephen hacked it up and added it to the stew they were making. Maredudd took greens he had gathered as we had walked and they were added too. With some dried venison they had with them a pleasant smell soon rose from the pot. Sean had found some wild thyme and that smell always whetted my appetite. John of Warrington returned with an ale skin which he shared with us.

It was not Sir Henry who came to us but another knight, Sir Edward Chorley and his squire. We had just eaten and I was taking the opportunity to study my father's falchion. He had never let me touch it and I was using my whetstone to sharpen it when the two men approached. Sir Henry was an older knight. Sir Edward was a young man and we learned that his squire, Geoffrey, was his son. I took him to be in his late thirties. He was a serious-looking man and, as we came to know very religious. We all stood and bowed.

He smiled, "I am Sir Edward Chorley, and this is my son and squire Geoffrey. His son looked to be close to my age, perhaps a little younger. "I am told that you seek employment for the campaign." We all nodded. "I need men," he glanced at me, "especially archers. The rate of pay is eightpence a day per twenty miles of travel."

Stephen nodded, "And when we do not march?"

"The normal rate."

"Arrows, my lord?"

"Will be supplied."

The two Welshmen looked at each other and then Sean said, "We will take your offer."

The knight looked at John who said, "Ale and food provided, my lord?"

"In reasonable amounts, aye but remember that God considers gluttony a sin."

John said, "Then I will curb my appetites, my lord. I am your man."

The knight's attention turned to me, "And are you a billman for you look too young to have trained?"

I was aware that my words had to be chosen carefully and this was no time for bravado or false claims. The last thing I needed was to be refused a post and sent back to Ecclestone where I would have to face my father. "I have trained, my lord, with the other billmen from my village. I am happy to show you my skills."

He smiled and nodded towards our tent, "And that would mean dismantling your home. Tell me truly, billman, have you trained to fight alongside other companies of billmen?"

I sighed. I knew what he meant. I had fought with my billhook and I knew how to wield it but I had not fought in a company of billmen and I shook my head As much as I wanted the adventure I would not risk other men's lives with a lie. I had lied enough, "No, my lord, but I am a quick learner and I swear that I have skills with a billhook."

"Do not swear for men do that too readily taking the lord's name in vain. I can see from your face that you do not speak falsely and believe you have skills. The battlefield is not a place to discover your deficiencies. However, I will take you on and I will speak with my captain of billmen, Giles Tarporley. I have a good company of billmen; he can train you and perhaps you may be of some use. We need all the men we can if we are to defeat these wild Irishmen and foreigners. I have others to see and I will find a place for you, my young billman."

He left and we saw him speaking to other archers who were camped close by. It was getting on to dusk and the smell of woodsmoke and cooking food filled the bailey. A sergeant at arms suddenly ran up to Sir Edward and he and his son turned and ran back to the castle proper.

Maredudd nodded, "Something is up. You never see a knight running." He was right and as darkness fell Sir Edward returned. He cupped his hands and shouted, "Those men I spoke to earlier, gather around me."

We all stood as close as we could. I saw that there were fifteen archers, and I was the solitary billman.

"This is our last night here. Be prepared to march."

Stephen asked, "Then they have landed, my lord?"

"There is a rumour that they have left Dublin and we will march tomorrow."

I asked, "To fight?"

Sir Edward smiled, "With just two hundred men? I think not. We march for York where Sir Henry will command the garrison there. The enemy will seek to put the pretender close to his supporters in York." He looked at me, "Can you ride?"

I knew that my answer would determine much, and I nodded. It was a lie, but I was unafraid of horses. "Aye my lord."

"Then you can act as a servant for my son and me. The enemy have come earlier than I had expected. Fetch your gear. You can sleep in the stables this night for you will be up while others are still abed."

I looked at my billhook, now supporting the tent and my cloak. Sean grinned, "Fear not, James, you will not need your cloak if you sleep in a stable. We will have both for you on the morrow and your buskins will not wear out as quickly as ours if you ride on a horse."

Geoffrey spoke for the first time. He was curt, "Come, we have little time to waste." I nodded and grabbed my sack which I had not unpacked, and I strapped on my falchion. I hurried after the knight and his son and we entered the castle to head for the stables.

Sir Edward did not stay with us but made his way to the Great Hall. He said not a word to either of us. When we reached the stables Master Geoffrey led to some stalls at the end. I saw a courser there and a good rouncy. Each had its own stall. In the stall next to them were three sorry-looking small sumpters. "These are the packhorses. There is no saddle," he gave me a mischievous grin, "but as you can ride there should not be a problem. They are Betsy, Eleanor and Scout." He pointed to each one as he named them and then Master Geoffrey shrugged, "I did not name them, but I am guessing there is a reason, but I care not. I will send a man to wake you early. You will not have long to sleep, and I would make the most of it." He pointed above the horses where there were hooks. "The panniers and the horse furniture are there. My father and I will expect you to meet us in the inner bailey with the animals where you will then load them." With that, he turned on his heels and left.

I looked at the horses and I recognised the breed. They were Galloways and could carry a good two hundred and fifty pounds. I knew how to attach panniers as I had helped my father do so when he delivered goods to the manor house. I would not have to ride, I could simply lead the animals. I had already worked out that the army would be moving at the pace of the archers and billmen on foot. We would make, perhaps, twenty-five miles a day. I would be travelling with the army and that meant I might be able to fight, and I would have my adventure. If this revolt was quickly quashed, then the opportunity might not arise again for many years.

One of the horses, Scout, nuzzled me and I tousled his head, "Well Scout, I have one friend at least. I have nothing for you yet but when I can I shall find you an apple, eh?"

Before I slept, I decided to bring down a pannier, traces, and reins. Using the compliant Scout I fitted them and then removed them. It was a relief that I did it so quickly and, that done I made a bed of straw and slept the sleep of the dead.

I was woken from what seemed a dreamless sleep by a rough hand and sharp voice, "You boy, it is time to wake. Your master needs you."

I sat up but the man had gone before I even opened my eyes. I did not like either term, boy or master. I was not a boy and Sir Edward was not my master. He was my employer. The sooner I could show him and everyone else that I could fight the better. I washed in the water placed for the horses and I fed them. It was in my interest to do so. I had just fitted the last pannier when Master Geoffrey came down. Part of the squire's duties was to prepare his horse and that of his knight. He looked surprised when he saw me leading the three animals from the stable.

"You can help me now. I thought that would have taken you longer."

I smiled at his discomfort, "There are many things about me that may surprise you, Master Geoffrey."

The two of us made short work of preparing the two horses. I saw that the knight's had a high cantle to prevent the rider from being knocked from his saddle while the rouncy had a simple riding saddle. I led the sumpters and Master Geoffrey led the two other horses. There was a great deal of hustle and bustle in the inner bailey. Master Geoffrey took me to a pile of war gear. There was plate armour, lances, swords, poleaxe, an axe and a mace. There were four bags that looked like they contained clothes and one that looked like it held food. There was a waterskin and an ale skin. I knew that I had to pack these correctly or they might injure the animals and I guessed that I was here on trial. I packed everything as carefully as I could. I picked up each item first to gauge the weight and when that was done, I balanced the load between the animals. I decided that Scout would be the one that I would lead and I packed the war gear on him.

Sir Edward did not appear until dawn, and he came directly to me to look at the animals. He nodded, "A good start… James is it not?"

"Yes, my lord."

"Go you now into the Great Hall, there are some scraps of food. That will be your breakfast. Then bring the sumpters to the outer bailey. You shall be with the baggage."

I had expected that. I headed into the castle. I had no idea where the Great Hall would be. I arrested a page and said, "Where is the Great Hall?" The boy, he was no more than ten, tried to pull away from me and I growled threateningly at him, "None of that or I will fetch you a clout."

The threat in my voice was enough and he pointed, "Down the corridor and on your left." To make it clear to me he tapped my left hand as though I did not know my left from my right.

When I entered I was amazed at the sight I beheld. Sir Edward said scraps but there was a veritable feast awaiting me. Other servants were already descending like a flock of pigeons and I muscled my way in. I was bigger than they were and they gave way. I stuffed a large chunk of cheese into my doublet and used my rondel dagger to shave the ham to the bone. The servants had no knives. I took a whole uncut loaf and put that within my doublet too. I then ate as much as I could. I would have been there longer but Master Geoffrey shouted, "James, now!"

I turned and nodded. I unhooked my costrel, my beaker, from my belt and poured some of the ale that was in the jug. I swallowed it in one and refilled it.

"Now!"

I turned and, still drinking, headed for the door. When I reached the squire I said, "Sir Edward said I was to breakfast, Master Geoffrey."

He looked at my bulging doublet and grinned, "It seems to me you have breakfasted and dined all at once. Come, we have far to travel."

The outer bailey was a maelstrom of activity. Most of the tents and hovels had been taken down and I saw captains organising their men. I knew by his size and the orders that emanated from his mouth which one was Captain Giles. He was the one I would have to impress if I was to become a billman.

Sean of Flint came over and handed me my billhook and cloak. "You have landed on your feet James of, where was it you made up, Prescot? I hope you continue to have such good fortune."

As I fastened my billhook next to the two lances I nodded, "And I thank you for all your sage advice. I hope we meet again, and I would like to fight alongside you."

He leaned in, "We may not be needed to fight. The word from our captain of archers is that we are to prevent the rebels from reaching York. As they have not yet landed, we should be able to manage that feat. Fare ye well."

I felt lonely as I fastened my cloak about my neck. I had made three friends and now lost them as quickly as I had found them. This would be my new world and I had to get used to it. I had made my choice and now I had to live with it for there was no going back.

There were many others leading packhorses, but all the rest were older and experienced. They were servants and I felt superior to them. I was being paid as a billman. Consequently, I gave only cursory replies to the questions thrown at me. Part of the silence was self-preservation for if I said little then there was less chance of others discovering my secret. There was another reason for my silence and that was the speed at which we travelled. It was nearer the pace of a man walking quickly than of foot soldiers. We stopped only briefly, and, when we did, I ate half of the food I had taken at breakfast. We passed Harrogate and still showed no signs of stopping. We did not camp until we were a few miles north of Wetherby at a manor called Allerton. When Master Geoffrey returned to me, he told me that it belonged to the Mauleverer family and that we had a camp to make. The knights and squires would be accommodated in the manor house, and I was told to fend for myself. So far my service to England and the King was not what I expected. I had expected men marching and merrily singing martial sons whilst boasting of the deeds that they would do. This was not that. Horse lines were put in place and guards were sent to watch them. I unpacked the sumpters and fed and watered them. I hobbled them so that they could not wander off. It was little enough I had to do but I did not want to incur the wrath of either Sir Edward or Sir Henry.

That done and after ensuring that the guards were Sir Edward's men, I left to find a fire to share. I would sleep by my animals, but I wished to speak to warriors. I found my three companions with another six archers around a campfire. They had a stew going.

Sean of Flint greeted me, "If it is not our young billman who can ride a horse." He nudged Maredudd, "A rare skill in a farm boy who has only seen a horse before." The other archers laughed. John of Warrington just waved. He was drunk again.

I realised that the banter was not meant to hurt me and I smiled, "Mea culpa." And bowed.

This time they laughed with me and not at me, "And he can speak Latin! Come, James, and share our fire. You have brought something for the pot have you not?"

I took out the remains of the ham and the bread. I had only consumed half.

Maredudd nodded and took them, "You have manners at least. Get some ale from the ale skin before the barrel that is John of Warrington consumes all."

I picked up the half-empty skin and poured some into my costrel.

Sean asked, "Have you learned anything at the rear?"

"Aye, Sean of Flint, how to avoid stepping in the horse shit." They all laughed once again. "And at the fore?"

The Welshman became serious, "That is that Henry Percy, the Earl of Northumberland who waits until a battle is almost over to choose sides, is to bring men from the north to help us. We do not have to rely on Sir Henry Clifford alone. We have two men who can make mistakes."

"You think they have no skill?"

"I know they have no skill but that is not the problem. They think they have the skill and that makes them both dangerous. Sir Edward knows what he is about, but he is not leading this army. I pray that de Vere, the Earl of Oxford, joins us soon for he is a leader."

The rest of the evening was spent in tales about the three leaders and I learned much. I had assumed that all knights had skills. It seems that while they all had courage, the skill was in short supply. What I also learned was the military knowledge of the archers. They revealed that they had heard that the enemy had landed and Sean of Flint was adamant that we were too far to the north, "Middleham was King Richard's heartland and the folk there still support him. They will not come to York but take the Wensleydale and head to the east midlands. If King Henry has support in the west, then it is the east that supports the Yorkists. I think we are all in for a long walk but at least we will be paid for wasting our boot leather."

In hindsight, he may have been right. We marched the next day to York and we camped outside the walls. We had barely had time to unpack the horses when a rider rode in to say that the rebels had been sighted north of Wetherby. Had we not marched to York we might have engaged them. Sir Edward and his squire rode into our camp to tell us. "Rouse yourselves. Your king has need of you. We march directly back from whence we came." The archers and billmen knew how to break camp quickly. The knight turned to me. "Leave all here but what I need for the battle. One horse will do and, to expedite matters you should ride." Wheeling his horse he and Geoffrey rode to join the knot of knights who were gathered around Sir Henry's banner.

Naturally, I chose Scout. When we had been at Allerton, I had stolen a sack of apples and I gave one to him as I packed him and spoke my thoughts aloud, "Well, my fine steed, today I ride to war. I pray that you are gentle with me." I leaned in and whispered in his ear, "To tell the truth I cannot ride, and a bloody coxcomb might tell the world that I am a braggart." I hoped the animal understood and he nodded.

Sir Edward wore his plate, but his shield, lances and spare weapons were to be taken on the panniers. There was a spare mail shirt. I had not yet asked who would wear it, but the metal looked ancient. I tied my sack and fastened my billhook ensuring that the load was balanced. There were no stirrups and so I led Scout to a low wall and used the wall to allow me to clamber on the horse's back. He waited patiently and I risked leaning forward to give him a second apple. I knew, for I had watched the knights and other riders, that I had to kick the horse in the flanks to make him move but the lances on one side prevented that. However, I found that the panniers held my body in place and so I felt more comfortable than I had expected. No one was paying any attention to me and so I had the opportunity to try things out. I used my voice, "Walk on, Scout." Miraculously, the commands I had used on the journey from Skipton worked and the horse moved on. I pulled the reins to the left and he obeyed. I tried it to the right and he obeyed.

Then I heard, "James, where are you?" I looked around and saw Geoffrey trotting towards me. "We await you. You are to ride with us so make sure that you keep up."

Walking Scout was one thing but trotting was another and I dreaded the motion. For the moment all that I had to do was to keep him walking. I joined the pages and squires who milled around behind the eight knights who led us. I had to concentrate just to keep Scout moving in the right direction and I was relieved that when I said, "Whoa!" and pulled back on the reins he obeyed.

I was ignored by the knights and squires for I was a human pack animal and I caught snippets of information.

"Did the ride from the Northumbrians say how many were in the army?"

"No, Sir Hugh, just that they recognised the bright uniforms of the mercenaries. Earl Henry is bringing his men with all speed and his Border Horses are keeping contact with the rebels."

"Who leads these Yorkists and Ricardians?"

"There is Viscount Lovell, the Earl of Lincoln as well as the Fitzgerald brothers from Ireland."

"And the Scrope brothers."

"All the rats gathered with the foreign rats they have hired." I saw Sir Henry Clifford look around, "Are they ready yet?"

The man I now knew was called Captain Giles Tarporley hurried over, "Aye, my lord. We are ready."

"Then keep up with us. Let us ride for time is not on our side."

I thought I was being ignored but as he passed me, he said, "And until I can train you, boy, keep your billhook where you can neither harm yourself nor others."

I had no time to contemplate his words for Sir Henry Clifford set off and I found that Scout tried to keep up with the other animals. I was bounced so hard that I was sure I would never be able to father children. When I had the chance, I would pad the horse's back for it was agony. The panniers gave me something which I could hold on to but the motion was alarming. We trotted the whole way towards Bramham Moor.

We stopped once, about halfway there at Long Marston. Even knights need to make water and as I dropped my breeks, I saw that my thighs were not just chafed but they were bloody. My foolish claim that I could ride would come to haunt me. It was summer and I deemed that I did not need my cloak about me, nor my jack. I took the jack from the sack and used that first and then folded the cloak so that it was padded. I saw Geoffrey smiling at me as I did so.

I decided to brazen it out, "I am used to riding with a saddle and stirrups, sir. This will make it more comfortable."

He grinned, "For someone who has never ridden a horse before you are doing a good job, James, and I am warming to you, but we have another seven miles to travel."

The padding helped but my breeks were now wet with my blood. I would have to use the salve that Mistress Gurton had given to me. Was she a witch and had she foreseen this? I put my hand to my dagger to touch the crosspiece.

I was exhausted when we reached the moor just north of Tadcaster. We had intended to get to Wetherby, but an army awaited us and we halted to prepare for battle. Its numbers were hard to discern as they appeared to mill around without any kind of order. I know not about the archers and billmen who had marched but I was in no condition to fight and when we saw the wild Irishmen, mercenaries and Yorkists arrayed before us then we knew that we would have to fight. I knew nothing about warfare but even I knew that our knights could not fight on the backs of their horses for there were too few of them. I also knew that we were not there to attack but to hold until Sir Henry Percy arrived.

That was confirmed by the orders given by Sir Henry Clifford, "Dismount and tether the horses yonder." I turned and saw a stand of young recently planted beech trees. Some farmer had obviously planted them to give shelter to his sheep in winter and give him a crop of nuts. "Have the billhooks line up before the archers and do it quickly."

I dismounted and, giving another apple to Scout, led him to tie him up with the others. Geoffrey led his own horse and his father's. I asked, "Will I need to unpack Scout, Master Geoffrey?"

"No, for we fight on foot." He nodded towards the Irish and added, "Despite your lack of experience I think that Captain Tarporley will need your billhook."

I would be getting the adventure I wanted; I would fight. I had the confidence of youth and did not think of death or defeat. I took my jack and donned it. There was blood already on it but it was my own. I would have to wash it but not yet. I put on my arming cap and then my sallet helmet. It felt heavy after the rabbit skin cap I had worn hitherto. My rondel dagger and my falchion were already in my belt and I took my billhook almost reverently from the pannier. "Farewell, Scout, and when I return, I shall have such tales to tell you."

I strode off towards the billmen and archers who were already forming up. There would be less than one hundred and forty of us. As I passed Sean of Flint he waved and shouted, "May God be with you and if you survive this day then you are truly James the Billman."

One of the billmen who was just ahead of me and hurrying to get into position shouted back, "If he survives this day, Sean of Flint, I shall bare my arse this night!"

The laughter which rang around made me even more determined not to let myself down. Captain Giles of Tarporley saw me approach and shook his head, "If we were not in such dire straights, I would send you hence, but today we may need every billhook no matter how badly handled. The enemy numbers mean that we must make two lines to protect our archers. You will be in the second line. Stand behind me. If I fall then the battle is lost in any case."

I saw now that the Irish were giving us no opportunity to form up at our leisure and were charging across the ground at a frightening speed. Behind me, I heard the captain of archers shout, "Draw!" I could hear the sixty bows as they creaked. "Loose!" The sound of the arrows flying over our heads was like a flock of birds taking flight. "Draw!"

Ahead I saw the first arrows as they plunged down. Some of the Irish had small round shields and holding them above their heads they were able to stop some of the arrows, but I saw one arrow drive through the shield and into the Irishman's arm. He did not falter, and I felt the first shiver of fear. Until then I had thought that the arrows would stop them but they kept coming. Barely a dozen fell and as the second flight was launched, I saw that we would soon be called into action.

It was then that the man next to me said, "Brace the billhook on the ground and plant your right foot behind it. Put the blade between the captain and Lucky Jack. Lean into the shaft and hope it holds."

My mouth was so dry that I did not trust myself to speak and so I just nodded.

He chuckled, "Just so long as you don't fill your breeks." I turned around to see if he was serious and he nodded, "Aye, at Bosworth, one man did just that." He nodded at the enemy, "He died. Now watch your front."

The Irish were now less than forty paces from us and Captain Tarporley shouted, "Brace!"

I guessed that was what my comrade in arms had just told me to do and I leaned into the shaft putting my weight forward. I suddenly recalled my father teaching me to do that, but I had almost dismissed the advice as I was more concerned with using swashing blows and hitting with the sharp blade. Now I saw the purpose in his training. I said to myself but out loud, "I am sorry, father. Forgive me."

The first Irishmen who struck us wielded long swords and axes but our billhooks were longer. With a spike and a wickedly sharp blade, they had two chances to hurt and to kill. My weapon was not yet called into use and I was able to watch the others, in the front rank, as they fought. I saw Captain Giles sweep his billhook diagonally across a half-naked Irishman. The sword, held two-handed, was still swinging down as the blade sliced deep into the man's chest. Unlike the Irishman with the arrows in his arm, this one was mortally struck, and he collapsed before my eyes. Amazingly six of the enemy were slain quite close to us but then disaster struck. An Irishman standing some way back swung his hammer and launched it. That he was then pierced by an arrow and fell dead did not help the man to the right of Captain Tarporley. The weapon struck him in the face and he fell. I guessed he was dead but I had no way of knowing. The man to my right lifted his billhook and took a step forward but the death had allowed a spearman to move up and he rammed his spear into the guts of my companion. The man who had given me advice was a dead man.

That was the moment when my blood took over. That was the instant where my father's drills and advice came to the fore. I stepped forward but unlike the gutted billman next to me I lunged with my billhook and drove it into the chest of the Irishman. I felt it grate off a bone, but I was moving forward, and my step pushed it up through his back. I saw another Irishman readying himself to swing his sword at me two-handed and I pulled the dying man's body across me as protection. It did two things; it released the body from my billhook, and it allowed the Irishman's sword to finish the job I had begun and slice through the dying man.

I was now in the front rank and wondered how long my luck would last when suddenly there was the sound of a horn and the majority of the Irishmen began to pull back. It was a miracle. We had been severely outnumbered and while we had killed a few of them it was a drop in the ocean for many more remained.

Captain Giles, who was now next to me, said, almost to himself, "This is a trick but what does it mean?" Then he turned and shouted, "Dress ranks and await orders!" He looked at me and shook his head, "I may have been wrong about you, but you still need to be trained."

I nodded, "I understand, and you should know that I am ever willing to be trained by you."

It was getting on to dark and we could not see the enemy. Was this, as Captain Giles suggested, a trick? Were they sneaking through the dark to outflank us? I was a novice but I realised that only about two hundred or so men had actually attacked us. The rest had watched. Why? The answer became clear as night arrived and we saw no campfires.

Sir Edward galloped up, "Lord John Scrope and his brother are heading for Bootham Bar. They attack York! Turn about and be prepared to march back."

I did as the others did and taking my helmet hung it from my billhook. As I fell in beside the others Sir Edward said, "Not you, James of Prescot. I have another task for you."

My heart sank to my buskins. Just when I had the chance to become a billman I would have to watch horses once more.

Chapter 4

I had to run behind Sir Edward and his horse. When we reached Scout, I saw that Geoffrey was in conference with Sir Henry Clifford. What was afoot? I was out of breath when I reached them, and I saw that Sir Henry's squire had taken the panniers from Scout and was fastening the girths of a saddle that now replaced them. Sir Edward said as he dismounted, "We have been hoodwinked. The rebels intend to take York and we, along with Henry Percy must face them. I am sending my son south to take word to the Earl of Oxford and the king. He needs a servant and, James of Prescot, it is to be you. Thus far you have acquitted yourself well. Do this and you will be well rewarded."

I merely nodded for events were moving too quickly for a brain befuddled by the battle and by tiredness. The squire waved me over and said, "I know you can ride panniers, but can you ride a saddle?" This was no time for lies and I shook my head. He nodded, "Honest at least. Use the stirrups to guide the horse and encourage him. Keep two hands on the reins." Scout turned to nuzzle me. I think he wanted another apple and the squire smiled, "The beast seems to like you and that will help." He took my helmet and fastened it to the left side of the saddle and then fastened the sack to the right. He looked at the billhook. "Do you want to leave this here?"

I did not want to be parted from the weapon that still bore the blood of the Irishman I had killed. "I would take it with me."

He laughed, "Then when you throw your leg over be careful, for one-legged billmen are of little use. Mount and I will fasten it for you."

"Thank you for your kindness."

"It is not kindness billman. You and Master Geoffrey must get through for the king only knows that the rebels have landed. London is far from here. There." He had fastened it so that the wooden haft faced forward, and the deadlier blade was next to Scout's rump.

I took off my cloak and fastened it around the head of the billhook and then, taking a deep breath, I put one foot in the stirrup and threw my leg over. Scout was being good and remained still. My injured groin, however, complained and I realised that I had not applied the salve.

Master Geoffrey nodded to Sir Edward and then said, "Farewell father. I will not let you down. Come James we have far to go this night."

I followed the squire and we headed off into the night heading for the road south. I was desperate to both stop and apply the salve as well as ask Master Geoffrey what the plan was but he allowed no rest. We had gone but two miles when we heard in the distance, to the north a roar and what sounded like a clash of arms. He did not stop, but looking around Geoffrey said, "I fear that the men we left have been attacked. My father suspected it and I think that it is one reason he sent me away. He sought to save me."

Having spoken it gave me the opportunity to speak myself, "Master Geoffrey, how far do we travel this night for Scout is no warhorse."

"We have thirteen miles to travel and we will rest awhile in Pontefract, but it will be only until our mounts have recovered. We are the harbingers of doom."

I suppose that if I had not been suffering from bloody, chafed thighs then the ride might have been exciting and the adventure I had craved. Scout proved a hardy horse and kept up with the better rouncy of Master Geoffrey. We were travelling on what had been a Roman Road and that meant it was cobbled. Whilst that made for a fast pace the jolting to my spine was painful and when Pontefract Castle hove into view, I almost wept with the relief of getting off the horse. Both horses were exhausted and I hoped that there would be stabling for them. The gates to the castle were closed but Master Geoffrey's title gained us admittance. Pontefract was a royal castle. It was where the second King Richard had died. There were Yorkist sympathies in the area, but the constable was a staunch Lancastrian Sir Richard de Lacy. We both ensured that our horses were fed and watered. There was a stable boy and I saw an assertive Master Geoffrey ensure that both animals would be well looked after.

We were taken to the Great Hall where, although it was late the constable and his family had not retired. Food was fetched for us and Master Geoffrey did me great courtesy. He did not ask me to take my food in the kitchen but allowed me to stay in the Great Hall. Admittedly, I was not seated as he was but my condition meant that was a good thing. Master Geoffrey was succinct and blunt. He spoke of the army heading south and intimated that he thought his father and the army of the north might have been roughly handled by the mercenaries and the Irish. Sir Richard promised to let the surrounding area know of the danger and to keep patrols out.

"And where are King Henry and the Earl of Oxford?"

"I was told to keep riding south on the Great North Road until I meet them, my lord. Sir Henry was adamant that I would find him. He knows of the danger and there is an army heading north but where it is…"

His wife said, "Husband these two young men are exhausted, let them sleep."

Master Geoffrey said, "Lady Anne, we must be away before dawn. Speed is imperative."

She smiled, "I will have you woken in plenty of time and there will be hot food."

For me, this was proving to be a real contrast to my life in Ecclestone. We ate well in my home, or so I had thought, but having eaten with the great and the good I now knew that whilst the plain fare had been wholesome and filling, the food the lords ate was like ambrosia from the gods. Although I ate with the others my bed was to be in the stable, but I did not mind for I wanted no one to see the condition of my body. After ensuring I was alone, I pulled down my breeks and stood half-naked. I used water from the water trough to clean away the blood. When I had dried it with a horse blanket, I applied some of Mistress Gurton's salve. The relief almost made me weep. I used it sparingly for it was a small pot. I put on my breeks, lay in the straw and with my cloak over me fell asleep. That night my dreams were of James the hero. I fought off enemies who were on foot and horsed. I had fought my first battle and survived.

Scout roused me for I was close to his stall and I had made water and fed both of our horses by the time the ostler came to rouse me. I gave Scout one of the last of the apples and headed to the hall for what I knew would be a feast.

We did not breakfast for long and were on the road heading for first Doncaster and thence Nottingham. Sir Richard assured us that the king would make for the royal bastion which guarded the road south. Having risen early I had applied a small amount of salve and I hoped that would make my ride easier. I also stole a small horse blanket that I folded up to place on the saddle. The salve had worked, and I was not as uncomfortable.

As we headed south Geoffrey said, "You have done well, James, if you would be willing, I would employ you as my servant on a permanent basis."

Shaking my head, for we were riding abreast each other, I said, "No, Master Geoffrey for I would be not just a billman but, in the fullness of time a Captain of Billman."

He nodded, "And I admire you for that resolve. You are turning down the chance to serve one who will be a great lord one day."

"I am resolved, Master Geoffrey."

We were not riding hard yet and that pleased me for the pace was easier on my thighs. The Yorkist army was on foot and we had a head start. The night ride had been hard and fast. It had hurt us, but we had gained the lead we needed. He shook his head, "The war between Lancaster and York is over. Men will beat their billhooks into ploughshares and there will be no need for warriors."

I knew that he may have been right but striking my father had meant I could not go back, and I did not relish the life of a servant who bowed and scraped. I smiled, "This war is not yet over, Master Geoffrey. We shall see."

We soon made Doncaster Castle which was another fortress that might slow down the enemy. We did not dismount but watered our horses in the bailey while Master Geoffrey relayed his news. Sir Edward Woodville, Lord Scales, was in the castle and I was relieved to see that he had with him a large force of horsemen. "You will find the king in Nottingham Castle. Ride with all haste to reach him. I will lead my horsemen and see if we can use the forest road to slow down their advance. God speed and England shall not forget this epic ride, Master Geoffrey Chorley."

His words inspired us, and we reached Worksop Castle just before dark. We had a dilemma for it was a mere twenty-four miles to Nottingham, but our horses were now too weary to continue and Sir William Furnival, the lord of the manor, pressed us to stay for the night. He assured us that he would rouse men to join either Lord Scales or King Henry, whichever reached him first. I was glad when Master Geoffrey acceded to his plea. I think that Sir William wished to hear, first-hand, of this rebel army. While the squire spoke, I ate; I was becoming accustomed to fine food and did not relish returning to the plainer food of the camp.

We were given food for the journey and having breakfasted well I put mine in the sack. We reached Nottingham before noon the next day and I hoped that there would be little more riding until I had recovered. The two of us were taken before King Henry. He was an astute man and his hawk-like eyes bored into a man so that you were certain he was reading your mind. I was not in his presence often but each time I was I feared for my life and yet, when he spoke, he addressed us both as heroes. I suppose that is the difference between kings and ordinary men.

It was Geoffrey who spoke, of course, although sometimes the king would dart a question at me to see if he could catch out the squire. It was in direct contrast to the way we had been received by the lords further north. It was only later I worked out why. King Henry had usurped the crown and he feared everyone. He knew that the imposter at the head of this rebellion was not a Plantagenet. The last of that line, Edward, languished in the Tower but he also knew that a figurehead could rally the opposition to his rule.

When Geoffrey had finished the king smiled, "You have both done well and I shall reward you. Geoffrey of Chorley, you shall be knighted. You will become a knight of my household and you, James of Prescot, shall have your wish. You may be young but from the words I have heard, you have the heart of a lion, and you should be given the chance to become that which you wish. I will speak with the Earl of Oxford, and you shall join his company of billmen." He waved over a liveried servant and took a purse from him. He counted out five pounds and handed them to me. "Wait without and one will come to take you to your new companions. I need to have conference with Geoffrey of Chorley."

I held the coins tightly. Five pounds was a small fortune but part of me could not help but wonder what reward had been given to Master Geoffrey. As I rolled the coins in my hand I realised I would not have to ride again but I was also sad for that meant I would be parted from Scout and I had grown fond of the sumpter. A billman does not ride. Many people came and went but none sought me. I was hungry and thirsty, but it would be churlish to ask for refreshment and I just studied the liveries and the weapons of those who passed me. I had food in my sack, but I dared not pull it out and eat it in the corridor of a royal castle.

The liveried soldier who found me an hour later had red and gold with diagonal stripes and white stars upon his tunic. I later learned that this was the livery of Sir John de Vere, the Earl of Oxford. The soldier was clearly a warrior with a scar running down one cheek. The grey flecked beard told me he had experience.

"You are the one who would be a billman?" He could not keep the incredulity from his voice.

I nodded, "I have fought with Captain Giles Tarporley, and I killed a man."

The words sounded pathetic even to me and he gave me a wry smile, "Aye, well I suppose David when he slew Goliath was not yet a man grown. I am Edward of Cowley, and I am the Earl's sergeant at arms. I will take you to the camp where your company resides. You have war gear?"

"It is in the stable, my lord."

He sniffed, "I am not a lord. Just call me Sergeant."

When we reached the stables, I saw that my gear had been piled to the side. The sergeant at arms nodded when he saw the bloody jack. "I can see that you have fought." I felt guilty but I could not tell him that the blood was my own. "Pick up your gear and come."

I slung the sack and helmet on the hook and then took the apple I had snaffled from the bowl outside the hall. I gave it to Scout, "Farewell my friend. I hope your adventures are over and you have a quiet life." He snorted and nuzzled me. I was sad.

As we headed out of the castle the sergeant said, "By the way you carry your sack you speak the truth and you are a billman. I shall tell Captain Jack Studley, who commands the Earl's billmen, not to judge on appearances."

The billmen were all camped a few hundred paces beyond the last house. The land was common grazing land but as Nottingham was a royal castle then the king's soldiers had priority. There were few tents and I saw that most of the billmen and the archers who were camped nearby had made hovels. It was June and whilst there could be a shower or two this was England, and it would not be cold. My father had taught me how to oil a cloak. I would not get wet.

I knew I was being studied by the billmen and they were judging me already. It had happened at Skipton Castle. The difference now was that I had fought and not run. I had been attacked and, most importantly, I had used my billhook with deadly force. There would be men before me who might have not yet used a billhook to draw blood. I was not the boy who had struck his father and run. I had been tested and not found wanting.

"Wait here while I speak to the Captain."

The Sergeant at Arms strode off to the Captain who rose from his own campfire. It gave me the opportunity to study the organisation of the camps. There looked to be eight men around each fire. It was not always eight for some had just six and one five. The billhooks for each tent were all stacked neatly. My billhook had my name carved on the shaft and an attempt by me to carve a gryphon. It was not a good carving and I now regretted it, but I had done the carving more than a year ago when my father had given me the billhook. I had grown a great deal in the last year and much of that growth could not be seen for it was inside. I had been dining with lords and their families yet I had not once drunk too much. That was a change. The youth who went to Windle to spend his coins, get drunk and fight was a different person from the one who stood patiently waiting as the eyes of the billmen bored into him.

Captain Jack came over and the Sergeant at Arms waved as he headed back to the castle. Captain Jack looked younger than the sergeant but he still had the look of a warrior who was experienced. His jack was not only padded but also studded with metal. I saw him weighing me up as he neared me. He leaned in to speak to me so that we would not be overheard.

"I have been told that the king wishes you to join our company." I nodded. "That will not sit well with my men for they are one company and are all close. You are a stranger and a young one at that. The Sergeant said that you had fought in the north and you will know that when you fight you rely on those around you." He paused as though choosing what to say next.

"And you, Captain, does it sit well with you?"

He smiled, "You have the courage to make such a thrust with your words. Let me consider." He rubbed his chin, "I suppose I see it as a challenge. Can I make a warrior from this raw clay? Who was the captain with whom you served?"

"Captain Giles Tarporley. I stood behind him and when the man to his right was slain and the warrior next to me killed, I stepped into the breach."

His eyes widened, "I was not told that."

"My story was not told to the king by me but one who did not see me fight. Master Geoffrey just said that I had fought and killed a man not how I did so."

"And it speaks well of you that you did not see the need to seek more praise."

Shaking my head I said, "I know how lucky I am for had the Irish not drawn off to trick Sir Henry then I might not even be here to give you a difficult problem."

He smiled for the first time, "I like you, James of Prescot. Let me see," he put his arm around my shoulders and surveyed the camp. His eyes lit on the fire with just five men around it. "Joseph of Didcot is the man who will help me mould you into a warrior. He is old enough to be a father, and he may view your youth as a good thing." He led me over, "Joseph, this is James of Prescot, and he is joining our company." His eyes glared around the others, "Do not judge him on his youth for he has fought and killed in the north and it was he brought us the word of the approach of our enemies." With that, he turned on his heel.

Joseph took my billhook and weighed it in his hands. He put his finger to the edge and it drew a tendril of blood. As he sucked the blood away he looked down at the name and the carving, "It is good that you mark your name upon your weapon and that it is sharp." He walked over to the other billhooks and carefully placed it so that the others did not fall down. He turned, "I will introduce the others. Have you any food for we were about to eat?" I took out the ham, loaf, and cheese I had been given in Worksop. He nodded and took them from me, "Good, for we share in our company. That is Tom the Wanderer." The billman looked to be in his early thirties and he nodded. "Next to him is Sam Sharp Tongue. Watch your words to him for he can read and write. He will pounce on any word you misspeak. Geoffrey of Aylesbury is next to him and the last is Stephen the Silent. Sit next to Stephen for he has only been with the company for half a year." I saw that Geoffrey was the largest man in the company and had a belly the size of John of Warrington's while Stephen looked to be little older than me.

I nodded, "I am James of Prescot, and I am honoured to join this company. I will do all that I can to live up to your expectations." I sat between Stephen and Geoffrey. Both looked to be young men who were barely in their twenties and sitting with them would disguise my youth a little.

The fire lit up the blood on my jack. Geoffrey nodded, "You have fought. Tell us the story of your fight, James of Prescot."

I knew I would have to wash the jack as men were making false assumptions. I told the story of the battle just as I had told Captain Jack. Joseph had divided up the food and we were all given an equal share. Tom the Wanderer came over, as I told my tale, with the ale skin and I held out my costrel for it to be filled.

When I finished Sam Sharp Tongue nodded, "So we fight wild Irishmen and mercenaries. Did they have pikes?"

Honesty would be my watchword from now on. I had done with lies which sought to trap you, "I know not for we did not fight them and it was dark. Sir Edward thought that they had pikes and harquebuses."

"And you did not see plate armour upon them?" I saw that Sam Sharp Tongue also had a sharp mind.

"No, for it was dark and all we fought were Irishmen. The man before me was slain by a hammer thrown at him and the man next to me was gutted by a spear." I took a drink from the costrel and said, quietly, "I had just met him and did not even know his name."

Joseph smiled and said, "Well, you know ours. Eat." As we ate, he said, "Prescot, that is in the northwest is it not?" I nodded. "It seems to me I knew a good billman who lived there, Walter of Ecclestone. Did you know of him?"

My attempt to be honest was about to fall apart before I had begun. I nodded as I rapidly concocted a story that might satisfy my new brothers in arms, "I trained sometimes with him on Sunday morning after church."

That seemed to satisfy Joseph who said, "He was a billman and was one of the heroes of Bosworth. I hope you picked up some skills from him, James of Prescot."

I nodded and said, truthfully, "Any skill I have with a billhook comes from him."

"Then I have high hopes for you."

Chapter 5

I had thought that we would break camp the next morning and march north to fight these rebels and mercenaries, but we did not. In fact, we had the whole day before word came to our camp that Lord Scales, whom we had seen at Doncaster, had encountered the army and that he had slowed it down. We were to march on the morrow. The day in camp was used well by me and I went to the river to wash the blood from my jack. Even when I had scrubbed, however, the stains were still visible. I would have to make water on the jack and wash it again to rid myself of the brown stains but that would have to wait. The men with whom we served were loud and boisterous. They happily traded insults and smiled when they did so. I became like Stephen the Silent and listened more than I spoke. When I saw Stephen the Silent smiling at their banter, I knew why he was silent. Like me, he was intimidated by these professional soldiers.

We were roused an hour before dawn by Captain Jack and, grabbing whatever food we could, we formed up with the other companies. We marched under the standard of the Earl of Oxford who, along with his knights rode at our fore. We marched ahead of the archers. As much as I missed the company of Scout, I did not miss the chafing and pain. Marching was much easier. I found myself marching next to Stephen and Tom the Wanderer. There was banter as we walked but the three of us were, largely, silent. The Earl of Oxford was leading the vanguard and we heard, from one of the riders sent back to deliver the news to the King and the Duke of Bedford, that the enemy had crossed the River Trent. We were moving far quicker than the army led by Sir Henry Clifford and that was because it was led by a better general, the Earl of Oxford.

Geoffrey of Aylesbury said, "Not too fast for you is it, James the Rider? Are you missing your horse already?"

I knew that such comments had to have a reply, or the rest would think it a sign of weakness, "No and I thank you for your interest, but the sight of your backside does remind me of the horse and makes me feel right at home."

I knew it was the right thing to say when Sam Sharp Tongue laughed, "Well said, James! You are clearly not a milksop!"

That moment saw a slight change. I was still not accepted, that would have to wait until there was a clash of steel, but I was no longer such a figure of ridicule.

At one point the Earl himself rode back and reined in next to me, "Welcome James of Prescot. My sergeant tells me that you were the one fought at Bramham Moor and brought the news to us."

"I am my lord and I thank you for the opportunity to serve England."

He nodded, "I am sorry to say that not long after you left the snake Lovell launched a night attack and many of Sir Henry's men were killed. It was fortuitous that you were not with them and that you were able to bring us the news."

I felt sadness more than anything else. The Earl could not know that my friends were the archers. I knew that Sir Henry had not been the best leader, but I had not expected him to be so roundly beaten.

Our pace was fast but to help us maintain it we stopped regularly, and it was at one such stop that we saw strange lights in the sky. I merely found them interesting but the companies behind us thought that they were an ill omen. Many of them fled.

Sir John de Vere and his sergeant at arms rode back with some mounted men at arms, "Are you women because you see strange signs in the sky? All that you need to know is that we have the right of this war and that we shall rout the enemy no matter how many foreigners they bring."

Joseph, along with the rest of Captain Jack's men all cheered. None of the Earl's retinue had even moved and it showed our confidence. Sam Sharp Tongue said, "So long as the lights stay in the sky I care not. It is when they fall to earth that I will begin to fear. We have the best men in this army and none shall stand against us."

I liked his confidence, but I was not so sure. I wondered if the lights had been from the harquebuses the mercenaries used.

When we found the enemy they were at a village called East Stoke and were arrayed on Rampire Hill with the River Trent surrounding them on three sides. As soon as we saw the enemy defences then the Earl deployed his men. He and his men at arms dismounted and joined us, the billmen, in three lines. My company was in the third line. We dropped our war gear and hurried to form our lines. We had marched in our arming caps and it was the work of moments to don our helmets and prepare our billhooks. I saw that Captain Jack and some of the other senior billmen wore metal greaves, poleyns and cuisse to protect their thighs as well as breast and backplate. His helmet also had a visor. Mine was an open sallet and I felt slightly more exposed when I saw the armour some billmen wore. I realised that until we were joined by the rest of the army, which was meandering its way along the narrow Nottinghamshire tracks, we would be outnumbered. Unlike Sir Henry, the Earl of Oxford carefully placed our archers, and there were many of them, before us.

Joseph turned to check that I was ready and said, "When the order comes to open ranks turn to your right and keep your billhook close to your body. The archers will pass through us and then loose from behind." I nodded. Being in the third rank meant that I kept my billhook upright.

What I did not know but learned that day, was that the bow easily outranged the harquebus. As I came to realise the gun, as it was also known, was loud and belched fire and if you were close to it then it delivered mortal wounds but anything more than eighty paces rendered it a noisy toy. The Earl went with his archers the better to command them. I saw that Edward of Cowley was with him. They were both plated from head to toe and both carried a poleaxe. I was close enough to see the enemy and they were in one single block. The Irish looked even more terrifying in daylight and some had limed their hair and wore bones in it. The mercenaries were even more frightening with brightly coloured and deliberately torn clothes. Some had pikes whilst others had the harquebus. The mercenaries and the Irish made up the majority of the enemy army. I saw their nobles gathered around a royal standard. I guessed that would be where the one pretending to be Edward was closely protected.

It was the Earl who began the battle and any lights in the sky disappeared as the arrows made a cloud of steel-tipped death descend upon the enemy. It was like Bramham Moor except that this time I could see the effect of the arrows. The Irish were struck and they were hurt. Most of the mercenaries had plate armour of some kind but the arrow storm was so relentless that I saw gaps and holes appear. After less than half an hour they decided that they had endured enough and a trumpet sounded the attack. We were still outnumbered for our army was still deploying and we would have to bear the brunt of the attack.

"Open ranks!"

As the archers passed through, one said, to no one in particular, "All wind and water! Stand firm and we will crenulate them!"

Sam Sharp Tongue snapped, "Decimate them! Typical archer: no brains and needs a good wall of billhooks to hide behind."

There were jeers from the rest of our company and, surprisingly, that put us in good spirits. As with Bramham Moor, it was the Irish who reached us first and unlike Bramham Moor, there were no archers to thin their ranks. The line before us reeled and Joseph of Didcot shouted, "Brace and hold them."

I realised then that he was in command of this part of the line. I suppose he was the equivalent of a vintenar or centenar in the archers. I pressed my shoulder into the back of the man before me. Although the sound of the harquebuses was loud I knew, I know not how, that the bodies before me would prevent any from hitting me and as they had few archers I felt immune. I pushed harder aware that until the rest of the army arrived there would be no comforting presence behind me for there were no ranks behind us. The archers were loosing their arrows and they would not be able to hold me. I was lucky for I found a few stones beneath my buskins and although Stephen the Silent slipped and moved back I did not.

The war hammer that smashed the skull of the billman in the front rank was a reminder that the Irish, and indeed the Swiss we fought, had weapons that could reach us.

Edward of Cowley's voice and the Earl's exhorted the ranks before us to hold firm yet I saw men fall in the front rank and as at Bramham that meant the rank before was promoted. That it was a bloody battle was clear to me as blood spattered from the front ranks and the din was like a weaponsmith's workshop.

I felt someone behind me as I was pushed forward into the second rank. Reinforcements had arrived. Bracing my bill hook as I had at Bramham I did not turn as I heard the king's brother, the Duke of Bedford shout, "Hold firm. Help is on the way."

The long Swiss pike that was rammed towards me had been intended for the man at arms in the front rank but the man had dodged out of the way and I only saw it at the last moment. I could not dodge but I could turn my head and the pike head rammed into the side of my sallet making my ears ring. I would have a dent that would need to be knocked out. The man at arms before me wielded his halberd skilfully and he either slew or wounded all who came close to him and for that I was grateful. I was now more involved and as the initial charge had now ceased, I was able to poke the spike from my billhook at the enemy. Our front line was no longer continuous but until the man at arms and billman before me fell I would not have to fight. I jabbed at an Irishman and was rewarded when the edge of the billhook sliced across the back of his arm. Blood spurted and he cursed at me. At least I assumed it was a curse, but it was in Gaelic. As I withdrew it the hook caught the arm of a German swordsman. Although unintentional it pulled his arm and sword to the side allowing the man at arms to slash his halberd across the German's face. Stephen, to my side, took his chance and rammed his spike into the centre of the German's nose. It drove through his skull and killed him. I glanced to my side and saw that my new comrades were all still alive. Indeed Sam Sharp Tongue was now in the front rank. Being so close to the enemy I saw the effect of the arrows as they rained down on the ranks behind the front rank. It was thinning them out.

Someone further along our line must have moved for there was a sudden shift and a gap appeared before me. I knew what I had to do, and I stepped between the man at arms and Sam Sharp Tongue. I watched the Swiss pike come towards Sam and I acted instinctively. I hacked down, biting into the wood and allowing Sam the opportunity to ram his billhook into the man's middle. I had no idea of how long had elapsed save that my mouth was dry, and my arms ached. It was at that moment that the enemy paused. Perhaps they were dressing their lines, or it may have been part of a preordained plan but it gave us the chance to fill the gaps. I turned as Edward Chorley placed himself between me and the man at arms.

Nodding but not taking his eyes from the enemy he said, "You have done well for you are still alive. It will get harder but we are almost there. Now the king will commit the other battles." Raising his voice he shouted, "Prepare to advance!"

I was terrified. It was one thing to move a pace or two and fill a gap but to attack the enemy meant using skills I was not sure that I possessed. I was helped by the noise which rose from all around me. Everyone but me seemed to be convinced that we were about to win. I had seen no dissipation in the resolution of the enemy but the cheers and songs that engulfed our men gave me hope that they saw an improbable victory that I did not.

It was the Earl of Oxford's voice which rang out and began our attack, "For England, God and King Henry! Charge!"

Charge is the wrong word for the enemy had realised what we were about and were bracing themselves just as we had. We lurched forward but we had movement and that gave me hope. With the billhook held before me as my father had taught me and my head dipped so that the front of the sallet gave more protection to my eyes, we moved forward. The Irish who had survived were still as unpredictable as ever and one detached himself from their lines to hurl himself the three paces towards us. I thought for one terrifying instant that he was coming for me but it was the Sergeant at Arms, Edward Chorley, who was his target. With a Scottish war hammer coming down towards him I was convinced that the man at arms would die but he calmly lunged with his poleaxe to skewer the Irishman and contemptuously flicked the body from his weapon before continuing his measured movement towards the Irish and the Germans who were before us.

The clash, when it came, was far worse than it had been at Bramham Moor. It was broad daylight, and I could see the faces of the enemy. They looked like warriors and I began to wonder what foolishness had made me think that I was their equal. Close by me I heard Joseph of Didcot shout, "Fight on boys! We are better than hired mercenaries."

I swung my billhook before me in a diagonal slash and I was lucky. I caught the head of the poleaxe with my hook and as the poleaxe came down Sam Sharp Tongue used his own weapon to smash into the side of the German's head. The man wore a sallet, but Sam's blow was a powerful one and the German fell. All along the line, our men were having the small victories that allowed us to advance towards the rebellious nobles who were allowing the mercenaries to die for their cause. I could not see it for we were in the centre, but the flanks were being assailed by King Henry and the Duke of Bedford's battles and when the enemy broke it was sudden and, in some ways, shocking. They were there one moment and then their backs were to us as they ran to escape.

It was then that our lines dissolved, and we became individuals each one racing to catch as many of the enemy as we can. At least that is what it seemed like to me but as we ran. Slashing and stabbing at those before us I realised that Sam, Stephen, Joseph and the others all flanked me. I could no longer see Edward Chorley but my brothers in arms were there. I realised that we were no longer fighting the mercenaries, they had all been slain and perhaps explained the collapse. The men we fought were Yorkists. Many wore the white hart or the white rose badge and we drove them towards the ravine where most died. There was no mercy and none of them even attempted to ask for it. Some hurled themselves down the ravine in an attempt to escape but all that they found was a rocky death. When the archers arrived and began to loose arrows at those trying to climb down then the sides ran with blood. Men called it the Bloody Gutter. I was there and a better name could not be found. I stood panting with blood and gore dripping from my billhook as I saw the last of the Yorkists die. I did not know them but Joseph of Didcot, who had been fighting them his whole life did and he pointed to their bodies as he named them, "There is the Earl of Lincoln, I do not see Lovell nor Broughton, but that Irishman looks to be Thomas Fitzgerald."

Sam darted a finger out and said, "And that finely dressed German looks to be Schwarz." He turned to me and took my helmet and sallet from me, "James of Prescot, you are young and fit. Before some other takes advantage, clamber down and relieve those dead rebels of any treasure."

All eyes were on me and when Joseph of Didcot said nothing, I took off my baldric and falchion and began to climb down.

"I will come with you, James. This is not something you should do alone." I looked around as Stephen the Silent emulated me and dropped his sword belt. The bodies were still warm, and blood seeped from them. All the ones we found had many wounds. The German, Schwarz had a smashed in skull that had ended his life while the Earl of Lincoln looked to have died from multiple thrusts from bladed weapons. We took their purses and their rings. It was grim work, and our hands were sticky with their blood by the time we had done.

"Quick, boys, King Henry comes!"

We heeded Sam's urgent plea and had just made the top when King Henry, flanked by his uncle and the Earl of Oxford arrived. He pointed to the bodies, "Have the bodies recovered. We will put their heads on the walls of Nottingham Castle."

Just then Edward Chorley came towards us with his hand in the back of a young boy of ten or so who was dressed in royal livery. "Here is the one who dares to call himself King Edward of England."

We were close enough to hear the words as the figurehead of the rebellion was brought face to face with the man he was supposed to replace. King Henry was remarkably calm and reasonable as he spoke. I had expected him to order the imposter's execution but he did not.

"What is your name, boy, and I want the truth for I have the real Edward in the Tower."

I think the boy's truthful answers saved his life, "I am Lambert Simnel, my lord, and I come from Oxford. There, Richard Symons, a priest, trained me to become a noble. He introduced me to Lord Lovell, and I was taken to Burgundy to meet Duchess Margaret. I can read, write, recite poetry and I know how to eat properly."

His innocent and honest replies seemed to work, and King Henry said, "Earl, have this boy taken to my castle and confined. He does not deserve to die but let no stone remain unturned to find Lovell and this Symons."

It was not to us that he spoke but his lords. Others fetched back the bodies that were now stripped of treasure and as we made our way back to our camp we were like carrion as we fell upon the bodies of the mercenaries we had slain. The Irish had no money but the Germans, Swiss and Flemish did. When they went to war they carried their treasure with them and by the time we reached the place we had begun our advance we had collected a large amount of booty. While Stephen and I lit the fire and fetched the water to cook our food the others, under the close scrutiny of Joseph of Didcot, divided the treasure into six equal piles. When we had cut up the salted meat and added all the other foodstuffs we had gathered into the pot, Stephen and I joined the others.

"You bring us luck, James of Prescot, and this day you have earned your place amongst us. You are now one of us."

I looked around and saw the smiling faces that were nodding at me. My father had spoken of the comradeship of war and now I saw it first-hand. "I thank you all."

He took one of the piles of coins and rings and handed it to me, "Here is your share. Use it wisely. Your sallet is badly damaged, sell it and buy a new one and have a jack made that fits."

It was wise advice. When Sam had taken my sallet from me I had seen that not only was there a dent but a small crack. I knew that it would not take another such blow.

Stephen and I went back to the food to add greens and I said, "Thank you for descending into that charnel house with me, Stephen, it helped."

He smiled, and it was a gentle smile, "You and I are the babies of this company, and we have to stick together. Until you came, I was not certain that I wished to stay a billman." He lowered his voice, "Sam is a good man, but he frightens me."

I thought of my own journey to get here and I asked him, "Why did you join with them?"

The smile had left his face as he said, "I come from the north, a tiny place you will never have heard of, Ancroft, on the borders with Scotland. It is two years since there was a raid. I was not at my home. I was with my mother visiting a sick aunt who lived in Morpeth. When we returned my father and brothers had all been killed and our home destroyed. My mother and I buried our family and returned to Morpeth. When my aunt died then my mother also took sick. I buried my mother and took my father's billhook. I was determined to get as far away from Scotland as I could. I ended up in Oxford and Joseph found me. He took pity on me and I joined the company. He gave me my sallet, jack and falchion. They had been his nephew's."

"His nephew?"

"Aye, he died at Bosworth." He leaned into me, "I think he sees the two of us as his sons and to be honest, I had adopted him as a father. He likes you and so you have become like my younger brother who died on the Tweed."

It was a strange confession and I wondered at the threads that bound all our lives together. Mistress Gurton was one thread and Scout the horse another. Perhaps my journey was pre-ordained by some higher power. I just knew that I was no longer alone. I had at least one friend and a sort of family to replace the one I had abandoned.

That night, after I had secured my treasure in my purse, I reflected that I had become a warrior, but I still felt like a fraud. My brothers in arms did not know my true name and I had been so afraid when we had fought that I was unsure if I could do so again.

Chapter 6

It was nearer to July when we headed back to Oxford and the castle that had seen so much action during the first civil war between King Stephen and Empress Matilda. Captain Jack had spent some time with us, but it was nothing to do with me directly. He was there to explain that not all the billmen who had taken part in the battle would be kept on over the winter. With just Lord Lovell from the Yorkist leaders unaccounted for it was thought that there was not enough of a threat to England to warrant the expense of maintaining archers and billmen. Some would be kept on, but that decision would be taken when we reached Oxford. However, the problem was not as frightening as I had first thought. The Earl of Oxford's men had taken the largest number of casualties. King Henry and his uncle had fed more men from their own battles to support ours and we had lost more men amongst both arms. In addition, some men had done as we had and taken from the dead and then decided to desert. My new companions were not dismayed by the news.

Sam, who I now realised was the thinker of the group, was remarkably sanguine about the whole thing. As we marched, at a leisurely pace, towards Oxford he expounded his thoughts, "We work well together and whilst few in number we are a force on the battlefield. Even our two novices have shown that they can acquit themselves well. We have money to spend a comfortable winter and there are many lords who will pay for good billmen." I learned that Sam was a natural teacher. He sometimes used deliberately difficult words and then taught Stephen and me how to use them,

Stephen the Silent had become a little more loquacious since the battle and he nodded, "The northeast always has need of such men. King James of Scotland casts greedy eyes on England. The Bishop of Durham and the earls of Westmoreland and Northumberland pay well. We could find work there."

Joseph of Didcot shook his head, "The Scots are as poor as church mice and it is far from where we know. Sam Sharp Tongue is right and even if the Earl does not keep us on there are more employers we could find closer to home than the wilds of the north. Let us not worry about that until we have to."

I wondered if I should return north to my family if that turned out to be the case. I had done enough already to be able to face them. I hoped to make my father forgive me but I did not relish the thought of bearding him. Even as the thought entered my head I dismissed it for I still yearned for adventure and I wanted to go home rich and famous. I prayed that we would be kept on.

"Is the rebellion over then?"

Sam Sharp Tongue said, "It was not really a rebellion, James of Prescot. You have heard of the princes, the children of King Edward?"

"The Princes in the Tower?"

He laughed, "That is what men called them, aye, Edward and Richard. They have not been seen for four years and it is assumed they are dead. This simpleton, Simnel, was portrayed as king but he is not. There is another prince in the tower now, another Edward, he is the son of George Duke of Clarence who was executed by his brother the late King Richard. So long as he is alive in the tower then men may well use him as a way to return a Yorkist king to the throne of England." He paused, "I would have him executed if I was King Henry."

I was shocked, "Executed, for what?"

He shrugged, "It matters not. What life will he have in the Tower? He will see no one and while he will be well fed that is no life, is it? He is a golden bird in a gilded cage."

It seemed to me that there were many benefits to being born poor and without a title. The fact that an uncle could kill not only his nephews but his brother and then imprison a child was something none in our village would even contemplate. Eternal damnation and roasting in hell were not enough of a punishment for ordinary folk.

The only city I had seen before had been York and that had been a brief visit before we had our fateful journey to Bramham Moor. Oxford had a city wall, but it was much smaller than York's Roman one. The castle had been a mighty one but now it was neglected and in need of repair. I was told this as we wound our way through the streets. The earl was cheered by the populace for he was well-loved and we acknowledged the cheers as conquering heroes.

"If the earl lives there then why does he not improve it?"

Sam Sharp Tongue was the cleverest and most well informed of us and he simply smiled, "His most powerful home in Essex, Castle Hedingham, is better positioned and closer to London. He will stay here but one night and then head to his real home, where the countess and his family live. We will be the guardians of the castle. For my part, I do not mind a leaking roof for that is a small price to pay for the freedom we shall enjoy."

Geoffrey of Aylesbury said, "If we are kept on." Geoffrey of Aylesbury was one who saw the pot as half empty.

"Have confidence, we shall be!"

When we entered the inner bailey or ward as some men named it, I saw what Sam had meant. There were piles of ancient horse dung and rubbish that had been deposited by other soldiers who had stayed there. No one had bothered to keep it clean. The earl and his retinue entered the keep and we wandered over to what I learned were the warrior halls. During the time of the civil war between Empress Matilda and Stephen the castle had been of great importance and had been well garrisoned. Since that time its importance had declined and while there was plenty of room, I saw what Sam meant. I saw daylight through the roof.

Joseph led us to a dry part of the hall and it was the latecomers who had to make do with the leaky roof. There was no rain but even I knew that there would be come the winter.

Perhaps because he knew that he would be letting go many of his men or maybe to say thank you we were supplied with plenty of ale and food. I had learned my lesson and drank sparingly. I was no longer the wild youth who drank too much and became a wild beast. It was strange to watch others behave foolishly. Geoffrey of Aylesbury was the one in our group who, having drunk to excess, picked a fight with an archer. It was a foolish thing to do for no matter how strong a billman thinks he is he will never be as strong as a longbowman.

Stephen and I were going to intervene, but Sam Sharp Tongue restrained us, "We will but Geoffrey needs a lesson or else he will do this again and allow the drink to control him."

When Geoffrey's face was a bloody mess we intervened, and the archer returned to his drinking. As Joseph tended to Geoffrey's face, I realised that had been me and I had been lucky. Other than the fight it was a jolly evening, and the food was good. Even more important to me was the joy of friends. Even when I had travelled to Windle and *'The Raven's Head'* I had not had friends. I saw that now. I had companions but they were not true friends. The other five I sat with now were and that made me realise why my father had gone off to war each time he had been called. It was the call of brothers in arms that made him leave. It also made me worry. What if the earl did not keep us on? The others had said there were always wars and disputes, but I was not sure. The other enjoyable part of the night were the jokes, riddles, and songs with which men entertained each other. It was Sam Sharp Tongue who had a never-ending supply of them. He loved words and plays on words. He would ask us a question and when we gave our answers, he would have us laughing when he gave us the answer.

"Tell me, my friends, what is the distance from the surface of the sea to the deepest part of the ocean?"

That taxed us all and we each suggested an answer. Joseph of Didcot did not and he just smiled.

When we had exhausted our befuddled minds Sam beamed, "Only a stone's throw."

We did not feel foolish at the answer, but we admired Sam for his cleverness.

"What is it that never freezes?"

I was determined that this time I would not look foolish, "The sun of course!"

Sam nodded and smiled, "True but the sun is not of this earth. What is it on this earth that never freezes?" As the others wracked their brains Sam leaned over and said, "You are a clever youth, James. That was a good answer and I never thought of it!" When none could come up with an answer Sam said, "Boiling water."

The one which had us all reeling was his last question, "What beast is it that has her tail between her eyes?" That had us all stumped and none could even come up with a single answer, "It is a cat when she licketh her arse."

The riddles were ended when the bagpipes and hornpipes were brought forth and dancing began. Geoffrey of Aylesbury's drunken capering with a bloody face made me laugh so much I had to leave the hall to make water. By the end of the evening, I could think of nothing finer than to spend my time with these heroes of King Henry.

The next morning reality set in when we were all gathered in the outer bailey. The Earl was there with his sergeant at arms and on a table were piles of coins. A scribe had a piece of parchment and we lined up to receive our pay for the work we had done. I had almost forgotten the payment for I had a bulging purse. I would be a rich man when I was paid for my war service. The men approached with those with whom they had fought. It was usually in groups of seven or eight. It soon became clear that the payment was only part of the purpose. We saw some of those who had been paid go to the warrior hall, collect their war gear and then leave the castle. Others did not. I followed Sam and the others to head to the table and waited with bated breath.

The earl nodded to the scribe who counted out six piles of coins. Joseph's was larger but I did not even bother to count it for I was waiting for the earl's words. He looked up and unlike the others he had paid off, he studied us carefully. I felt uncomfortable when his eyes lighted on me for I felt sure I had done something to incur his wrath.

"Joseph of Didcot, you and your billmen fought well at Stoke Field and Edward of Cowley has impressed upon me the need to keep you on the roll." He smiled, "He seems to think that the youth of your men will help us in the future. You are to be kept on the roll. You will remain here until twelfth night after which you will leave and join me at Hedingham. Does that suit?"

"Aye, my lord, and we are honoured to continue to serve you."

He nodded, "You will need to be attired in my livery and each looking identical. My sergeant at arms will arrange it. We cannot have the Earl of Oxford's men looking like vagabonds, can we?"

I knew that his comments were directed to me for despite my efforts with my jack the brown stains still showed the blood, but I cared not. I was to be a liveried billman. My father had often said that such men were the best of his profession. I would, when time allowed, be able to return to Ecclestone and present myself dressed in the livery of the Earl of Oxford. I felt honoured when, that night, I saw how few men had been retained. There were just forty archers and a mere twenty billmen. There had been some resentment amongst a few of the ones who had been allowed to leave and most of it was directed towards Stephen and me, we were the youngest. Even Geoffrey of Aylesbury defended us, and I felt that I truly belonged. Over the next weeks, we were fitted and kitted with new helmets, jacks, and liveried tunics. When we walked the streets of Oxford wearing the Earl's coat of arms, we were treated with respect in the earl's home city.

Tom the Wanderer remarked upon it, "Make the most of it James, for in other parts of the country we would be spat upon and abused. Our allegiance to the cause of King Henry does not sit well with many folk. The war might be over but there is still resentment. There are Yorkists and others who do not like the king's taxes. The money that was paid to us came from taxes and while those in the north and the midlands may think it money well spent to keep them safe those in Kent, Dorset, Devon and Cornwall might not."

We did, of course, continue our training for Tom was right and whilst the war was over the pretender, Lambert Simnel had shown how quickly resentment could flare into violence. We worked with the archers. They had their own practice, but we came together once a day where under the watchful eye of Edward of Cowley we practised manoeuvres such as passing through lines and either standing before the archers or behind them. When we worked as billmen under Captain Jack I discovered that he had very high standards. The lowering of a billhook would result in a blow from his stick. I learned that it was the haft of his first billhook and had been sliced through at the battle of Towton. Reluctant to let it go he had smoothed the end and now used it as a form of punishment as well, I have no doubt, as a reminder of what could happen in battle.

As Christmas approached, I spent some of my coins in the Oxford market. I bought new buskins and a spare cloak and the oil to make it waterproof. I bought some better clothes for sometimes we liked to visit alehouses not as billmen but as men who wanted a good time. I even had my first visit to a whore, one of the Oxford geese. When Sam learned that I had still to know a woman he had laughed and insisted that I visit a doxy. Sam felt that he had to spill his seed regularly for he believed it kept him healthy. Joan was a comely lass and younger than most, but she had begun whoring at the age of twelve and as a sixteen-year-old knew all that there was to know. She was, however, kind and when I spilt my seed quickly, she did not mock but was sympathetic. The deed done I knew that I would wait and save my coins as the act had seemed somewhat overrated. I was also a little worried as two of the archers visited another of the Oxford geese and had a goose bite as a result. The healers applied the disgusting ointment which marked their shame and made them itch.

The celebrations for Christmas were an enjoyable time but were tinged with the sadness that I was not with my family and this was the first time such a thing had happened. Had I been able to write I suppose I could have written to tell them that I lived but I could not and there was little point in worrying about something I could do nothing about. I enjoyed the dancing and the caroles and the food. Although much of the food at Christmas was made up of fruit and meat which might have gone off by December, the spices and brandy in the castle meant that it was as tasty as any food I had ever eaten. We also enjoyed, thanks to Edward of Cowley, mulled wine. I drank sparingly but enjoyed this brief elevation to the life of the nobility.

Then, all too soon, it was time for the six of us to leave the castle and head across England to Essex. Edward of Cowley furnished us with coins for our accommodation and a warning that as we wore the earl's livery then no misbehaviour would be tolerated. All eyes were on Geoffrey of Aylesbury.

I had learned from my time on the back of Scout. The panniers I had used and the sacks to hold them had given me an idea to make life easier on the road. I had also seen the gardyvyans of the archers and, my helmet apart, I used my old cloak to make a bag to carry all. My helmet could still hang from my billhook covered with a hessian sack but with leather straps around my gear I was able to carry it on my back and the walk was easier. After the first day of marching along a sleet and rain covered road from Oxford to Aylesbury, Geoffrey's hometown, they had all decided to emulate me. The oiled cloak kept everything dry and I was the only one who did not have to dry all his clothes out before the fire in the inn. I just dried the clothes in which I had walked. My spare hose and breeks were as dry as a bone.

As we ate Joseph told us, once again, of the need to uphold the name of the Earl of Oxford.

"There are still many who oppose King Henry and do not like his taxes. The fires of rebellion are not yet doused, and they still glow. A simple act such as the Earl of Oxford's men behaving badly could fan those flames."

"And how far do we have to walk? I know the north but not the road to the east of here."

Tom the Wanderer smiled, "Aye, well, Stephen, it is a hundred miles we have to travel and not all of it will be as safe as the first part. Before I joined and I walked this land oft times I would be forced to walk for twenty or thirty miles a day. Many times the shelter I took was not from the elements but bandits and brigands."

Geoffrey of Aylesbury was the most belligerent of our company and he growled, "They would get short shrift from attacking a company such as we."

Our leader shook his head, "You forget, Geoffrey, that many of the bandits are more than mere brigands. They are the men we fought at Bosworth and Stoke Field. We wear the Earl's colours and are marked men. We have to pass London and as we all know that is a cesspit and nest of vipers. No, we shall drink sparingly and be vigilant. We are summoned to Hedingham for a purpose. Let us ensure that we are able to carry out the task the earl has in mind for us."

That night as we slept my last thoughts were questions. I had thought we would just guard the earl's castle, but Edward of Cowley and Joseph had been closely closeted before we left. Was there another motive? Growing up in the backwater that was Ecclestone we had only heard of the murders, treachery and treason of King Edward and King Richard. It was like the tale which starts at one end of the village and by the time it is retold at the other end, bears little relation to the original one. I knew that the Earl of Oxford was now the most important man after the king in the realm and that was a dangerous position. I thought him loyal but King Richard had thought that Percy and

Stanley had been loyal but both, in their own ways, had betrayed him. I now understood why my father had left the world of war.

The weather did not improve and though by the third day of our walk the sleet had stopped, the wind from the east found gaps in our cloaks. By then, however, the others had all managed to fashion sacks such as mine. Our reception in the inns at which we both ate and slept was mixed. The civil war was still a raw wound. Lancastrians welcomed us but Yorkists were openly hostile. We learned to look for subtle signs such as white roses climbing up the outside of Yorkists taverns or the sign of the boar, King Richard's sign. Despite our fears, we reached the Earl's mighty castle on the sixth day after leaving Oxford. I felt closer to all the men I thought of as brothers. Stephen and I had become particularly close. He was no longer silent although he was still addressed as such. My friendship with him also made me feel guilty about striking my father. He had lost his family and was an orphan, but I had chosen to abandon my family. Perhaps God had sent him to make me reflect upon my sins.

The earl did not have a large garrison. Most of his retainers were still in Oxford and we had plenty of room in the warrior hall. Edward of Cowley was already there having ridden by a different road and it was he who greeted us. "Welcome and I hope, Joseph of Didcot, that you had a journey free from incident."

"We did."

"Good. You have a week of what will pass for leisure although I will be working you each day and then we shall be off once more." He grinned as though he had a secret, and he was enjoying keeping it from us.

When he had gone and we began to unpack the gear Sam asked, "What should we know, Joseph? Why have we been summoned?"

Joseph was an honest man and he shifted uncomfortably as he answered, "The Sergeant at Arms spoke to me in Oxford and said that the Earl might have a task for the six of us. That is all. He asked me if any of you was considered unreliable." He jabbed a finger at Geoffrey of Aylesbury, "The fight you embroiled yourself in tainted the whole of this company. It almost cost us our places."

Geoffrey looked down, "I have apologised, Joseph of Didcot; can we not leave it at that?"

Sam asked before Joseph could reply, "And this work for which our services have been promised, is it warrior work?"

Joseph spread his arms, "You know as much as I do. I am guessing that we have a week to discover its purpose." He smiled, "It will, Sam Sharp Tongue, be an occupation for our minds and hands and you of all people know the value of such activity."

Slightly mollified he nodded, "Yet I am still unhappy about being used."

Stephen and I did not care. Although he was older than I was by a year or so we were both still young enough to view any variation from a daily routine as exciting. We would be doing something different and that appealed to me.

Chapter 7

The next morning we breakfasted well. Although we did not eat the same food as the earl and Edward of Cowley, food was cooked for us and we enjoyed freshly baked bread as well as fried slices of salted ham with cheese. They set up a man for the day ahead. We picked up our billhooks and headed to the outer bailey where we were told that Edward of Cowley awaited us. To our surprise, we were told to stack our billhooks. We did so and stood expectantly. Four men at arms appeared with what looked like wooden clubs. They deposited them on the ground and then stood, grinning, behind the sergeant at arms.

"You will learn new skills this week. The first is how to use a sword." He picked up one of the wooden clubs and I could see that it had a guard and was a practice sword. "This is what we will use." He smiled, "We would not like any of you to be hurt, would we?" I saw Sam begin to open his mouth but Edward of Cowley silenced him by picking up a second practice sword and throwing it to him. "Instead of using your famous sharp tongue, let us see how you use a wooden sword. Try to hit me."

Sam was a clever warrior; I knew that from the times we had practised with a billhook but this was different. Edward of Cowley was a man at arms. Geoffrey of Aylesbury would have rushed in to use his superior strength and size to defeat the man at arms but Sam was too clever for that and I saw him weighing up the man at arms whose sword hung almost lazily from his right hand and he appeared to be inviting a quick strike. I could not see a reason why he should not and, eventually, Sam stepped in and brought his wooden sword around to smash into the arm of the man at arms. Had the blow connected it would have hurt. It might, perhaps, have broken the bone but it got nowhere near and Edward of Cowley pirouetted on one leg so that Sam's sword struck fresh air while Edward of Cowley's wooden sword cracked into Sam's back. Sam winced and I knew that it had hurt.

Edward said, "Good, you did not rush in but you risked all in the hope that you might catch me asleep. Any warrior who faces you with a weapon pointed not at you but the ground is trying to trick you." He patted Sam on the shoulder. "You did well and I know that each of you can use your falchion or your short sword but the Earl wishes you to be able to use them as well as your billhook."

Sam asked, "Why?"

Smiling enigmatically Edward of Cowley said, "You have all been chosen to be the best of the earl's billmen. Captain Jack is making the rest of the Earl's company better billmen, but you all showed, even the younger ones, that you have skills and work well together. The earl wishes to harness those skills. Now pair up and let us see how you can fight each other."

Naturally, I sparred with Stephen the Silent, and we were well and evenly matched. The man at arms and his men came around us to place our feet better and to improve our posture. I was slightly quicker on the uptake than Stephen and that helped me to score a couple of minor victories. It spurred him on and soon we were both rapidly improving. When I saw the smile of satisfaction upon the face of Edward of Cowley, I knew that he was happy with our progress. By noon we were all a little battered and bruised; I began to dread an afternoon that would only see us increase the pain. To my surprise, after a pleasant food break, he led us back into the inner bailey and I wondered if we had finished for the day. We had not.

"Step forward, James of Prescot."

I wondered why I had been singled out but I went to the fore albeit reluctantly.

"The earl was also impressed that while he had patently never ridden before James of Prescot managed to master riding a horse from York to Newark to bring news of the rebels. The earl wonders if the rest of you could learn such skills."

My comrades were behind me, but I could feel the resentment from their eyes boring into my back. Edward of Cowley whistled and six ostlers led hackneys from the stables. These were not Scout, they were not slow-moving sumpters, they were riding horses. I now wondered if we had been asked to wait at Oxford so that the Earl or his horse master could procure the mounts. That they had been selected was clear for one was much bigger than the others and that had to be for Geoffrey of Aylesbury.

"James, fetch a saddle from the stable and choose a horse. Show the others how to saddle a horse."

As I headed into the stable, I put all thoughts of the feelings of my comrades from my head. I dared not make a fool of myself. The saddles were all hanging from hooks, and I chose not the newest one but the one with the softest leather. I also chose the thickest horse blanket that I could. As I went out of the stable, I examined the horses. I ruled out choosing the largest horse for obvious reasons. Still holding the saddle I walked down the line and when the mare nuzzled me, I knew that I had been chosen. I stopped and said to the ostler, "What is her name?"

He was younger than I was and as he stroked her mane he said, "Molly and you have made a wise choice." He lowered his voice so that only I could hear, "If a horse chooses you then it is a foolish man who ignores that." He spoke normally as he said, "She is a good horse and is two years old. She may not be the fastest of these horses, but she is the most surefooted."

I nodded and placed the blanket and saddle on the ground. I put my face close to hers as I stroked her mane. When I spoke to her it was as though she was a person and no other could hear us. Scout had taught me that, "I have ridden but one horse so you needs must be patient with me. When I can I shall find you some apples and carrots but until then be gentle, my lovely." She neighed and I saw the ostler smile and nod. I placed the blanket on her back and ensured that there were no creases. Then I fitted the saddle making sure that the girth was as tight as possible. I did not want to slip off. Taking the reins from the ostler I walked around the inner bailey. I had learned enough from Master Geoffrey to know that all horses try to trick their riders for most horses do not like a tight girth. I saw Edward of Cowley nodding his approval as I led the mare back and then tightened the girth a little more. I stood with the reins in my hand and Edward of Cowley nodded. Taking a deep breath I stood in the stirrups and mounted. As I had expected the stirrups were the wrong length. The ostler came to adjust them.

Patting her rump he said, "She is ready, billman."

I dug my heels in and said, "Walk on." When she obeyed I could have cheered. This was, however, no time for overconfidence and I just walked her around the inner bailey. I knew that my style was not correct but I cared not. I stayed in the saddle and that was all that mattered.

Edward of Cowley waved me over and I stopped Molly next to him. He stroked her mane and nodded. When he spoke it was for my ears only, "You have a natural eye for horseflesh and whilst your riding style would make a knight squirm it will suffice. Well done, James of Prescot." He turned, "There, that is how easy it is. If the youngest of your company can do that then by the end of the week you shall all be as proficient. However, I will choose your horses while James here gets to know his mount a little better." He waved towards the gate to the outer bailey and said, "You have half an hour. Use it wisely."

I wheeled Molly to the left and dug in my heels. We headed through the gatehouse and across the outer bailey. I saw the surprise on the sentries at both gates as I did so. Although I had no intention of being foolish, I knew that, at some point, I would have to trot and I did not relish falling from my horse before the gaze of others. I left the village and headed down a quiet track rather than a road. The earth was softer than the cobbles of the road.

"Well, Molly, time to trot. Ha!" As she trotted, I found myself hanging on but the time on Scout's back, even though it had been lower to the ground, came to my aid and I found that not only could I hold on but the pain from my thighs was not as bad as it had been the last time. Perhaps Mistress Gurton's salve had some property that hardened the skin. I kept the pot in my purse with my coins. It was as valuable as gold. I wheeled her around and kept her trotting all the way back to the castle. As I entered the inner bailey, I saw that Geoffrey of Aylesbury had been deposited on the ground. The cobbles of the inner bailey would have hurt but his pride would have suffered more as the rest of our company, all mounted, laughed at him. That became our routine for the week. In the morning we bruised our arms and heads and in the afternoon, we bruised our buttocks and in most cases, our pride.

That first night, after we had eaten, I was questioned heavily about my experience of riding Scout. Tom the Wanderer could not believe how far I had ridden whilst still untrained, "My thighs are chafed already and we barely had an hour in the saddle."

I shrugged, "The message had to get through and besides, I had little choice in the matter."

Joseph of Didcot said. "There is more to James of Prescot than meets the eye. What tips have you for Edward of Cowley made it quite clear that we have but a week to master the art of riding?"

Every face, even Sam's was turned eagerly towards me. I gave them as honest an answer as I could, "Get to know your horse and make him like you. In my limited experience, a horse responds better to kindness than blows. If you can find apples or carrots then give them to your mounts. Make sure that the girths are tight. Master Geoffrey showed me how to do so and I am grateful to him." I paused so that my next words would sink in, "Thus far you have walked. Believe me, when you trot and then canter, staying on the back of the horse becomes a far harder task."

I saw that sink in. We all retired early that night; there was neither banter nor games. We all knew that the next week would be hard.

I was not wrong but it was also a rewarding time for the men at arms who taught us to use swords knew their business. They encouraged us to look on our swords and falchions as a shorter version of a billhook and once that idea was planted it took seed. There was a point we could use but, as with the billhook, a backslash with the blade could be equally deadly. Of course, we were only using the wooden swords, but we all grasped the concept. The riding came slower to some, especially Geoffrey of Aylesbury who I doubted would ever be a horseman. However, I gleaned from snippets of conversation that the skill of riding was merely to enable us to travel quicker but it intrigued me for where would we be going that necessitated horses?

Our master did not relent all week. I could have offered the salve to my comrades but there was little enough to go around, and I did not want to play favourites. The small pot still resided in my purse. I suggested all sorts of remedies such as padding the saddle and breeks. They worked to varying degrees but none were as effective as Mistress Gurton's salve. It was the last day of the training that the men at arms brought us real swords with which to practise. They were short swords and we all established, by the use of our thumbs, that they had no edge. They were notched and pitted, clearly, the weapons used by the garrison. As soon as I held mine, I knew why we had used the wooden ones. Even the ancient, pitted iron in our hands felt more like a weapon than the wooden one. It was balanced and lighter.

I faced up to Stephen, but Edward of Cowley's voice rang out, "We use the pel. Today we show you not how to fight a man but how to use the blade."

The pel was a wooden stump buried in the ground. It was the height of a man and each pel, there were ten of them, bore the scars and wounds of previous training. We then used the blunted edge to hack and slash at the pel. We were not given the luxury of time for our master's voice gave the rhythm and the order for the blows. His men at arms had willow switches to whack at us when we were tardy or made the wrong strike. It was the hardest training any of us did that whole week as you were waiting for the savage whip from the willow switch when you made the smallest of errors. Edward seemed satisfied and the food that was brought out seemed to be better than the fare normally served.

We were sent to fetch our horses. By now we all knew how to saddle them and even Geoffrey of Aylesbury was able to speak to his horse. I liked Molly. Given a choice between Scout and Molly, I would have been hard pushed to make a choice. Molly edged it because she was a hackney and a much better horse for what we intended. I had known for some time that giving us such horses meant we were heading to war. They would not waste six horses just to get billmen to the battlefield quicker. As we had not used our billhooks then our purpose would not be to use billhooks but swords. I was intrigued. We led the horses to the outer bailey where we had practised for the last two days, and we waited. There was just Edward of Cowley, his willow whackers were not to be seen. "Mount!"

We clambered aboard and I saw the hint of a smile as we all managed to do so almost as one. He then led us, not around the outer bailey but through the gate towards the village. I glanced over to Stephen who had the same surprised expression. It was like being let out of gaol. Stephen and I had been given the position just behind Edward. It was not a place of honour it was so that the others could hide behind us and Edward of Cowley would just see our mistakes and not those of the others. We walked through the village, Edward acknowledging the calls and waves from those who knew him. Ignoring the cobbled roads he took us on a track and shouted, "You will keep up with me for the rest of the afternoon. There will be no commands."

Now I was glad for our position. I would be able to see the feet of the sergeant at arms. When we would be going faster, he would dig in his heels. I watched him as he did so and I said to Stephen, "Now!" I dug my heels in and Molly responded. We were trotting. I did not glance behind, but Edward of Cowley did.

"Sam Sharp Tongue, are you asleep? Keep up."

I smiled to myself for Sam would hate to be highlighted as having made a mistake.

Edward of Cowley kept up the trot for quite a while. I saw a gate ahead to the right leading to some open fields in which a few sheep were grazing. Suddenly Edward of Cowley swung his horse through the gate and into the field. He almost caught me unawares and had I not seen the gate a moment earlier I might have missed it. As we went through, I saw him dig his heels in and I did the same as we went through the narrow entrance. He was cantering and, as the field was a long one, I guessed he would use it to gallop. I was no longer next to Stephen whose horse was directly behind me. The cantering was hard, and I barely managed to keep hold of both the reins and my seat, but I did so. The grazing sheep scattered at the sound of the thundering hooves. When he began to gallop, I feared the worst. I pressed my knees into the saddle and leaned a little towards the back of the saddle as the slope was heading down to a brook. When I heard the cry from behind, I feared that someone had fallen but I dared not look around. I suddenly realised that Edward of Cowley had no intention of slowing down. He intended to jump the water. I was two lengths back and I watched him sail across and land with plenty of ground to spare. The ground had flattened, and I was able to lean forward and to say, "Go, Molly. Show Master Edward what we can do." Molly had a better idea of what to do than I did, and she sailed across. In hindsight, I should have stood in the stirrups as we jumped but I merely clung on. The landing was so heavy I feared once more that any chance I had of fathering children had disappeared with the collision between the saddle and my crown jewels. Edward had reined in and turned around. I pulled back hard on the reins whilst pulling Molly to the right to avoid the sergeant at arms. Thankfully I stopped, I turned a panting Molly and rode next to Edward of Cowley who was grinning.

He pointed up the slope. Halfway down the field, Geoffrey of Aylesbury's horse was grazing while its rider lay writhing on the ground. As for the others? They had made the brook. Sam and Tom had obviously tried to stop and been unhorsed. Joseph and Stephen were still astride their horses on the other side, Edward turned to me, "You have courage and even if you do not know it, you have natural skill. I thought to turn and see all four of you on the other side."

"Four?"

"Aye, James of Prescot, when I heard the cry then I knew one had fallen. It matters not for we can accomplish this with one less. Now let us jump back over the stream eh? This time lift your reins and stand in your saddle. It will make your landing easier." He rode around in a circle and urged his horse on. He took the narrow stream at a canter.

Knowing that I had time and had done it once before made it easier for me. I stood and sailed across. I realised that it was a very narrow stream and when I landed there was no pain.

"Not bad and we have found the weak piece of mail. Your training is done, and we shall return to the castle. Groom your horses well for tomorrow we leave Hedingham. Let us go and see how Geoffrey of Aylesbury fares."

Our largest billman had fallen badly and broken his arm. Joseph fashioned a sling and that done we helped him into the saddle. I was given the task of leading the horse of the wounded warrior. Once in the inner bailey, he was whisked off to the physician while we saw to our horses and Gerald's. As we groomed them, we could not help but speak of both the day and the future.

"Well, James of Prescot, I think that you are something of a dark horse." I groaned at Sam's pun, but it was to be expected. "I thought I could best you in all things but today you showed me you could do something I would never attempt in a hundred years."

I shook my head, "He did not expect any of us to attempt what he did. I was foolish and I should have reined in. I know I am, at times arrogant."

"No, James, God gave you a natural skill and it is a sin to waste such talent." Joseph was always our leader and knew the right thing to say.

"Aye but Gerald broke his arm. Do you think that the sergeant intended that?"

I shrugged, "Perhaps, Stephen, perhaps not but whatever is intended that we do, will be without Gerald."

Stephen asked, "What do you mean, James?"

"We leave Oxford tomorrow, and it will be by horse and without billhooks. Does that not intrigue you?"

Sam Sharp Tongue laughed, "And now, James of Prescot, you show me that your mind works quicker than mine. I heard the sergeant's words but did not put it all together. You are right. Why would we be leaving in the middle of winter? There is no snow on the ground but there might be soon. We are not going to war or else we would be taking our billhooks. I am intrigued."

We were all even more intrigued when we were taken by a liveried servant to a small private dining room just off the Great Hall. There were six places laid and Edward of Cowley stood with the Earl of Oxford. The earl smiled, "You may sit. I am not intending to stay but I thought you should know the reason for your recent training."

We sat and I saw that there were no servants in the room and that the door had been closed behind us.

"Firstly, you are my men and your loyalty is, first and foremost to me." I did not see it, but I guessed from the next words that Sam Sharp Tongue had reacted. "And of course, to your king. That goes without saying, Sam Sharp Tongue, and nothing that I ever ask you to do would be considered treasonous."

Silence fell upon the table and Edward of Cowley smiled and said, "Drink while the earl speaks."

I took the beaker of ale and sipped it. It was strong ale; good but strong and I would drink sparingly.

"My wife, Countess Margaret, is a Neville. Her brother Richard, Earl of Warwick, was killed at Barnet and his body was displayed in London before being buried at Bisham Abbey. His sword was kept hidden, and it is now in my possession. My wife, who was the youngest sibling of the great earl, wishes the sword to be taken, in secret, back to Middleham Castle where it will be kept until needed again." He smiled, "You will all be rewarded when you return." He glanced at Edward of Cowley, "With a reward commensurate with your position. I will leave you now so that Edward of Cowley can complete the giving of instructions."

He left and servants entered. Looking around I saw the questions on every face, but we knew we could not ask them until we were alone. That the servants had been instructed was clear for they laid all the food on the centre of the table with fresh jugs of ale and without saying a word, left.

Edward of Cowley said, "Eat. I will answer all questions when I have satiated my appetite. The ride this afternoon was entertaining and has made me look forward to this feast. Enjoy, for once on the road I know not if we will have such fine fare."

And it was good food. There were fowl and game birds as well as an old sheep which had been slow-cooked so that the meat slipped from the bone. Some spices had been used to cook the beans and had we not had the ride north hanging over us I think all of us would have thought that we had died and gone to heaven. Edward of Cowley enjoyed his food, and I took heart from that. He saw the task as within our compass. When the savouries and then the sweetmeats had been devoured the sergeant at arms drank deeply from his beaker and said, "And now the questions."

We all looked at Sam for we each knew that his mind would have been sifting through all the information to come up with the most pertinent question, "Why now, Sergeant? It is almost seventeen years since Barnet. Where is the urgency that necessitates a ride through winter when the days are short, and the weather will fight us?"

"You are well named, Sam. The countess is unwell and she has been asking for the return of the sword to Middleham since its discovery in April. The earl seeks to please his wife and while it is kept here then the enemies of the earl may use that knowledge to discredit him with the king."

Tom the Wanderer snorted, "The earl won Stoke Field for him. He is safe."

Shaking his head Edward Cowley leaned forward, "No one is safe. The struggle for the crown has been going on since King Richard the Second was killed in Pontefract Castle, perhaps even longer. The sword has to be taken somewhere and Middleham Castle seems the best place."

Sam nodded, "And yet the Earl died without a male heir."

"Sharp, Sam, very sharp. Aye but if the countess and the earl had a child…"

We all knew that the earl and his wife were trying for children and that made sense. The answer seemed to satisfy almost all. Joseph said, "And Geoffrey of Aylesbury?"

"I have always viewed him as the weak piece of mail that made up your company, Joseph of Didcot. It was not just the fall from the horse but the temper and his fighting. He will be moved into another company of billmen when he is out of the hospital." He paused. "He is leaving your company."

"You are breaking up the company?"

"Until James of Prescot came you were a company of five. Who is the better warrior, Joseph, Gerald or James?"

The brief pause and silence gave me the answer and Joseph's defence of Gerald was purely out of loyalty, "Gerald is a good man."

Edward of Cowley nodded, "And he can be replaced. You know yourself that even when the arm heals, he will never be the billman that he once was."

More silence followed. We all picked at the sweetmeats and treats that lay on the table. The jugs were emptied. I felt bold enough to ask my question, "Sergeant, I have ridden this road to the north although I was travelling south. Even if we were not carrying a treasure such as this then it would be a dangerous

82

road. There are bandits and brigands. Sherwood Forest may not be as dangerous as once it was but..."

He nodded, "And that is why you have been trained with swords and taught to ride. I expect that somewhere along the road we will have to fight." He leaned forward, "I speak amongst warriors and so I will be honest with you. I expect word of what we carry to be common knowledge before we have reached the next village. The earl has kept secret the knowledge of the sword but there are men here who are not warriors. There are men here who will seek the opportunity to make a friend somewhere else. Not all the Yorkists were killed. I have heard of another, in Flanders, who purports to be King Richard."

Sam snorted, "He died with his brother Edward in the Tower."

"And the bodies?" That silenced Sam. "Lord Lovell is still abroad, and he hates both the king and the earl. Whatever reward we are given, believe me, we shall have earned it."

Joseph asked, "And can we ask not to go?"

The sergeant smiled, "You can ask but if any choose that path then they will have dark days locked away until we return." His words were sinister enough for me. I was quite happy to go on this adventure, but I could see that it did not sit well with Joseph of Didcot. He did not like having little choice over the matter but that was the reality.

There were no more questions and, as we made our way back to our beds, I spoke with Stephen about it, "How do you feel?"

He shrugged, "I will be closer to the land of my birth. I always feel like a foreigner here in the south besides, it is employment. You should be happy for you can ride well and I have bruises to show me the skill you have with a sword. Whatever else happens you will survive and for that I am pleased."

I had not thought of that, but he was right. I was the best horseman and, I suspected, the best swordsman. Perhaps this might be the making of me.

Chapter 8

Edward of Cowley was a careful man, and he did not divulge our route until we were well on our way and even then he only gave us the waypoints. We were on an open stretch of the road that led to Cambridge before he told us our first bed for the night. "We will stay in Godmanchester this night. I have an old comrade who has an inn there and we will be safe."

I was increasingly in awe of the sergeant at arms. He had cleverly hidden the sword in plain view and it hung along his saddle beneath his leg covered by a sheepskin. His cloak disguised the pommel and hilt. It would not be considered as a treasure and would be seen as normal for he had another sword hanging from his belt. The longer sword beneath the saddle was a battle sword and not a weapon for protection along the road. Stephen and I rode just behind him and I took that to be an honourable thing and showed that he trusted us. Joseph of Didcot rode behind us and Tom and Sam rode at the rear with the sumpter laden with supplies and a tent. The tent signified that at some time we would sleep rough, and I was not looking forward to that as the days were already cold and the nights freezing. I resigned myself to the discomfort, telling myself that it would all make me a better warrior.

Edward of Cowley was taciturn and silent as we headed towards Cambridge, but he did turn and say, to all of us, "Silence when we ride through towns. Better that they wonder than they hear words that might give them clues as to our identity. If words are needed, then I will speak them. All of you will become the silent billmen!" I heard the chuckle as he laughed at his own joke.

We wore no badges. The tunics, doublets, and hose, not to mention the leather jerkins had come from chests kept in the warrior hall. They had all belonged to men who were no longer alive but they made us anonymous. We wore our own cloaks, and I had my rabbit fur hat to keep me warm. My spare cloak would come in handy when we were forced to camp.

It was as we passed through Cambridge that I saw how clever our sergeant had been. Although we said nothing, I heard the guards at the gates say, as we were allowed in, "More swords for hire looking for a master now that the war is over." He could not keep the contempt from his voice, and he spat as Joseph passed.

We watered our horses in the town and Edward bought us some freshly made pies. We only spoke again once we had left the town and headed along the open road. "If there are pies all the way north, Sergeant, then I shall not complain." Tom liked his food.

Edward of Cowley chuckled, "Aye well, Tom the Wanderer, make the most of any such delicacies for when we are north of Lincoln the fare will become less wholesome for the land there is not as rich as here around Cambridge."

The inn, *'The Infanta of Castile'* was an old one and had plenty of rooms as it was on the main road north. Gerald of Wednesbury had a maimed left hand and he bore the scars of combat on his face but he and our sergeant were old friends. That was clear for we had unsaddled and taken care of all seven horses and yet Edward and Gerald were still in close company. Edward turned as we entered, "These are my men. This is Gerald of Wednesbury."

You are welcome. We are busy but I have a room I keep for lords and the like. You shall have it. There is a bed for Edward, but the rest will have to make do with the floor."

That did not bother any of us for we would be warm and most of us were unused to soft beds.

"I will make up for the hard floor with find food. Hob, show these men to their room and tell Tom to clear away the big table for them."

"But master there are men sitting there drinking!"

He laughed, "They are tosspots who nurse an ale for an hour. If they choose another inn, I shall not miss their custom. Tell Tom!"

"Aye, master." As we passed another servant Hob said, "Clear the table, Tom. Master's orders."

Tom merely nodded and headed to the table with three old codgers sitting around it.

Sam said, "Your master knows his own mind then, Hob?"

The servant laughed, "He maimed just his left hand, and all fear his right. We are the only inn that does not need someone to keep peace and the doxies are clean. It is a good alehouse and you have chosen wisely."

We organised the room ourselves and Stephen and I took the floor on the narrow side of the bed. Tom and Sam took the other side and Joseph of Didcot the bottom. I used my old cloak as a bed which I padded with the spare clothes I had brought. If I needed it, I could use my new cloak as a blanket but the chimney from the main room passed up through the room and I could feel its warmth from the bricks. Gerald of Wednesbury had done well to afford an inn with a chimney.

By the time we returned to the main room the three old men had been shuffled off to a smaller table further from the roaring fire. They cast us venomous glances and I knew that we would be the subject of curses and derisory comments. It was the same in *'The Gryphon'* in Ecclestone. There it was four old men who spent every hour that they could be seated at the table close to the fire. Edward was seated alone at the large table. Stephen had taken his gear to the room whilst Joseph had secreted the sword amongst his own chattels.

Edward had already paid for a jug of ale. We knew that the earl had given him plenty of coin to pay for whatever we needed. "Here boys, enjoy the ale and Gerald is bringing us some hunter's stew." He tapped his nose, "He was always the best of cooks. It will be fine fare."

The beer was good, and the warm fire made all seem cosy, When Gerald returned with Tom and Hob and platters of food, I knew we were in for a treat. The landlord would dine with us and that guaranteed that we had the best food and the best ale. Even better was the fact that it cost us not a single coin. The earl would pay. The stew was a game stew; I knew that there was rabbit along with the beans and the sausage but they had also used a ham hock and some offal, I think it was pig's liver. The result was a delicious stew and a gravy so thick that you could spread it on bread. Stephen and I were both young enough to still have very healthy appetites and I was sparing with the strong beer. We ate and the others chattered while they ate. As we finished our platters and were mopping up the gravy with our bread Gerald waved a hand and Hob topped us up. We kept eating and they talked.

"Have you been kept busy then, Gerald?"

"Aye, the war might be over but there is still unrest and men moving from one place to another. They want no trouble from me and so they keep quiet and pay promptly. That in itself tells me that they are up to no good."

Sam was ever inquisitive, "But where are the paymasters?"

Gerald leaned forward conspiratorially, "Whenever there is trouble in England you can bet that the Scots are rubbing their hands. I heard that Lord Lovell has found a new master in Scotland and is busy trying to raise an army. The man still has money and supporters. Hob, another jug of ale." Hob waved and Gerald rubbed his hands, "It is good to talk to men I can trust. I normally have to be close-mouthed for you never know who you can trust."

For some reason that made me sit straighter on the bench and I know not why.

"Just the Scots then Gerald?"

Shaking his head as he poured some of the fresh jug of ale in his beaker he said, "Visitors have told me that Margaret of Burgundy and Maximillian are supporting the Yorkists you defeated, and I have heard rumours of another pretender. Then there are the Cornish. They did not side too often in the war and enjoyed a pleasant time. Now that the king is demanding taxes the men of the West Country are becoming a little boisterous, shall we say."

He was a mine of information and I saw Edward taking it all in. Living in the castle of the Earl of Oxford meant that people were judicious in what they said to him. Here he knew it for the truth.

"And the route north of here?"

Gerald leaned back and said, "It goes without saying that I would not venture forth without a company of mailed men at arms." He smiled at us, "No offence, gentlemen."

Sam had drunk sufficiently for him to grin and say, "None taken."

"I have not asked, nor will I ask what the purpose of this winter ride is. Better that I know neither the destination nor the purpose. Wherever you go in the north you have to pass through Sherwood, and it is still a vast forest. I know that much of it is being hewn down to make ships for the king and grazing for sheep but it would take a hundred lifetimes to make a dent in that mighty forest. The inns and the castles where you make your beds will be safe but for the rest? Keep your swords sharp and ready to be drawn."

Those sobering words were the last we heard before we retired. The adventure I had keenly anticipated now seemed less attractive. Edward of Cowley must have sensed the collective gloom for he said, "I know my friend does not lie but he does not know you. If I had chosen a company of mailed men at arms then all would have known what we were about and there would be the enemies of the king and the Earl already gathered to take the sword from us. We have bandits and brigands with which we will have to deal and I am confident that the men who fought so well at Stoke Field will have the measure of them. I trust you and that is all you need to know."

As we headed north, the next day Edward of Cowley gave us his plan, "I intend to avoid Nottingham and the forest north of there. Instead, we head to Stamford and Grantham." He paused, "It means travelling close to Stoke Field but that cannot be helped. If we can get to Doncaster where the king still has great influence, then we might avoid the worst of the forest."

Sam waited and then said, "But not all."

Knowing that a loose word might spell disaster for us we were all close-mouthed as we stayed in the inns at Stamford and Grantham. We skirted the battlefield where we had defeated the Yorkists and stopped for barely half an hour in Newark. We headed for Lincoln. That city had always been a king's city and all of us were happy to be staying within the walls of such a strong fortress. We could have stayed in the castle but that would have involved too many questions and instead, we stayed in an inn close by the north gate. I did not like it. I saw too many of the young men I had consorted with in Windle. They were what my father had called bad uns although at the time I could not see it. One tried to pick a fight with Stephen but when we gathered ranks then he backed off, but I saw them admiring our swords, boots, and clothes.

The next day, as we left, I saw the wisdom of Edward of Cowley's plan. We were far to the west of any vestige of a forest, and we would not have to negotiate deadly trees and ambush. We had a different problem. The land was flat and to fight the wind the locals had planted hedgerows. The blackthorn, elder and rowan stopped the wind flattening crops, but they also gave places where an attacker could hide.

The attack came at the village of Scampton. There we were to take the road north and west rather than the road heading north. We had passed the forest which lay like a great shadow to the south and west of us. The gang that attacked us had to have left early to race along the road and arrive there before we did. It was our horses that were attractive to them. These were not the bandits of the forest but the bandits of Lincoln. The youths we had seen were their scouts. The first we knew was when Edward of Cowley drew his sword and shouted, "Treachery! Defend yourselves." I still know not how he knew they were there.

I was still the best rider amongst our company and I had my falchion out almost as quickly as the sergeant but, for the first moment or two, I saw nothing. Then I saw a shadow move towards the rump of Edward's horse and my fist fights in Windle came to my aid. I slashed, almost blindly, at the shadow and was rewarded by a scream. Edward of Cowley had a hand and a half sword, and he almost severed the man in two with his blow.

"Drive at them! They are the scum of the earth and cowards who attack from ambush."

I wondered at his words but then realised he was attempting to antagonise the bandits and make them come at him. He was a very brave man. I whirled Molly to my right, slashing my sword as I did so. I was lucky for the youth who had tried to pick a fight with Stephen launched himself at me from above. My falchion's curved blade tore through his middle and guts and blood poured forth as he fell dying at my horse's feet. Edward was right. Our horses were a weapon, and I dug my heels into Molly's side. She leapt at the would-be robbers who were now pouring from the hedgerow. We were outnumbered but I was damned if I would go down quietly. Edward had three men clinging on to him and I rode Molly at them. I knew they had no mail, and their weapons were knives and, from the odd arrow I saw sticking from Edward's mail, bows, but we had swords. The time at the pel had not been wasted and I cut through almost to the backbone of one of the men clinging to Edward's horse. I then used, for the first time, the tip of the sword. It drove through the ribs and into the chest of the man trying to wrestle Edward from his horse. I saw the tip emerge from his shoulder and he fell to die in an ever-widening pool of blood.

Behind me, I heard a scream and saw Tom the Wanderer as he was hewn almost in two by an axe. For the first time since the alehouse in Windle, I saw red and I galloped at the killer who was trying to pull the corpse from the saddle. Standing in the stirrups I brought my falchion down so hard that I split his skull in twain. The spattering blood, bone and brains had a shocking effect on the men who had survived. They turned and ran but we were in no mood to let them get off Scot free and we charged after them. Admittedly I was at the fore for I was the better rider but the other three all followed me and we had slashed at the backs of the fleeing men to inflict horrible wounds before Edward of Cowley's stentorian voice brought us to our senses, "Back here! Now!"

I reined in Molly and headed back. The bloody corpse of our comrade took away any sense of victory. One death was one too many.

Edward of Cowley had sheathed his sword and he nodded, "You all did well but never ride after fleeing men unless I order you to." He smiled at me, "James of Prescot, you are a wild cat and I am glad you fought with me this day. I owe you a life. Now bind poor Tom in his cloak and we will bury him when we get the chance."

Stephen asked, "And the robbers?"

"They will have company this night when the rest of the carrion come to feast on them and when we return, I will speak with the landlord of that inn and the constable. It is a rat hole that needs to be mended!"

We did not stop until we reached Gainsborough. While we visited the priest Edward went to speak to the lord of the manor. For a small payment, the priest was happy to bury Tom in his graveyard. Our friend would wander no more. It was good that he was laid in holy ground and a priest spoke Latin. I did not understand it but I guessed that God would and it gave me comfort. We headed north and west at a faster rate and in silence.

We had passed our first real test as warriors, but it had cost us dear. We rode into Doncaster just as the gates were being closed for the night. Lord Scales had been here the last time I had passed through, but it was now another who was acting as constable. Guy de Ferriby knew Edward of Cowley and was most concerned that we had been attacked.

"This is England! And a man cannot travel a few miles from the king's castle without being attacked?"

We had spoken about this on the road and Edward of Cowley had a theory. "It seems to me that this gang are cleverer than most. They attack those heading north. Who knows how many have been attacked and murdered on their way north? We chose the route as we thought it safer than the forest. There were many of them and they seemed determined."

"You may be right. King Henry has a monumental task if he is to bring order to this land but tell me, why do you and this handful of men travel in the depths of winter? Is the matter urgent?"

Edward de Cowley was enigmatic in his answer and I was learning from him, how to use words like a weapon to deflect questions and obfuscate the answers. "Urgent no but necessary yes." He turned to me, "Do you remember this youth who rode south with the son of Sir Edward Chorley last year?"

He studied me as though I had suddenly appeared before him, "Now I look I do. Are you not the boy who rode a ragged sumpter?"

"Yes, my lord."

"I thought that a brave enough act, but this is its equal." He suddenly made a leap that was not there and clapped his hands together, "Just so, you return him north. Still, it could have waited."

Edward of Cowley shrugged, "We had little enough to occupy us in Hedingham. Could we stay the night, Sir Guy?"

"But of course. There is room in the warrior hall for these four and I will have a chamber in the keep prepared for yourself. On the morrow, I will send a few men north with you to see you safely beyond our walls."

"That will not be necessary. It was my fault for not staying in Lincoln Castle and risking an inn I did not know. Even an old hand like me can make mistakes, my lord."

Laughing Sir Guy led him away, "The captain of the Earl of Oxford's men does not make mistakes. Let us say you were unlucky."

We were taken to a half-empty warrior hall. Like many castles, the garrison was allowed to be run down in winter. Men were given permission to spend the winter with their families. Cold and disease took their toll and there were plenty of men who could be found to replace any who did not return. We had many comrades in Oxford who, come the campaigning season, would seek work.

"So, now there are just four of us." Sam was acting as the spokesman. The death of Tom the Wanderer had upset Joseph and I knew that his heart was no longer in serving the earl. When Geoffrey had been taken from us, he had not been happy and now he withdrew into himself.

Stephen was more of his own man these days and he spoke up, "It seems to me that we are too few to be able to fight on our own as billmen and will need to join another company."

Joseph shook his head, "This has taken away my appetite, Stephen. When we return to Hedingham I shall ask to be released from my contract."

Sam had, I knew, served with Joseph for many years, "You cannot do that. We need your wise hand to guide us."

Shaking his head Joseph said, "I have grown old following lords who fight for this land. I should like a piece of it for myself. When we are paid off, I will add the sum to that we took at Stoke Field. I can find somewhere, I am sure."

The adventure was turning sour and soon I would be left with two companions, and they would hardly give me the companionship I needed and which my father had said was vital for billmen. The food we were served was good, but I did not taste it.

The next two days were hard ones as the weather deteriorated and rain flecked with snow and sleet drove in from the east. We now had a spare horse and were able to change horses more frequently, but it was still a hard ride. The land we passed through was no longer verdant and tilled. This was sheep country and with the snow-covered hills, all that we saw were sheep and snow. There appeared to be few people here. Edward of Cowley was not downcast by events. I suppose he knew neither Gerald nor Tom very well. We were a means to an end for him. He tried to cheer us with his words and the optimism of a fine reward at the end of this but the four of us rode in silence wrapped as much in our own thoughts as the two oiled cloaks and fur hats.

When Middleham Castle loomed in the distance I did not know what I was viewing. I had not passed it on my journey south and it seemed to me too big to be stuck here in the wild north. It dwarfed the tower at York and yet the village appeared tiny. This had been the favourite castle of King Richard and the heart of those who supported him. In the end, it had availed him little and he had been butchered in a little field called Bosworth. Had he retreated here I doubt that any could have shifted him.

Although we were expected and, indeed, welcomed, the purpose of our visit was unknown. Baroness Alice Fitzhugh as the senior member of the Neville family was in the castle. She was the sister of two kings, Edward V and Richard III. She had with her a large entourage and the castle bustled. I did not see much of her but she was a gracious lady and she made us feel welcome as soon as we stepped across the bridge that led into the massive keep.

"Welcome. I pray that the earl is well and that this visit does not portend dire news to follow. We knew you were heading north and assumed you would be coming here for the road goes nowhere else and we have wracked our brains for the purpose of the visit."

Edward of Cowley frowned. It was clear that he had expected another to be here but he smiled and ploughed on. "I have brought a gift from the earl. When time allows, I will fetch it to you but we are dirty and stained from our travels."

She was a real lady, "I understand. I am here merely to put the affairs of Anne, who was Queen of England and a Neville into some sort of order. Enough time has passed since her death and that of her son, Edward of Middleham, to allow me finally put an end to the conflict that has plagued our family." She turned to her steward, "Ralph, take these men to the warrior hall.

I will speak with Edward of Cowley in my solar when he has cleaned some of the dirt from his clothes. Have wine and food fetched for us."

"Yes, my lady."

"James, when you take the horses to the stable bring me... well you know what it is."

"Aye, sergeant." I felt elated that I had been chosen to deliver the sword. The bailey was the smallest I had ever seen, and I wondered where the men practised. I led Molly and the sergeant's horse.

Ralph pointed to the stable, "You can leave your horses there and bar the door. We have no ostler at the moment." He saw the look on my face, "They will be safe. This castle is the safest in the north of England."

We deposited our gear in the half-empty warrior hall and went back to the stable. Despite the fact that there was no ostler there were oats and freshwater. When the horses had been attended to, I wrapped the sword in the sheepskin and said to Ralph, who waited impatiently without, "Where is the solar?"

"That is for the Baroness and not some boy who can barely shave."

Ralph was full of his own self-importance, and I stepped up to him. Then he saw that I was much bigger than he was. "I was given a command to take this," I held up the sheepskin, "to the Sergeant. The carrying of it cost us a friend so do not annoy me, little fat man, for you are nothing to me. Take me to the solar."

I saw my three companions smiling as the pompous little man led me back into the castle and up the stairs. The castle was well apportioned and had windows with glass. Such a thing I had rarely seen. The Nevilles had been a rich and powerful family before their fall. Perhaps they were still rich and powerful. How would the likes of me know who actually ran the country? In the end, I did not need to find the solar for we came upon Edward of Cowley who was following a liveried servant up the same stairs to which we were headed.

He smiled when he saw me, "Speedy work, James, you have done well." As I handed the sheepskin wrapped sword to him, he caught the expression on Ralph's face and he smiled, "I see you have been upsetting the Baroness' people."

"Sorry, Sergeant."

He nodded, "You see, Steward, this young man has little knowledge of castles and manners. In fact, the only reason to keep him around is that he is a killer, and I knew that if I asked him to do something then it would be done. He might be young, but he has the blood of more than a score of men on his blades." He wagged his finger and said mockingly, "Mind your tongue, James!" I knew the man and I heard the humour in his voice. Like me, he had little time for pompous officials.

"Of course, Sergeant, I am sorry if I spoke a little harshly to you, Ralph."

He turned and led me down the stairs finishing up outside the stables where our companions awaited me. Sam had his hands on his hips, and he faced the steward, "What time do we eat?"

I think Ralph wanted rid of us as soon as he could and he said, "The Baroness likes to dine later than most and we follow her. It will not be until two hours after dark."

Sam nodded. We had ridden hard for the last few miles and eschewed a stop for food. "And are there alehouses?"

Eager for us to be gone the steward nodded, "Aye, there are four all around the square and the cross."

"And from your girth, you know them; which is the best?"

He pointed to the right, "*'The King Richard'* has the best ales and is almost the closest to the castle. It has the sign of the white rose and the boar."

As we left Joseph said, "And it will be a hotbed of Yorkists. James and Sam, try to control your tongues. The last thing we need is a fight."

We turned between two houses to head down a narrow alley to the square. Stephen asked, "How do you know?"

It was Sam who answered, "An alehouse named after a dead Yorkist king and emblazoned with his crest? They will think that Bosworth Field never happened. Fear not, Joseph, I can curb my tongue and marvel at the stupidity of these northern yokels, and I think that James has purged his mouth of the need to pick a fight."

Despite the sign and the obvious hostility towards King Henry we kept our voices low and with Stephen and I having northern accents scant attention was paid to us. The ale was the

95

best we had enjoyed in a long time. Stephen and I were northern lads and preferred northern beer. Even Sam who defended all things southern had to admit that the ale was good. I enjoyed two large beakers of ale and would have had a third but knew that it might just tip me over the edge. We nibbled on snacks we purchased; the roasted and salted skin of the pig was delightful as were the little cooked balls we called faggots. Sam and Joseph had never eaten them but we assured them of their quality and we were proved right. Neither purchase made a hole in our appetite but went well with the beer. There were smiles and nods when we left and returned to the castle. Our task had been completed and, as we ate with the other servants and soldiers, I began to look forward to our journey home.

Chapter 9

Except that we did not go home, not directly at any rate. We spent the first full day in the castle at our leisure and that was something we rarely enjoyed. Edward of Cowley was noticeable by his absence. Ralph sent a young servant with a message, "Ralph the Steward said to tell you that your sergeant will be closeted with the Baroness this day and you are to amuse yourselves." He grinned, "I was told to tell Sam Sharp Tongue and James of Prescot to mind their manners." We both laughed and the servant said to me, "I am guessing that you are the one that put Fat Ralph in his place."

I nodded, "And I have been chastised for it."

He shook his head, "You are now a friend to all those who work in this mighty castle."

Sam asked, "And what is there to do in this village in the north in the depths of winter?"

He pointed south, "This was not always the castle and if you head south you will see the remains of the first castle. It is interesting and, I am afraid, all that we have to offer in the way of entertainment save the alehouses."

Joseph shrugged, "It has stopped snowing and a good stretch of the legs might help me to forget the back of the horse. I thank you, young man." We wrapped in our cloaks and walked down the hill to the road that led to the mound just under a mile from the castle at Middleham.

There was little to be seen on William's Hill of the castle and it took the keen eye of Joseph to discern the features. "See the dips and hollows; they would have been the ditches and lined with wood. There would have been a wooden keep at the top. I have seen such castles before although few are lived in."

"But why did they rebuild so far away, in stone?"

Joseph had enough patience to be a schoolmaster and he explained to Stephen, "This would have been a good site to defend but if you need a hall in which you are to be comfortable then you need a larger area. The present castle is just as elevated, but it has more room. I can see why they moved."

We explored and then, becoming bored, headed back. It was as we entered the main gate that I saw a second entrance but the access was restricted and I saw when we neared it that that they had built lime and tile kilns there. I could see that in the short time since the death of King Richard the castle had lost some of its grandeur. Now I saw why the Baroness was here. She was securing what was valuable and leaving a caretaker in charge. I wondered if that would be Ralph. It might explain his high-handed attitude. That night, as we ate I said, quietly, to Joseph, "What will they do with the sword now? It seems to me that there will be no lord living here."

"Who knows? We have done our part and soon, I hope we shall head south again. The north is too cold for my old bones."

We did discover the answer the next day when Edward reappeared. He gathered us and led us up the stairs to the chamber used by the lord and now the Baroness. It was empty. "Stephen, close and bar the door."

Intrigued we followed, after the door was barred, Edward who led us to a small door in the far side of the bedchamber. When he opened it, we found ourselves in a small candlelit chapel often called an oratory. There was a simple altar and a cross. "Today, you will swear an oath never to reveal what we are about to do. Only the Baroness and we five know of it and if any other speaks of it then I know whence the words will come." I noticed that, in one corner, stood the sword and in another a bag of tools. He took the sword and laid it so that all could touch it. "Swear!"

I put my hand on the sword which I had carried before but now it seemed to tingle, and I knew that what I was doing was a most serious thing and not to be taken lightly. Sam seemed unwilling to touch it but he did.

Edward said, "Repeat after me. I swear that neither drink nor torture will make me reveal the final resting place of the sword of the Kingmaker on pain of death and eternal damnation."

"I swear that neither drink nor torture will make me reveal the final resting place of the sword of the Kingmaker on pain of death and eternal damnation." It was the place, the sword and the seriousness of Edward of Cowley that made me shiver. This was beyond an adventure. I was swearing in a chapel and risking my eternal soul.

That done Edward said, "Lift the rug and just enough floorboards so that we can hide the sword in this chapel where it will rest unseen. The countess will pass on its whereabouts to her heirs when she sees fit. That will be her decision and not ours."

We were all handy and working together we soon removed four floorboards. We even managed to salvage half of the nails. We were about to begin hammering the boards back in place when Edward said, "We will sing Te Deum while we do so. It will mask the banging." He was a careful man, but we managed to make little noise. We had swept all the damaged wood and the like into the resting place of the sword and when we replaced the rug then it was impossible to see where we had worked.

"James, carry the tools. Sam, open the door to the bedchamber and ensure that we are not observed."

While he did so Joseph asked, "And do we now go home, Sergeant?"

Shaking his head as Sam nodded that it was safe, he said, "Next week and we escort the Baroness to London first. There we take her to meet with the Queen of England and then our work is done."

I am not sure the real reason we were chosen to escort the Baroness back, but we were treated well by all in the castle as a result and, when we visited the alehouse we were accorded local status and greeted as friends. I suppose it was because this was a Neville stronghold, and our gesture was valued. When the four of us spoke of it there was much debate although I think that Sam had the right of it. His sharp mind was far quicker than ours.

"It cannot be that there is a danger to the Baroness. Men might be attacked but not ladies."

"Aye, Stephen, you are right. I cannot fathom why they need our small band to go with them."

Sam shook his head, "Remember why the Baroness said she was here? She is putting in order the affairs of Queen Anne who was a Neville. Her grandfather was Richard, Duke of York and he was related to the Neville family. It does not take any great wit to discern that while she was sorting through the detritus of a queen that she should find something pertinent to the present queen and a relative, albeit distantly. Our King Henry is a careful man and my guess is that Edward of Cowley takes us to escort her for our mutual safety."

The complications of the interbred nobles and their families made my head ring, but I accepted the reason as an answer.

Surprisingly we were not relegated to the baggage. Our spare horse and sumpter were led by the Baroness' servants. She had with her just eight men at arms under the command of a sergeant at arms. With four ladies and six female servants, I saw why she needed extra protection. She was, however, a Neville, and she rode. I had dreaded going at the speed of a carriage with all the added problems of wheels being damaged and the slow speed of a horse-drawn wagon that would be forced to stay on cobbled roads, especially in winter. Even so, the journey south was slow but we stayed each night in a castle. We had to sleep in the stables at Pontefract Castle and Nottingham but I did not mind for it was warm. We saw little of Edward of Cowley on the way south and he rode with the Baroness' sergeant. The two of them flanked the lady. By now the other three had learned to ride and grown used to their horses. With my thighs and buttocks well acclimatised I dreaded going back to a walking pace. I knew that one day we would. Once we were again in a company of billmen we would march to war and fight on foot. During the ride south on Scout I would never have imagined that I would prefer the back of a horse to foot but I did.

When we stopped and tended to the horses we got to speak to the Baroness' guards and learned that another reason we were with them was that she had been impressed by the story of the way we had fought off the attack outside Lincoln as were her guards. My youth particularly intrigued them.

"From what your sergeant said you have fought in but one battle, the Battle of Stoke Field."

I shook my head, "No, I fought at Bramham Moor, but I was not there when Sir Henry Clifford was defeated. I was there until the rebels tricked him."

That impressed them too. "Have you not thought of becoming a man at arms? You clearly have the skills that are needed." The soldier who spoke to us waved an arm around, "You all have for you can ride and to fight off so many bandits is impressive."

Sam said, "Not that impressive. They had numbers but had not the courage and as for being a man at arms? I prefer to fight with my billhook. I have done so my whole life. When I give it up then I give up war."

Joseph nodded, "And that is my intention too."

The warriors turned their attention to Stephen and to me, "You two are young enough."

Stephen looked at me and I knew that if I agreed then he would, "I have fought twice let me have a few more battles under my belt and I might consider it, but the expense of plate worries me."

"Aye, but whilst we might need billmen in times of war, in peace we do not. There is about to be peace and then you may be unemployed."

I said nothing although the thought terrified me. I would have to go home and face my father. Too long had elapsed for it to be a comfortable meeting. I prayed for war. We rode directly to the Tower. This was while the apparent and last legitimate heir to the throne, Edward, Earl of Warwick, and son of the Duke of Clarence, still languished as the king's guest and before King Henry began to make Richmond Castle on the Thames his chosen residence. One of the Baroness' men, as we unsaddled the horses, confided in me that it allowed King Henry to keep a closer watch on the fickle city that was London. It had supported both sides in the civil war. It was a monumental structure and dwarfed even Middleham. Here we were housed in the barracks that lay close to the river gate. It was crowded but we were few in number.

This time, when Edward came to speak to us, he did not advise us to go into the city rather he counselled the opposite, "This is London and I fear for my safety here let alone yours. We will not be here long."

Joseph, who was anxious to quit the service of the Earl of Oxford, take his money and leave this life spoke, "I thought that when we fetched the Baroness here, we would return to the Earl. We have exceeded the time for which we will be paid."

I think that Edward misunderstood for he smiled, "Do not fret, the Earl is coming here and you shall be paid for the extra work. I do not doubt that there will be a bonus. I hear that there is to be a tourney here soon and I suspect the Earl comes for that. The king may well pay you to attend. "

Thinking that he had done us a favour he hurried off to the tower where he would be accommodated. That the king was in residence was clear from his bodyguards. These were the same men who had kept him safe from the suicidal attack of King Richard at the Battle of Bosworth Field and even the cynical Sam was in awe of them. We did, however, heed the advice of our sergeant and explored the parts of the castle that we could. There was a great deal to be seen and the only parts forbidden to us were the tower and its entrance. King Henry had done a great deal of work on the castle already and was building a second court in the eastern bailey. Guns now lined the river which I seriously doubted would ever fall. I heard, from one of the sentries, that in the time of the second King Richard rebels had simply walked into the defences. That was impossible now and the son of the deceased Duke of Clarence was as safe and secure as a man could be anywhere in England.

After three days we were bored and contemplated going into the city but, perhaps at the instigation of Edward of Cowley, a pursuivant of the King's Court found us. "I understand that you are Edward of Cowley's men?"

Joseph was still our leader and he nodded, "Aye, sir."

"And are available for gainful employment?"

Sam smiled, "So long as the pay is satisfactory."

It was the pursuivant's turn to smile, "You will not be disappointed. We need labourers to erect the stands for nobles and their ladies."

Joseph looked at us and when we each nodded, he replied, "Yes, but tell me, Pursuivant, why does the king hold such a tourney? I have never heard of one for many years."

He said, conspiratorially, "It is Emperor Maximilian, you know the one they call the Last Knight, he holds them regularly and being opposed to our king and close to the avowed enemy of all things Lancastrian, the Duchess of Burgundy, then this is a way to spite the Emperor who will not, of course, be able to attend." He pointed to the Tower Green that lay to the west of the tower. "Make your way there and you will be given your orders." He suddenly stopped, "Can any of you ride?"

Sam laughed, "Ride? Yes, but are we horsemen, no." He pointed to me, "James is the best of us why?"

On the day of the tourney, Saturday, we will need men to aid the ostlers and squires. If you are willing, James?" I nodded, "Then you shall be paid a silver shilling for the day."

I saw Sam's eyes roll into his head, if he had thought there was so much pay involved, he would have lied.

We headed to where a carpenter and his apprentices were sawing wood into lengths. Our task was simple; we carried the sawn timber and held it while it was hammered into place. We were human pack animals and it suited us all for it was easy and, at the end of the day, we would have coppers in our purses. For Joseph, who had now set his heart on retirement, then any extra coins would make his life much easier. I was already richer than I had ever dreamed the day that I had left Ecclestone. In fact, I had so much that I began to fear that another might steal it. Joseph had left the bulk of his money at Hedingham with the priest. I had not liked the priest's eyes for they were too close together and I had carried mine with me. The king had asked for the men of the castle to be used as labourers for his own safety and peace of mind. He knew and trusted all those within the walls whilst any from outside might be a traitor or a murderer. We heard from some of those brought in to build the structure that there was another claimant to the throne, this time in Flanders. It was said he was the Edward kept in the Tower. All eyes swivelled to the whitewashed building as the idea was broached.

Stephen said, "Then all that the king has to do is bring forth this Edward and say that the one in Flanders is false."

Sam's sharp mind snapped out an answer, "If he was to do that it should have been when he became king and not now when it might be seen as a deception upon his part."

It all seemed overly complicated to me, and I put it from my mind but that evening, as we ate, the subject was brought up again. The carpenters were dining with the garrison, and it was they brought up the matter. We paid scant attention to it, but a couple of the older apprentices were from Flanders originally and they seemed, and I know not why, proud of the fact.

We learned as we dined on the most excellent fare provided by the king, that the new pretender was one Pierrekin Wezebeque. One of the apprentices said his name boldly but one of the garrison burst out laughing, "Is that a name or have you brought back some of the food?"

We all laughed. The apprentice coloured, "Perkin Warbeck is the way you might say it. Why is it that the English can speak no language other than their own?"

Sam turned to me and said, "Most can't even speak their own very well."

It was left to the carpenter to silence his apprentices, "We don't need to, for we have a king and warriors that make other nations take note of us."

It silenced the room but Sam said, quietly, to the three of us, "In the days of kings like Henry the Fifth that was true but since then, and our present king apart, we have had a succession of men who were just clinging on to power and doing little to make our nation great again."

The next day, when we arrived at the construction site, we found that the two apprentices were no longer there. No explanation was given but the other apprentices and the carpenter kept their heads down and would not respond to any of our questions. There were twenty other men from the garrison all working and as we had all heard the comments we were intrigued. No answers came and that night the presence of the constable of the Tower ensured that the topics of conversation were safer. When alone we speculated as to their fate, and it was Sam who offered an answer. "They will have been taken to the Tower and tortured or probably executed. Our king clings to power like the others before him. He is building a land much like this wooden stand, but it takes time and until the structure is erect it is in danger of simply collapsing upon itself."

We finished our part the next day. The structure was erected, and labourers were no longer needed. The pursuivant paid us and I added the coins to my growing collection. This was better than I had expected for my father said that often billman sought an employer and had times of hardship. I appeared to have landed on my feet.

The following day the Earl of Oxford arrived along with many other high-ranking nobles. The king was not only cocking a snook at Emperor Maximilian by holding the tournament, but he was also rewarding his supporters. I saw the banners of Henry Percy and Sir Henry Clifford amongst those arriving. Would I see Master Geoffrey? That it was an important moment became clearer when Edward of Cowley came to see us after we had dined. He had not spoken to us or seen us since he had warned us off leaving the castle.

"You should know that tomorrow the Earl will reward all of you." He turned to Joseph, "I know, old friend, that you tire of this life and I hope that the reward you receive might induce you to stay on but if not there will be enough there to give you a comfortable life. As for the rest," he could not contain himself and I saw a rare side to the sergeant at arms, he beamed like a groom on his wedding night, "I am to be given my spurs and knighted. Think of the honour, the king himself dubs me!"

We all said, dutifully, "Well done, my lord."

I am not sure if our replies were not what he expected but he added, "And for the rest of you, there is a chance to serve me as my own men and you shall be at the heart of a company of billmen I will raise. The king and the Earl intend to make war across the Channel and that means profit for all."

I realised we risked offending our paymaster and I tried to make up for my earlier lack of enthusiasm, "Well done, my lord, and I look forward to serving with you. Shall we wear your livery?"

It not only placated him but set him to thinking, "You know James, I had not thought of that but you are right. I daresay we are in the right place to determine what my livery should be. For the morrow, when I am to be knighted, you shall all wear the livery of the Earl of Oxford. You are still his men until you accept my offer." He looked at the other three, "I would be sorry if you did not join me but there will be a place for each of you with the earl."

He left and Sam shook his head, "Now things become clearer. He knew about the knighthood before we left yet he could not confide in us."

Joseph said, "Would it have made any difference Sam Sharp Tongue?" Sam shook his head. "And besides he might have considered it bad luck. I do not begrudge a man luck."

"You may be right but still," Sam looked at me and grinning said, "and you were quick enough to stick your nose…"

I held up my hand, "Do not say it Sam Sharp Tongue for if you do we shall fight and I do not wish that. Let us just say that I am happy for Edward of Cowley and if that means advancement for me then why not?"

"Aye, you were not stabbing any in the back just leaping over them." He held up his hands as I bunched mine, "Just my sharp tongue."

Knowing the import of the day we were up early and bathed in the river. We had carried on the sumpter our liveries and after combing our beards and hair to remove livestock we dressed and tied our hair back with ribbons. I wore my new buskins and we displayed our swords and daggers. The caps we wore were just the ones used for sentry duty, but their red colour was bright having spent most of the time in our sacks. We were warriors and not sentries.

The morning was crisp and clear. We had all commented on the fact that the weather this far south was far more clement than in the north and now that it was March there were signs of Spring everywhere. The wooden stands were now decorated with flags, banners and the livery of the king; he was showing the world he had arrived. From the castle's many towers flags fluttered and all said the same; Henry Tudor was now the King of England. We joined the rest of the earl's men. Captain Jack still commanded. He ignored Stephen and me but greeted his old friends Sam and Joseph. I did not see Geoffrey and I wondered at that. Edward of Cowley was finely dressed as I had expected him to be and his hair and beard were not only combed but oiled too. The king and the earl, along with the Queen were amongst the last to arrive.

As I would come to know over the next years such events were exploited by kings, rulers, and lords. Edward of Cowley was not the only one to be rewarded for his services to the crown and the speeches were used to warn enemies that dire retribution was still hanging over them. I knew that was a reference to the lords, Broughton and Lovell, who had disappeared. They were also a warning for the sister of the dead King Edward, Margaret, the Duchess of Burgundy. Most importantly they were an inducement for nobles and commoners alike to serve their king well in the hope of reward. I was not totally taken in and that was because I was next to cynical Sam who snorted and sniffed at every piece of hyperbole, yet I knew I had done well from King Henry. Indeed I had done better than my father even without the money the earl would give us. I had earned as much in a short time as my father had brought back from Bosworth.

With the rewards given and the newly knighted men seated it was time for the joust to begin. I had totally forgotten that I was part of it until the pursuivant roughly grabbed my arm and said, "I have no time to go searching for you. Come you are needed to hold the horses!" I just ran with the painted popinjay and found myself in the area close to the stables and the castle wall. Our stables were small and mean and closer to the river wall. These were grand apartments for the best of horses. He pointed at a liveried ostler and said, "That is John the Stablemaster. Present yourself to him."

I did so and, whilst barking out orders he glanced around, "You are the boy who can ride a little?" I nodded. "Can you count?" I nodded again. "Then count four stalls from the bottom and fetch me the horse." He stopped and jabbed a finger at me, "Attach long reins and be careful. He is no sumpter but a warhorse and he bites!"

Nodding I said, "And what is his name?"

I thought he was going to fetch me a clout but instead, he laughed, "You have ridden. He is called Warrior."

At the last feast we had attended there had been marchpane. I am not fond of the stuff myself but I knew that Molly might enjoy it. Now I took out the piece I had saved for her. I knew that horses have a sweet tooth and I intended to ingratiate myself to the horse. I stepped into the Stygian gloom of the stables and counted up four stalls. The horse that snorted and stamped at me towered over me. I think Scout could have fitted under his belly. I did not try to enter, instead, I spoke gently as I sought out the long reins on the wall of the tack room. "Good boy, Warrior is it? A fine name and I do not doubt that you are a good horse."

The stable was well organised, and I found the long reins which I took. "I have a horse, Molly, but she is just a riding horse. You might like her although I know not the tastes of such horses as you." He had stopped stamping and I took the opportunity, as I jabbered on, to step into his stable. "I suppose the king gives you your choice of mare, still, Molly is a fine horse and suits me." Holding the reins in my left hand behind my back I proffered the marchpane. He was curious but also cautious and he sniffed at it, "You will like it, I swear." Holding my hand flat I raised it to his nostrils so that he could sniff. Seemingly satisfied his tongue rolled out and he licked the sticky sweet into his mouth. He nodded and I took the opportunity to stroke his ear, which I knew horses liked and to slip the reins over his head. He gave a derisory snort as though to tell me that he knew what I had done but allowed me to secure him. "Good boy, let us go so that King Henry may see what a fine animal you are."

It was as we stepped from the gloom of the stable that I saw Warrior in his true colours. With a white blaze, his chestnut coat shone like gold, and I saw that he had three white socks. Someone had once told me the rhyme about the luckiness of the number of socks, but I had long forgotten it. I saw that the other boys who were fetching horses were running and so I did. I worked out why; it was to warm up the horse.

I reached the stablemaster who looked at me in surprise. He looked at my hands and grinned, "There is a surprise. Warrior has a temper on him and I was sure that you would arrive without a finger or two. Well done. Now take him to the tent with the red chevrons and yellow finches. Warrior is Sir Lionel's horse. He is Sir Lionel of Stroud." He said it as though I should know the name. I did not.

I spotted the tent and saw a knight already being prepared to mount another fine charger and I led Warrior to the squires and pages who were tightening the plates on the knight I took to be Sir Lionel of Stroud. The horse was also covered in plates. The squire was an older man than I had expected. I had thought them all to be like Master Geoffrey and young men seeking to become knights. This man was as old as Sam. He looked up when he saw me and nodded, "At least they sent one who knows horses. Walk Warrior around the tent to keep him warm but do not let him near another horse. He kicks and one blow from one of his hooves might break your leg."

"Yes, sir."

I knew that I was in elevated company and everyone I met was my social superior. It was safer to say sir than risk censure.

"Come, Warrior." Avoiding other horses was easier said than done as there were many other horse handlers doing as I was. The difference was that they were younger and smaller than I was, and Warrior was one of the larger horses. As I trotted through the congested area of tents, they tried to avoid me. I worked out that Sir Lionel was a professional knight who had a spare horse to guarantee a chance of winning the prize. Sam had told me, while we were building the stands, that there was a lucrative living to be made by knights who could unhorse an opponent.

"James! James of Prescot!" I looked up and saw Master Geoffrey on the back of a plated horse. He was now a knight and taking part in the tournament.

I dared not stop but I slowed as I answered, "Congratulations on the knighthood Sir Geoffrey. Your father must be proud."

"He is. When I am done here, we must speak. I am interested in your adventures and wish to know how you ended up as an ostler at the Tower of London!"

When I returned to Sir Lionel's tent, the knight, his squire, and his horse had gone. One of the other squires said, to me, "Warrior seems to like you." He shook his head and held up a gnarled finger, "He likes to bite me. Keep his head still and talk to him or sing to him. Peter the squire does that. We will fit the plate."

I had done so already in the stable but now it felt foolish. However, a shilling was a shilling and so I jabbered, "You have a fine day for it Warrior, I would not like to be any horse that has to face you. Why the very sight of your magnificent frame would make me concede the fight instantly. I doubt that you will even need to go at more than a canter." I continued in the same manner and saw the smiles on the faces of the squires and others who laboured to fit all the armour that the horse would need. They were smiling with me rather than at me. I reflected, as plate after plate was fitted, that Warrior, strong horse though he was,

109

would not be able to ride for long with such a weight upon his back. Then it came to me, it was unlikely that Warrior would ever have to go to a real war. Sir Lionel was a professional knight. He would not risk such a valuable horse in a battle where a billman such as I could take the legs from the horse. It was why we were feared on the battlefield and being so close to a warhorse showed me how to defeat such an animal. The protection was on the head and chest. The need to charge meant that the horse's legs were unprotected and being such a large horse a billman could simply duck beneath a lance to hack through flesh and bone. A horse cannot run with just three legs.

There was a roar from the stands and the others, who had just finished fitting the plates looked up. I continued to sing to Warrior. The man with the gnarled finger shook his head, "Peter is leading Zeus, and he is limping. It seems he will need Warrior."

The squire I had first met led the injured horse, I could see the plate hanging down and the blood dripping from the wound. He shouted, "Is Warrior ready?"

The man with the gnarled finger shouted, "Aye and in good condition."

Sir Lionel of Stroud dismounted and came over to Warrior. He had already taken off his plated gloves and he stroked Warrior's ear much as I had done, "I had hoped to spare you this last battle before you are put to stud, old friend, but that Flemish knight has no honour and struck at the plates. Come we have to go to war once more." To my surprise, Warrior not only nodded his head but lowered it so that the metal plate over his blaze gently touched my nose. Sir Lionel of Stroud smiled, "You are the boy they sent to fetch Warrior. They made a good choice. He likes you and I take it as a good sign. What is your name?"

"James of Prescot, my lord, a billman."

He laughed, "A youth who is a billman and knows horses. You are a rare find. Stay here and when we are done, I would speak with you."

He mounted and Peter led Warrior away from the tents. Sam and the others would all see what was going on but I felt privileged to be with these professionals. The man with the gnarled hand handed the reins to me, "Here do as you did with

110

Warrior. Zeus is hurt and we must tend to him. He cost Sir Lionel of Stroud much gold and this was his first tourney. We hoped to spare Warrior." He made the sign of the cross as he said, "Fate has a fickle finger and Sir Lionel must risk his favourite horse one more time."

I used almost the same words and tone as I had with Warrior and Zeus seemed to respond. When his headpiece was removed, I put my fingers into the pouch that had contained the marchpane. It still felt sticky and I brought out my hand to let Zeus lick it. He did so gently and long after any stickiness was gone. The man with the gnarled finger laughed, "Are you a magician, my friend. You have a gift and yet you seem not to know it. You are wasted as a billman. You could earn a fortune if you joined us."

When the plates were all taken off then the wound was cleaned with vinegar. Zeus baulked a little but I think he knew it was for his own good.

"We will let Peter finish the healing. The wound is clean, and the blood is clear. We will not have a lengthy wait, I think. Warrior cannot fight a long time now."

There was a huge cheer and the others all looked up. I continued to stroke the head of the injured horse. The others cheered, as did the other knights and retainers as Peter led a victorious Sir Lionel, holding his helmet under one arm, astride Warrior. The squire with the gnarled finger punched me good-naturedly in the upper arm. "He won! You bring us good fortune!"

The knight dismounted and came directly to me, "You must have some gift for Warrior was inspired this day." He nodded to Peter who went into the tent. "Take this as a reward for helping me to become the champion of this day." Peter emerged and handed me a gold coin, I had never seen one before and the head of the king did not look English but I was speechless. My father had never earned gold. "And if you would join my company then there will be more."

It was a tempting offer but there are unspoken oaths and I could not simply leave Stephen and Sam without speaking to them. Then there was the oath I had taken to the Earl of Oxford. I was honour bound to make a clean break and an honourable one. "I thank you my lord, but I am the Earl of Oxford's man at the moment. Could I have a day or two to make my decision?"

He beamed, "Better and better. A billman who understands honour and service. Of course. I will be here until the tourney is over for I have high hopes of winning the long swords."

I left to head back to my companions.

As I did so I saw Sir Geoffrey, I assumed, of Skipton, limping towards me and leading his warhorse. He shook his head ruefully, "I should, perhaps, curse you, James of Prescot for I know not what you did to Sir Lionel of Stroud's horse but no man could have faced him and survived."

I had not seen the fight but talking to Sir Lionel's men I knew that he was an excellent knight who excelled on horseback. Sir Geoffrey was a rural knight but I nodded my agreement. I had learned with nobles that you disagree with them at your peril and a nod is always the acceptable answer to any question. "And what do you do now? I assume from your garb that you are still a billman, but I am intrigued as to why you tend the horse of a tournament knight."

"To earn money, my lord." I proffered the coin. I had not been paid by either Sir Geoffrey or his father for my service. The fact that others had was neither here nor there. I had been under their command when I had ridden south.

His eyes widened, "That is more than a fair payment. And you are still a billman?"

"Aye, I serve Sir Edward of Cowley, the Earl of Oxford's knight."

"I now have a manor, Settle, and I seek men to follow me. I can offer you a post there."

My services, it seemed, were in demand from all. I gave the same answer that I had given to Sir Lionel and I saw the disappointment on Sir Geoffrey's face. "I pray that you will give consideration to my offer. You are a good fellow and despite your youth fought well at Bramham. I would have young men around me."

I put the coin back in my purse. I had kept it out so that he knew that I would not be cheap, "And I am honoured that you wish me to join you. If I can leave my lord with any kind of honour then I will give your offer due consideration." I had no intention of following the young knight.

When I reached my companions, now in the hall and drinking the ale supplied by King Henry, I felt that if my head swelled any more I should have to duck to get into the room. I was, of course, brought down to earth by Sam Sharp Tongue. He wafted his arm, "Watch out boys, James the Horseman is here and he stinks of horse. Did you groom it boy, or try to mount it?"

The others in the room laughed and I smiled. He was right and I did stink, "I shall bathe just as soon as I have quenched my thirst." Stephen shifted over to allow me to sit next to him. "It is thirsty work earning gold."

I sat down and Sam became serious, "Gold?" I did not want others to see and so I slipped the coin out and held it below the table. Sam said, "A French crown; that is rich payment indeed. Perhaps I should learn how to tend horses."

Joseph smiled, "You do right, James, to seize opportunities when you can. Do not drink too much for Sir Edward wishes to see us after our meal and before his feast. I think he wishes to make us an offer and such matters are best considered with a clear head. We can drink later."

I nodded and Sam said, "Have you not noticed, Joseph, that the one who never drinks too much is James and yet I know he likes his ale. There is a story there."

I drank down half of the beaker of ale that Stephen had poured, "And that is good Sam Sharp Tongue. Secrets are like gold and best hoarded rather than shared. It makes us all more interesting." I seemed to have more than my fair share but I was now in a better position to make the right decision. Whatever Sir Edward offered me, I had two more attractive offers to take.

Chapter 10

The food was as good as I had expected and, once again, when the precious marchpane was brought out, I slipped a piece into the small bag I kept attached to my belt. It would keep for weeks and I could always give it to Molly. The others devoured theirs and licked their fingers. I thought of Warrior's tongue as he had cleaned my hand completely.

We wandered over to the Tower Green where liveried servants were cleaning up the detritus of the day. That was not a word I would have used when I lived in Ecclestone but Sam Sharp Tongue liked to give us the precise word when he could. Already I had enjoyed a better education with him than I had before I had met him. When we watched one of the servants pounce, as he swept where the nobles had been seated, we all knew that he had found a coin. Even wandering the hundred or so paces from the hall Stephen had picked up a half penny. In the jostle of the crowd and the excitement of a tourney, it was easy to lose a coin or two. The gold piece in my purse, Sam had told me it was a French crown, meant I did not need to grub for coppers. I think Sir Edward must have been watching for us for he left the Tower to head over to us before we had even begun to think of turning and walking back.

The rosy glow told us that he had been drinking. He beamed, "Well my good fellows, I have earned my reward for our service and here is the first part of yours." He took out his purse, "Hold out your hands." He began to drop coins into them. They were silver. "Here Joseph, you are the leader and for you, the earl has given you ten shillings."

"Thank you, my lord."

"For the rest, it will be the same amount, five shillings each."

Had I not been given a gold crown I would have been delighted but I smiled and kept the slight disappointment from my face. We all slipped the coins into our purses. We all counted to make sure we had not been cheated but did so subtly.

"And now another offer. I would have the four of you become the first of my men. You, Joseph, shall be the captain of my billmen and you will get to choose the men."

Shaking his head Joseph said, "A kind offer, my lord, but one I cannot accept as I wish to leave the path of war and choose a more peaceful one for my latter years."

Although I saw that Sir Edward had hoped for a different answer, his nod told me that he had expected the one he had received. It was confirmed with his next statement, "Then, Sam Sharp Tongue, would you become the captain of my billmen?"

"I will earn extra pay and get to choose the men?"

"Of course and wear my livery. I intend for all my men to have jacks studded with metal and the best of helmets upon their heads. As captain, you would have a breastplate."

The offer was already generous enough, but the offer of plate armour was too much to even consider a refusal and Sam nodded eagerly.

Turning to Stephen and me Sir Edward said, "And you two?"

Stephen could hardly answer quickly enough, "Aye, Sir Edward, and gladly!"

All eyes swivelled to me. The opportunity to tell them of my other offers had not arisen and I did not answer directly. The beaming smiles left the faces of Sam and Stephen. Sir Edward said, "Just so. I heard that young James here was offered two other positions by Sir Lionel of Stroud and Sir Geoffrey of Settle. He is in much demand." He shrugged, "I can pay more than Sir Geoffrey but not the coin, fame and glory that would be forthcoming from Sir Lionel. Is that what you wish, James, to hold the reins of a horse and never fight for your country again?"

Until that moment I was going to take Sir Lionel's offer for I could see no bad side to it. Now I realised that the risk and adventure would all be Sir Lionel's and that I would be a spectator; a rich one but a spectator, nonetheless. I saw the disappointment on Stephen's face and then thought about the two of them fighting without me. I was torn.

Sir Edward thought I was still going to take Sir Lionel's offer as he said, "I can offer you the chance to fight in Flanders. I know that you all did well from Stoke Field, and I am happy to look the other way after all our future battles. I was not born a noble and I understand what a man must do to better himself."

I had already decided but the last offer convinced me, and I nodded, "I will take your coin, Sir Edward, although as Sir

Geoffrey did not tell me how much he would pay me I know not if my pay with you will be better."

He laughed, "You have a cunning mind, James. You and Stephen shall be paid more than my other billmen, but I would not go around boasting of that."

I then realised that I would now have to tell two knights that I would not be serving them. I decided to get it over with. "I will return with you and speak to Sir Geoffrey and Sir Lionel."

He smiled, "There is no need. I shall tell them. Go enjoy London's inns. The king's guards are patrolling the streets and the inns close to the walls will be safe." I think he would enjoy telling two men who were his superiors that he had been chosen over them.

We turned and headed for the Lion Tower and the gate to the city. I did not need others to tell me the reason for Sir Edward's offer, I knew so myself, but Sam liked to be precise and show his sharp mind, "Of course had you gone to speak to the two knights then they might well have increased their offer."

"I know," I put my arm around Stephen and Sam, "but what would you two do without me to save you in battle?"

Sam laughed, "One battle and a fight with bandits and he thinks he is Richard the Lionheart."

I turned to Joseph, "You have enough money for what you intend, Joseph? I have more than enough should you need more."

"And that is a kind offer but I have enough. I have a place in mind, and I do not think it will be expensive. My needs are small. There are many widows out there and not all are Yorkists. I shall find one still able to bear children and see if I can make good men and women as I have made good billmen."

We had a good evening although Sam was less than happy at the prices we paid for what he considered second rate beer. It made a small dent in the pile of coins I had and I did not mind. It just felt exciting to be in the greatest city in England. We spoke mostly about our future and Joseph's in particular. We learned that he was headed for the village of Frilford. It was between Oxford and Didcot. Joseph had been planning his move whilst still in Oxford and everything was well thought out. He gave the three of us advice about serving abroad. He had done so and knew the pitfalls.

"Don't worry about the language; they all speak too many anyway, French, Flemish, German. It is all Greek to me. Sir Edward is quite right, there is much bounty on foreign fields but watch out for fake coins. It doesn't matter if you are robbing a corpse but watch your change. All foreigners are thieves. You can only trust an Englishman."

Sam laughed, cynically, "And then only a Lancastrian."

By the end of the evening, I was quite excited about the prospect but wondered when we would be leaving. Sir Edward had just three billmen. As far as I was aware, he had no squire. He would also need archers and men at arms. Action seemed a long way off.

Joseph rose early the next day and left as soon as the gates opened. The horse he had used was Sir Edward's but he allowed Joseph to take the sumpter we had used for our gear. He would not have to walk. We were men of war and there were no tears but the arm clasps were firm. His last words were, "If you pass through Frilford, then ask for me. You will always be welcome, and I would like to know how you fare. You three were always the best of the men I led."

The three of us packed our gear and headed for the stables. I slipped the marchpane into Molly's mouth and looked towards the stables of the warhorses. Would Warrior remember me?

Sir Edward rode from those stables even as we led ours from our humbler accommodation. He said, cheerfully, "We have a hard fifty miles to ride this day. We head back to Hedingham. The earl has said I can offer employment to some of his men. We will cast our net at Hedingham first and then ride to Oxford. We take a ship for Flanders in September."

There were fewer billmen left in Hedingham and Sam found none who were suitable. All had families and lived locally; clearly, they would choose to stay in England rather than come abroad with us. We resigned ourselves to a trip to Oxford. Sir Edward was more successful. There was a young man at arms who had caught Sir Edward's eye and William the son of Edgar leapt at the chance to better himself and become a squire. His inclusion brought us another four men at arms who were friends with William. He was a popular man. Sir Edward had, like me, been careful with his money and he now spent it on horses for the others. We still had one spare horse but mounted men moved faster and wasted less time on the road. After a week in which we were all dressed in Sir Edward's new livery and with some of our own money spent to make us more secure, we headed back to Oxford.

William rode with Sir Edward who began the training of his squire as we rode. We got to know the four men at arms. Jack, Martin, Dick, and Egbert had all heard of Sam Sharp Tongue and that helped us to get to know one another on the road. Unlike many men at arms, they did not look down on billmen. The four of them had plate armour and good weapons but they knew that in battle they would have to rely on the greater numbers of billmen to protect them from the enemy. Sam and Jack, the most experienced of the four spoke and we listened as we passed a land burgeoning with new growth.

"War has changed, Sam Sharp Tongue. When King Richard's charge failed at Bosworth then that marked the end of horsemen initiating an attack. If knights are to ride their horses into battle then the enemy will have to be softened up first."

"You are right and what do you make of these new weapons, the harquebusiers and cannons?"

Martin snorted, "They frighten the horses but, in my experience, you have to be unlucky to be felled by their missiles. Deadly, I grant, you but so inaccurate."

Sam nodded, "And the smoke means that when they have discharged them then the ones using them cannot see and it takes longer to reload them than a crossbow."

I ventured, "But might they not become better? They are a new weapon and there might be men making improvements?"

Egbert nodded his agreement, "Aye, I fear that England may be behind the times. After Stoke Field, we questioned one of the Flemish men before he expired. He told us that had they had cannons from their homeland then the outcome would have been different."

Sam snorted, "Of course he would say that. I agree with Martin. We billmen can move quickly on a battlefield and when they have fired we simply run at them and use our blades to end their lives. Then you men at arms can charge across the battlefield and slaughter those fleeing."

"Aye, while you rob the dead."

Sam was not put out by the words, "And that is the right of those valiant enough to face death quickly. Our former leader, Joseph of Didcot, reaped enough reward over the years to buy himself a home. Even now he is close to Oxford and becoming a man of leisure. Is that not the hope of us all? We have each used war to come this far and what is the purpose of all the fighting? I will tell you, to become richer than when we began so that we rise a little higher in this life than where we began."

I was silent. My father had done that, and I had spurned the life. The smallholding he had bought would be similar to the one Joseph was now buying. I began to think about my motives and realised that what I had really wanted was an adventure. It had taken until now to realise it, but everything made sense. My wild youth, getting into fights in Windle through to seizing the opportunity to make a friend of Warrior all showed that. I was determined to continue to seek adventure and danger; those two companions made me feel alive.

Stephen said, quietly, "You are not your usual self, James; what ails you?"

I beamed, "Nothing for our life is what it should be eh, Stephen? We have good companions, coins in our purses and ahead of us the adventure of war. Are we not the luckiest of men?"

The warrior hall at Oxford was as depressingly ruinous as it had been when we had left. There were, however, men left there who had endured enough of garrison life in Oxford and when they were offered the chance to join Sir Edward's retinue then they jumped at the opportunity. Despite our youth, Stephen and I were considered Sam's lieutenants and we helped in the selection of billmen. The fact that many wished to join us did not guarantee that we would take them all on. Sir Edward needed just twenty billmen and so we helped Sam to whittle down the applicants. Some were easy to dismiss. During their time in Oxford, they had drunk too much and trained too little. There were others who resented the youth of myself and Stephen, the seventeen almost chose themselves. Billmen have to work together on the battlefield but they also need the ability to think for themselves. The seventeen who joined us seemed perfect.

However, we had to remain in Oxford for a week or so while Sir Edward sought his archers. They were harder to find and it was during this time that we found other problems I had not anticipated. There were enough empty buildings for Sam to find one for our billmen. He was keen to make them all part of his company. He was now Captain Sam. The ones we had rejected refused to call him that and rather than risk confrontation he sought the Constable's permission to take over a derelict stable. It was warm and had a roof. We were happy. We practised each day in the outer bailey and Stephen and I were given five men each to command. Sam had this idea of breaking down the unit into smaller parts. As he said to us, the night before we began the training, "Remember why Joseph was so successful? There were just a handful of us, but we all worked well together. Let us try that with these seventeen. I trust you two to do what I wish and if you can control your five then we have more flexibility."

He had been proved right and I got to know my five billmen well. Over the time we were in Oxford we devised new strategies such as Sam and his men holding while Stephen and I flanked an imaginary enemy. At other times we would use my men to hold the enemy. We developed a formation with billmen on three sides so that we had an impenetrable wall of billhooks.

The trouble came one Thursday as we headed back to our stable. Sam had gone ahead and I was at the back with my men. Stephen had tarried to work with his five men. He had grown as a result of the responsibility thrust upon him. We passed through the gate to the inner bailey and I gave my billhook to one of my men, "Ned, take my billhook and I will wait for the others."

In truth, I needed to make water. There was a garderobe in the gatehouse for it was used at night by sentries. The smell, in the dark, directed me to it and it was a relief to finish making water and get back into cleaner air. It was as I emerged that I heard heated voices. I recognised one of them as a man we had rejected. Tad of Easingwold was a huge bully of a man and I had never liked him. As I stepped out from the dark I took in immediately the situation.

"How come a stammering milksop like you gets to say who may or may not be a billman?" He punched Stephen in the shoulder. Stephen did not respond for he was a gentle soul.

"What do you do for Sir Edward that he keeps you on? Does he mount you like his mare?" He punched him in the shoulder again trying to make Stephen respond.

I could see from the expressions on the faces of Stephen's men that they were unsure of their reaction. The three men with Tad of Easingwold were enjoying the moment and laughing. As Tad pulled back his arm to punch again I arrested the movement from behind and said, quietly, "Stephen take your men back to the barracks and I will deal with this Yorkshireman," I was deliberately insulting him.

Despite his name, Tad hated being associated with the Yorkists and he whirled to face me, his fists ready. He grinned, "Even better I have the boy before me. I hear you like horses, boy."

I shook my head and readied my fists, "You seem obsessed by what we all get up to at night, Tad, do you secretly desire us?" That made his friends laugh at him and as his face reddened and he lunged at me I said, "Stephen, go."

The fights in the inn at Windle had hardened me and gave me reflexes that enabled me to deduce what an opponent would do. Sure enough, the lumbering bully tried to plough into me. I flicked away the flailing fists with my right hand, his weight helping me to fool him and then I brought my left hand hard into the bully's ribs. It was a blow I had learned early on and when I heard the rib crack, I knew he was hurt. I stepped back so that I had room in the inner bailey. Darkness was falling but the watch had yet to be set. Whirling, Tad brought out his rondel dagger.

One of his friends said, "Tad, is this wise?"

"Shut it, you. I will mark this baby-faced boy so that all will know him for what he is."

I smiled, knowing that it would infuriate him, "And what is that Tad of Easingwold, a better warrior than you? They know that already."

This time he lunged at my middle with his blade. The timing was all and I used my left hand to grab his right. Even so, the edge tore into my jack and caught on one of the metal plates. I pulled back my right hand and punched him twice in rapid succession in the left side of his head. I saw his eyes roll and when I pulled back my hand for a third time it was to hit him hard under the chin. He collapsed to the ground just as Sam and Stephen, along with Sam's men, appeared. I reached down and took the rondel dagger. "Tell Tad that any time he wishes to reclaim his dagger all he has to do is to ask me," I smiled, "nicely."

Stephen must have told Sam all for Sam said, coldly, "Pick him up and tell him that if he is still in the castle on the morrow then I will report his words and actions to the constable and Sir Edward. I am sure that they will wish to prosecute the matter."

The one who advised Tad to cease the conflict asked nervously, "And us?"

Sam looked at me and I said, "Choose better friends or follow this one from Oxford."

When they had gone Stephen said, "You had no need to interfere, James."

I shook my head, "I know how to fight men like Tad. You are a fine billman, but he would have hurt you."

Sam said as he led us to the barracks, "And you have made an enemy."

"That is what you do when you protect friends. No one hurts my friends and escapes my justice."

I know not how but Sir Edward heard of the fight and the three of us were summoned to his presence and that of the constable, "Tad of Easingwold has fled the castle." We said nothing as the constable spoke. "He is now sought as a thief as he stole some plate from the chapel. He will be found but I understand from his friends that you were the cause of it, James of Prescot."

Stephen shook his head, "No, my lord, I was the cause. Tad tried to provoke me to fight."

Sir Edward nodded, "Knowing that you have a gentle nature and impugning my honour." My eyes widened, "Aye, I heard and I thank you, James of Prescot, for defending both my honour and your friend but no more. If there is another such incident, then walk away. That is a command."

We all chorused, "Aye, my lord."

When we returned to our practice, somehow, the fight had made us closer. We were Captain Sam's men and felt ourselves to be superior.

Chapter 11

In the end, we found all the archers we needed within a couple of days of the fight. Sir Edward liked symmetry, another word Sam taught me, and so we had twenty archers who were mounted on ragged sumpters. We then left for Southampton and the muster. We passed within a mile of Frilford, but we had no opportunity to visit Joseph. It was sad as we had thought to visit with our old leader in a day or so. It taught me never to procrastinate. From that moment on I did what I wished immediately without delay. It made some men think me reckless, but I was not. I was a considered billman who weighed up each move and thrust of my weapon but when it came to life I knew you only had one chance to make things right. I had not told my mother or my father that I loved them and now it was too late. You can never undo bad deeds.

There were other companies on the march to Southampton. We made better speed than most as we were all mounted. I commented on this to Sam, "How can Sir Edward afford to mount all these men? The horses are not the best but we must feed and stable them."

We fight under the banner of the Earl of Oxford and the king pays him. He will pay Sir Edward and part of the contract is that any horses that are lost are replaced at the earl's expense. At the moment Sir Edward is paying his own money but once we are at Southampton then the expense will be the earl's. Why should we worry? He pays us and our purses are full."

The problem was I did worry not only about the fact that if our pay dried up I would have to use my own funds and secondly that I now carried what I would have viewed as a small fortune before I became a billman. I solved the problem on the road to Southampton. A tanner in Abingdon was selling offcuts of hide at the side of the road. I bought a couple and my nimble fingers managed to sew a series of pouches that I made into a belt. I spread my coins around it and from that moment on spent every waking moment with the belt around my middle beneath my padded and metalled jack. The different pouches meant that the weight was well distributed, and I had a thin extra layer of

protection from hide and metal coins. I worried less about being
robbed after that.

We passed Captain Jack and the earl's billmen as we neared
Southampton. It was a time for us to slow down so that the two
old friends, Sir Edward and Captain Jack could speak. We also
chatted with billmen alongside whom we had fought. Sam knew
them better than we did, but we chatted amiably. A billman I did
not know suddenly said, to me, "I would like to thank you,
James of Prescot, for that apology of a man, Tad of Easingwold,
made my life a misery at Oxford and you rid this land of him."

Others nodded their agreement, and a second said, "Aye, he
would make up stories about a man and threaten to spread them
abroad if we did not give him a share of our pay."

I shook my head, "If they were lies then why pay?"

"They were lies but a man's name is important and better to
pay an odd penny than have a name besmirched and impugned."

I looked at Stephen. He was a quiet man, and I could see how
he might have been bullied into paying someone like Tad. He
was lucky that he had joined Joseph's men and now Sam's, but I
determined to watch over my quiet friend. He had been my first
real friend and I felt I owed it to him. It was as we neared
Southampton that I remembered my father talking of shield
brothers. At the time I had not understood the reference; billmen
bore no shield but now I did. A shield brother was one with
whom you fought. He had spoken of men dying to save shield
brothers which I had thought, at the time, a foolish thing to do
but now I understood it. A man did not choose to die but if in his
dying he could save another, then his life was not wasted.

Southampton was heaving and there were no rooms to be had.
We camped where we could. We were lucky to find a wall in the
outer bailey of the castle and we quickly improvised cloak
shelters and began to cook. As with Joseph's men, we shared all
that we had, and we soon had two fires going with our cooking
pots filled with all manner of foods we had gathered. The two
pots had been provided by the constable at Oxford. With the
diminishing numbers of the garrison, he had no need of them and
he was an old friend of Sir Edward. I think he would have come
with us had he been asked. Life in Oxford Castle was not one for
a warrior.

Sir Edward, his squire and men at arms were accommodated in the castle and so the billmen and the archers made our own enclave against the wall. Joseph had given us plenty of advice about campaigning abroad and we used our time wisely for the four days we awaited our orders to embark. We procured hard cheeses with good rinds that would last six months or more. We bought a spare ale skin each. Before we embarked, we would buy the best ale that we could. It would eke out for just a week or so and then we would have to endure what Joseph had called the foreign muck that they drank over the Channel. It was while we were sampling the ales on offer that we heard of the next pretender to the crown. Perkin Warbeck had been seen in Ireland where he had proclaimed that he was the rightful King of England. The mayor of Cork, John Atwater, a Yorkist, gave credence to the story that he was indeed the rightful heir. However, when soldiers were mobilised to arrest him, he fled back to the court of the King of France who supported him.

As we headed back to the castle Sam tapped the end of his nose, "Now I see the method behind this campaign. He wishes to rid himself of the threat of Warbeck. The king does not need Boulogne for Calais is ours and is stronger, but the French need it." It seemed to please him that there was an apparently good reason for a siege. The veterans amongst us had told us that a siege was not a good way to fight. Disease could strike a camp of besiegers and there was little profit. Stephen and I were anxious to see how our men would perform in such a battle.

We embarked on cogs which took us across the water. We left our horses in the castle and that confirmed the king's intentions. He only needed horsemen if he intended to range into France. None of us enjoyed the voyage as the choppy seas and uncomfortable motion of the cog meant most of us were sick for at least half the voyage. As at Southampton, the twelve thousand troops were too many for the castle in Calais and we made camps outside the city. It was October and although slightly warmer than in England, the weather was just as troubled, and we lived under our oiled cloaks until the time came to march down the road to Boulogne.

We had seen little of Sir Edward and the men at arms. They had procured horses when we landed at Calais and rode with the king and the Earl of Oxford. As we neared Boulogne Dick rode back to speak with us, "Not far to go. Boulogne is just ahead." He shook his head, "This will be bloody work. There is a lower wall and a citadel; worse, the French are prepared. We are to camp to the south of the town as close to the river as we can manage. It means we have a longer journey than most as we have to avoid the defences and they bristle with cannons." He wheeled his horse and headed back to the van.

I knew that we had cannons with us and that they would be used to batter the walls but others, far more experienced than I was, had told me that they were inaccurate and whilst firing on a flat trajectory could break through walls, an elevated target was harder to hit. A citadel suggested elevation. I was desperate to ask Sam how we might be used but after the incident with Tad, I was keenly aware that I was still considered young, and I did not want to fuel the opinion that I knew not what I was doing. I would speak to him when we were alone.

I smiled as I turned to my men, "It is good that they are prepared and that they have spoken to God. It does not do to kill a man who has not been shriven."

They laughed at my confidence, and I felt pleased with myself. Then my mind did its normal trick of planting doubts and then watering them. I did wonder about camping by a river. Freshwater was always useful, but it also brought the risk of insects and disease. Those who camped upstream would have already soiled the water if we were close to its mouth. My handful of men seemed unaware of such matters, and they laughed easily. I had put them at their ease but not myself. Why could I not take such matters in my stride? Was it because of my father? When he had come back from the wars, I had begged him for stories. He had done as I asked but these were not the stories of heroism and brave knights. His stories had been about the real war, the brutal one. They had been for my ears only and neither my mother nor my sisters knew the true horror of war. That picture had not dismayed me for my father had also spoken about fighting for the right. He believed that fighting for the true king was God's work. I had to keep that thought in my head.

The town appeared in the distance. We were to ride all around its circumference to the river. Not as large as Calais I knew that since they had lost that port to the English, they had improved the defences of Boulogne. The fleet which had carried us across were now blockading the port, we could see their sails, and that meant the only help to the town had to come from the east. Sam had already hinted that there would be two battles to fight: one to take the town and the other to repel the attempts to relieve the siege. From Dick's words, it seemed likely that we would be called upon to do the former. I think that I would have preferred to fight against other soldiers rather than risk climbing a ladder and facing all manner of missiles. A herald directed us from the road to trek across fields to our allotted position. Sir Edward's banner was a good marker and we walked over recently harvested fields that had already been turned to sticky mud. It did not bode well. We crossed the river, which was just thirty paces wide and as it was low tide merely came up to our waists. It cleansed the mud from our boots but soaked our breeks. Sir Edward waved us over. William son of Edgar had already tethered the horses on a patch of grass. The grass would not last long.

"This is the best camp that I could spy," Sir Edward waved his arm around, "It is slightly higher than the rest but I fear that the water will soon become too foul to use."

Sam pointed to a farmhouse just half a mile from the walls. It was too vulnerable to be used as shelter as cannons could destroy it and had been abandoned, "My lord, let us find barrels in the farmhouse. If we fill them now, we shall have cooking and washing water. Who knows, they may have left pots there."

"Good man, take your men and see what you can find."

Sam said, "James and Stephen see to our camp. Come my fine fellows let us take this war to the French."

I envied Sam for our task was not one I relished. Taking our daggers, I used Tad's, we hacked down thin branches from the trees and bushes which lay close to the water. We were lucky that there was one willow, and the pliable branches were the best for making hovels and tents. While Stephen's men procured the wood my men and I stripped the branches and buried one end in the ground. Using ivy we bound the tops of the branches so that there was an apex. That had been one of the first words given to me by Sam. I then sent John and Alf to the river to fetch river mud which we plastered along the sides of the hovel and then use more ivy and smaller branches to cover it. When it dried it would keep us warm but as I knew from Sam, it would have to be repaired after rain. Each hovel could hold six men. It would be cosy and a tight fit. If we had to be here for a long time, I knew that we would build more and Stephen, almost anticipating that, stripped the willow of every usable branch. We stored them in the hovels. The archers had made their own hovels and we were finished while the men at arms were still erecting the tent that they and Sir Edward would use.

As we used the discarded pieces of wood for kindling and lit a fire Stephen nodded towards the willow hovels, "You know that the wood will start to sprout?" I nodded. "Long after we are gone there will be a stand of willows here. If nothing else, they will mark our passing."

I laughed, "You are a deep one, Stephen."

He nodded, "Losing all your family will do that to a man. I spend a lot of time contemplating the hereafter."

In contrast, I had not lost my family, I had discarded them.

Sam and his men came back laden. They had two barrels and whilst they were not large, they would be useful to store water. He had also found a small barrel of beer and that would augment our supplies. Although they had not found any food, they had found two large metal pots that were too big for the farmer to take and we filled them with water and began to prepare our food.

This was my first campaign and it seemed to move inexorably slowly. It took two days for King Henry's army to arrive and men were still building their camps the next day. Sir Edward was a cautious man and he had us, having built our camp already, form a sentry line along the boundary of the small farm that Sam had pillaged. The Earl of Oxford's men emulated us and there was a thin screen of billmen and archers along the southwestern side of the port. The French decided to sortie while we were still establishing camps. Sharp-eyed John, one of my men spotted them as the gates open and they sallied forth, "Stand to!"

Grabbing our helmets and billhooks we ran to the entrance of the farm. I made sure the helmet was securely fastened. I did not want it knocked from my head. This was where our practice paid off and we formed two lines of billmen anchored by two men at arms on one side and two men at arms and Sir Edward on the other. I was at one end of the front line with Sam at the other. Stephen stood in the middle of our second line. The archers spread out in a long line which overlapped us. I heard Captain Tom shout, "Nock!" They would not draw until they were commanded. Pulling a warbow was something I had only attempted once, that was before the battle of Bramham Moor, and the laughter of the archers still haunted me. I ran my eye along my line of men and saw that they were all doing as we had practised. I then looked at the French. They had men with harquebusiers as well as men at arms, pikemen, and spearmen. By my estimate, there were more than a hundred and fifty men running at us. Other parties were attacking our lines too.

Sir Edward said, calmly, "When you are ready, Captain Tom."

The archers knew their range better than any and as some of the harquebusiers were raising their weapons it seemed a good time to loose. "Draw! Release!" There was just a heartbeat between the two commands. "Choose your own targets." The third command came while the arrows were plunging down. Some found sallets and pot helmets, but the harquebusiers wore no plate and three were struck in flesh. More arrows descended and then the primitive firearms belched forth their charges. The air reeked. Human urine was used to make the gunpowder and when it was ignited then the air was filled with its pungent stench. I heard a cry, but I kept my attention on my fore for the French, emboldened by their firearms were close enough to charge. A phalanx of six pikemen with men at arms guarding their flanks ran at us.

I heard one of Stephen's men behind me as he moaned, "Dear God, protect me."

Stephen said, "Fear not, Wilfred, he is with us and we have stout comrades before us. Remember the training."

The six pikes were thrust at us. Sam shouted as the pikes were drawn back, "Sweep!" The command was unique to us but we all knew what it meant. Sam had designed it as a way to defeat pikes. The longer weapons were dangerous but also vulnerable as, unlike our billhooks, had no metal protection for the head. The sweep was a simple move, and all ten billhooks were swept left to right at the same time. We had practised it but never used it. Now, as we did so for the first time, I was amazed at its success. Not every billhook found wood, but every pike had three feet hewn from its end. While the jagged stump could still hurt it could not kill and, for the French pikemen, they would now be on the receiving end of our own billhooks. "Billhooks, strike!" We had practised this one too and we all stepped forward on our right feet to ram our spikes into the middles of the pikemen and men at arms. Even as I felt my spike find flesh the stump of a pike scraped and scratched along my sallet. I was glad that I had fastened it well.

Sir Edward shouted, "Stand firm." I knew why he gave the order. It would have been tempting for our billmen to charge on, but we had a wall protecting our flanks and we had enjoyed the better of it. The French began to withdraw and I wondered if it was over but all that they were doing was allowing their harquebusiers to fire at us again. In the time it took for their comrades to pass through them and for them to raise their weapons, Captain Tom's archers sent their arrows not to plunge down on helmets and shoulders but, loosing on a flat trajectory, to hit faces and chests. Barely four harquebusiers fired. It was then that the French finally withdrew but it was a costly withdrawal. The archers reaped a heavy harvest. We stood firm while the rest of the French attacks were beaten off but when the gates were slammed shut then we were ordered forward. We left behind our billhooks and took swords to end the lives of any French who still lived. It was not out of cruelty but kindness. If they could not leave the battlefield then they were too badly hurt and we had no means of healing. The archers retrieved as many of their arrows as they could. Even ones with damaged shafts had something worth salvaging, the heads. We stripped the bodies.

It was as we returned to our own lines that we saw the cost we had paid. Egbert the man at arms was dead. He had been unlucky and the stone from the harquebusiers had found his face. Hob, one of Sam's men had also been killed. His death had not been as swift. The stone had hit his middle and he had died while we had still been battling the pikemen. Alf, one of my men had lost his eye. The stump of the pike had taken it. The earl had healers and John took Alf to them. I knew not what they could do but my man was not dead and that was something to be grateful for.

When Alf returned, he had a bandaged head, and I could smell burning hair. The surgeon had simply used a burning brand to seal the orb. John told us that Alf had mercifully passed out and the surgeon had given him a flask of brandy to help dull the pain when he did awake. I nodded, "Your task, John, for the next few days is to tend to Alf. Keep him cheerful and do not let him alone."

"Will he be able to wield a billhook?"

I shrugged, "I know not but I doubt that he will be called upon to fight for some time."

I told Sam and Sir Edward all when the knight held a council of war. "We were lucky that they did not come at night or else things might have gone ill for us." he pointed north, "Sir John Savage was killed yesterday when he and Sir John Riseley were scouting out the enemy. The sooner we make siege lines the better. I want one man in four on duty all night. Captain Sam organise your billmen and Captain Tom the archers. We will bury Egbert."

Sam nodded, "And we will do the same for Hob."

I think the French found the exchange had been too costly for that was the last sortie that they tried. Two days later we moved back to the farmhouse and began to dig the ditches and trenches to enable us to bombard their walls. Gunners arrived with two bombards. The walls of the farmhouse allowed them to build a protective cover for the gun and to give the structure support. Our task was to dig two diagonal trenches that would allow us to get within two hundred paces of the walls. We filled baskets with soil, they were called gabions, that were placed above us and they allowed us to dig while we had some protection from the soil-filled baskets that acted like the crenulations of a castle. It was hard work and dangerous too. The French had guns on the walls and Ned and I were grateful for the baskets of soil when a stone, fired from the wall, smacked into one. Although the soil held the missile its integrity was gone, and we had to make another. As we dug the soil we piled the surplus up to make a parapet. It was the task of the billmen and men at arms to dig. The archers had the more dangerous task of keeping the walls clear of the enemy. They duelled with the crossbowmen and harquebusiers on the walls. We just dug and after five days of digging, we were close enough to begin work on the main trench that would run parallel to the town wall. The digging had strengthened our arms and we had learned the techniques. When we began the parallel trench we used some of the willows we had kept from our hovels to make a double wall above the trench and we filled that with earth. We soon learned to fill the wood at night for it was more dangerous during the day. When we joined our trench up with the ones to the side we had a reasonably safe walkway and we put away our spades. The task of reducing the walls was now down to the engineers, sappers, and gunners. We would be the interested observers. As soon as the walls were ready for assault we would take our billhooks and ladders and force the walls.

Alf had recovered enough, after a couple of days, to ask to be able to perform some useful function. We made him into a cook. He was philosophical about the loss of his eye, "I still have one eye and I have lost none of my strength. When I become accustomed to having just one orb, I will join you again. I now have good reason to fight the French and as they say, an eye for an eye." It was the right attitude to adopt.

We still had our night duties, and it was when I was in command of the trench that we spied movement from the walls. As well as digging our trenches we had also dug pits before us and they were to trap the unwary. When we saw the movement from the town, I tapped the sentries next to me and drew my sword. The shadow looked like a giant spider as it descended the walls. It moved across the open ground, and I nodded to the archer close to me to take aim. The sudden scream in the night told me that there was no need to waste an arrow. Whoever it was had found a trap.

"Au secours! M'aidez, s'il vous plait!"

The voice sounded young and I guessed it meant that whoever it was needed help. I sheathed my sword but drew my dagger as I clambered out of the trench and headed towards the trap. The Frenchman had not known where it was but I did and I headed for it. I was ready for a trick or treachery. When I reached the pit I saw that it was a boy of no more than ten years of age. He was weeping and, from the angle of his leg, it was broken. He was no threat and I sheathed my dagger. I held my hands out. He looked at me fearfully. I had no time for this, "Come boy or the rats shall have you."

I am not sure if he understood me but he put his arms up and I pulled. As his leg moved he screamed and this time there was a response from the walls. Two harquebusiers fired. They missed but added urgency to my actions. I hauled him up and slung him over my shoulder. The movement made him scream again. I ran back to the trench and jumped in the bottom. "John, take charge. I will take this one back to our camp."

The boy moaned and wept for most of the way but when I slipped, in the dark, and he banged his leg on the wooden fascine he screamed and then went silent. The cries and gunfire had woken the camp and Sam and Sir Edward awaited me. "This boy fell into one of our traps. I think his leg is broken."

Sam nodded, "Better we splint it now while he is asleep." He looked at Sir Edward for his approval.

"Aye, and then we can question him on the morrow."

He headed back to his tent and Sam said, "You had better help me, James." We carried him closer to the fire and Sam shook his head, "He is a boy! What was he doing?"

I shrugged, "I know not. We shall have to find out, eh?"

Sam knew his business. Broken limbs were common on the battlefield either from falls or blows from blunt instruments and the break appeared to be clean. He cleaned it rigorously with vinegar and smeared honey on the open wound before first bandaging it and then, while I held the splints in place, he put another bandage around it. The boy would not be moving for some time. We woke Alf so that he could stand guard on him and I returned to the trench. It was a warning for us that the French were not simply going to wait for us to attack. They had plans of their own.

When we were relieved, at dawn, we returned to the camp and some welcome food. We would sleep for just four hours before going back to the trenches. The night watch was every four days, and we were growing used to it. The boy was still asleep and even Alf, who hated all things French felt sympathy and said, "Poor little thing. He must have been desperate to escape the siege, eh?"

I was intrigued but there was little point in speculating. We ate and then went into our hovels which were still warm from the nighttime occupants. Of course, there were just two of us in ours and it was comfortable. The camp, by the river, was not as unpleasant as I had first thought, and we were far enough from the siege to have relative peace. That was until that day when King Henry ordered the bombards to begin to fire. The two by the farmhouse were not the only ones but they were the closest to our camp and when they began to belch their dragon-like fire then all thoughts of sleep disappeared. Luckily the wind was from the south and blew the smoke and the stink towards the walls of Boulogne. With no chance of sleep and no desire to be upwind of the guns until I had to be, I went to the campfire.

Alf gestured at the French boy, "He is awake. He started jabbering but I could not understand a word."

I took some small beer and poured it into my costrel. I went to the boy and offered it to him. He looked at me suspiciously and so I drank. I offered it again and he accepted. I decided to try to speak to him. I pointed at myself and said, "Me, James." I pointed to him, "You?"

"Pierre."

It was a start. I used a mixture of sign language and words I thought were French to speak to him. Sir Edward came back from the trenches and came over to us. "How is our little French friend?"

"From his face, in pain. I know his name and that he is nine years old. That is about it, my lord."

"Let me try. I speak some French although the French language they speak here has many Flemish words. I can try." He began a conversation and after a short time seemed satisfied, "The boy's motives were innocent enough. He was here with his father who was killed in the nighttime attack on our defences. He was lonely and just wanted to get home to Desvres. It is ten miles east of here. His mother and grandparents live there with his sisters. There is little chance of that until his leg heals. I told him that he can go when he can walk and until then he can help around the camp. Tell the others to be kind. The poor child is terrified that we will eat him. They are spreading stories that Englishmen eat babies for breakfast."

And so each day I learned more French as he learned more English. Only Stephen and I seemed willing to try to learn to speak to him. Whatever the reason we mutually benefitted.

It was a relief to do something kind for the rest of the siege grew both more dangerous and nastier. There were no more sorties as such but two nights after the boy had fallen into the trap and when a large section of the outer wall had been destroyed by the bombards, the French sent a party of men to damage the guns. The gunners slept close to their weapons, but we were the primary defence as our trench had to be crossed before they could get to the guns. We were more alert, and we heard them. I tapped the men next to me and the news was passed down the trench. I drew my falchion. Once more the pits we had dug trapped the unwary although they did not scream as Pierre had done. We heard the grunt and the sound of metal scraping on metal as they fell. As soon as that happened the French stopped worrying about being seen and simply ran at us. They were brave men but we knew our trenches and they did not.

We stood with our backs to the side of the trench facing the French so that when they jumped into the trench intent on spearing us, we were behind them. The spear that was rammed into the soft earth of the other side of the trench rendered the weapon impotent and I used my falchion to kill a man. I slid the blade up under the ribs of the Frenchman. It grated off a bone and I turned the point a little until there was no resistance. I had no thought that I was killing a man. This was self-preservation. I was stopping him from hurting me. When his body went limp I pulled out the falchion and he fell at my feet. The next man had seen my position and he tried to spear me from above. My helmet saved me, and the spearhead scraped down the side of the sallet. I was already turning and lifting my sword while my left hand grabbed the wooden haft of the spear. I pulled the man down and as he overbalanced, he fell onto me and my sword. I was knocked to the bottom of the trench but the falchion had done its job and the man lay dead. When Sir Edward and the rest of our men arrived the survivors turned tail and ran. We had lost no one and they had left twenty of their own dead.

I was woken the next morning by the sound of the bombards as they began once more to reduce the walls. The night attack was the last one and on the third of November, the siege ended as the French sued for peace. Our siegeworks had proved to be too effective and as the French were unable to relieve it King Henry had won. The treaty was called, we later learned, the Peace of Étaples. The siege had proved to be a successful show of force and King Henry was offered very favourable terms by King Charles of France, including the end of French support to the pretender to the English throne Perkin Warbeck who was also expelled from the country. The terms of the treaty also included us accepting French control of Brittany, and the French paying King Henry an indemnity of almost three quarters of a million crowns, payable at fifty thousand crowns per annum. For the loss of a few men, King Henry had achieved all that he might have hoped and was in profit.

Of course, the treaty took some time to be ratified and that meant we did not go home, but we had no night watches and no fighting. Even better was the fact that we did not have to endure the stink of the two bombards. I thought my war was over, but I was wrong.

Chapter 12

We had all got to know Pierre well and he was grateful that we had not eaten him. I could now speak some of the language and I enjoyed his company. When he was well enough to travel Stephen and I sought permission to take him home. I had wanted adventure and travelling just ten miles to his home in my first foreign country seemed like such a one. We used Egbert's horse and Stephen and I took turns to ride with the boy on the beast. It was not a long journey and we made it in less than two hours. The reunion was touching and made me yearn to have such a one with my mother and father. After hearing her son's story, Pierre's mother was grateful to us, showering us with kisses on the cheeks and insisted upon feeding us. We enjoyed a convivial time in Pierre's home and it showed us that while we had some French words we could not speak the language yet. His mother was patient and corrected our mistakes. We were back at our camp by evening and I had enjoyed our day away from war not to mention one of the best meals I had ever eaten. It showed me that a kind gesture is never wasted. We could have been cruel to Pierre, in fact, many of our comrades would have been but we were kind and the result was we had been rewarded.

It was as the army prepared to move and return to Southampton that I was summoned by Sir Edward. "You and I, it seems, are needed by King Henry. Leave your billhook here. I cannot see that you would need it." I donned my cloak and strapped on my sword.

As we headed for the king's quarters which were situated in a large house he had taken over back in October, I asked, "Have I done something wrong, my lord?"

"Far from it. Your name has been lauded by all as a resourceful warrior who was instrumental in saving the bombards. Had they been taken we might still be fighting. I daresay he wishes to reward you." He smiled and put his hand upon my shoulder, "You are a good boy. Do not be so fearful."

There were just two guards at the house which was remarkably empty. I had not seen much of the king but when I had passed his quarters it seemed to be a hive of activity. There were no servants and that worried me too. King Henry was

137

known to be a ruthless man although for the life of me I could not see why I should have come to his attention. One of the guards remained at the main door while the other took the two of us inside. I saw a frown crease Sir Edward's face and that confirmed that he did not know what was going on. We were taken to a small room and the guard did not knock but opened it and gestured for us to enter. We did so and the door closed, ominously. There, at the table were the Earl of Oxford and King Henry of England. I began to run through every misdemeanour I had committed but I could think of nothing so heinous as to warrant such a meeting.

"Sit." There were two chairs, but I hesitated. I knew little of court protocol but sitting in the presence of a king seemed to me to be forbidden. "I give you permission, James of Prescot, to sit." He said it with a smile.

Sir Edward asked, somewhat nervously, "Is aught amiss, my lord?" The question appeared to be addressed to the two men.

The Earl smiled, "I hope not." He took a piece of parchment from a pile and said, "I have a letter here from the lord of Windle." He smiled at me, "Close to your home, I believe?"

My heart sank and I murmured, "Yes, my lord." I was tempted to blurt out the whole story but did not.

Sir John began to read, "One of King Henry's billmen, Walter the Rat Slayer has visited his lord."

Sir Edward could not contain himself, "I knew him! A fine fellow and a real hero of Bosworth Field."

The king nodded, "A great warrior. Continue, my lord."

The earl coughed and found his place again, "Walter went to him because his son had run away to fight the Yorkists, and he wished to know if he lived or died. He said that his son was James of Ecclestone. There is here," he tapped the letter, "a description of both the youth and the arms he took from his father. Both match you, James of Prescot. What say you?"

My head drooped. All my good work was to be for nothing and I would be dismissed from the company. I would lose my friends and that made me sad, "I am James of Ecclestone, my lord."

I studied the pattern on the polished table. It was an expensive piece of furniture. Whoever owned this house was a rich man. I was aware that silence reigned in the room.

King Henry's voice was soft when he spoke, "James, are you loyal to your king and your country?"

I looked up and defiance replaced the sadness, "Aye, King Henry. Did I not fight well at Stoke Field and here at Boulogne?"

The king nodded, "And would you do all that your king ordered you to do?"

"Of course, my liege. My father earned a great name, and I would earn one too."

"What if the work you were to do for your king and your country was unrecognised and no one knew of it except, let us say, the three men in this room?"

Sir Edward could contain himself no longer. "King Henry, what is it that you ask of this boy?"

The king held up his hand for silence, "James, answer honestly. I care not that you took a different name you are quite right, and you have earned our thanks. I ask you again, is it fame and glory that you seek or are you loyal to the crown?"

It was a good question and I did not answer it straight away. When I had left Ecclestone I had sought fame and fortune as well as the glory of success in battle but I was no longer the same youth. War had changed me. The men alongside whom I had fought had moulded me too. The conflicts I had encountered had helped me to grow. I found myself smiling for even the words I used were now different and that was thanks to Sam Sharp Tongue. I nodded at the king, "Although I still seek fame, I am more willing to be a servant to the king and to do all that he wishes me to do although, King Henry, I cannot see what a lowly billman can do for England that necessitates such a clandestine meeting."

The king nodded, "You are right, de Vere, and he may be the very chap we seek." He nodded to the falchion hanging from my belt, "Take out your sword and swear on the hilt never to reveal what is asked of you and to fulfil the orders I am about to give."

To draw a sword in the presence of a king was also serious and I did as he asked. Reverently kissing the crosspiece I said, "I swear that I will never reveal what is asked of me and I will strive to do that which is asked of me."

The two men smiled, and I sheathed the weapon. I could tell, from his face, that Sir Edward was confused. The king said, "Sir Edward, you need not know the details of what we ask of James. Indeed, it is better that you do not. You shall not see him for some time." He paused, "If things go badly, you may never see him again. You will return to your men and tell them the part of the story of the letter from Windle and tell them that James of Prescot or Ecclestone, is to be returned to his family."

"But…"

The earl said, "Edward, I know that you are loyal. What we ask James to do is for England and will save lives. The youth is willing to risk his life for the king and that should be sufficient for you. We are all servants of the crown."

Defeated he stood and, turning to me, held out his arm, "James, whenever you have completed this task then return to me for there will always be a place for you in my retinue."

I nodded, "And tell the others…" I suddenly realised he could tell them nothing, "Stephen will be sad, my lord, try to help him for he is a kind soul and my one true friend." I stood and lifted up my doublet. I knew not what the king and Earl thought but they watched, bemused as I removed the hide belt. "There are all the coins I have earned thus far, Sir Edward. I would have them given to my family if I do not return."

As he picked it up, he felt the weight, "There are plenty here. You trust me?"

I smiled, "I do but, in reality, I have little choice, do I? I cannot speak with Sam and Stephen whom I do trust for I swore an oath."

Nodding the knight took the belt and left.

The earl and the king seemed relieved that they could speak openly, "You know that the French have now abandoned their support for Perkin Warbeck?" I nodded. The king continued, "He will now head for Burgundy and my avowed enemy, Margaret of York, Duchess of Burgundy. This is not over, and an army will be raised to put the puppet on the throne. I want you to join his army and be my spy in his army." I thought I was going to be sick and to do so before a king was unthinkable. He saw my

reaction and smiled, "It will not be as hard as you think." He
tapped the letter, "You managed to fool all your comrades about
your identity. Now that I know the connection, I can see your
father in you, but you managed to keep up the pretence for years.
You are a natural spy. All we ask is that you adopt the identity of
the son of a man killed at Bosworth. Instead of becoming James
of Ecclestone or Prescot, you become James of Yarm. You have
a northern accent and the men you meet will not comment. Your
father, Geoffrey, was a billman who died at Bosworth."

"Is there such a man?"

"There was and he died. He even had a son who was about
your age, but he died at Stoke Field. You make your way to
Burgundy and seek service. They will take you on for they are
desperate for any who will follow the white rose. Margaret of
York is a desperate woman. All that we need from you is the
news of when Warbeck plans to attack. I daresay that you will be
treated well by the Burgundians who would rather Yorkists died
while fighting me than their own men."

"And how do I get the news of their proposed attack to you,
King Henry?"

The Earl of Oxford said, "That is the hard part. You will need
to desert the army but in such a way that they do not suspect you
are King Henry's spy. You make your way back to England and
you find me. You are known at Hedingham, and my people will
tell me when you have come."

A sudden thought came into my head, "Was that why I was
kept on and sent to Middleham?"

The earl smiled and nodded, "You did all that was asked of
you and more. I needed to know if you had the steel to serve the
king. And you do. We have known of this Warbeck for some
time. Do not fear James, for there are other spies who will be
doing as you do. You will never know who they are and that is
for your mutual benefit."

I knew that my father would wish me to serve the king, but he
would prefer it in a more open manner. However, I was resigned
to die, serving England. Perhaps my face gave away my doubts
for the king asked, "What is it that troubles you? Would you
withdraw your offer?"

"No, I gave my word and humble though I am I believe that a man's word should count for something. I will do this for you and for my country, but I do not think I will be returning home."

The Earl of Oxford leaned forward, "We do not send you to your death and we do not ask you to get close to Perkin Warbeck or whatever he calls himself. Just become part of his army. Take the coins they give you and when the time is right then return to me with news of the time and place of the invasion. You will be rewarded."

"Aye, well, my lord, coins do a corpse little good, do they? A pauper and a lord may have different graves but they are both dead."

The king smiled, "Perhaps this pessimism might help with the illusion. A youth who lost his family would have such an attitude and we are not fools, James of," he glanced at the parchment before him, "Yarm. We have clothes for you to take and, when you are close to Burgundy, to change into. My barber will crop your hair and remove the hair from your face. The falchion you bear will be replaced by a short sword such as the men of the north country use and we have a sallet taken from Bosworth that has a narrow slit for the eyes. The only fear the earl had was that one who escaped Stoke Field might recognise you."

This was going to happen come what may and I was emboldened enough to speak again, "Then send for your barber but do you not fear that he will be a party to the plot, King Henry?"

He smiled, "He is a blind barber and so long as you remain silent then all will be well. I like that you think of problems, James. You have yet to ask what your reward shall be."

"As I do not think I will be alive to claim it I am unworried. If I survive then I will have a reward although life itself may seem a worthy reward as well as serving the king of England."

"There will be a purse with ten crowns waiting for you. Here," he pushed a purse across, "is a bag of coins so that you can feed yourself while travelling to Burgundy. They are all taken from dead Yorkists and will not betray you as a spy. We also have a ragged sumpter for you. It means you can travel faster but there is little likelihood that others will try to take the beast from you." He stood, "I will leave you now and see you whenever you return."

He left and I remained with the earl, "You are not the only spy we are sending into the camp of the enemy, but you know not them, and they know not you. Trust no one."

"And where do I go? I assume I leave today."

He nodded, "This night under cover of darkness. Warbeck and his retinue are heading east. They will stop in Paris first for that is where they were accommodated and then they will head for…" he shrugged, "We know not where. It may be Lyons in the southeast or perhaps north for the duchess likes Mechelen. You may catch up with them or with others of a similar bent. Keep to your story as you did with the James of Prescot one. It fooled many."

There was a knock on the door and the earl put his finger to his lips, "Come."

By the tools of his trade, the man who stood before us was the blind barber. He said cheerfully, "I was told there was one who needed a close crop and a close shave. I am here to do both."

"Come, the man is before you on the chair."

The man came behind me and used his hands and fingers to explore my face and hair. He was behind me, and I could not see him but I heard him for he talked non-stop, "You have good hair." He sniffed, "But you do not wash it often enough. Still, my crop will help it grow stronger. I will start with the beard although from the feel you are not a man grown and it should shave easily." I started for I feared he might deduce too much. He took the wrong meaning, "Do not fear a blind barber, young man. I have never so much as nicked any and a crop is the easiest of haircuts. I was a barber long before God took my eyes. I know not why I was cursed but there you are. I may have committed a sin too many. Still, I make a good living and my nose and fingers tell me more about a man than ever did my eyes. Eyes can deceive you know."

I thought about Alf. If I should ever see him again, I would tell him of the blind barber. Then I felt fear, would I be able to tell any of the men?

The warm soap on my face was pleasant and then he began to use his shears to trim my hair. His hands and shears appeared to know what to do and I resigned myself to the change in my appearance. I consoled myself with the knowledge that it would grow again.

"This will not take long, and I can use my razor on your head. I guarantee that any lice that wish to take up residence will fail."

He continued in such a manner until, after using a towel to wipe my head and face he said, "There you are, young sir and you may run your hands around your head and face, if you find a single drop of blood then my fee is halved."

The earl stepped forward and pressed some coins in his hand, "Thank you, barber, you have done a good job."

I heard him sniff, "A skilled man likes to hear praise from his customers."

The earl was quick thinking, "Just as you have no eyes my nephew has no tongue. He thanks you."

"Oh I am sorry young sir, still like me you can make the best of God's curses."

When he had gone the earl went to a chest, "Here are your travelling clothes and the Yorkist ones for Burgundy. I shall leave you for a while. Edgar guards the door, and I will return with your food."

Left alone I realised that the two men were not taking any chances and that my task was one that was important. I put the chair behind the door so that I would not be disturbed and then I took out the clothes and undressed. They were better clothes than mine. I guessed the former owner had been a nobleman. The boots were also finely made and showed little wear and tear. That done I examined the clothes of the warrior I would adopt in Burgundy. There was a good jack and a well-made arming cap. There were also mailed gauntlets. Someone had provided a bag to carry the spare clothes and, that done, I put my old life in the chest. I transferred the coins I had been given to those in my purse. The pot of salve was now too big to keep there and I placed it in my bag. I removed the chair and sat upon it and waited for my food. I was starving. My head and face felt naked and cold. I would have to use the arming cap in lieu of the rabbit skin hat I preferred.

The earl entered and he was alone. He carried a tray. I felt self-conscious to be served by an earl. "Eat. It is almost dark now and Edgar and I will take you to the stable where your steed awaits. While you eat, I will add details to the story that might save your life. You have spent the last few years trying to serve the Yorkist cause. You were at Stoke Field, but you were too young to fight, and you held the horses. That is how you escaped. You came to France and found employment in Calais. The only leader we know of who survived both battles is Lord Lovell. He may be dead, and he might be hiding in Scotland or, more likely, Burgundy. Lord Lovell has royal livery with a rampant beast in the centre wearing a crown, but he is also known by the sign of the silver wolf." He stared at me, "Sir Edward said you have picked up a few words of the local language." My mouth full I nodded, "Good. You have been trying to join the man who calls himself Richard of Shrewsbury, the Duke of York. You killed a man to get the horse. That will explain both why you are mounted and why you are fleeing east. Tomorrow we will spread a story about someone killing one of our men and stealing the horse. The description will be of you, without the name, of course."

So, I was to be hunted by my own side and the only ones who would know were Edgar, the earl, and the king. We left the house like thieves in the night. All of us were cloaked and I had a large bag containing my new helmet and spare clothes. To any who viewed us, we would have looked like men who had just robbed a house. Edgar led us to a stable and I saw that whilst there were other horses there was no ostler. The earl was being careful.

It came to me, as Edgar held my bag and I mounted the tired-looking sumpter, that Edgar might have an idea of my identity but I seriously doubted he knew that the youth he was helping was King Henry's spy. He smiled as he handed me the bag that I placed across the saddle, "The horse is called Goliath," he chuckled, "I think it was given as a joke, but he seems a good-natured beast and he has rested this last week. He can carry you far." He took two apples from his doublet. "These may help and God speed, whatever it is you do." I put the two fruits in my own doublet.

He slipped outside to keep watch and the earl stepped closer, "The closer you are to Boulogne the more danger you are in.

Make as much time as you can whilst it is dark and be discreet. The part you play is a hard one but James of Yarm would be a careful man. I pray I shall see you again."

I nodded, "And if not, you will pray for my soul."

"Just so."

I put my feet in the stirrups and mounted. Edgar gestured for us to leave and I dug my heels into the sumpter's side. He moved amiably enough, and we headed into the night on the road to Paris. I did not glance back for my world now lay to the south and the east. I would have to follow Warbeck and go to Paris. Each step would take me deeper into a land filled with enemies. I was leaving friends and heading into a world of enemies. I doubted that I would chance upon a Mistress Gurton. Had she been some sort of witch who had set me on this path all those years ago? I made the sign of the cross. Such thoughts were unwelcome to a youth alone and already terrified beyond words.

Chapter 13

There was little point in feeling sorry for myself; I had been chosen by the king and what greater honour could there be than to serve him? Of course, I did not think it likely I would survive but at least, in my dying, my parents would be made much richer. I realised even as the thought passed through my head that it was unlikely that the king would pay crowns if I did not succeed and died but there was a gold piece from Sir Lionel that would make them realise I was not a total failure.

Goliath was a steady plodder, and whilst not fast he ate up the miles, albeit slowly, as we headed south for Paris. The reason I was heading there was not just that I might meet some other Yorkists, but I had heard that the city was even more wondrous than London and if I was marked to die, I might as well enjoy my last days or weeks on this earth. The woollen arming cap I had been given kept my newly shaved head warm but it itched. As I scratched my head, I saw more and more flaws in this plan of theirs. Firstly Duchess Margaret had to provide funds and men for the pretender. I could be away for years. On the other hand, there could be an army already and if they left quickly then I would not be able to outrun them. The more I thought the greater became my fears and I concentrated on watching the mileposts as we passed them to mark my journey to Paris.

By the time I reached Montreuil, it was dawn. The small town was waking up and the smell of fresh bread could be discerned. I took a decision. Although I had been told that the early part of the journey would be the more dangerous, I had to become the Yorkist as soon as I could. If I was who I said I was then I would need food and travelling so early would necessitate questions if I just rode through the outskirts. I dismounted and led Goliath towards the smell of bread. I slipped an apple to the horse which chomped upon it happily.

My time with Pierre and at the siege had given me a few French words and I knew please and thank you. There were many kinds of bread that the French ate and I could not be sure of identifying the correct one. After tying my horse outside the bread shop, I entered and was engulfed by the comforting smell of warm bread. As soon as I spoke and then pointed to the loaf I wanted, I knew that I had been identified as English. The baker asked for payment, and I did not understand a word nor could I read the French script. I reached into my new purse and took out a couple of coppers. I handed over three and the baker gave me one back. I was learning and the next time I had to buy bread I would offer just two coins. After thanking him I headed out of the bakers and led Goliath through the main street of the small town. Being on the road to Paris meant it was wide and cobbled. I put half of the loaf in the side bag of the saddle and ate the other half while it was still warm. It seemed to make me look normal and the nods and salutations were, generally, friendly. I suppose a man eating a loaf and leading a tired horse were not out of place. I led Goliath to the water trough in the centre and let him drink while I finished off the bread. It was delicious and I was tempted to finish it all off but I knew that would be a mistake.

I saw a small, laden wagon emerge from the side street opposite and the man leading the horse brought it to the trough. The man was old enough to be my father and had a grey beard. He nodded as he approached, and I moved Goliath out of the way so that his horse could drink. He thanked me whilst saying something else and pointing to the sun rising in the east. I had heard a phrase used by Pierre's mother, *d'accord*. I think it meant I agree with you and when I used it, he nodded. Goliath had not finished drinking and I was forced to stay a little longer than I might have wished. The wait invited conversation and he asked me something else. I deduced that he was asking me where I was going and I gave another one-word reply, "Paris." Speaking one word at a time masked my accent but if I had to speak a sentence then I was in trouble.

As luck would have it his horse was satiated at the same time as Goliath and we both turned to head south out of the town. I was tempted to mount Goliath and put distance between us but that would have aroused suspicion and until we were out of the town I needed to behave as though I was an innocent traveller on the road. He walked his horse next to me and began a conversation with me. I picked up, perhaps one word in three and I responded as best I could with nods and shakes of the head.

We had just left the town and I was about to mount the horse when he suddenly spoke in English. "You are an Englishman, are you not?"

There was little point in denying it and the relief of being able to speak made me smile. "Yes, how did you know?"

He smiled, "When I asked you if the sun had warmed you last night you nodded. Besides your accent is appalling." He nodded to my sword, "You can use that?"

I nodded, "I am a soldier."

"And as you are heading away from the English army then either you are a deserter or a mercenary. Which is it?"

"I have not deserted, and I am not part of the English army."

Perhaps there was more aggression in my words than I had meant for he held up his hand, "I care not, my friend, so long as you do not fight France and as your king has just signed a peace treaty then all is well. The reason I ask is that it is a long way from here to Paris and the road can be dangerous. I have some pots in my wagon and I would like to get them there safely. If you would ride with me and use your sword to protect me then I will feed and house, you. It will take four days for us to reach Paris and I will save you having to use your purse."

I was suspicious although the memory of the carter and his son on the road to Burnley made me warm to his offer, "How is it that you speak English so well?"

He smiled, "I have a workshop in Calais and while I am a loyal Frenchman, I know how to get on with those who are my masters."

"And suppose I am a deserter and leading you into a trap?"

He laughed, "You have a good imagination." He stared at me, "You have a secret but that is not it. You would have ridden away once we left the town, I could see that. I am Jean."

"And I am James. I will ride with you, at least part of the way to Paris but I wish to get there sooner rather than later. I will accept your offer but if I draw my sword and have to use it then there will be a payment."

"Of course, but I wonder what your business is that is so urgent." He held up his hand, "Do not tell me. I like puzzles and I can, perhaps, help you to improve your French."

He appeared an honest man and I liked him. I could detect no threat to me from him and the proximity of his wagon made me and my mount almost invisible. When others approached from the south, we both got out of the way and our speed meant we rarely had to overtake any. The speed also suited Goliath. Had I ridden him hard I might have ruined him. As it was, although we only made another twenty-five miles that day, I could not have made it further without Jean's company. We stopped in Abbeville, and I confess that I was exhausted. The boots I had been given were better than my own, but my feet were unused to them. I would need the salve from my bag.

Jean negotiated a price for a place for us to stay. It was the yard of an inn and although they had no rooms the owner was happy enough, for a fee, to allow us to use his yard. I unsaddled Goliath who looked as weary as I was. I gave him the second apple and placed the saddle and my bag beneath the cart. Jean had suggested we sleep beneath it in case of rain. The innkeeper had provided feed for our horses as part of the price, and they ate from the pails he provided.

"Come let us go within and have a meal. I know not if it will be good or not. I have not used this inn before."

I had learned, as we walked, that the pot maker had been sending most of his wares to England. The wars between the houses of Lancaster and York had meant that the supplies of English pots had been in shorter supply. King Henry's peace meant that the prices in England were lower and Jean was looking to make more from the Paris market.

The main room was crowded but Jean knew his way around such places, and he led me to a table I had not spotted when we entered. It was close to the kitchen and meant that one of us, in this case, me, would have to endure the servers as they fetched food from the kitchen. Jean shrugged apologetically, "It is a small price to pay for a table and our food will come all the quicker." I nodded and he lowered his voice, "Perhaps, James, it will be safer if from now on we speak in French. It will improve your skill and make us both less noticeable."

I had seen a couple of men stare at us as we spoke in English, and I nodded. Jean was a good teacher and he corrected me each time I made a mistake. As we drank and then ate the stew, which

151

seemed to me to be largely offal augmented by huge quantities of
bread, he told me his story. His wife had left him ten years
earlier and run off with a younger, richer man, and his two
children. He was philosophical about the whole thing, "It was
my fault for I married a pretty woman who liked beautiful things.
Take my advice, James, and choose plainer women. They are
less likely to look for a better man. When I am rich enough, I
may take another woman who can warm my bed but she will not
be painted and slender."

I was listening more than I was speaking and as I listened I
used my eyes to scan the room. Few seemed to take any notice of
us but for two. One was a weasel-faced man and I saw in his belt
a wicked-looking knife. It was the kind Sam had said was Italian
in origin and called a stiletto. The other was a huge brute of a
man who looked more like a bear than a man. His broken nose
and scarred features suggested a fighter of some kind. It was
when Jean took coins from his purse to pay for the food that the
weasel-faced man nudged his companion. Jean's purse was a fat
one.

Jean patted his belly and said, "I enjoyed that food. Perhaps it
was not to the English taste, but it was wholesome and filling."

I nodded, "It was the sort of meal my mother might have
cooked." Even as I said the words, I knew I had made a slip. It
might have been the drink that did it.

Jean did not pursue the matter but said, "As I saved money
with the food let us indulge myself and you." He waved over a
server and rattled off an order. I had not heard the word before
and I frowned. He spoke slowly as he explained, in French,
"This is a warm drink made with honey and butter. It is made
from a local spirit a little like brandy. We call it grog. It will
keep us warm tonight and, although we need no inducement, will
help us to sleep."

When the steaming drink arrived, I sipped it, a little
nervously, I confess. As was my practice I had drunk sparingly
of the beer but when I felt the heat from the drink, I feared it
might make me drunk again. The carter drank his far faster than I
did and when I continued to sip it asked, "Do you not like it?"

"I do but I fear it will go to my head."

He laughed, "And that is the point for it will induce a deep sleep."

The inn had begun to clear by the time I had finished, and I was relieved to see the weasel-faced man and the bear had gone.

My first days after leaving Ecclestone added to the hovels we had made at Boulogne had ensured that I knew how to be comfortable at night. I used my bag as a pillow and I arranged it so that the helmet and heavier things were at the top end while the clothes at the bottom made a good pillow. A cloak had been provided by the earl and I folded that one to make a bed and used my own oiled one as a cover. Jean was asleep before I was. He had consumed not only ale and the hot spirit but also wine. He was a snorer. I fell asleep quickly enough, but I was awoken, not by a sound, but by the need to make water. I rose and slipped out from beneath the wagon. It did not do to make water close to where you slept and I went to the stable where the other horses, not ours, were housed. I saw a patch of wet straw and added to it. The ostler would get rid of it in the morning. Our horses were closer to our wagon but far enough away not to disturb us. I went to Goliath and stroked his head. I knew not why I had an affinity for horses but I did and already Goliath was becoming as precious to me as Scout and Molly.

It was as I stroked him that his ears pricked as did Maria's, Jean's horse. I stiffened and my hand went to my dagger. One was lying on my bed but I had a spare and I drew it. One horse becoming alerted might be nothing but two were worth investigating. I stood stock-still and saw the two shadows clambering over the roof and down towards the yard. Even in the dark, I could recognise the bear and the smaller man had to be the weasel. For such a large man, bear was both agile and silent. I saw, in his hand, a club. A glint told me that weasel had his stiletto. I saw them heading towards the wagon and I slipped silently between the horses. I was familiar enough to them that they simply moved. I was torn. Did I shout a warning and lose surprise or risk Jean being hurt? I was confident enough to choose the latter. I was behind them both and about two paces from them with my back to the wall of the inn when I saw the club swing towards the two beds. I knew I had miscalculated. Even as I stepped forwards I heard the dull clang as the club hit not Jean's head but my helmet in my sack. I lunged with my dagger and finding the rear of the bear slashed sideways. His scream woke not only Jean but the inn.

Everything happened really quickly after that. Weasel had been about to slash Jean's throat but the scream woke Jean who rolled to safety. Bear swung, more in anger than anything and his wild swing with the club went over my head. I slashed at his right hand almost blindly and heard another shout as I was showered with blood when I cut to the bone. Weasel saw me and came at me with his stiletto. He knew how to use it and while Bear tried to staunch the bleeding Weasel slashed at my throat. The practice with the wooden swords had helped and I reacted quickly. It was not fast enough however and although he did not manage to cut my throat, his stiletto tore through my cheek and I felt salty blood in my mouth. By now there was noise inside the inn and lights appeared. Weasel grinned at me evilly, "I will do for you boy!" I was amazed that I understood every word. He flicked out a second knife and waved them before him. Suddenly he froze and I saw the tip of my sword emerge from his front. I whirled around but Bear had gone. Weasel's body slipped to the ground. He was dead.

Torches filled the yard as the innkeeper, his son and a guest appeared armed with short swords, "What goes on here?"

Jean pointed to the dead body, "This one and a huge fellow tried to kill us. The other was wounded and fled."

I saw a moment of guilt flick across the face of the innkeeper and then he nodded, "Gaston and Guillaume; I am sorry, sir, I let them drink in my inn because they always pay but they are bad men. I will recompense you for any loss."

Jean sniffed, "As well you might." He saw the cut on my cheek and snapped, "And how do we compensate for that?" He knelt down and tore the scarf from Weasel's neck. "James, staunch the bleeding. Well do not just stand there; fetch a doctor."

The innkeeper looked confused. His son said, "Father, there is a doctor staying here. I will go and rouse him."

In England, there were many doctors who travelled from town to town. Some were charlatans while others moved on before their incompetence could be discovered. It appeared to be the same in France.

The innkeeper said, "Come inside and I will fetch ale."

Just then we heard a cry from the main street. Jean said, "It looks like the other has been apprehended."

As we went inside, I feared that my attempt to be a spy for King Henry had lasted just a day's ride from Boulogne. The authorities would question me and the best I could hope for, bearing in mind that I was a hunted man, was that they would return me to Calais.

When the doctor came, I guessed he was an incompetent, but he was sharp enough to ask for payment before he stitched my face. Jean said to the innkeeper, "You will pay."

Reluctant to pay from his own purse he said, "I will have your bill, doctor."

The doctor laughed, "There will be no bill!" Like me, he knew that the innkeeper was complicit in the attack.

Defeated the innkeeper nodded and he proceeded to clean my face of blood and begin to stitch. Perhaps he had been a tailor before he became a doctor for his stitches were small and neat. He smeared honey on the wound and said, "Let the air get to it. In ten days or so have someone remove the stitches."

We were about to retire when the night watch arrived. There were four of them and they looked at my face and then ignored me. They addressed the innkeeper, "Monsieur Leblanc, we have found one of your regulars in the street. The one called Guillaume has bled to death and the blood trail leads here. Explain."

Jean spoke and did so slowly so that I heard every word, "My companion and I were sleeping when two men tried to slay us in our sleep. The youth here managed to wound the one you found and I slew the other. He is in the yard."

They looked at the innkeeper who said, simply, "Gaston."

The sergeant who led them nodded and then addressed Jean, "You have done Abbeville a great service, sir, for these two men have preyed on the weak long enough." He glared at the shamefaced innkeeper and added, "Until now we had no evidence and so I thank you but now we know how the two operated." He turned to me, "Yesterday we had news of a deserter from the English army that fits your description." He smiled, "It cannot be you for the man we sought had long hair and a beard, added to which he was a murderer. I hope you do not meet him on the road." He knew who I was and his eyes told me that. "Still Englishmen are different from us. Have a safe journey. We will rid you of the bodies."

The next morning my face ached. The stitches had been neat but they were painful. Jean's money was refunded, and we headed south from Abbeville towards Amiens. We were the subject of much comment as we headed through the town. Word had spread and my vivid red scar would keep tongues wagging for a while. So much for my remaining a secret.

Jean waited until the road was clear before he questioned me, "James, I thank you for last night but I cannot travel with you if I do not know the truth." I said nothing, "You know how to fight, I saw that and the helmet marks you as a soldier." I still said nothing, "In your pack, I saw, when you took out the salve for your feet, the sign of the white rose. It was disguised but I live in Calais and know it is the sign of the enemies of King Henry. Speak."

I nodded, "I seek the Yorkist rebels and that is why I am headed to Paris."

"That is better and now I know your secret I can help you. I care not who rules England, Calais will still be an English port. I know where the Yorkists are to be found in Paris." My eyes widened and I regretted it as it hurt the stitches. "Do not ask how I know save that I am a man with many friends. I owe you my life and I will try to help you if I can."

The rest of the journey to Paris was easier for me. I did not have a double-secret to keep. Jean knew one and that satisfied him. I had wondered about the danger of carrying the white rose but the Earl had been insistent that it could only help me.

Chapter 14

Paris was exotic; from the smells of the streets to the architecture, it was like nothing I had ever seen before. Jean had been more than kind to me on the journey from Abbeville. He had ensured that I tended to my wound and that I was fed. As he told me, when we saw the towers of Notre Dame rise in the distance, "It was luck that brought you to me and good luck at that. Had you not been there in that courtyard then it would have been my skull that had the dent and not the sallet in your bag. I am grateful to you. If you wish to work for me I will pay you well." I said nothing. "My own sons are gone, and I like you. When I make my fortune, you shall have half."

It was a tempting offer but I had sworn an oath. I could not tell him of the oath and so I smiled, "Let me find out if I can serve the Duke of York first and if that does not work out, I know where to find you."

He shook his head, "Calais, where you are a marked man." He gestured to my scar, "The scar tells the world who you are for that sergeant in Abbeville will dine out on the story of the youth who slew the bear. You can never go back."

"I know." I also knew that the story would help me to get close to Perkin Warbeck.

He shrugged, "If you seek me, my house and workshop are on the Rue de Gravelines close to the harbour."

I nodded, "I will remember."

The first thing we did was to deliver the pots to the merchant who was delighted to have them arrive in an unbroken condition. I saw the gold exchange hands and hoped that Jean had some means of holding on to it. We stayed to the south of the cathedral close to Sorbonne University. It was a lively place, and I would have avoided it, but Jean tapped his nose, "This is where those who ferment trouble live. The authorities know it and so long as that trouble is for the enemies of France then it is ignored. There is a tavern not far from the walls and the Abbey de St Germain. I have heard that the white rose is welcomed there. I can stay one night and try to help you and then you are on your own."

"And I thank you, Jean, you have been more than kind."

Shaking his head he said, "No, my friend, for if I was kind, I would lock you in a room until this madness had left you. All young men seek this type of adventure. For most, it ends in death."

"I must do what I must do."

He shrugged and led me into the tavern which was filled with both people and noise. As soon as we entered all noise ceased and every eye swivelled towards us. We were being assessed as a threat and, later on, I realised that this was the most dangerous moment of the plan. Even before I had opened my mouth, I could be deemed an enemy by one or the other of the people in the room. Perhaps Jean was right. My feet, however, propelled me towards the bar. Jean seemed unconcerned by the apparent hostility and when a man stood and approached us, Jean smiled. I feared the worst.

"Jean le Casserole, what brings you to this den of thieves?" The man's outstretched hand was intended for Jean, but his eyes were fixed on me.

"Guy, it is good to see you." He lowered his voice, "This is an Englishman, James, and he has been of great service to me. He seeks friends."

Guy nodded and led Jean to a table at the back of the room. The three men who had been seated there moved away quickly and we sat. Guy waved his hands and a pichet of wine and three beakers arrived. "We all need friends."

While he poured the wine Jean said, "Nothing happens in this part of Paris without the knowledge of Guy le Rouge. This is his bar. I was of some small service to Guy some years ago."

Guy laughed, "Some service. That is modest of you. When the men of Flanders put a price on my head it was you and your wagon that spirited me away, but I am intrigued, Jean. This young man looks scarcely old enough to shave and yet bears a scar, which, unless I am mistaken, was made by an Italian stiletto."

"There is more to him than meets the eye. He saved my life and killed one man twice the size of your bodyguard. It is said he fled Boulogne after killing a man. I trust him, Guy."

Guy looked at me, "Drink some of your wine. It is not poisoned."

I was not overfond of wine, but I drank some. It was red, rough, and strong. He examined my face and then said, "Why did you shave your head and face?"

"So that I would not be recognised. I had to leave Boulogne in a hurry."

"And yet you took the time to change your appearance. You are right, Jean, there is more to this one than meets the eye." He turned his attention back to me. He had eyes like a hawk, and they were just as threatening, "And whom do you seek?"

"The white rose."

He laughed, "You English keep fighting each other. You once had kings who fought for lands and now you have those of lesser blood who struggle to grasp the crown. You know you cannot win?"

"I am sorry?"

"This man who pretends to be the Duke of York he will be like the other your king defeated. You need an actual heir to the throne."

I was being tested for his voice was raised so that others could hear. The babble we had heard when we had entered was now down to a murmur. There were Yorkists in the tavern and Guy le Rouge was letting them hear me. There would be no introduction; if the rebels did not like what I said then Guy would feign ignorance of any who could help me.

I nodded, "Just so but my father fell at Bosworth Field, and I owe it to his memory to at least raise a sword for the house of York."

He nodded, "And if I cannot help you, what then?"

"I will continue to the court of the Duchess of Burgundy for I believe that I will be welcomed. I may not have much experience, but I have a sword and I have killed. That must count for something."

He nodded and said, "I will let people know that you seek employment, but you must understand I am a mere tavern owner, but I will try to help." He waved over one of his servers, "Bring them out the stew." He smiled as he stood and went back to his friends, "It is my treat."

I appeared to have passed the first hurdle. I toasted Jean, and said quietly, "Thank you, my friend."

"As I said, I would not do this, but you seem to be fanatically determined, almost as though you have a death wish."

I did not for I was serving my king and I did not want to die but I would, in the service of my country. "Le Casserole?"

He smiled, "I make pots and my speciality is the dish that cooks stews. It is more of a nickname than anything, but it sells my product." He pointed at the servers, one of whom carried a large pot and the other two bowls and wooden spoons, "This is one of my pots."

The stew might have been delicious, but I was too nervous to enjoy it. I had to hope that I had been right and that Yorkists were listening. We finished the stew and I allowed Jean to consume the rest of the wine. The noise had risen again but, as we left, a lull descended. Once on the street, we headed to the yard where Jean had secured his wagon. His horse was precious to him, and he did not mind sleeping close by it. We had covered barely fifty paces when three men ghosted up alongside us. As soon as they spoke, I knew that they were English.

"If you wish to serve the Duke of York, then come with us."

Jean turned and said, "Where are you taking him? Do not go, James."

One of the men growled, "If he is who he says he is then all will be well, and, on the morrow, he will come to your wagon to collect his horse and belongings. If not, then you will never see him again and you will have gained a horse."

"But…"

Jean got no further. A dagger pricked his throat, "Go."

I was not as afraid as I should have been. I was more impressed. They had obviously spent the time we were eating to discover who we were. They were not as reckless as I might have expected. They took me down a narrow side street. There were too many of them for me to work out how to escape and they all led to the river where a body could be disposed of very quickly. The men suddenly stopped and whirled me around. The one who was the leader, the growler, lifted my chin so that he could see my eyes, "Now speak. Who are you and what is your story?"

I had decided to keep my story as basic as I could and as close to my own. I knew the dangers of being caught out in a lie, "I am James, and my father was a billman who fought at

Bosworth Field." I was speaking the truth and there was no lie in my eyes.

"His name?"

"Geoffrey of Yarm."

Growler looked at the man next to him who nodded and said, "I know there was a Geoffrey of Yarm; he died with the king."

"And you? What of you?"

"I wish to avenge my father's death and that of the king. I tried to follow Lord Lovell to Stoke Field. I had no chance to fight but I held horses."

The man next to Growler said, "Where did Lord Lovell trick the Lancastrians?"

I answered straight away, "At Bramham Moor. He sent the Irish in and when they fell back we ambushed the billmen and archers."

The man said, "His story is true. Only those who were there would have known that."

Silence fell and then Growler said, "Go to your friend, the potman. Tomorrow, be at the Pont Neuf with your horse and gear when the bell tolls the hour of ten. You will be contacted."

"But..."

Growler smiled and I saw that he had teeth missing, "You will have to trust us. Two of King Henry's spies were caught last week trying to join our army. He must think us fools. You will be taken north to meet with... well you shall see."

"North but I thought..." I had been told that Dijon was where the rebels were gathered.

"What you thought and what is real is as different as chalk and... Wensleydale!" He laughed at his own joke.

The three disappeared so quickly that I thought they were wraiths.

Jean had not gone back to the yard, and I found him on the street off which the alley had led, "Are you hurt?"

"No, I am safe." I did not mention that two others who had tried to join had fatally failed.

He kept looking over his shoulder as we headed for the yard and once there, he paid the owner an extra coin to keep watch on the gate. He was worried but I was not. My story, which had seemed implausible to me had passed inspection. I would have to remember to tell it, in the same way, each time. Once safely under the wagon, I told him of my plans.

"I am to meet one tomorrow who will take me north. I had thought Dijon or Lyon would be my destination but the Yorkists, it seems are north of here."

"You are in a dangerous world, James, and I hope you know what you are doing. Those men you met tonight are killers."

"Yet I am still alive and had they wished me dead then my throat would be cut and I would be in the alley." I had to convince him that I was a Yorkist in case he was questioned after I left, "I have to fight for the white rose. Geoffrey of Yarm will sleep easier in his grave knowing I fought for York."

"Your father would rather you lived; I am sure."

The story, false though it was came out easily. I had become the spy. "Yet he died fighting for the cause. Jean, I hope not to die and if our cause fails then I may well seek you out, but it is something I have to do."

I slept well knowing that this would be the last night for some time where I would be close to a friend.

It was almost a leisurely morning for me. My gear was all packed and we ate a hearty breakfast. I still had plenty of time to ride the short distance to the Pont Neuf that crossed the Seine. It would be the start of my journey north. Jean slipped me five silver coins as I mounted my horse, "Here is a little money in case you have to flee your new friends." He patted Goliath's rump, "I would rather you had a better horse for Maria is less likely to flee than Goliath here."

"He will suit my purpose and he has an easy disposition. Take care, Jean, you are a good man, and I would have been proud to have been your son." I saw that my words had an effect. He nodded and waved as I headed out of the yard and into the maelstrom that was Paris on a busy morning. Most of the ones I met were on foot and riding a horse, even a sumpter, gave me some advantage. The bridge crossed the narrowest part of the Île de la Cité. As such it was a busy crossing for those heading for the right bank of the Seine. I could see why it had been chosen. I would stand out on my sumpter and I could be watched to see if this was a trap. I smiled to myself as I headed for the centre of the bridge. I was now thinking like a spy and I had developed a suspicious mind. Perhaps the king had chosen well. There were small embrasures along the bridge, and I occupied one and dismounted. I knew not how far we would have to ride and I did not want to weary Goliath unnecessarily.

I was there early and when I heard the bell toll for the hour of ten, I looked for, well, in truth I knew not whom to expect. For some reason, I doubted that it would be one of those I had met the night before. They would have described me. I was deliberately bareheaded so that whoever sought me could pick me out; the stubbled head and scar marked me out. When the bell tolled for eleven, I became worried and wondered if they had decided not to use me. That would mean I had failed and could return to the king but that thought did not make me feel happy for I wanted to succeed. I had come so far and whilst not exactly enjoying what I did I was finding it an adventure. When the men had not slain me in the alley I had felt a success. Now, as I waited like a jilted bride, I felt sad.

The voice next to me made me start. It was an English voice and when I looked around, I saw a man on a horse staring down at me, "The White Rose."

I was so startled that I almost forgot to speak and then I realised this was almost a password and I had to reply correctly, "The White Rose."

He nodded, "Mount your nag and follow me."

As I swung my leg over the saddle, I saw that the man was about thirty years of age and he rode a good horse. In my time on the road, I had come to know that judging a man's age helped. He was older than me and that meant he could have been at Bramham Moor and Stoke Field. I would have to be wary about what I said. I had rehearsed, in my mind, the story of both battles from the Yorkists point of view, on the road to Paris. As we meandered our way through the northern part of the city of Paris I did so again. I saw that the man's sword was a good one and that his boots bore the marks of spurs. He was a knight but trying to hide the fact. He had a bag, similar to mine, across the rear of his saddle and that told me he was not just taking me to another courier but was my guard.

We neither stopped nor spoke until we were north of Saint-Denis. We had been travelling for about an hour and from the mileposts I had observed we were eight miles from the bridge. We stopped at the tiny hamlet of Gonesse. There was a water trough, but I saw no sign of any villagers. The man dismounted and led his horse to drink. He waved me to copy him. He was a cautious man and looked around before he spoke, "You need not know my name and you can address me as, my lord."

I let Goliath's reins drop. He would not move while he could drink, "Yes, my lord."

"I will be taking you to the court of Duchess Margaret where others will decide if you speak the truth or not." He smiled, "I happen to be travelling there and you are not getting any special treatment. The men you spoke to last night believe your story but then it might be that you are a spy and it is well-rehearsed. We have one hundred and eighty miles to travel and I intend to ride hard and make it in four days. You may well find the journey on your nag uncomfortable. Regard it as a test for your worthiness to fight for the Duke of York."

"I will pass any test that you wish to make, my lord." He could not know that my thighs and buttocks had been hardened on the ride from Bramham Moor to Stoke Field.

He nodded, "We shall see. When we stop each night you shall sleep in the stable with the horses. You will eat with me. As for conversation, do not bother, you are baggage I am forced to take with me so do not hold me up."

I nodded and, as he mounted I did so too. The nights spent in the stable would be another test. I was being given the chance to run. The stubble on my head, the scar and my horse would all make me easy to find if they needed to. I spent the next four days just watching the swishing tail and the rump of Gerard, the knight's horse. I watched it as it dropped its dung, which Goliath neatly avoided, and I watched it as it flicked out a hoof should Goliath get too close. I learned a great deal about the horse but little about the man. From his accent, he did not come from the north but the land they called the Midlands, close to Leicester. There were many Yorkist sympathisers there. I learned that he was careful with his coin and although the food we had was wholesome, it was, generally, the cheapest available. He did not drink as much as Jean and just paid for small beer for me. He studied me each time we stopped. I was asked questions that seemed innocent enough but I knew they were tests. I was glad it was small beer for my mind remained sharp and I always answered as James of Yarm. His questions and my answers also told me that he did not know the north well and, most importantly, that he had not been at Stoke Field. That came when he asked me how I had escaped at the end of the battle when everyone had died or been captured. When I described my escape with a faithful description of the battlefield his questions told me that he did not know it all.

It became clear, as we crossed into Flanders, that we were heading for Mechelen. In fact, I was told so when we were a day away. "The Duchess of Burgundy holds her court at Mechelen and there our forces are gathering."

"And the Duke of York?"

He laughed, "You have other tests to pass before you get to meet him." He reined in his horse and turned to look at me, "Few men come as you do, alone. Most of those who wish to join us come in groups and they are known. You may be who you say you are but until your identity can be verified you will be viewed with suspicion. Do not worry, James of Yarm, you will not have long to wait once we reach Mechelen. When my cousin sees you that will either mean you join us or…"

I knew what the silence meant. Who was his cousin and how would he know if I had been at the two battles? For the first time since the inn in Paris, I began to feel fear.

We rode into the Burgundian town, and I saw that it was a town preparing for war. Armed men drilled in the square and I saw horsemen practising their skills. We rode, not to the castle but to a large house close to the castle walls. We dismounted and a groom said, "Welcome, Sir John, the Viscount has been expecting you."

"Good to see you too, Ralph. Stable this man's horse and watch his belongings. James, come with me."

There were armed guards on the doors and whilst they saluted and smiled at the man I now knew was Sir John, they regarded me with suspicious eyes. We reached a guarded door and Sir John said to the guard, "Watch him." He headed inside.

I wanted to run but knew that would be a disastrous mistake. I had to brazen it out. I forced myself to breathe steadily and

concentrate on remembering every detail of the plan and my
character. After an inordinate length of time, Sir John emerged,
"Leave your sword and your daggers here, all of them."

I removed them including the one in my boot. He took me
inside and there were four men. One was young, he looked to be
about my age and the other three were older. One of them had a
silver wolf around his neck and had royal livery surmounted with
some kind of rearing beast. I thought it might be a gryphon, but
it could have been a lion. No one spoke until Sir John said,
"Now, do you recognise any of the men here before you?"

I answered straight away and pointed at the man with the
silver wolf, "Of course, that is Lord Lovell whose brilliance won
us the Battle of Bramham Moor and nearly won us Stoke Field."

That it was the right answer was clear when they all smiled,
especially the one I had identified and flattered. He nodded,
"You were right to bring him here. He is perfect. I do not
remember the face but it was some years ago he looks to be of an
age with the Duke of York here." He gestured towards the young
man. This was Perkin Warbeck. He looked to be a pleasant and
personable youth. Was this the enemy King Henry feared so
much?

Sir John turned to me, "I apologise for my mistrust, James of
Yarm, but we have had many men trying to get close to Lord
Lovell and the Duke of York. I am Sir John Bardolph and Lord
Lovell's cousin."

Lord Lovell said, "Sit." I did so but I was confused. Did
every recruit have such a grilling? I was not introduced to the
other lords and I did not recognise them but they were obviously
senior men in the conspiracy. Lord Lovell leaned forward,
"This," he gestured to the young man to his right, is Richard of
Shrewsbury, Duke of York and rightful king of England. He was
supposed to have been murdered with his brother in the Tower
but he was spirited away by our supporters and brought up in
Flanders." The story sounded like mine, well-rehearsed.

The young man said, "I am pleased that you wish to join us."
He had an accent and if he was an Englishman then I was a
Barbary ape.

Lord Lovell continued, "We are raising an army and next
week we will take the duke to introduce him to his aunt, the

166

Duchess of Burgundy." He leaned forward, "There will be some who try to trip him up. Some Burgundians do not wish to support us. When we heard of a young supporter of the White Rose who wished to join us we realised that you have been sent from God. The duke's accent is due to his upbringing, and, in addition, he knows little of England having been fetched from there when he was barely a toddler. James of Yarm, we would employ you to be his friend and to teach him the words he may not have heard in Flanders. You will be attired as a gentleman and live in chambers close to the duke. What say you?"

I was not a fool and I realised that this might be another trap to discover King Henry's spy, "I am honoured, and I will do all that you ask but I came here to fight and I would not sit and watch as others die for our cause and the duke."

That was greeted with applause from the duke and a beaming smile from Lord Lovell, "Better and better. You shall fight but not until we set foot on English soil."

"Then I am honoured, and I agree." I turned to Perkin Warbeck, "And what do I call you, Duke Richard?"

"My lord will do."

"Good, then all is well. Sir John, take him to the bath chamber and have him bathed and dressed in the clothes we furnished."

I stood, "And my weapons, my lord?" He frowned and I explained, "I have killed men and a man is more comfortable with his own weapons."

Sir John smiled, "You are a true warrior, and I can see no hindrance." As we left the room and headed up the narrow stairs, Sir John said, "What my cousin forgot to say was that when Duke Richard is crowned in Westminster Abbey you shall be awarded a manor in the north of England for your efforts."

I doubted that would ever happen, but I pretended that it might, "I am honoured. I do what I do in memory of my father and with no thought of reward."

"And that alone deserves a reward."

Servants were already filling a tub with boiling water and one of them came over to help me undress. I had not been undressed since a child and I stepped away from the man. Sir John said, "You will have to get used to servants. The duke's servants will also tend to you but, for the present, undress yourself. Henry, have James' clothes cleaned and placed back in the bag he brought."

By the time they had finished, I barely recognised myself although until that moment I had only ever seen my reflection in the water. There was a polished mirror and I looked at a young gentleman who was dressed in silk hose and fine breeches. I was given an undershirt and something that Sir John called a swete bagge. It was a hessian bag similar to my money pouch and worn beneath the breeches. It contained fragrant smelling herbs and petals. The leather jerkin I wore over my linen shirt was also made of calf hide and was as soft as a lady's hand. The doublet I was given was also made of linen and all was topped off with a red gown. The hat upon my head was made of red velvet. If such expense had been wasted on me to make me look like that which I was not then how much had been spent upon the pretender, the Duke of York?

Sir John seemed satisfied but, before we descended, he had a warning for me, "The duke will learn from you but there are lessons which you must learn yourself. You are a gentleman. Look how the other young gentlemen eat and drink and emulate them. Now strap on your sword and let us begin the work that will bring us the crown of England.

Chapter 15

Flanders 1493

It was a whole new world that I entered. I was lucky in that my time with Sir Edward and the Earl of Oxford had introduced me to the world of nobles but I had to keep my wits about me and my abstemious behaviour helped as had Sam and his lessons in language. I also had to continually correct Perkin Warbeck for his misuse of common words. In my mind, I always used that name and I simply addressed him as, my lord. He was a quick learner and grateful for all that I did for him. I found that I liked him and we became friends, of a sort. I must have been a quick learner for Sir John only had to correct me once or twice when I made a mistake. I was also called upon to teach him to use a sword. He had never been trained and it was easier for me to spar with him and have Sir John correct him. My training with Sam and Sir Edward's men at arms made me look a better swordsman than they had expected. After all, an orphan who had trained himself would not have the skills I did. I rose in the estimation of all so much so that I was soon considered an integral part of the machinery that would propel Perkin Warbeck to the crown of England. Perkin had not had the best education and he had lessons in reading and writing; an English priest taught him and I learned too. It was unexpected but it made me a better person.

The first test was the stiffest. Perkin had to persuade the Dowager Duchess of Burgundy and his supposed aunt, that he was who he said he was. Margaret of York, despite having been a widow for the last twenty odd years and being childless was still the most powerful woman in Europe. Even King Henry's mother, Margaret Beaufort, was in awe of her. She was a passionate enemy of all things Lancastrian but she was no fool. The night before we were to leave for her castle I was excluded as Lord Lovell and Sir John were closeted with the would-be king. They were drilling him so that he would not make a mistake. It convinced me that they knew he was an imposter but one that suited Lord Lovell.

The nerves of the leaders were clearly in evidence as they fussed about every detail before we left our home in Mechelen to head for the palace. I was told to remain silent throughout. That would be easy as I was already petrified before we were ushered into the presence of the great lady. In fairness, she only had eyes for the pretender.

"Come here, nephew, and let me look at you. The last time I saw you was when you were but a babe and then only briefly. Come close and let me see you. My eyes are not what they were."

I could almost feel the Yorkists who were there holding their breath.

"So where have you been these last few years?"

I heard the sigh before he spoke, "I was hidden by loyal Englishmen in the Netherlands." He reeled off the names of three of them. All conveniently dead at Bosworth. "When I was left alone, I took what little coin I had and sailed to Ireland. I had been told that they would give me support and they did. I am grateful to the Mayor of Cork for his help. King Charles of France also believed my tale and he agreed to finance an army to retake my throne. The recent peace ended that hope."

The Duchess was shrewd and I saw her eyes narrow, "And you would have me finance an army too?"

This was the moment that would make or break the attempt by Lord Lovell to foster another rebellion. Perkin Warbeck had skills. I was a good liar but he was better. I began to believe his words. He dropped to one knee and took her hand in his, "Duchess, God has denied you a child and our enemies have denied me a father and a brother. I would be as your son and I would raise the standard of York over the Tower of London where my poor brother and father were murdered. I would do this so that York would be great again!"

It was stirring and I saw tears spring from the Duchess' eyes. She pulled him to her bosom and held him tightly, "You are Richard of Shrewsbury and you shall be King Richard the Fourth of England."

The joy and relief on the Yorkists was something to behold, they had won.

Over the next months, I accompanied the would-be King of England as the Duchess began to teach him about his history and the York court. I was there and I am still unsure if she believed he was the rightful heir or if she merely hoped he was. He was treated as heir apparent. I was used more as a servant, but the work was easy as it merely involved fetching and carrying books. I still practised with Perkin and his skills did improve but there was no chance of him surviving a real battle for he had no training as a warrior and when we practised I saw that he had no skills whatsoever with a sword.

I saw little of Lord Lovell and the conspirators for they were busy building an army. Perkin Warbeck began to rely on me as his only friend. I think he knew that I knew he was an imposter and, in many ways, that helped him. It meant he could relax in my company. He was good to be around. He could tell jokes and sing but only in my presence for a future King of England did not do that.

My hair had grown, and I had been given a fine horse. I kept my chin shaved as that was the fashion in the court. It also helped to disguise me. I still feared a face from my past recognising me. Poor Goliath enjoyed a stable but no company. I saw my horse whenever I could, but I felt a traitor as I rode the fine chestnut hackney given to me by the Duchess. Like the putative King Richard, I now wore plate armour and had a sword made in Spain. The sword was presented to me by Lord Lovell who was increasingly grateful to me. I was not the boy who left home with his father's helmet, bill, and falchion. I was someone I doubted that my father would even recognise. Sir John visited more frequently than his cousin and each visit saw him spend time with the two of us. He was a soldier and spoke of war more than politics, "There is money for mercenaries, but I like it not. I think it is better to hire men such as you, James of Yarm, men of true heart. We have begun to hire men who are disillusioned with England and its new king. Did you know that the king has raised a tax to pay for a war against us? It has alienated many men both noble and peasant. There are rumours of uprisings. I believe, Duke Richard, that we have a good chance of success."

The talks gave Perkin confidence and he began to believe that, one day, he would be King of England. I truly believe that Sir John believed his own words. I had seen no evidence of an army that could face King Henry's. Was I doomed to be trapped in this golden palace in Mechelen for the rest of my life?

There were other knights who visited and all flocked to see Duke Richard. I knew, from the way some looked at him, that they were making a decision as to the truth of his identity, but I also knew, because I overheard pieces of conversation, that the truth mattered not to most; they all wanted Henry Tudor gone and even a puppet would be better than a Tudor. And he would be a puppet. When Lord Lovell came it was as though he was a customer coming to inspect the progress on a piece of furniture he was having made.

My position also improved for they saw me as having the ear of the next King of England. They saw not the son of a billman but a young gentleman dressed in fine clothes who was always at the side of the man they called Duke Richard. I was flattered and bribed. James of Ecclestone would have rejected both the coins and the flattery but I was King Henry's spy and playing a part. I accepted both with a greasy smile. That part was growing increasingly tiresome. It was not Perkin Warbeck's fault. I genuinely liked him and had I not been the spy might have suggested to him that he should flee the court and seek a life that was less dangerous. It would have been pointless. He loved the life where he could play politics and his opinion, as well as his favour, was sought. Duchess Margaret saw that he wanted for nothing. After the funeral of the Holy Roman Emperor, there could be no going back.

One summer night as we walked around the grounds of the castle, two of the Duchess' personal guards less than twenty feet from us, he said, "We are to travel to the Empire, next week, to attend the funeral of Emperor Ferdinand. We shall be travelling to Vienna. I do like to travel. It is exciting, is it not?"

It was and I nodded but I wondered if and when I would get back to England. There appeared to be little prospect of an imminent invasion and whilst I was relatively safe, I yearned to be back with my real friends.

"It certainly is."

He lowered his voice, "And there is more. King Maximilian of Rome, the Duchess' father-in-law will be there and the Duchess has said that I will be crowned in the cathedral there as King Richard of England for it is hoped that he will be the next Emperor. Soon my dream will be realised."

I nodded but decided to try to pour some water on his fiery enthusiasm, "I am sorry, my lord, but being crowned and achieving the throne are two separate things. I was at Stoke Field and know how hard it is to defeat Henry Tudor and his Lancastrians."

He smiled, "You are ever my touchstone and speak the truth. Fear not, an army is being raised and next year our friends in England will begin to rally the support we need so that soon, perhaps next year, we shall invade England and you and I will fight alongside each other. They will be glorious times."

Vienna was another revelation to me, and I began to see London as a poor copy of these other great cities. The funeral was, to us, almost an irrelevancy. The Emperor had been almost eighty when he had died and the mourning was muted. The coronation, in contrast, was attended by kings, princes and dukes. Sir Robert Clifford, a prominent Yorkist, had come over with Lord Lovell and the other conspirators who lived abroad. He wrote, in our presence, a letter to other lords in England confirming that King Richard was alive and well and living in Flanders. No matter what King Henry did or said now he would have to fight once more for his crown. I knew then that I would need to keep my ears open for things were coming to a head. From that moment the term King Richard was used at every opportunity.

Over the next year, we barely had time to think. Duchess Margaret and King Maximilian, who was later elected Holy Roman Emperor, placed the funds of their two lands at the disposal of the Yorkists. Lord Lovell was rarely seen and I gathered that he was in England, organising that side of the invasion. The details were not known but the Yorkists wanted their supporters across the country ready to rise. There was a conspiracy and plotters were to be found all over England; including the court of King Henry.

We had just celebrated Christmas when Sir John Bardolph arrived for a surprise visit. He was the conduit of news from outside the cosy court we enjoyed. As they sat in the opulently apportioned chamber we used I was acting as a servant while the two of them spoke.

Sir John smiled at me, "Well James, the scar on your face has healed well and now gives you an air of mystery. With your fine clothes, you could be mistaken for a noble."

"And I thank you, Sir John, for giving me this chance to better myself."

"Nonsense. We are indebted to you. You have been more than good for the king. You can be proud of what you have done." He turned to the man I still thought of as Perkin, "And you, King Richard, how goes your life?"

"I feel as though I should be doing more, Sir John. When do I get to lead my army?"

We had enjoyed Christmas but the man feigning the identity of Richard of Shrewsbury yearned to be in England and ruling that country. Perkin liked to think of himself as a general. He was not. I knew I was not one and yet I understood far more of strategy than he did. Sir John tried to explain the plans that were being formulated by those who had such skills, "We have the advantage that Henry Tudor does not know where we will land." I noticed that they called King Henry, Henry Tudor as though that invalidated his coronation. "We have allies in Scotland and King James is keen to support you, King Richard, but he will not break his peace until we land in England. We have also fermented discord in Cornwall. As they are not known as Yorkists, Henry Tudor will not be expecting an attack there."

I saw that Perkin Warbeck was confused and he confirmed it when he said, "But what does this mean for me? When do I get to land in my homeland?" He had persuaded himself that he was the King of England.

Like a patient teacher explaining a new concept, Sir John went through what he saw would happen, "King Richard, we have, as yet, but five hundred soldiers and while we do not need a large number, for the people will rise, we need more than that. We want England to be riven with taxes and discord. We will wait."

"How long, my lord? Three months? Six months?"

"Perhaps August or September, we shall have to wait on events but fear not King Richard, we shall invade, and you shall lead your armies into England. Over the next months, we will choose a place where we can land and that landing will ignite the fuse that will blow Henry Tudor and his supporters back to Wales."

It sounded bold but nothing I had seen led me to believe that it would succeed.

"And you and young James here, who has proved to be a most valuable asset, can continue to hone your skills. In April we will have your bodyguard ready and the two of you can work with them."

That satisfied Perkin who liked the idea of playing at war. I was not taken in by Sir John's flattery. I had fooled them and done as King Henry had asked but I would leave the court the moment I knew when and where this landing would take place. I would be sad to leave the side of Perkin Warbeck for we got on well but he was not Stephen the Silent and Sir John was not Sam Sharp Tongue. I wanted to go home.

When the first of the bodyguards arrived, all of them mercenaries, they also brought unwelcome news. King Henry's second son had just been awarded the title, Duke of York. It told the world that he believed Richard of Shrewsbury was dead and that the man falsely crowned as King Richard was an imposter. Sir John did not elaborate but speaking to some of the men at arms he brought I gathered that support in England was waning. I wondered then if I should simply return to England. I could not see an invasion materialising. The thought left me when we began to train with Sir John and the mercenaries. Some were English but most were foreign. There were twenty, initially, and they came from Italy, Germany, Switzerland and France. My skills as a horseman had improved for as part of the preparation for my charge to become king, Sir John had insisted that we ride every day so that the King of England would appear comfortable in the saddle. I had ridden a variety of horses and I now knew how to ride well. My training with a billhook had also prepared me for the use of a lance and even the mercenaries became impressed by the skills I used.

Sir John was also impressed, "James, you are a natural with a lance and it seems to be part of you. Of course, when we go to war you shall carry the standard of the king."

If he thought I would be disappointed, he was wrong. I had no intention of being with this rebel army when it landed, "I am honoured."

He leaned closer to me, "We both know that the king does not have martial skills. Your task will be to guard him although I hope that these bodyguards will perform that task and you will not be needed."

I liked Sir John and did not want him to die and I knew that die he would if they met an English army, "Sir John, will we have enough men? I was at Stoke Field, remember, when we thought we had enough hired swords, we lost."

He nodded, "And my cousin is aware of that. It is why we delay until we have enough men. There are five hundred men ready to sail with us but until we have at least two hundred bodyguards for the king there will be no invasion. The news of the appointment of Henry's son, Henry, as Duke of York is a setback, no more."

I got to know a couple of the bodyguards well. There are always natural leaders and Robert of Guisborough, and Giuseppe di Torino were two such men. Perkin Warbeck was also keen to learn as much as he could about his bodyguards and often, as we headed back to our quarters from the training fields we would talk. Giuseppe was keen to improve his English and listened more than he spoke. His Flemish was better than his English and, thanks to my time in Mechelen, I could speak it well. I helped to translate the English words he did not know into Flemish for him. Sir Robert had been a condottiere and had fought all over Europe and he knew the reality of what we undertook. I learned much from the mercenaries. They gave me a lesson in weaponry and fighting. They made me a better warrior.

He was brutally honest when he spoke with Perkin and me, "Unless we have guns, both bombards and harquebusiers then we have little chance of success. Giuseppe and I have fought all over Europe and know that a hardcore of professional soldiers can do well but only against another professional body. James and I know that England still trains its archers, and they are the weapon that can turn a battle. We need far more men, King Richard."

"But we have God and the right on our side."

Robert laughed, "That puts heart into a man but does not win battles neither does courage alone. King Richard the Third was a brave man. He hacked his way into the heart of Lord Stanley's men to get at Henry Tudor, but he failed." I saw him look at Giuseppe and then he said, "Whenever we attack, I beg you not to be at the fore. Keep your banner behind as a rallying point." All of us could see that the man they called King Richard was not convinced. Robert said, "Tomorrow let us take the practice to a higher level. We will divide into two and use wooden weapons to hold a mock battle."

Perkin was eager but I knew that Sir John would not be, and I was right. When he was told his face reddened and he was adamant it would not take place. "We cannot risk you, King Richard. In such a mock battle you could fall and be hurt without any intention of malice or harm."

I knew the real reason was that it would show up the pretender's frailties.

For the first time Perkin asserted himself, "If I am to fight for my land surely, I should experience the danger of war? I am determined. Robert, Giuseppe, make it happen."

Sir John, defeated, took the two mercenaries outside. I guessed what was being said.

The next day we prepared for war and for the first time since Boulogne I dressed for battle. The difference was that I was now plated like a knight. The armour was not as heavy as, when I had been a billman, I had thought. Perhaps that was because I wore it regularly. My horse, Zeus, was a warhorse and had barding to protect him. I used a lance and found it much easier than a billhook. I would not be the standard-bearer.

Sir John was not happy and he would fight alongside Perkin and me. Robert and Giuseppe would lead the smaller half of the bodyguards. Sir John had chosen the best for us. I know why Robert had suggested the mock battle. It was to show King Richard that he could not fight in a battle. I did not care for I would have the chance to show my skills off. To the annoyance of Sir John, many of the court came to watch the spectacle. You cannot hide a hundred men or more on horses. We would be on public display. Wearing the plate meant we did not need shields and for that I was grateful. I had improved as a horseman but the thought of holding a shield and guiding my horse with reins was a step too far. The wooden lances had no tips and the swords we held had neither point nor edge. Sir John had made it quite clear that he wanted no hard blows struck at King Richard. When he said that I saw Robert shake his head and I fully understood why. If Perkin Warbeck came away feeling he could fight, then this would all be in vain.

We faced each other at the ends of a large open field eight hundred paces long. My sallet restricted my view of the other horsemen and I yearned for my open one. With Perkin between Sir John and I, we began to advance towards Robert and the smaller number of bodyguards. I knew when we had travelled but fifty paces that Perkin did not have full control of his horse. A horse is sensitive to its rider and Perkin was excited. More, he was a poor horseman with no natural ability. His reins were not held tightly enough and the horse, also a warhorse, was eager to open his legs. Perkin lost control and the horse suddenly leapt forward and as we were just a hundred paces from Robert and his men it was a potential catastrophe. I think because I had anticipated it, I was able to react the quickest and in fifteen strides I was level with the rump of Perkin's horse. When I saw his helmet turn in my direction I knew he was seeking help. Even if he was shouting I would not have heard him through his helmet and above the noise of thundering hooves. The men charging us could not know that this was not planned although when I saw Robert and Giuseppe rein in, I knew that the two leaders did. The others were keen to impress the man they saw as King Richard and came at us. I aimed Zeus to cut across Perkin's horse's head. It would make him slow at the very least. It would, however, expose me to the wooden lance of one of the bodyguards. It could not be helped. I liked Perkin and I feared that if struck by a lance, however softly, he would fall from his horse and with war horses charging from behind that did not bode well.

The two bodyguards were not aiming their lances at me but the man they saw as their future leader. I pulled back my arm to strike at the nearest of the two and by leaning forward and using Zeus' momentum I was able to get between their lances and Perkin's horse. My lance struck a bodyguard in the shoulder and threw him from his saddle but the lance was shattered. The fact that I was hit by two lances at the same time actually prevented my fall but they hurt as they came from two different directions and one negated the other. The one from the man I had unhorsed was a slight one but the other felt as though I had been punched by Geoffrey of Aylesbury. Perkin's horse was forced to turn and, as we did so Sir John arrived and placed his horse between us and the other bodyguards. My right hand was now free and I grabbed the reins of Perkin's horse, tearing them from his hands. I led him back through the rest of the men on our side to the rear. The charge had calmed Perkin's horse and when we reached the starting point, he was shaking but the urge to gallop had gone.

Taking off my helmet I patted Zeus' neck, "Good boy, you did well."

I saw that Perkin was shaking as he took off his helmet, "I feared I would die! You saved my life, James, and I am grateful."

I shook my head, "Robert does not want you to risk yourself in war and neither do I. I am sorry, King Richard, but you are not a warrior. Even had we been fighting on foot you would not have lasted long." I waved my hand around for there was no one within fifty feet of us, "I say this here in private for I like you and do not wish to see you die."

He nodded and gave a sad smile, "You are right, and all thoughts of martial glory were driven from my body by that wild ride. I fear I shall never ride a warhorse again. I will stick to hackneys. Let us keep this between ourselves, eh, James?"

"Of course, my lord. I am ever your servant."

I wheeled Zeus and we watched the rest of the combat. These were all professional soldiers and now that the king was gone they could be warriors. They might have been using wooden weapons, but they were intent on hurting each other. I saw Robert unhorse Sir John and wondered what would happen as a result. Eventually, tiredness kicked in and they stopped fighting. I knew that there would be recriminations and so I said, "Let us return first and rid ourselves of this plate. I know not about you, my lord, but I need a bath. I am sweating like a pig!"

He laughed, "And I too."

By the time a bruised and battered Sir John returned to the hall Perkin and I had bathed and were enjoying wine and ham. They had good ham in Flanders and I had grown accustomed to the wine although I just sipped and nursed one small goblet.

Sir John came to me first, "Thank you, James. I thank God that you were sent to us. But for your quick reactions, we would have lost our king before he could see his homeland."

"I was glad to be of service." I knew that if he heard about it, King Henry would be incandescent with rage. I could have allowed the pretender to the throne to die and end the threat. There was no way I could have allowed that to happen.

Sir John turned to King Richard, "And you, my lord?"

Looking around to see that we were not overheard he said, "Have no fears Sir John, all thoughts of riding to glory ended this day. When we invade, James and I will be with the standard and I will let others do the fighting."

The relief on Sir John's face was clear for all to see.

Chapter 16

That day marked a change for all of us. It drew Perkin closer to me and ensured that I had the complete trust of Sir John. Robert and Giuseppe were also impressed for I had unhorsed a good man who, rather than being unhappy about it saw it as some sort of compliment. To the bodyguards, I was almost a noble, a gentleman. It is true what they say, clothes maketh the man. Inside I was still the boy from Ecclestone but the clothes, the words and manners I had acquired, all gave me the appearance of what I was not. Perkin bought me a signet ring to wear as a mark of his appreciation. It also saw an increase in the number of men joining us and I believe we might have made plans to attack England in the autumn of that year but events, or rather King Henry, conspired against the Yorkists. Sir Simon Montfort, Sir Thomas Thwaites, Sir William Stanley who was the Lord Chamberlain, Sir Robert Clifford, William D'Aubeney, Thomas Cressener, and Thomas Astwode were all suddenly and simultaneously arrested by King Henry's men and were to be put on trial. The trials were set for January and left the plans made by Duchess Margaret and Viscount Lovell in tatters. The Yorkist leader arrived in November and in secret. He looked gaunt and ill. I was desperate to ask how he had escaped but I did not wish to draw attention to myself.

I was privy to the meeting held in the castle and presided over by Duchess Margaret. Also present were Sir John, Viscount Lovell and one of the men I had first seen in Paris. He was the growler. I learned that his name was Quentin d'Urse. I met him, outside the meeting room, as he greeted the man he called king. Then he turned to me and chuckled, "I confess young man that I had you for a spy. I was all for slitting your throat had not Ned spoken up for you." I was grateful to Ned. "It just shows how wrong you can be. Still, the other four we caught were all Tudor spies and the fishes in the Seine fed well from their bodies and I from their purses." I shivered for that could have been me.

I later learned from Sir John that Sir Quentin was a soldier of fortune with Yorkist sympathies. He was a doughty warrior and as he stayed with us in our camp, I was able to see his skills when he sparred with the bodyguards. The only one he could not defeat was Robert. I, of course, was not seated at the table when they spoke. I did not mind. King Richard demanded that I be present and so I acted as a servant, fetching wine and food. Along with the other men present were the leaders of Duchess Margaret's men who had volunteered to come to England.

Viscount Lovell began proceedings, "It is clear that we cannot attack Henry Tudor yet. My cousin tells me that we have just a thousand men and while they are all good warriors, without the support of men in England we cannot hope to win. Our plans have been upset and that is all by these arrests. I suspect that there are spies in England. At least the people in this room can be trusted for none of you have had any contact with England in the last months."

That was chilling as I worked out it meant that Viscount Lovell had spies here in Burgundy.

The Duchess of Burgundy said, "That is all very well but we cannot put the invasion off indefinitely. Now is the time to strike for it shows that Henry Tudor is fearful."

Quentin spoke for the first time, "You need a larger army than I have seen and that may mean accepting those who are, perhaps, not as patriotic as others."

We were all curious and I paused mid pour to look at him.

He gave a sinister smile, "There are many men who will serve a master in the hope of loot. They are neither knights nor men at arms. Some are billmen while others are swordsmen. Some may be crossbowmen or even archers. The point is that they are expendable and would give us greater numbers. The mercenaries you have hired are the best but they are expensive. The men I would seek are cheap. They would happily accept food and lodgings so long as there was the promise of loot at the end of the day."

Viscount Lovell said, "I would prefer men who wished to put King Richard on the throne."

"As would we all but if we were to wait for that to happen then young King Richard would be in his grave. The people need prompting." He drank some of the wine I had just poured. "Let me gather such a band at Boulogne. There we can find malcontents from Calais with a grudge against England and

Boulogne and Dunkerque are the two ports through which come dissidents from England. I will happily fund them."

Sir John said, "What is in it for you?"

"I will be honest, when I joined this illustrious body, I did not think it would take almost three years to launch an invasion. I, too, need money and this seems the best way to achieve that end."

Sir John smiled, "And if we do not invade then you can use your band to serve another."

Silence descended and Quentin said, affably, "Just so."

Duchess Margaret was a clever woman, "Then do it. I will make funds available to you Sir Quentin and we will use these brigands to make the first attacks."

Sir John said, "And that just leaves the question of when and where."

Viscount Lovell said, "Not before next summer."

"That is a date, at least." Quentin was keen to have a date of any description.

"The where is more of a problem. We have support in the east and could land men on the Humber. On the other hand, there is always the malcontents of Cornwall who might join us."

Quentin shook his head, "Both of those involve a long sea voyage and that is always tricky. Why not the shorter route; land in East Anglia or Kent? It is the shortest way to get to London."

The Viscount said, "I had not thought of that but it is too early to make such a decision. It will be one of the three but I know not which one yet. We work to landing in England in July or August."

That seemed to satisfy everyone. I suppose I could have left immediately for I would be able to give the king a one in three chance of meeting the enemy. I dismissed the idea immediately. East Yorkshire and Cornwall were too far apart and spreading his numbers might guarantee that the king failed. I would wait. I had until the summer to continue to play this dangerous game.

The mock battle had made Perkin more serious about what he had to do. I am not sure but I think until the moment that his horse leapt away he thought that this was all a game, however that, and the news that his supporters had been arrested made him realise that he could die as a result of his ambitions. News

reached us in February that all the conspirators had been
sentenced to death and that too made Perkins pale. Even when, a
month later, we discovered that six had their sentences
commuted he was still a shaken man. We knew that soon we
would be leaving the safety of Mechelen and the lively evenings
we had enjoyed hitherto came to an end and he began to spend
the evenings talking with me. He knew he would have his most
critical audience once we landed and he was acclaimed king. He
also worried that his soldiers might fail and that his life of luxury
would end. I had to be the confidante who made him feel better.
In doing so I felt worse for it seemed to me I was deceiving him.
I did not like being a spy.

We learned that we would be heading for the coast at the end
of May. The final destination was still a secret and to be honest, I
do not think that any had made the decision yet. We had not seen
Lord Lovell since the last meeting, and he seemed to be the one
masterminding the attack. Perhaps he was in England and was
securing the support that he would need. Perkin had servants and
they packed all that we would need for the journey in our chests.
This would not be like my journey here, on the back of a
sumpter. We would head for Dunkerque with wagons, horses
and servants. In the time I had been at Mechelen and as I thought
back I realised that it was years and not the months I had
assumed it would be, I had collected coins for I knew the day
would come when I would have to find a way back to England
and that would cost money. Thanks to Jean I had not had to eke
into the purse of coins given to me in Boulogne. The coins I had
accumulated since then dwarfed the pathetic purse. I had made,
in secret, another of the belts and that was my constant
companion. I still had my two rondel daggers and they both
resided in my fine boots. All else that I had brought was long
gone. Goliath still resided in the stables and would be going with
us, carrying my plate and for that I was glad. He was tougher
than he had first appeared.

That last night, after the servants had left us and when Perkin
returned from the meeting with the woman he called aunt, he
joined me to enjoy some wine and fine ham before we retired. I
know not what his aunt had said but whatever it was it had made

him reflective. "James, you are an honest man and will tell me the truth rather than that which I wish to hear."

"Of course, my lord."

"If we win the crown and I sit on the throne of England, will the people support me?"

"If you are crowned, my lord, then does it matter?"

He gave me a rueful look, "England it seems is riven with factions. I have not lived there, as you know, and, from what you have told me, you are not of noble stock." I nodded. "The ordinary folk, those who toil in the fields, fish the seas, gather the wool, all of those, will they accept me?"

It was a good question and I felt I could give him an honest answer that would not jeopardise my chances of returning to England, "England just wants a good king, my lord. You have to go back to King Henry the Fifth for the last English ruler that the people gave their hearts to. He almost conquered France and had he done so then who knows. His son was not a good king and that allowed others to steal the crown." I knew that I was speaking of the Yorkists but I believed that Perkin deserved the truth. "Henry Tudor took his chance to take the crown but as our gathering army shows, he is not without enemies. I would not do what you do, my lord, but I admire you for trying. I tell you now that it will not be easy."

He smiled and raised his goblet to toast me, "Thank you, James, for you have said almost exactly what my aunt said, except, of course, she, said that Henry Tudor took the throne that was rightfully mine. She also said to keep you close. I am glad that you will be with me."

I did not sleep well that night. I was torn for while I had my duty to perform for England, I genuinely liked Perkin Warbeck. I knew that he would fail but I could not tell him that. He had stepped onto a path that led in one direction. Having begun his walk there was no way to retrace his steps. I finally consoled myself with the thought that he might end up like Lambert Simnel, a meat turner for the king.

The thousand men who were with us were cheered and applauded all the way to the camp at Dunkerque where Sir Quentin, Sir John and, so we heard, Lord Lovell awaited us. To the rest of the army, Lord Lovell was still hidden; none knew where he was. Since Stoke Field, he had not been seen and that was deliberate. Sir John had told me that his cousin wanted the anonymity of a supposed death so that he could continue to work for the cause. I was one of a privileged few who had seen him. That in itself showed how successful I had been in my role as a spy.

The future King of England did not have to endure a tent or a hovel like the bulk of his army and a fine house was provided for him by a supporter. As it had no stables it meant that our horses were kept with the horses of the other nobles closer to the army. The army that would land and invade would not be horsed. Sir John had made that clear on his last visit. We were limited with the size of the fleet we would use to land us. I would be one who would have a horse. It became my job to check on our horses each night and I used both my time and my position well.

The Burgundian who was in charge of the horses was a good man who knew horses and I got on well with him. I sought him out when I first took our horses to him and asked him where the sumpters were kept.

"The sumpters, my lord? You ride with the king and will not need sumpters."

I nodded, "As you know when we land in England there will be few horses. I need a sumpter to carry spare armour for the king."

"Ah, I see. I will pick one out for you."

"No, it is my appointed task and whilst I trust your judgement you will not be the one responsible. I wish the sumpter I choose to be close to my horse, Zeus and the king's."

"As you wish, my lord, if you would follow me."

He led me to the line of hackneys and sumpters. I spied Goliath immediately. At Mechelen, I had ensured that he was well-groomed and well fed. I think I had amused the horse master and his grooms. I went to a couple of others before I settled upon Goliath. "I will have that one." Goliath recognised me and nudged my arm.

"A good choice, my lord, for he likes you. You know your horseflesh for he is the one I would have chosen."

As I made my way back to the house, I began planning for my escape. I needed Goliath for anonymity, and I had him now.

However, I knew that I would be missed, and I needed to affect an escape that would arouse neither question nor hue and cry. That was a dilemma but as there were no finalised plans, as yet, then I had time.

Lord Lovell arrived at the end of June by which time the camp was bursting with men. Perkin now had fifteen hundred men he would be able to lead. Although not a great number, one thousand of them were good men, mercenaries, while the other five hundred, Quentin d'Urse's men, would cause havoc in any English town. The number of soldiers who came with Perkin Warbeck was almost immaterial. They just had to be sufficient in number to be the heart of a rebel army. Sir John had made it quite clear that he hoped for thousands, rather than hundreds to flock to the banner of King Richard the Fourth.

Annoyingly Lord Lovell did not give his plans immediately. He insisted upon a parade of the men we had so that he could view them. I knew he must have been in Ireland for the numbers of the army would be swollen by two hundred wild Irishmen he had brought with him. I saw now how he had evaded capture in England and Ireland. He did not wear the livery I had seen in Mechelen but was dressed in Irish livery. Like me, he was playing a part. Perkin and I had to dress in our plate although we did not don our helmets. I carried the standard and that day, which was a windy one, I learned the hazards of carrying a large banner.

It took some time for the eclectic collection of soldiers to be arrayed in rows so that we could ride along their lines. Lord Lovell, Sir John, and Quentin d'Urse followed the king and I rode behind them with my banner. I had learned to ride Zeus one handed but as the wind caught the banner and made it swirl around me I was forced to change hands so that I could grip the bottom of the flag and stop it fluttering before my face. I did not wish to ride into the back of the three horses before me. It was as I grabbed it that I spied a face I recognised. It was Tad of Easingwold and he stood with some of Quentin's men carrying a halberd. I was saved from scrutiny by the standard for it was fortuitous I chose to change hands when I did. I let it flap a little to disguise me. We rode all the way along the line and then back to the centre. King Richard faced them and Lord Lovell placed his horse next to him. It meant I was hidden behind those two, Sir John and Quentin. With Zeus stock still, I allowed the banner to blow before my face. I caught the words of the rousing speeches from the king and the puppet master. They told the army that within a month they would be sailing to England to reclaim the crown of England. One of my tasks had been to help Perkin use words that would appeal to patriots and he was a quick learner. Not only that he had a fine speaking voice and between the two of them they whipped the army into a fanatical fury. Had we sailed for England that instant I believe we would have defeated any who faced us.

That night Lord Lovell held a council of war and as King Richard's gentleman and trusted confidante, I was privy to the meeting. "We attack in August. My cousin, Sir John, will sail to Kingston upon Hull where we have many men who are willing to join us. They will march to York." Lord Lovell smiled, "This is not the main attack but is intended to draw King Henry's army north. We will later land at Deal in Kent and landing unopposed means that we can march quickly to London and take the city. London seethes with rebels and they will all be happy to throw off Henry Tudor's shackles. What think you?"

He was really asking the other leaders and, in particular, Quentin d'Urse who was the professional soldier. The growler nodded, "I like it and as it was I who suggested landing in Kent I can find neither fault nor flaw. However, you are wrong. We will be opposed for there is a garrison at Deal and they will see us land. However, the men we have will sweep them from the field and then we can take the castle and have a base from which to operate." He nodded to Sir John, "The danger lies with you, Sir John. You have to draw men to you and hope that you can escape."

He smiled, "My cousin has made his plans well. I will escape, believe me, and I would not throw my life away carelessly but you, King Richard, you have said nothing. What is your opinion?"

Perkin glanced nervously at me and I gave the slightest of nods, "I believe that this will give us a good chance but I would not have men waste their lives for me. Sir John, you say that you can escape but what of the men you lead?"

"I will not divulge all of the plans King Richard, but King James of Scotland has promised not only support but a safe haven for those of us who are forced to flee. The men I lead know the risks and are willing to take them for you."

My mind was now elsewhere. I had to act sooner rather than later. Sir John would be leaving before we did. He had to be in position first and that meant I had to reach Hedingham before he landed in Yorkshire. I would have to risk a hue and cry. I had already discovered that I would have a thirty-mile ride and that I needed to leave at night. I did not think I would need food but plainer clothes would be essential. I decided that I would buy some in the local market. It would add a day to my departure but as Sir John was still in camp, I had time. I also had to be as normal as I could for those in the house. I did not want to arouse suspicion.

Perkin thought that my idea to visit the local market was a good one and he accompanied me. It complicated matters. Robert and Giuseppe also accompanied us and as we wandered the stalls of Dunkerque market I wondered if I would be able to buy any clothes at all. I saw light when Robert and Giuseppe spied some old comrades drinking in one of the taverns in the market square. They begged leave to enjoy a drink with their friends. After assuring the two that we would not leave the square I went with Perkin to see if I could manage to buy some poorer quality clothes to aid my disguise. I still had my oiled cloak and that would cover a multitude of sins. I bought some loose breeches, cheap hose and a buff jerkin as well as a plain cap.

Perkin asked as we headed for Robert and Giuseppe, "Why, James, do you want such clothes? You have fine apparel and enough money to buy much better ones than this."

I smiled and the easy lie spilt forth, "When we are in England, my lord, it may be necessary for me to spy for you. After all, Henry Tudor will still have supporters and wearing such garb will help me mingle with them. Putting the crown on your head is only part of our task. We have to keep it there."

The answer seemed plausible enough for him to accept. Robert and Giuseppe were still too full of the conversations they had enjoyed and did not think to question the bundle beneath my arm. Once back in the house I put the clothes somewhere safe. I planned to leave that very night. My greatest fear was not that I would be caught but that they might deduce I was a spy and change their plans; then the years I had spent with the rebels would have been in vain. Of course, in reality, they were not wasted. I had learned more skills as well as languages. I had lived the life of a gentleman and while I knew it would end once I returned to England the experience would always lie within me. Lord Lovell dined with us that night and it was then I learned that Sir John would be leaving the next day. He was not leaving from Dunkerque but heading further north to a smaller port where we would sail in a day or so. The ships gathering in Dunkerque harbour were a clear indication of a gathering army and a small ship leaving the port might draw attention. I had to leave.

I had to draw on everything that had happened to me since I had left England to make it through the meal. I had grown close to Perkin and Sir John and I knew that it would be unlikely that I would see either of them again and that made me sad. I cared not for Lord Lovell and if I never saw him again it would be too soon. It was clear to me that he was using poor Perkin for his own purposes while his cousin genuinely believed in the cause. Lord Lovell just hated being on the losing side. I helped Perkin to his bedchamber. Sir John's early departure meant that the night was relatively young when we retired.

"So, my lord, soon we shall set sail for England. Are you excited?"

He nodded, "And yet a little worried also. That practise battle shook me." He looked around, although we were alone, "You will not tell anyone will you?"

"Of course not. That reminds me I should take the breastplate that was damaged by the lance and get it repaired. I have put it off. It is early yet. Perhaps I shall do it now for the weaponsmith may have time to repair it before we leave."

"Is there urgency?"

"I know not how long it will take to beat it out." The two lances which had struck me had managed to hit the same spot and the dent was deeper than it should have been.

"Very well. I shall see you on the morrow."

"Yes, my lord."

I went to my chamber and undressed. I donned the cheap clothes I had bought and then the damaged breastplate. If I was stopped, I would say I was heading to the weaponsmith at the camp. Then I donned the livery of King Richard and finally my cloak. I put on the fine cap and rolled the cheaper one in my belt. I had my two daggers and my good sword. I left the house. The two guards at the door winked at each other. Perhaps they thought I was heading for a doxy.

I had been right, it was early but the sun was setting and the camp of soldiers was filled with the fires and the smell of food being cooked. With the hood of my cloak over my head, I hoped to move almost invisibly through the camp. I also chose this time because the horse guards would be preparing their food. There would be a visit to the horses later on but that would be when the grooms and horse master had eaten and drunk well. There had been a buzz around the camp that the army was to embark soon and experienced soldiers knew that you ate and drank when you could. I had my best opportunity to escape at this hour.

I had an apple for Goliath as well as one for Zeus. My plan, which was not perfect by any means was for me to ride Zeus and Goliath. I intended to head due east and then change horses, allowing Zeus to graze. There I would leave my plate and hat and hope that when my disappearance was discovered it would take them time to find out which way I went. Heading east would confuse them. As I had anticipated the horse lines were deserted. I gave the apples to the horses and saddled Zeus and then, as an afterthought, Goliath. I wanted as much confusion as I could manage, and two saddles and two horses would confuse the ones who would seek me out. I hoped that it would work, and I could escape back to England and report my news to the king. I was just about to mount when I heard a voice from behind me. I vaguely recognised the voice, but the words left me in no doubt that I was in trouble.

"So James of, where was it? Prescot? When I saw you in the market the other day, with your fine clothes, I knew that Fate had given me the chance for vengeance, and by God, I shall take it." He laughed, "If you thought that shaving your face and dressing in fine clothes would disguise you then you were wrong for your face is burned in my memory."

I turned and saw Tad of Easingwold and he held a short sword in his hand. Even as I turned my hand was reaching for the dagger I had in my belt, but I knew I would not be able to draw it in time.

Lunging at me with the sword he said, "Your purse and fine sword shall be mine."

Chapter 17

I was not the same youth Tad had fought before. I was stronger and had been trained with a blade. I had learned well and knew that until the sword entered my body and found a vital organ, I had a chance, and I brought my dagger around in a wide sweep. Tad's sword was a short one and a little longer than my dagger, but it tore through the cloak and then struck the breastplate. The metal on metal sound screeched as the sword slid along the breastplate. By that moment Tad was so close, we were roughly the same height, that I stared into his wide eyes. He had thought that even a glancing blow would end my life. I could smell the drink on his breath and the stink of his body. I rammed my dagger up between his ribs. As the razor-sharp blade scraped off a rib, I twisted it a little and drove it harder towards his innards.

He shook his head and blood began to drip from his mouth, "Cunning little…" The light went from his eyes and Tad of Easingwold died. I wiped the dagger on Tad's shirt and sheathed it. I was about to mount my horse when I had a thought. I could use Tad and his body to my advantage. Slinging the corpse on the back of Goliath and putting his sword back in its scabbard I mounted Zeus and after checking that Tad had come alone and I was unobserved I rode away, to the south and east. I passed through the open gate of a farmer's field and emerged at a small road. I had seen it when I had been riding with Sir John and Perkin. The people of this part of Flanders stayed within doors at night and as I walked the two horses none came out as they might have done had we galloped.

I knew not what I was looking for except that I had to make it look as though Tad had suffered an accident. The road I was using was a narrow country lane with twists and turns. There were some stone walls lining the road and when I had to duck my head beneath a beech branch that jutted from the side, I knew I had found the best place to stage my accident. The spot was about a mile from the nearest house. I tethered Goliath and then removed Tad's body. This first part would be distasteful but had to be done. I took my ring and placed it on Tad's finger. I removed my breastplate and fitted it on him followed by the livery of King Richard. I jammed my fine hat upon his head. I did not want to do the next part but knew that if it was discovered that James of Yarm had fled to England then Lord Lovell might change his plans and my time in Flanders would have been wasted. I went to the wall and found a large loose stone at the top. I returned to the body and lifted the stone high. I dropped it to smash down on his face. There was little blood for he was already dead, but the stone was covered in what blood there was as well as brain and bones. I replaced the stone on the wall with the gore uppermost. Tad's face was unrecognisable. We were roughly the same height and build. Our hair was a similar colour. I hoped that by the time the body was discovered firstly I would be in England and secondly the body would have begun to stink and any examining the body would spend as little time doing so as possible. I hefted the body so that the smashed skull lay on the stone. I hoped they would believe that the rider had struck the tree and when he had fallen smashed his head on the wall.

Mounting Goliath I led Zeus for a mile or more down the road until I came to a field with an open gate. I led Zeus in and patting his neck said, "Farewell, old friend. I would have taken you to England but it would tell all that I was a spy and I must remain a mystery." There was grazing in the field and such a fine horse would soon be discovered. I whipped Goliath's head around and took the road which would lead me to the main road to Calais.

As I rode I wondered at Fate's intervention. It was now clear to me that although Tad had not seen me at the parade of men he had spotted me when I was buying my clothes. I had no idea what had brought him to Flanders except that I had robbed him of an income in England and the theft had made him a fugitive. He was one of Quentin's desperate men. When the body was found the livery would ensure that it was taken to Perkin. By then Sir John would be on his way to Kingston upon Hull. Had he been at Dunkerque he might have examined the body closely. Perkin would not. He would see the ring and breastplate and ignore the clothes and the sword and assume I had suffered an accident. I had staged it a mile or two from the camp and that would raise questions, but I hoped that it would not prevent the invasion. All I had to do was to get to England.

It was dawn by the time I reached Calais and I was leading Goliath by then. I was dressed in the clothes of a poor man, all except for my fine boots. Luckily for me, the two sentries at the town walls did not look at them but Goliath. One laughed, "Well, friend, do you wish directions to the knacker's yard to dispose of the beast?"

I was relieved they were both English and spoke English. I shook my head, "No for my master, Jean Le Casserole, would be most unhappy."

They recognised the name and the sentry nodded, "Aye, it looks the sort of beast he might use. Pass friend although I do not think your master will have risen yet."

The other laughed, "Aye, for since he wed that pretty young thing, he spends more time in his bed-chamber than making pots."

I had used Jean's name merely to gain entry to Calais but knowing he was in the port gave me hope that he might help me again. It was a chance I would have to take. The port did not keep normal hours. The tide determined when ships arrived and left. The streets, especially those close to the harbour were busy and I was able to find out where Jean's house was located; the Rue des Gravelines was close to the harbour as befitted an exporter of pots. My French, especially the dialect spoken around here, was now perfect and I aroused no suspicion. Jean's people were already working in the workshop. I could see the smoke rising from the ovens and hear the buzz of conversation. There was a water trough close by and I tethered Goliath to it so that he could drink then I boldly walked up to the door and rapped sharply upon it.

To my great surprise a young woman, about my age and heavily pregnant answered the door, "Yes, can I help you?"

I took off my hat and bowed, "I seek Jean le Casserole."

She nodded, "If you seek work, young man, then see the foreman." She said it with a smile but it was a command.

"I beg you, madame, to tell him that James the Englishman is here." I raised my voice a little when I said, 'James the Englishman' and it worked.

Jean rushed to the door with a look of joy on his face, "James! You live! Come inside! Come inside!" I stepped inside and the door was closed behind me. "Marie, this is the young man I told you about when first we met."

Her eyes widened, "The young man who saved you from death? You are most welcome, sir, and I apologise for my cold reception."

"No apology needed, madame, for I know my appearance makes me seem like a wastrel."

"James, this is my wife, Marie." Just then a small boy, no more than two toddled out of a room leading off from the hall. He was dressed in his nightshirt. "And that is my son, Jean. Marie, have the servants fetch us food and ale. James, let us sit for I can see that you have a tale to tell."

Marie whisked the boy away and Jean led me to a large room with a fine table and a comforting fire. He waved me to a seat and said, "I thought you dead."

Shaking my head I said, "No, I have survived but I need to get to England as soon as I can."

"You are hunted?"

"Better that you do not know. All I ask Jean is that you trust me for I swear that what I do is honourable."

He laughed, "Aye, I knew you had a secret, but I care not. I do trust you for I look in your eyes and see honesty. I also see a confident man grown and not the boy I left with those I thought would slit his throat for pennies."

A servant returned with Marie and Jean. Food and drink were placed on the table and Marie said, "Little Jean needs milk. I will see you later, James."

I stood and bowed, "Perhaps."

She smiled, "Such manners. I hope I do."

When she left, I cocked my head, "Your wife?"

He smiled, "That was down to you. When you left, I could not get you out of my head and I thought that I had lost another son. I found Marie begging the first day after you left and it seemed like a sign. She had lost her parents and needed help. I swear that I just did as I did with you and gave her shelter. I had no intention of taking advantage of her."

His voice betrayed emotion and I put my hand on his, "Jean, I would never think such a thing. We knew each other but briefly and yet I know that you are honourable."

He nodded, "Aye, but others did not and tongues wagged. It drove us closer together and, well, I am no longer young but we fell in love and I married Marie. It was only then that I lay with her despite what others might have said," He raised his beaker, "Here is to you, James."

"And to you, I am pleased you have found happiness."

"And now, what do you need?"

"I need to leave Calais this day and be in England as soon as I can." I held up my hand, "As I said it is better you do not know the details of my life since we left. Let us say that I am a better man now than I was."

He nodded, "Say no more. I will go to the port when we have eaten and Marie returns for she would like to speak with you I know. I have often mentioned your name and your story. If you are to be with us a short time, I would like you to talk."

I nodded and put some ham on the bread I had just smeared with butter, "And I need passage for Goliath."

He laughed, "You still have him?" I nodded, my mouth full. "You are a loyal fellow and I like that."

When Marie and a now dressed little Jean returned, Jean dabbed his mouth with his napkin and said, "I will do as you ask, James, although I would have wished we could have spent more time together."

"I now know where you live, Jean, and when time allows, I can return."

When he left Marie sat down and began to feed the boy with pieces of soft bread she tore from the inside of the loaf, "You are not staying the night?"

I shook my head, "I have urgent business in England or else I would stay here."

"Jean will be sad for he often speaks of you. He told me that your tale was what drew him to me and so I am grateful to you for a life I did not think I would have."

I nodded as I realised that I had spurned my family and she had lost hers. I was a selfish man. "Jean is a kind man, and I was lucky to have met him."

"Yet without you, he would have died. It is strange is it not?"

"As I have discovered, madame, life cannot be predicted and there are twists and turns in this life. A man does well to react quickly."

"It is Marie, James, and you are right. Who knew when I begged in the suburbs of Paris that the kind man with the old horse and wagon would change my life?"

We spoke of Jean and his business. In contrast to the disparaging remarks made by the sentries, Jean had not neglected his business, rather he had made it grow and he now used others to make the journey to Paris. As Marie said, they were amongst the richest folk in Calais and she knew she had been lucky.

Jean was not away for long and he returned with good news. "I have found a ship sailing on the afternoon tide to London. The captain is a good man and he is carrying some of my pots that are destined for King Henry. He will take you. We need to have you at the quayside by noon. I told him you were taking the sumpter and it may take time to load him. Until then let us talk for it is good to see you."

I smiled but inside I feared that the afternoon tide might be too late. What if the body was discovered already? I had counted on some delay to make the body look more like mine. I resigned myself to my fate. If I was meant to be taken then so be it. We talked as though old friends although I had just met Marie and not seen Jean for years. That is what happens with true friends and it made me yearn for not only conversation with Stephen and Sam but also my family. Whatever happened I would return to Ecclestone and take whatever censure was due to me. Watching and listening to the two of them as they spoke of their hopes for the future and their children, I could not help but wonder how a man almost old enough to be my father and a girl just a little younger than me could have found such happiness together. As I have often heard, God moves in mysterious ways.

When it was time to leave Marie hugged me as though she had known me a lifetime and not just a morning, "I pray you to come back and see my next child. Everything Jean said about you is true." She ran her finger down the white scar that marked my clean-shaven face, "One day you shall find a woman and she will see what I see, a gentleman." She smiled, "In every sense of the word."

Jean walked next to me as I led Goliath to the port, "Marie is right, my friend and it is not empty words when I say you are always welcome, no matter what you have done."

I nodded, "And I can say with hand on heart that I have done nothing of which I am ashamed, and I have served my country."

"Then that is good, and I doubt not your word."

The ship was a small cog and the captain a Frenchman. Jacques, however, was a practical man who knew that alliances could be made and broken but men had to make a living, and while he was a loyal Frenchman there was peace between his country and mine and he was happy to carry me and my sumpter. Jean and I had little time for goodbyes as the captain was keen to set sail. The busy quay was also not a place for words that meant something. We both waved as the cog left Calais harbour and headed west. We had barely cleared the harbour when I discovered that before landing at London, the ship would be calling at Tilbury. My knowledge of the area was hazy but I knew that Tilbury was closer to Hedingham than London. The captain was happy to disembark me there. As I stroked Goliath, who was not happy about the choppy seas, I saw another advantage. I knew that there were many Yorkist spies and sympathisers in London. I had seen some as they held clandestine meetings with the duchess and Lord Lovell. Although I doubted that they would recognise me without my fine clothes I was happier knowing I would not have to take that chance.

The passage was not a swift one and it was dawn when we passed Canvey Island. I had slept, fitfully, close to Goliath and had been awoken by a ship's boy with wine and bread. It was a French ship and that was how they breakfasted. The captain pointed to the northwest as I fastened my breeches having made water, "Tilbury is but an hour or so away for the tide is on the turn and helps us as does the wind."

"Thank you, captain. I am grateful for the passage."

"Do not thank me, Jean le Casserole is a valuable customer, and I was honoured to do him a favour. My purse is fatter thanks to him."

For the first time in a long time, I felt that I might survive this adventure. Goliath seemed eager to be back on solid ground and, waving farewell, I was on the road within half an hour of us docking. I asked for directions once I reached the edge of the town and found that the main road went from Brentwood, through Chelmsford before reaching Hedingham. I was told it was over forty miles and while that seemed daunting, I determined to do it in one journey. I would walk Goliath when I could and ride him when I needed. I intended to make plenty of stops. The one thing I had in abundance was money for my purse was full. Strangely I feared neither brigand nor bandit. I had faced murderers and killers and survived. It took some time to become accustomed to hearing English spoken again. Of course, Perkin, Sir John and I had spoken English all the time but around us, it had been Walloon, Flemish and French. I had learned to dip in and out of languages with ease. Now I had to attune myself to the rhythm of English. The food and ale were also different. Something as simple as bread, cheese, ham and ale can taste totally different in lands separated by a mere twenty-two miles of water. I reached Hedingham about an hour before dawn and I was weary while Goliath appeared to be totally exhausted. He was getting old. I waited at the green in the village where Goliath could both graze and rest while I looked east for the rising sun. The first villagers to rise looked in surprise when they saw the man and his sumpter but I gave them a cheery greeting and as the sun peered over the horizon and I heard the church bell toll I headed to the castle.

The gates were, of course, closed and the walls manned. I waited patiently. The sentries, whom I did not recognise, saw me but I appeared not to be a threat. My clothes also meant I was not considered important and so the two men on the gatehouse chatted. Eventually, the gates were opened and a Sergeant at Arms came forth. He had his head down and did not see me at first. When Goliath neighed he lifted his head, "And who are you? What is it that you want? We have no need for vagrants and beggars."

I smiled, "Gerald of Wednesbury is that any way for you to speak to an old comrade in arms and a shield brother?"

He screwed his eyes up and then they widened as he recognised, "James of Prescot! I thought you dead." He frowned, "I heard you killed a man."

I shook my head, "I am neither dead nor a murderer. Is the Earl within?"

He shook his head, "He was summoned to London by the king. Yorkists have risen in Yorkshire."

I was too late and I had tarried too long, Sir John had not waited as long as I might have hoped and the invasion was on.

Chapter 18

"And Sir Edward?" Even as I asked the question, I knew he would be more likely to be with the earl than in the castle.

"Aye, he is here and is the castellan until the earl returns. He is raising the local levy to face the rebels."

"Then I beg you to take me to him. The news I have concerns the safety of the realm."

I saw the debate in his head and eventually, he nodded, "I never believed that you would be a killer, come and I shall take you to him but if I am reprimanded for disturbing his breakfast then I shall fetch you a clout to remember me by."

I left Goliath in the stable and slipped a coin to the groom to tend to him. We reached the Great Hall where the knights and squires were dining. All conversation ceased when we entered, and I saw Sir Edward frown.

Gerald of Wednesbury announced, "A man is here to speak with the Earl on a matter of the safety of the realm."

Sir Edward strode over and when he was just ten paces from me smiled and said, "James of Prescot! Is that you? I would barely have recognised you."

I saw a young man close by him and I guessed that he was his page. "Aye, Sir Edward but Gerald is right, the news I bring for the earl is of the utmost importance." I looked around, "And not for such a public place."

He nodded, "I wondered what you were about when I took you to the earl and the king. Come, there is a small room we can use. Sergeant, thank you, send for Captain Sam and Sergeant Stephen. Have them wait outside my chamber as sentries." As Gerald hurried off Sir Edward turned to his squire and said, "William, as a precaution, go to the stables and prepare my horse."

"We will be leaving, my lord?"

"This is James of Ecclestone, and he is ever the harbinger of potent news. It is always better to be safe." When Sir Edward used my real name I felt a huge sense of relief. I was no longer a spy and I was not living a lie. I felt cleaner.

"Yes, my lord." He scurried off.

"Sam and Stephen will be glad to see you. They never believed the story of murder. I knew it was untrue, but the Earl swore me to secrecy." We reached the room and after checking that the corridor was empty, he closed the door, "Speak what you can but if the words can only be spoken to the earl then we will ride there immediately."

"I have been in the service of the king since last we met and I have been at the pretender's court to discover what I can. The rebellion in Yorkshire, my lord, is a ruse. The real landing will take place in Deal." I blurted it out and felt such relief. Even if something happened to me now then others would know.

He nodded, "And the earl and the king are raising an army to march north even as we speak. I would ask if you are sure but your face and what I know of you tells me that it is true. That you have been away for years and come back with such a tale is fantastical."

I nodded, "When time allows, my lord, I will happily share my story, but I acted under the orders of the king and the earl. It is to them that I must report the full details of my task."

Sir Edward was a decisive man, "You have travelled hard?" I nodded, "Then I will send food to you. When you have eaten, we shall take fast horses and ride to London where the king and his council debate the issue. I just pray we are in time although as the news only reached us yester afternoon and the earl left at dusk I think you may have arrived in time." He pointed to the jug of wine and goblet, "Help yourself."

He left and I poured myself half a goblet. I would have preferred ale but my mouth was dry.

I heard words without and then there was a tap on the door, "Come."

The door opened and a liveried servant with a tray stood there. Behind him were Sam and Stephen. The servant laid the food down and as he left and was about to close the door I said, "It is sad that while I recognise old friends, they do not see me before them."

Their jaws quite literally dropped when they heard my voice. Sam said, "We were told to guard the door for Sir Edward had an important visitor. You?"

I laughed, "Aye, I am sorry that I disappoint you."

Stephen said, "You do not but we both thought you dead. Where have you been?"

Shaking my head I said, "All that I can say is that I served the king and the earl. When I have their permission then I will tell you what I can, but I will say that I am pleased to see you both."

Sam nodded, "Then we shall be patient and wait. Enjoy your food and know that you are safe while we are here."

I had barely finished when Sir Edward returned, "Come, James. Whatever you have not consumed you must eat while we ride."

I grabbed the ham and the last of the bread. Who knew when I would find time to eat again?

"You two shall come with us. We must be fast but I would have us protected on the road. I do not doubt your words, James, and if what you say is true then there will be enemies closer to hand than Yorkshire."

I saw Sam and Stephen exchange a look. I had left them a youth, a billman like them but from Sir Edward's words, I had returned as something different. I had, however, had enough of this new world and I would, as soon as I was able, return to the life of a billman.

The four horses that Sir Edward had found for us were the best in the stable. His squire held the reins of Sir Edward's, "Are you sure I cannot come with you, my lord?"

"No William, I ride quickly, and you shall follow with my war gear." He threw him a purse. "This will be a test for you, eh? Let us see how you fare without my eagle eye on you."

"Yes, my lord, I shall not let you down."

I threw another coin to the groom, "Keep Goliath safe!"

Sam laughed, "That is a tale you must tell me, James of Prescot, how you acquired such a beast."

As I threw my leg over the saddle I said, "And we can start our friendship anew. I am not James of Prescot but James of Ecclestone. I am sorry for the deception."

Stephen said, "Does it make a difference?"

As we dug our heels into our horses Sam said, "Aye, it does for Walter the Rat Slayer came from Ecclestone and I believe that James is his son."

Sir Edward shouted, "Ladies, we serve the king! Let us save such words for a time when England is not in danger!"

I had not given Sir Edward the full details but he was a clever man and knew that if King Henry sent his men north to meet a foe that did not exist then he could lose his capital and with it his crown.

We had a fifty-mile ride and I knew that our horses would not be able to keep up the pace we set for the first twenty miles. We stopped in Great Dunmow to water the horses and to allow us to make water. Sir Edward said, when I asked about the horses, "Do not worry about them. I will use the Earl's authority to get fresh ones at the castle at Chipping Ongar."

Sam rubbed his backside, "And is there any chance of getting me a new arse, Sir Edward?" He would not have spoken thus before the earl but Sir Edward was different.

The knight laughed, "I think we will all need a new one by the time we reach the Tower!"

Our ride was as frenetic a one as I could remember. Even riding with Sir John to Mechelen we had travelled at a more sedate pace. Nothing overtook us and when we reached Chipping Ongar and changed, our first mounts were so exhausted and lathered that I doubted they would be ready to ride in three days' time. Our speed meant that we reached the Tower before dark. We could see, already, the preparations for the supposed northern attack. The Tower Green was filled with horsemen, billmen and archers. We were waved through to the inner bailey.

"You two find the sergeant in charge of the barracks. Have the horses stabled and find a bed for the three of you."

We rushed inside and up the stairs. We were stopped by a pursuivant at the entrance to the Great Hall. Sir Edward was blunt, "Tell King Henry that we have news of the rebels and James of Ecclestone has returned."

The pursuivant looked down his nose at me. After almost three days in the saddle and not having had the opportunity to bathe I stank of horse and me. "I think this man needs a bath before he can be taken into the presence of the king."

Sir Edward's voice became heavy with threat, "Either tell him or I will!"

The man hurried off clearly terrified by the wild-eyed warrior.

It was the earl who returned. His first words seemed to be the ones everyone used, "We thought you dead, but I am pleased you are not. You have what we sought?" I nodded. "Come with me. The king and I should hear of this in private." He looked at Sir Edward, "You know?"

"The bare bones only, my lord, and James has done nothing wrong." I did not need defending but I was pleased that Sir Edward did so.

We were taken up some stairs to a small chamber. It looked like it would barely hold the four of us although I saw that there were four chairs there.

"Wait here. It will take a few moments to clear the hall."

Sir Edward smiled as the earl left, "When I was asked to take you to the king and the earl I thought, like you, that we had done something wrong. I know, without you telling me, that you have been a spy for King Henry and that, in itself, is remarkable. You have a name now, James."

"A name I do not want. I wish for neither fame nor honour. I would be a billman once more."

"You can never go back, James. I know not what you have done but I see a change and not just the knife scar on your face. The way you talk and move makes you a completely different warrior from the one I left at Boulogne."

Before I could reply the door opened and the king entered. We both leapt to our feet. The king and the earl sat, and the king said, "Sit and speak!"

I did not tell him how I came to be at Dunkerque but gave him the details of the attack and the numbers. I gave the names of the leaders that I knew. The two men sat and listened while Sir Edward just gaped in amazement at the names and numbers I reeled off.

"So you were close to the one they call Perkin Warbeck?"

I nodded, "I was given the position of being his teacher to coach him in the ways of England."

The king laughed, "That is a fine jest. Lovell the Dog escaped us and then hired my spy to help his man. Do they know he is an imposter?"

I nodded, "I believe that some think he is Richard of Shrewsbury, but most have their doubts."

"So Sir John Bardolph did not die either. This Quentin d'Urse, I have not heard of him."

Sir Edward ventured, "I have heard the name. He is an adventurer."

"So they land at Deal."

I nodded, "The plan was to sail a day or so after Sir John had landed."

"Then we have no time to waste." The king said, "De Vere, begin the men to march to Deal."

He stood but said, "What if James is wrong and the northern invasion is real?" All eyes swivelled to me, "What if James here was turned by Lovell and sent back to give us false information?"

I saw the doubt on the faces of the king and the earl. I was about to speak when Sir Edward came to my defence again, "King Henry, I have looked into the eyes of James of Ecclestone, and I believe he speaks true but even if I am wrong, we can reach Deal before we could reach Yorkshire and the message has already gone out to raise the northern levies. Clifford and Percy will have to deal with the northern attack."

The king nodded, "You may be right but so might the Earl. I want James of Ecclestone closely guarded until we determine if he speaks the truth or not."

I was angry and I stood, "King Henry, I have done all that you asked of me. The other spies you sent were all caught and killed. Would this have been their fate if they had returned? Lock me in a cell here in the Tower and then, if I am wrong, come back and hang me. As for me, I have had enough riding."

The king's eyes narrowed. I would not have spoken like that had I not been so close to nobles and those with royal blood. I had seen that they were the same as us. Henry Tudor was king through a distant bloodline, and he had been lucky to gain the crown. I thought I had gone too far until a smile creased his face, "You may be right, impertinent youth, but we will have you guarded for that way you are protected and as for no more riding...you shall ride!"

I was given my third horse of the day. Sam and Stephen had managed to be fed while I had not. Being King Henry's spy had never been a job I sought and now I wished I had never come to his attention. As I mounted the chestnut I wondered if, when Jean had made the offer, I should have taken it and begun to work for him. As we clattered out of the postern gate by the Byward Tower I knew that I had to have done what I did. If I had done other, then Jean might not have met Marie and Perkin would not have had a companion. I knew that now he would be alone for I had been his only friend. I was resigned to my fate but at least I knew that I had spoken the truth. Of course, if my desertion was now known then there might be no attack at Deal and a rope would await me.

Our journey was even longer than the one to London and it took all night for us to get halfway to the castle on the coast. It was almost sunset when we reached Deal Castle. The king and his advanced guard of five hundred men were the only ones to reach the castle. The rest were still on their way from London and it might take them another day or more to reach the beach. However, riders had reached the constable and the lords of the manor had been summoned. There would be another five hundred men, including four hundred archers. More men were on their way. Sir Edward obeyed his orders, and I was taken by Sam and Stephen, now my gaolers, with the king and the earl to the Great Hall and the constable.

The constable bowed, "King Henry, when I received your orders, I thought someone was playing a joke, but I obeyed them and mustered the lords and their men. When, this afternoon, a fishing boat reported a fleet of ships heading for the coast from France I realised that you had shown wisdom and foresight. There is an army coming. By my estimate, they will be here by dawn."

Men who are not kings might have apologised to me, but King Henry just said, "It looks like you were right, James of Ecclestone and you did speak the truth. Constable, find a room for these four men. They have ridden hard in my service."

If this was what the gratitude of kings looked like then I had done with kings.

Sir Edward sensed my anger and when the door to the chamber was closed said, "Kings are not like mere men, James, and King Henry has suffered many friends who have become enemies."

I nodded as I took off my boots, "Aye, Sir Edward, and if he treated them as he treated me then I can understand it. And what of the earl? He is not a king and it was he who suggested that I was a traitor."

Sam was a clever man and, unlike Stephen, had pieced together the threads of my story to make sense of it, "James, spies are never trusted by any neither their masters nor their friends. Put your spying days behind you. Stand with men with the billhook. Those men you can trust."

His comments were aimed as much at Sir Edward as me. I nodded, "Aye, and as it has been so long since I slept, I will have an untroubled sleep."

I was wrong of course for I was haunted by the face of Perkin Warbeck. You do not decide your dreams and I know not whence they come but his voice pleaded with me to help him as a laughing King Henry hung a halter from his neck. When I woke the others were all dressing. Perhaps their noise had woken me, but I was glad to be free from the nightmare I had endured. It was a frightening thought, but I preferred the man I knew to be a pretender, Perkin Warbeck to the cold and heartless Henry Tudor. Of course, if Perkin was successful, he would be a puppet and I hated Lord Lovell even more than Henry Tudor. I would fight.

The sun was yet to rise when we entered the Great Hall to breakfast but neither the king nor the earl was present. There was a buzz of conversation and we learned that more men had arrived while we slept and that when we had eaten, we were to march to the beach where the local garrison soldiers were already arrayed. The ships had been sighted but they would not attempt to land until daylight. Even a landsman like me knew that. They would have a shock when they were greeted by not only the garrison of the castle but a hastily mustered army. Thanks to my intelligence the king knew the numbers and the quality we would face and with the Earl of Oxford leading his men he believed he would win.

A liveried warrior came to find us, "The king demands that James of Ecclestone joins him on the beach. You are to arm yourself."

Sam snorted, "Aye and his shield brothers will be with him."

Sir Edward added, heavily, "We will all stand with him this day."

The others had their plate and jacks, but I had nothing save the good sword given to me by Perkin Warbeck. There was an armoury, and I was fitted with a leather jack and a good sallet. They would do but I confess that I missed the comforting protection of a breastplate. Mine now resided on a corpse. The three of us took a billhook each. They were familiar weapons to the other two and I would fight alongside my friends.

The beach lay just paces from the castle and when we made our way there, I saw the problem we had. Apart from the couple of hundred men he had brought from London and the garrison of the castle, the rest of the men on the beach were local men armed with bows and billhooks. The best soldiers we had were the twenty bodyguards of the king.

Sir Edward said, "We should speak with the king. He sent for you, James."

"Perhaps he has me here to test my loyalty, Sir Edward."

Sam laughed and Sir Edward shook his head, "Do not be so bitter, James. What you did was for England, and it was a noble thing."

"And yet, Sir Edward, there has been no word yet about my reward for the almost three years I spent living a lie."

"That will come when time allows." A sudden thought struck him, "I still have your belt at Hedingham Castle."

"And I thank you for keeping it safe."

I followed Sir Edward to the side of the king who said, "I am pleased that you have come too, Sir Edward. The earl and I will withdraw our men to the castle. If this pretender sees our banners, then he may not land and I would have him caught. The Constable will command but you can be an able lieutenant. James of Ecclestone, you alone know the identity of the pretender. I want you here so that you can identify him." I nodded. The king smiled, "And I have not forgotten my promise to you. There will be rewards when this danger is gone."

My fate, it seemed, was irrevocably bound with that of Perkin Warbeck. Until he was in chains, I would not have my life back.

The king and earl left with their men to return to the safety of the walls of Deal Castle as we could now see the ships emerging from the bank of sunlit clouds to the east. Sir Edward went to speak to the Constable and Stephen turned to me, "You shall have your reward then, James."

"Aye."

"And then what?"

"And then I go home to see my family."

"Aye but after that. Will you return to be a billman with us?"

I heard the pleading in his voice and for his sake, I was tempted but that would mean serving the Earl of Oxford and I felt a little betrayed by him. "I know not; perhaps and I would be in your company Captain Sam, for you are a good man and the two of you are my only friends this side of the Channel." They looked at me in surprise and I smiled, "Aye, the spying was not all hardship and I have some friends." I pointed to the ship which I could now see bore the standard of King Richard the Fourth, "And one of them is there."

Sam grabbed my arm, "Keep your voice down for you speak treason."

"Sam, until you have lived the life do not criticise. I will do my duty and my sword will be as bloody as any this day, fear not."

Sir Edward returned and said, "I am to command the right wing and the Constable the left. The men we brought from London will be in the centre. Sam and Stephen, you should guard James."

I laughed, "You think I have not drawn my sword for the last years? I will fight, Sir Edward, fear not and the three of us will fight together. I will have no man risk his life for me. We are brothers in arms and there is an end to it."

Sir Edward shook his head, "You have changed James of Ecclestone. Aye, you are right. When I was given my spurs it changed me, and I remember fighting with shield brothers. As you will."

I saw that it was low tide and that meant the ships would be out of range of the guns on the walls of Deal Castle. The ship with the banner did not close with the shore. Perkin had remembered the mock battle. I knew that the ones that landed would be good men and led by either Sir Quentin d'Urse or captains Robert and Giuseppe, either way, it would be a hard fight. I looked along the line and saw that we faced them with a forest of billhooks and pole weapons backed by archers. The centre had our only plated men.

As the first ships ground onto the beach the Constable shouted, "For God, King Henry and England let us drive these invaders from our land. Forward."

We began the march down the beach as the first mercenaries jumped from the ships and began to form ranks. I saw that there were three battles being formed. One, in the centre, was commanded by Captain Robert. The right, which faced us, had Sir Quentin and his men while Captain Giuseppe had the left. I recognised them by their surcoats. The full face sallet would disguise my identity.

"Halt!"

The Constable halted our line when we were just one hundred paces from the enemy. The archers, who were behind us, would have to send their arrows almost two hundred paces and as the men who had landed were all plated it would be the polemen who faced them.

I said to Sam and Stephen who had flanked me, "The ones we face are the scum of the earth. Their leader is the huge man with the full plate armour. He is Sir Quentin d'Urse and he is a killer. Give him no quarter. The others are even worse and they would take the coins from the eyes of a corpse."

The mercenaries did not race at us. They saw men without armour and some without helmets. I had trained with these men and knew that they had supreme confidence in their own ability. What they did not know was that the king had reserves already waiting to be fed into the battle. The local warriors were deemed expendable by a king desperate to hang on to his crown. I had to fight. If I did not then there would always be doubts about my loyalty.

As I had expected Sir Quentin and his men charged us. The two captains had a more measured attack up the sandy beach. I had not fought in many battles but what I had learned was that each man fights his own battle. What happens twenty feet away should not concern you. The three of us had not fought together since Boulogne but the training we had done meant that our actions were almost reflexes and as the five mercenaries, wildly swinging their swords, came at us we all jabbed in unison. The billmen around us also jabbed forward although not as smoothly as we three. They were warriors for the working day and for us it was our living. Our spikes and blades tore into the five and three were struck. One, pierced in the eye, fell writhing to the ground while the other two could not continue.

Sam shouted, "Sweep!" and the three billhooks swept from side to side, tearing into shoulders and necks.

Just then I heard, "Loose!" and the sky blackened as the archers sent their missiles into the men in the rear ranks. They were concentrated on the centre, and I heard not only the rattle of arrowheads on metal but the screams and cries of those who were struck.

Sir Edward shouted, "Forward and drive them into the sea!"

I knew that this was not what the king wanted. He had hoped that we would be driven back and that would encourage more of the rebels, including the pretender to land. Sir Edward was too good a soldier to let that happen. He wanted to drive the enemy back and end the battle with as few losses as possible.

Stepping forward the three of us stabbed again. Some of those in the second and third ranks did not wear plate and the spikes on our billhooks drove into flesh. My billhook found a gap in the plate and my hook caught the metal. I jerked the man towards me and lowered my head, he had an open sallet and my helmet smashed into his face. As I raised my head, I saw that he had dropped to his knees. I stepped back and used my full force to smash the blade of the billhook through his helmet and into his skull.

Sir Edward, like the three of us, had advanced and the four of us were in danger of becoming isolated. For Sam, Stephen and me, we had mutual protection and Sir Edward, fighting one mercenary was suddenly struck on the side of the helmet by Sir Quentin d'Urse's poleaxe. Sir Edward fell to the ground, stunned. As Sir Quentin raised his poleaxe to end Sir Edward's life I shouted as I lunged with my billhook, "Face me, murderer!"

Even through the grille of my helmet he recognised my voice and he turned, "You! I knew you were not dead. You shall die here."

I had seen him fight and knew that he was skilled. Stephen and Sam were straddling Sir Edward to protect him, and I would have no help. I would have to fight and face Sir Quentin alone. I was aided by the fact that while I had seen him fight with a pole weapon, he had only seen me fight from the back of a horse with a lance. He was overconfident. Our weapons were similar. Both had protection for the shaft. His advantage was that he was plated and I wore a leather brigandine. He thought to either batter my body or hack through the leather. He chose his war hammer for the first blow and brought his weapon from on high. Instead of blocking it, I swung so that I deflected the hammer head to hit the ground instead of my head. It missed my shoulder by the thickness of a piece of parchment but that was enough. I feinted with the spike at the grille behind which he peered. It is a natural reaction to jerk your head back. It made him readjust his feet and then raise his poleaxe again. This time I saw that he would use the axe head. I swung my billhook at his knee and I spun at the same time. Had I tried the same manoeuvre in plate I might not have made the turn. As it was I not only hurt him but my hook caught on the back of his poleyn and I jerked my billhook as I turned. He lost balance and fell heavily. I had told my companions not to give quarter and I would heed my own advice. I brought my billhook down to smash into his skull but he had quick reactions. He managed to move a little. The billhook smashed into his upper left arm. His scream told me I had broken a bone and the blood that seeped from the wound that I had penetrated the plate.

He rolled and rose. He hurled his now useless poleaxe at me. All around us more men of Kent were fighting deadly combats with the brigands and bandits but for me, this was the only battle. D'Urse drew his sword, "You are not without skill but let us see how you fare against my sword."

He suddenly lunged at me and I had to bring up the billhook to block the blow. The top half had protection but his, as yet unused and sharpened sword hacked through the wooden haft of the billhook. It was now useless. I dropped it and drew my own sword which I knew was the equal of his although he had more skill. My one advantage was that I had a left arm and he did not. I pulled my rondel dagger as he brought his sword down to end this combat quickly. It was a powerful blow and I barely managed to stop it, but my left hand drove up beneath his armpit. There was no plate there and the dagger's point went through the mail undershirt he wore. I forced my right hand to keep his sword from sawing down and hacking into my neck as I twisted and turned the blade into his flesh. The feral scream echoed inside his sallet and when my hand was sprayed with warm blood I felt the resistance from my sword disappear. I did not give Sir Quentin quarter, but I did end his life mercifully quickly. He collapsed in a heap at my feet.

I stared around and saw that the Battle of Deal was over. The survivors were fleeing back to the fleet that had brought them. Perkin had not even landed. I saw at least one hundred and fifty enemy bodies littering the beach. The men of Kent had lost far fewer. I turned and saw Sir Edward groggily rise to his feet supported by Sam and Stephen.

Taking off my helmet to allow cool air to my face I walked towards them, and Sam shook his head, "James, you left us a boy and an apprentice but you have returned a man and a master."

Chapter 19

Sir Edward took off his helmet and said, "Once again I am in your debt, whatever reward the king has for you it will never be enough."

Sam, ever practical said, "And there is plate armour for you. Take it now before another does so. We will search the other bodies we slew."

We all knew that mercenaries would be paid in advance and carry their coins with them. Whatever we took would be shared amongst the three of us. That was our way. The king and the earl arrived before the ships had even hoisted sail. He came directly to me, "Well? Is his body here?"

I had not examined the bodies, but I had seen his face at the stern of the ship that flew his standard. I shook my head, "As I suspected, King Henry, he did not land." The king's face clouded over, and I continued, "He is not a warrior and a figurehead only." I pointed to the body of Sir Quentin, "One of your enemies lies dead but the other mercenary leaders live yet."

"Then I have yet to scotch the snake!"

The earl said as he pointed out to sea, "They sail not north but west, my king. Perhaps they go to Ireland."

"Or Cornwall?"

All eyes swivelled to me, "What do you mean?"

"I mean, King Henry, that if Lord Lovell hears that the Cornish are unhappy he may go there. I know that he has spies everywhere and he would know of such discontent.

"Why did you not say so before?"

"Because, King Henry, that was speculation and I told you just what I knew for certain."

"Hm." He studied me, "You were a good choice as a spy. Perhaps I should use you again."

I shook my head, "A spy is only useful, King Henry, so long as he is anonymous." I waved my hand across the beach, "They will now have an idea that their plans were leaked and my faked death will be viewed with suspicion. More to the point, I do not wish to be a spy."

"You would not serve your country?"

I held up Sir Quentin's sword, "King Henry, I thought that was what I did this morning."

"You have grown impertinent."

"I am sorry, King Henry. Perhaps I should take myself from this place if I cause offence."

"Perhaps you should. I do not like ingratitude."

Sir Edward ventured, "I believe there was talk of a reward for my billman, King Henry."

The king nodded, "What was it, de Vere?"

"A purse of ten crowns, my lord."

"Then give it to him so that he can quit my sight." I began to pick up the plate armour. Stephen started to help me. "But until Perkin Warbeck is in the Tower of London, you are at my beck and call. I would know where you are each and every day. You are the one who will be able to see through any disguise he uses." He nodded to Sir Edward, "You, Sir Edward are responsible. De Vere, go with them and pay the spy." He said it as though he resented having to make the payment.

"Aye, my lord. Sir Edward, I will follow. I need a word with the king in private first." I hoped that the earl was showing the same kind of loyalty to his man as Sir Edward had shown.

The four of us headed back to the castle. Sam saw that Sir Edward was unsteady on his feet and said, "You should see a healer."

"And I will. First, we eat and then ride back to Hedingham. Like you, James, there is a stench around here I like not and it is not the stench of battle but of ingratitude."

We all knew he was not speaking of the dead bodies which were beginning to add to the stink of seaweed but of the king. We were all loyal Englishmen and we served him, yet he seemed to have no respect for us or our efforts. Lord Stanley had discovered that to his cost. He had gained the crown for Henry Tudor but one remark that he would not fight Warbeck if he discovered he was one of the princes from the Tower cost him his head. A man could not speak his mind in this Tudor land.

The earl arrived not long after us and he sent for the healer himself. While we waited, he handed me a purse with the crowns. As he counted them out from his own purse, I guessed that the king had ordered him to pay. He spoke to us all quietly,

"You are loyal men and should know that King Henry was distracted when he spoke to you thus, he had hoped to end this threat but so long as it hangs over us like a sword of Damocles, then he cannot be himself." We all heard the genuine sincerity in his voice and nodded. We had fought alongside the earl. "Sir Edward, you four will be the ones who will ride wherever in this country that we suspect this pretender to be."

"Even Ireland?"

He shook his head and gave a wry smile, "Ireland is Ireland and filled with Irish. If he is there attempting to ferment trouble he will hardly be noticed. Nor do you go to Scotland. He may ally himself with the Scots, but we will not provoke a war with them. Cornwall is a different matter. When I return to Hedingham I will give you a pass to enable you to use royal castles. It is the least that the crown can do." The healer arrived and he left.

By the time the healer had tended to Sir Edward, it was noon and we headed back to London. We would not make Hedingham and so, Sir Edward took the decision to stay in the Tower. While we rode, my plate on a sumpter we had taken, I gave them the details of my adventures from the attack in the inn to the clandestine meeting in Paris through to Mechelen and beyond. When I spoke of Tad, as we neared London Bridge, Sam shook his head, "I knew he was a bad 'un but had he not tried to kill you, James, then you might not have succeeded."

"Did I succeed? The king does not think so."

Sir Edward laughed, "You predicted where and when they would land. If the king had a fleet then perhaps it would have ended. You could have done no more."

The horses we had ridden from Hedingham were still in the stable. When we left the next morning, we took not only those horses but also the ones we had ridden to Dover. As Sir Edward said, it was a reward for our labours and if we were to ride all over the country seeking the pretender then we needed good horseflesh.

I surprised them all when, upon our arrival at Hedingham, the first thing I did was to go to Goliath. "But he is just a sorry sumpter!"

"And that sorry sumpter was a friend when I was a spy. You do not discard your friends just because you no longer need them. I may ride the fine horse we brought from Deal, but Goliath will have just as much attention and will accompany me where I go."

The earl arrived just four days after we did. He brought us news that ships had reported the rebel fleet heading for Ireland. I nodded when I heard the news, "Then, my lord, do I have your permission to visit my home? If you recall it was the letter from my father that brought me to the king's attention. That was almost three years since and my family have had no news." I was determined to go with or without permission. My time in Mechelen had given me a mind of my own. In the event, however, the earl allowed me to go but for no longer than a month and he insisted that Stephen accompany me. He did not want my life risked on the road. That suited the two of us and it was Sam whose nose was put out of joint. However, he had the task of training new billmen. The earl knew that we would have to fight again and soon. Sam and Sir Edward would prepare the men for the war that was not yet over. Sir Edward gave me my belt of coins and added to that which I had from Mechelen, and the ten crowns made me a rich man. I took my father's sallet, falchion and billhook and left my newly acquired plate armour with Sam. We used Goliath as a pack animal and left for the two-hundred-mile journey home. Sir Edward gave us the pass from the earl, and we left on a fine July morning.

I confess that the journey was one of the most pleasant I had ever had. We had good horses, the weather was fine and taking the route through Leicester and Stoke meant that we had no high ground to cover. More, Stephen and I made up for the lost years. He told me of his life, the girls he had met and in two cases bedded since we had parted. I told him more about Jean and Marie as well as Perkin.

"How could you like him, James? He is a traitor who has tried to take King Henry's throne."

I knew that I had changed when I had lived in Mechelen. I tried to explain, "When I was with the pretender, I was able to study the family trees of the kings of England and believe me, Stephen, they are complicated beyond belief. The thrones of

Scotland, France not to mention many other countries in the Empire are all related to the throne. Any one of them has a claim to it. It seems to me that a man may grab the crown through many different methods but he needs to use force of arms to hold on to it. Is Perkin any different?"

"But he has no legitimate claim!"

I shrugged, "He is not the prince who was murdered in the Tower that is for certain but who knows if he has some tenuous link to the crown?"

"But that could be true of any man."

I nodded and said, after a suitable pause, "And that is the conclusion I have come to." I smiled, "You know there are men who study these ancient family ties and one said he could trace the lineage of Richard of Shrewsbury back to the Queen of the land whence you came. He said that he was descended from Queen Cartimandua of the Brigante who ruled before the Romans came. How far back does a man need to go? How many of those descendants married not nobles but ordinary folk and sired children? Could not they rule?"

"What you suggest is treason."

"No, Stephen, I am loyal to the crown and King Henry is as good or as a bad a king as we have had in recent years. Thus far he has not murdered and having traitors executed is understandable. I will fight for him but what I am really fighting for is England. I will fight those who threaten it and what I know of those behind Perkin Warbeck is that they are not loyal Englishmen. Perhaps Sir John Bardolph but the rest? Self-serving and manipulative men."

Stephen laughed, "You know I can hear Sam's words coming from your mouth. You changed while you were away. Do not get me wrong, you are still my dearest friend, but you are different, and I fear that you will outgrow me."

"Ah, that is where you are wrong, for my enforced absence made me realise that the most valuable things I possessed were not money or power but friends and family. I go to visit my family with my friend, and I am the happiest man in the realm and would not exchange places with the king at any price."

However, once we neared Ecclestone, I became nervous. I stopped our horses frequently ostensibly to check for stones but really to delay our arrival. Stephen knew what I did and became exasperated as we passed through Sutton, just three miles from my home. "James, these delays just mean that we will travel in the dark and arrive, perhaps, when all are abed. Is that what you really wish? You either want to see your family or you do not."

He was right and when I remounted, I dug my heels in and we covered the last three miles in under half an hour. I was not sure if any would recognise me as I rode through the farms and outlying houses. We were, however, a point of interest for we were two well-dressed warriors with swords on our belts and we were strangers. Had we just passed through we would still have been the talk of the village for a week. I spied smoke from the small holding and saw a bent old man heading towards it, a bundle of faggots on his back. I thought to hurry and help the man for I could see that he was struggling. As I dug my heels into my horse his hooves clattered on some stones and the old man turned. It was my father. The hale and hearty man I had left almost nine years earlier had become an old man and it was all my fault.

I let go of Goliath's reins and raced to my father. He looked up, not recognising his own son, "Can I help you, my lord?"

I threw myself from the saddle, "Do you not recognise your own son, father? It is James."

He dopped the faggots and I thought he would faint. He shouted as I held him in my arms, "Mother, it is our son, God has returned him to us."

I held him tightly and, as tears coursed down my cheeks, wondered where the mountain of a man had disappeared to. My mother came out of the house, her hair now white and so small I felt I towered over her. She held her apron to her mouth as she wept and hobbled towards me. She buried her red cheeks in my chest and sobbed. I felt the tears coursing down my own and I cared not who saw me thus unmanned.

A voice said, quietly, in my ear, "I will take the animals into the yard and unsaddle them. Go in the house, James. I will see to all."

I nodded to Stephen and led my parents across the small yard and under the low lintel into the humble house that was their home. Everything seemed tiny. How had my memory so deceived me? The room my mother called the parlour was a small room but it was cosy and the fire sparked away. Their two chairs, made by my father, were on either side of the hearth. As I put my mother into her seat she said, "No, my son, you should sit here."

Shaking my head I said, "No mother, I am content for I am home." I dropped to my knees and took my father's right hand in mine, "Forgive me father although what I did to you was unforgivable. I am sorry." I rested my forehead on his knees.

He used his other hand to stroke the hair on the back of my head, "James, I forgave you the instant I woke. I was angry with you, but I would rather have had a malcontent son than lose him. Whence did you go?"

I stood, "That is a tale that shall be long in the telling."

My mother suddenly started and made to rise, "Walter we have company, James has a friend. I have a bed to make up."

"Mother sit. While Stephen and I are here we shall take some of the burden from you. I will be here but a month and I have years to make up for. Where are Alice and Sarah?"

Mother smiled, "Married and with bairns. Alice and John live in Parr and Sarah and Michael live all the way out to Pendlebury."

"I shall find the time to speak with them."

"Are you wed, son?"

"No father. I have been in the service of the king since I left this home, and I am still his servant. I was given leave to visit my home by the knight I serve, Sir Edward of Cowley." The door opened and Stephen shily appeared. "And this is my shield brother Stephen."

Stephen bowed, "God save all those in this house."

My father stood and held out his hand, "Welcome Stephen. You are welcome to our home. The two of you sit for I can see by your clothes that you have ridden hard and we would be poor hosts if we did not fetch food for you."

When we had passed through Warrington, we had called at the market there and made purchases for I had not wished to impoverish my parents. Stephen said, "I have put the ham, cheese, bread and beans we bought in the kitchen. There is plenty there for a meal this night and will take no preparation."

My father smiled and nodded to me, "It is good that you have given up your wild ways and now consort with good men. The two of you take off your cloaks and sit."

They left us and as we did as we had been asked Stephen said, "Your parents are kind folks." I nodded as I looked around at the things I had not seen for nearly nine years and which now seemed so small. Had I grown so much? Stephen said as he sat in my mother's chair, "Wild ways?"

"Indeed," I stared into the fire, "aye, I did many things I now regret. I drank and hung around with reckless youths. I fought and I dishonoured my parents. I am here to make amends."

"You have more than made up for that, James of Ecclestone. Your father will be proud when you tell him."

I shook my head, "How can any man be proud of a son who was a spy and betrayed those who became his friends? I fear that when he hears my tale, he will wish me gone again."

My father entered a short time later with three beakers of ale. We stood. He gave one to Stephen and one to me, "Your mother makes up the beds and the table is laid. Let us drink to the prodigal son returned for my heart is now filled with joy."

We lifted our beakers and drank. I drank but half. My father asked, "And Stephen, are you wed?"

"No, sir, for like James I serve Sir Edward of Cowley."

"I thought the wars were over."

"No, father. It is not long since we fought the Yorkists at the Battle of Deal."

He frowned, "I had not heard of the battle."

Smiling I said, "Kent is far from Lancashire, Father, and word will come. Of course, when it does the tale will bear no relation to the actual battle."

He laughed, "Aye, I have heard tales of Bosworth Field that make me wonder if I was there at all."

My mother opened the door and said, "All is ready. Stephen, forgive our humble abode but while it is mean it is ours and you are welcome to stay as long as you are able."

We sat at the homemade table in the kitchen, my father at the head and he bowed his head, "Dear Lord, we thank you for answering our prayers. We shall now sleep at night. You have kept our son safe and brought him home. We thank you for this bounty. Amen."

The Duchess of Burgundy had given me an ornate eating knife and as I used it to carve off some ham my father said, "I have never seen such a beautiful knife. It looks almost too fine to use. Is there a tale to it?"

Stephen laughed, "Sir, as with everything to do with James, there is a tale that will make your hair stand on end."

My father smiled, "It is Walter, Stephen and as I have few hairs left on my pate, I will risk the hearing."

My mother said, "First my son will eat and when I am satisfied that he has eaten enough then he may talk. Talking while eating shows great disrespect for God's bounty."

Suitably chastised I nodded, and said, "Yes, mother."

My father smiled and I could see that he was content. We had bought good food and it was appreciated but my careful mother, when we had all finished, carefully wrapped what remained. She was ever frugal. As the parlour would be too small for us, we sat at the table in the kitchen warmed by the cosy fire on which my mother cooked everything. I began at the beginning and told all from Mistress Gurton to John of Warrington and the battles of Bramham Moor and Stoke Field. I was judicious in my description to avoid offending my mother, but I saw my father filling in the blanks that I had left. I spoke of the siege of Boulogne and then the result of the letter my father had sent.

He stood and poured more ale, "Had I known it would have an effect I would have sent it sooner. And you came when you received it?"

I shook my head, "That was some years since, Father, and the result was that King Henry chose to make me his spy at the court of the pretender, Perkin Warbeck."

My mother's hand went to her mouth and she made the sign of the cross. My father shook his head, "Then I wish I had never sent it. A spy?"

"You served the king, father and fought his enemies. If you had been asked would you not have gone?"

"But to be a spy is to live in constant fear of your life."

I nodded, "Aye, I know and I am done with that life. I shall be a billman where your enemies are all to your fore and not behind your back."

My mother put her hand on mine and squeezed it, "My poor bairn."

I decided to end my tale there and I stood dramatically, "Aye, well, your poor bairn did not come back a pauper. I reached beneath my doublet and my mother's hand went to her mouth again. Stephen laughed, "James! Mistress, he just takes out his hidden belt. Be not alarmed."

I looked at Stephen, "How did you know?"

"We all knew before we sailed for Calais. We respected your secret."

I took off the belt and laid it, with a thud, on the table. I emptied each of the pouches to make a pile of coins. Reserving but ten I said, "Here father. Take these in recompense for the hurt I caused you."

Their eyes widened and he said, "This is almost a king's ransom. How did you come by this?"

I isolated the ten crowns, "These were payment from the king for my time as a spy." I put another pile to one side, "These were payment from Burgundy for helping them and the rest were taken," I looked my father in the eyes, "after our battles."

He nodded his understanding and then shook his head, "This is too much. We cannot take it."

I sat back. "But you can for we earn good pay from Sir Edward and there will be more like this."

"But they will come when you fight and, as I know, a man has only so much luck and time on a battlefield."

I remembered Jean and Marie, "Do not worry, father. When Perkin Warbeck is in the Tower then I can give up the billhook and begin a family."

He gave me a sad smile, "Then I pray that this poor unfortunate is soon in the king's hands; God help him." He made the sign of the cross.

It was good to be home and the next day as Stephen and I helped my father around the smallholding we were constantly interrupted as the villagers all took it in turns to come and speak with me. I was a five-day wonder. At the end of the sixth day,

Stephen and I mounted our horses so that I could go to visit my sisters. Parr was an easy ride, but Pendlebury would necessitate a whole day. I was mindful of how little time I had but the visits were joyous. They had both married good men and I had two nieces and two nephews. All four were toddlers but I enjoyed bouncing them and throwing them in the air. I gave each of the four a silver coin. It was considered good luck. I managed one more visit to each sister before it was time to return to Hedingham.

The night before we left my father took me to one side while Stephen helped my mother to wash and dry the pots we had used. "Son, it is good that you came home but do not stay away too long. Your mother and I grow old, and I would like to see you wed and with a family before the Good Lord takes us to his bosom."

"And I promise that when my work is done, and I can leave King Henry's service, I shall be home so fast that it was though I rode Pegasus."

"Then I am content."

I left Goliath with my father. The ride north had shown me that he, like my father, was getting old. I wanted his last days to be contented. He could help my father fetch faggots from Ecclestone Wood and my father would show him care and affection for I now knew just how kind my father was. How had I not seen that when I lived at home?

When I returned his helmet, falchion and billhook he said, "I shall never need these again. Keep them."

Stephen said when my father looked doubtful, "He needs them not, Walter for he has a suit of plate, a German helmet and as you can see he has the sword of a gentleman."

I nodded, "Keep them in remembrance of the service they did us both."

He nodded.

I forced myself to be strong as I mounted my horse to ride the two hundred miles back to Sir Edward. Mother wept and I saw my father's rheumy eyes were wet also. I lifted my hat from my head and swept it in a grand manner, "Fear not, father, mother, I shall return and when I do it will be to make a home."

Chapter 20

January 1496

In the months after we returned from Ecclestone, Stephen and I had to adjust back to life in the castle. We were kept informed, through the earl, about Warbeck. He was reported in Ireland and then disappeared. I was restless. My visit home had made me yearn to be close to my parents in their last years. Hedingham never felt like home. I had been there too infrequently and the way I had been used by the earl seemed to put a barrier between us. Sam had acquired new billmen and I threw myself into the daily training. I was a little rusty, but the regular routine soon brought back the familiarity of the weapon. I no longer used my father's billhook. I had bought a new one or, rather, had one made by the weaponsmith.

Once we were back then the three of us, Sam, Stephen, and I became as close as we ever had been. Stephen had endeared himself to the cook in the castle and that meant we were given all sorts of treats while we trained. She had her eye set on him but Stephen seemed to be oblivious to her charms. Sam tried to take advantage of her interest and to bed her but she would have none of it. It was either Stephen or none. We would normally take warm pies, freshly made, with us to train. If the other billmen resented it, they did not show it but then again they were all younger men. Time takes its toll and some men had died, not all from wounds, whilst others had left to begin families or rejoin abandoned ones. We three were the constant and, once I had recovered all my skills, it was Stephen and me who were, once more, Sam's lieutenants.

However, I was mindful of the way I had joined and when I saw a billman, roughly my age, show more skills than the others, I nurtured him. His name was Michael and he had much in common with Stephen and me. He was solitary but diligent. My nurturing was not gentle. I intended to make him the best of the rest, the equal of we three. Each day he became better and responded well to my comments and advice. So it was that a month or so after our return William, Sir Edward's squire, came to find us and said, "Captain Sam, his lordship wishes to see the

three of you in the Great Hall." He did not need to name us for
all knew the three were as one. Someone had called us the
Trinity but we had stopped the use of that name. We did not wish
to offend God.

Sam nodded, "Keep on training while we are away."

As we left I thought it might be interesting to see who took
charge for they were all equal.

The knight's face was careworn when we entered and he was
scrutinising a parchment. One of the things I had learned at
Mechelen was how to read. I could even read French and
Flemish, or some, at least.

"William, guard the door and let none enter."

Disappointed the squire said, "Yes, my lord."

Holding the parchment up Sir Edward said, "Warbeck is in
Scotland, and he has with him an army. It may not be one that
can threaten us yet but he is in Scotland and King James may
well choose to side with him. The Scots and the French are as
thick as thieves." He looked at me.

I nodded, "At the court of the duchess I often saw both
French and Scots. They were ever eager to ferment trouble for
England and it seemed to me that their joint endeavours were
fuelled by a common hatred of England."

Stephen nodded, "The land all the way to the Tees and
beyond is often subject to the raids of the Scots even when we
enjoy what is supposed to be peace. If Warbeck is there, then it
will not be long before they cross the Tweed."

Sir Edward folded the parchment and placed it upon the table,
"And the king and the earl concur with that opinion. We have
been ordered to ride north and alert the Earl of Northumberland
although I do not doubt that he will already be aware of the
danger. Our task is to find Warbeck and, if we can, fetch him to
London."

Sam laughed, "We? I am confident that we are the best of
billmen, my lord, but I feel that there may be a few hundred of
his supporters who may try to stop us."

"Your tongue is as sharp as ever. We will work with the lords
of the Northern Marches but James here is the only one who
knows Warbeck on sight. Remember Deal? He did not land and

all we saw was his livery. He is a fearful foe and may well hide from danger. What say you, James?"

I nodded and recounted the tale of the mock battle, "Until his horse took flight, he was convinced that he was Alexander reborn and after that, a nervous doe nibbling grass at the edge of a forest. He will flee at the first sign of danger."

Stephen said, "And as James knows, we have a monumental journey north. At this time of year, it will be hard going."

"Aye, we will have to take two horses each. William will have to act as servant and squire for the horses. Sam, you will need to leave one to lead the billmen. The earl wishes his men to be ready to respond to any danger."

"Aye, my lord. When we return to the practice yard, we may well see one we can promote."

I asked, "And when do we leave?"

"This afternoon. I know we can make but a few miles north, but we cannot tarry. Each day will see us travel forty miles or more. We have more than three hundred miles to reach the land close to the Scots. It will be eight days in the saddle."

Sam shook his head, "I pray, James, that you have more of your magic salve for if not my backside will look like Beelzebub's face!"

When we reached the training ground, we saw the men drilling and there was order. Michael was shouting out orders and Big John, the loudmouth of the group, sported a bloody nose. As we neared them then I saw that Michael's knuckles were also bloody.

Sam gave me a knowing look and said, "We have our leader. You must have trained him well and I did not know he was so handy with his fists. Knocking Big John down must be like felling an oak." We stood before them and Sam put his hands on his hips, "Well, ladies, I can see that words have been exchanged." Both Michael and Big John put down their heads. "Whatever the cause, although I can guess, it ends now. Clear?" There were mumbles from the two of them and Sam shouted, "I want to know that all of you heard me. Is that clear?"

They all stood to attention and shouted, "Yes, Captain."

"Good. Now Sir Edward has decided that we three have done such a good job that we deserve a little trip away with him. We shall be leaving for a short while. In our absence then Michael will be corporal and paid accordingly." Michael's head shot up and he had a shocked look on his face. "You will continue to train every day and when we return then be prepared to march to war."

Roger of Dauentre asked, "Whom do we fight?"

Sam beamed, "Why the king's enemies, of course, but does it really matter so long as you are paid and Sir Edward satisfied?" He waved to Michael, "Come and speak with us." He came over and we moved a little further from the rest. "I did not ask you if you were happy with this. Speak now. Are you content to lead and can you handle them?"

"Yes, Captain. I am just surprised is all and I thank you."

Sam laughed, "Leading is a lonely post, Michael. You lose friends when you are given command."

He said, innocently, "Yet you three are as close as brothers, captain."

He nodded, "I am lucky and gifted with a honeyed tongue. You may not be so lucky." As we headed to gather our war gear Sam said, "He will do."

"Aye, and I am pleased for I like him."

In the end Sir Edward took the decision to allow Geoffrey of Aylesbury to train the men. It was a mistake but I knew that Michael would use the time to hone his own skills.

This would be the first time since I had returned to England that I might, once more, be in harm's way. I took Sir Quentin's plate with me. William the squire would be leading a sumpter with Sir Edward's plate and we used mine to counterbalance his. We did not bother with billhooks; we would be using swords. We had our helmets and they hung from the spare horse we each would lead. We also took spare clothes and food. We were all experienced campaigners. We still had the pass from the earl and could stay in royal castles but who knew when we might have to endure a cold camp. William led Sir Edward's spare horse and the sumpter. It did not do to have a knight leading a horse. For his part, William was just happy to be part of the adventure. He had arrived too late for the Battle of Deal, and he was desperate to show Sir Edward that, one day, he would earn his spurs. He saw this ride north as his opportunity. For my part, the thought of knighthood did not even enter my mind. I was happy with what I was. I had lived the life of a noble but preferred the life with my friends and my family. It was simpler.

In the end, it took us ten days to reach Alnwick. The old Earl of Northumberland had been murdered seven years earlier and his son, the new earl was but ten. The Earl of Westmoreland, Sir Ralph Neville was at the Percy castle to begin the muster. Our letter from the king and the Earl of Oxford gained us entry into the fortress. As was to be expected we three billmen had to wait in the inner bailey while Sir Edward and William entered. There was a time that I might have felt slighted but no longer. This way meant I had to bow and scrape less than had I entered the Great Hall. We chatted with the men who were also waiting outside. A couple wore Percy livery, but the others were spearmen, billmen and men at arms gathered from the north. We led our horses to the water trough for they were thirsty having ridden hard.

One spied the livery of the Earl of Oxford. Since Bosworth Field, it had become well known and he came over to speak to us. He had the look of an old campaigner. His plate was not the latest fashion and he wore mail beneath it as it was not as good as the plate I had taken from Sir Quentin. His sword had a plain scabbard but he also sported a hatchet and a knife; both were the weapons of a fighter. "What are three southerners doing all the way up in the north? Are you lost?"

Sam was going to answer but Stephen answered. Since we had crossed the Tees, his Northumbrian accent had returned, "Watch who you call southerners. I was born not twenty miles from here."

The man at arms eyes widened, "No offence meant my friend. I am Gerard of Etal and I serve in the castle on the Tweed, Norham."

Stephen nodded, "Then I am surprised you are here with the rebels and the Scots so close."

He laughed, "The King of Scotland, it seems, has found a bride for this pretender. There will be no fighting until he has married Lady Catherine Gordon and they have held a tournament. We have time to muster but the earl only arrived last night. Since the Earl of Northumberland was murdered the Scots have raided at will and our castles are all short of men." He looked beyond us, "Are there more of you?"

It was Sam's turn to speak, "Friend, we fought at Stoke Field and Boulogne. I do not think a few hairy arsed Scots will cause us too much trouble."

"You would think so would you not? Your friend here," he paused.

"Stephen."

He nodded, "Stephen will tell you that in a pitched battle we will trounce the Scots any day of the week and twice on Sunday but that is not how they fight. They sneak across the river like pack rats and ravage where they deem us to be the weakest and then trot back home with the sheep and captives that they have taken."

I asked, "Will this not be different? They have Perkin Warbeck with them, and he seeks to be King of England."

"That is true, and it is why we wait to gather more men. We need to be able to strike wherever their largest force is gathered. I am here with Sir Simon of Norham. He needs to know that if Norham is attacked support will be forthcoming."

We then chatted about the local food and ale for, until our betters returned, any words we used would be idle chatter. I began to curry my two horses while we spoke. When I had been at Mechelen I had learned that nobles often judged a man on how well his mount was presented. I had found that even a sumpter like Goliath responded well to such care and I did not like having idle hands. I was also hungry, and the smell of pies, stews and breads being cooked wafted over from the kitchens.

"What is the food like here?"

"Plain but wholesome fare. This is the north." Gerard pointed to the gate that led to the outer bailey. We had entered through the town gate and barbican. The outer bailey drifted down to the outer walls and the river. "There is a veritable sea of tents and hovels yonder. We have but five hundred men yet and the Percy family is keen to show that despite having lost the earl, the family is still generous. You will not be disappointed. I saw, this morning, wagons coming from Warkworth, and they were laden with shellfish. At the very least we shall have a fish stew this night and, who knows, perhaps some of the shellfish."

We spoke of the mussels we had enjoyed in Boulogne and then spoke, as soldiers do, of our favourite fare; the food we had enjoyed and the best ales. A tap on my shoulder brought me face to face with a liveried equerry. He was from the Earl of Westmoreland, "Are you the one they call James of Ecclestone?"

"I am."

"Then I pray you to accompany me. His lordship would have conference with you."

Stephen said as I followed him, "If they serve food then we will save a platter for you." Stephen truly was a friend who was always looking after my interests.

The sentries parted their halberds as we approached, and we headed up the stairs where I could hear the hubbub of voices as nobles and gentlemen discussed the threat. What I noticed was that there was no hysteria. Calmness prevailed and the volume of noise was just the numbers of voices giving an opinion. These lords were used to danger and lived cheek by jowl with Scots who constantly threatened to try to take back the land they thought was theirs. Perkin Warbeck was but another burr beneath the saddle. I now understood more about Stephen who had ever been calm in battle and viewed adversity with a philosophical attitude I could not emulate. Now I saw why.

The equerry deftly parted the nobles like Moses at the Red Sea. He did so politely but firmly, steering a course to the dais where the Earl of Westmoreland sat as did the child Earl of Northumberland. William was standing apart and looking very uncomfortable. Standing nearby with his head close to the older earl was Sir Edward. The movement of the ones betwixt drew us to their attention and stopping their conversation Sir Edward pointed at me. The older earl was a hardened veteran of the north. I had not seen him at Bramham Moor but that was because Sir Henry had not waited for the earl who was bringing men to our aid. In the bailey, the talk had been of his steadfastness and his ability to thwart the Scots. His eyes bored into me as I bowed,

"My lord."

"Sir Edward here tells me that you know this Warbeck by sight."

"Yes, my lord."

"A spy, eh?" Shaking his head he said, "I wished we did not need them however from what Sir Edward has told me but for your efforts, then a landing might have been made in the south so I suppose your courage paid off."

I knew, from my time at Mechelen, that often it was better for inferiors to remain silent while their betters spoke on.

He leaned forward, "And have you the courage to risk your life again?"

I nodded, "My lord, I swore to serve the king and to protect England, aye."

His eyes never left me as I answered and seemingly satisfied, he said, "You are right, Sir Edward, the man has steel. For my part, I would rather face a dozen men sword to sword rather than sneak around, but I suppose we must do all that we can to nip this attack in the bud." He looked at Sir Edward, "And the king wants this Warbeck prisoner?"

"He does, my lord."

"Then whilst I am confident that I can defeat them in the field I am not certain that we can guarantee Perkin Warbeck will live."

I coughed and then ventured an opinion. I had seen courtiers do that at Mechelen. They coughed and spoke. At first, I thought they all had the winter sickness but later learned it was a way of announcing their intention to venture an opinion. I looked the Earl in the eye as I spoke, "My lord, you need not fear that Warbeck will be in the fore wielding a sword. He will be a spectator."

The young earl leaned forward and spoke, "But we heard that the King of Scotland gave him a shining suit of white armour and that he was at a tourney."

I smiled, "My lord, he will wear the armour and play the part of the hero. He might even have pranced and posed in the tourney but if he struck a blow then I am a Frenchman."

Ralph Neville smiled, "Your words sound true, and I can see you know this man. You may be the best chance we have of doing as the king bids us." He nodded as though he had made up his mind, "The Scots are still north of the Tweed. We have fought them of old and know whence they will come. We have four castles that block their favoured route south, Norham, Etal,

Twesilhaugh and Heaton. They will attack one of them and if they have enough men, all four. Norham they shall never take. The Bishop of Durham has improved the defences and, while they may besiege it and pound at it with these infernal bombards, it will not fall and any siege will allow me to bring my army and crush the Scots. The other three, however, are small and weak. The de Greys left Heaton to a constable and live in Howick. Etal is but a strongly defended keep. Twesilhaugh is the one most in danger as whilst it is a good castle it is closest to the border. Sir Edward, I would have this James of Ecclestone cross the Tweed now before the Scots have finished celebrating the wedding and building up the courage to cross to England. You need not accompany him but he will need a companion, preferably one who knows this land, to fetch me word when the Scots have crossed. I want you, James of Eccleston to be on hand when we attack so that Warbeck can be identified. If what you say is true, then he will be in little danger from the fighting, but you have been in battle and know that once the blood is up it is often hard for men to restrain their arms. You must be on hand to see that Warbeck lives."

Sir Edward said, loyally once more, "My lord, I will not send one of my men to do aught that I will not. I will take all my men. There be but five of us and yet I would say they are the equal of any conroi of northern knights."

"Boldly and bravely spoken Sir Edward. Very well." The equerry had hovered close enough to be summoned but far enough away not to have heard anything and when Ralph Neville waved him over he was at his lord's side as though he was a noonday shadow, "Fetch Sir Simon." As the equerry disappeared into the brightly liveried throng the Earl said, "Sir Simon has come from Norham. Return with him. The men of Norham know the best ways across the river and the secret places men may hide. I fear that five of you may be hard to hide but you seem to know your business."

A young knight approached with his squire a step or two behind and bowed, "You sent for me, my lord?"

"Aye, I have the orders for the constable. I would have you return hence and take with you Sir Edward and his mesne. They act under my orders and those of the king."

The knight looked at me and his eyes widened but he nodded and said, "Yes my lord. When do we leave?"

"Stay until you have eaten for I hold a feast this night and you can leave first thing. Which road shall you take?"

"The coastal route will be the quickest and the one where we are the least likely to find danger. If these men are to get to Norham I would take them there safely."

"As you will." The hand dismissed us and bowing we walked backwards before turning around.

I walked behind the two with William and Sir Simon's squire. Sir Simon spoke quietly to Sir Edward, "That you were taken directly to the earl bespeaks well of you and tells me that despite your appearance your mission is urgent. You were sent by the king?"

Sir Edward nodded and said, "Aye, Sir Simon, but this is not the place for conversation. I impugn the honour of no man here but we both know that there are northern lords who find it politic to keep a foot in Scotland whilst living in England."

Sir Simon turned to look at me and he smiled, "You have a sharp mind and I wonder that a simple billman is afforded a conference with the two earls. I will await enlightenment, but I confess that I am intrigued."

Sir Simon looked around for his man at arms and I said, "Is it Gerard of Etal that you seek, my lord?" He nodded and I pointed to where he was. Stephen and Sam flanked him and the sudden laughter told me that Sam had regaled them with another of his stories.

"You are sharp, billman and I look forward to hearing your tale. John, tell Gerard that we leave on the morrow and to be ready before dawn. Until then the time is his." His squire nodded and hurried off, "Sir Edward, perhaps we should adjourn with our squires so that I might be apprised of all that I need to know. The earl's words were sketchy at best."

"Of course." He turned to me, "I will see you and the others in the morning." I saw, like Sir Edward did, the surprise on Sir Simon's face. Sir Edward smiled, "I need say no more to James of Ecclestone for he and the others can be trusted to both hold their tongues and their ale. When the morning comes, they shall be ready. This short hop of thirty miles is as nothing after the three hundred we have ridden thus far."

That Sir Edward trusted us so much and was so complimentary about us made me feel almost like his equal. I was not but Sir Edward always remembered whence he had come.

As I neared my friends Sam and Stephen affected a bow, "Ah, my lord, you have deigned to grace us with your presence. How was it at the high table?"

I laughed at the banter, "Let us say, Sam Sharp Tongue, that I was not out of place!"

Sam laughed and shook his head, "The earl will need to enlarge his gatehouse so that you can get your big head through it. Come, food is about to be served and there is a comely northern wench that has caught my eye. She appears to have pies that appeal to me." He winked, "And breasts that could nurse a wild boar!"

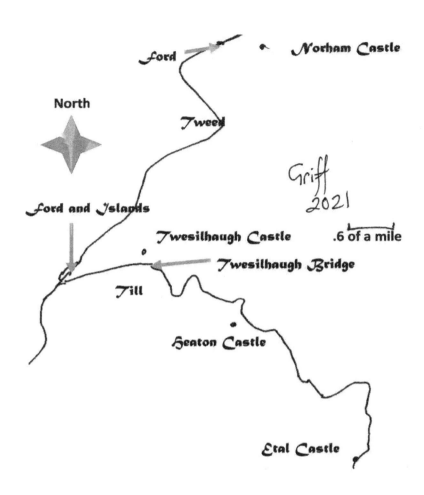

Chapter 21

You meet some people and you care not if you ever see them again but there are others who are different and, from the moment you meet, you are firm friends. So it was with Gerard of Etal. He and Sam, in one night of drinking and joking, had become as close as Stephen and me. More, the three of us felt that we could trust Gerard with our lives and was, although we had never fought alongside him, a shield brother. William, Sir Edward's squire, was a good fellow and we liked him but he had his eye on a greater prize than friendship with billmen. The Earl of Oxford had pressed Sir Edward to take him on as a squire as a favour to a friend for he was the third son of a noble who was a little impoverished. So, as we rode north, the two squires had their heads closeted together, as did the two knights and the four of us rode easily at the rear, the three of us from Hedingham leading our spare horses.

"How did you come to own such good horses? I am a man at arms and mine is as a sumpter compared with yours."

Sam happily told him the tale of our wild ride to London and thence to Deal. He tapped his nose, "The horse master at the Tower did not ask for them back and so we kept them. It was a small price for the king to pay to save his kingdom."

I shook my head, "I do not think that Warbeck threatens the kingdom. He is being manipulated by others."

Sam shook his head, "James here has a jaundiced view of this Warbeck, he likes him."

"Had you met him you would too. He is a fool but a pleasant fool." I smiled, "You two might get on... if you could be pleasant!"

Everyone laughed and Sam joined in, "I am what I am and people take me for that. I have a sharp tongue I confess and that is why I do not suffer fools gladly."

Stephen turned, "Are my ears deceiving me, James, did Sam Sharp Tongue just say we were not fools?"

Sam laughed, "Not as foolish as most."

I broached the subject that was closest to my heart, "Gerard, when we cross the Tweed, will we be able to use our horses?"

We all became serious once more as he answered, "You could but it would be a mistake. You will be using the trails and the woods. Horsemen stick to the roads and your horse dung would warn those who watch the Scottish bank that enemies were abroad. You will have to use your feet, I fear."

"But is there not a great deal of ground to cover? We might miss our prey."

"The enemy when they come will use the road. From Norham to Twesilhaugh which is the other castle close to the Tweed, it is but three miles. They will attack either Norham or Twesilhaugh first and then move on to Etal and Heaton. We are strong enough to survive but the others? I would place yourself close to the ford where the River Till meets the River Tweed. To be honest you need not cross the Tweed but do not tell my master I told you so."

I shook my head, "This land is unfamiliar to me. Why does the Earl place so much faith in me?"

Stephen said, sagely, "Because Sir Edward has belief in what you can do. If we suggest we stay on the English side of the river then he will heed our advice."

Gerard looked at us, "A knight, heeding advice?"

Sam said, quietly, "Aye, Gerard of Etal, for many years he was a man at arms such as you. He did not suck at a noble's teat when he was a bairn. He is hewn from the same rough clay as we."

I said nothing but since my time in Mechelen, I wondered if there was such a difference and if having noble blood made any difference. Warbeck seemed, despite his humble beginnings, to have as much nobility as most and more than many of the nobles I had met.

The road we took was a relatively gentle one and the sea was always just a few miles east of us. We spied the royal castle at Bamburgh and the monastery on Holy Island. The air was bracing but with the sun shining and good company it was a pleasant ride and certainly the thirty miles passed quicker and easier than the journey north.

At one point Stephen looked to the north and said, to me, "My former home lies north of here. This land has both fond and frightening memories for me. When the Scots came, they destroyed not just the homes but many lives. That part of this land will be forever haunted." He turned his head and I saw that his eyes were wet.

Norham rose from the trees with its massive donjon dominating the skyline. I saw why Gerard was so confident about the fortress but as we passed through the gatehouse and headed for the bridge over the ditch, I could not help but notice there were few guns and the ones I could see looked small in comparison to the bombards we had used at Boulogne. Was this scrimping from the Bishop of Durham? Certainly a couple of northward facing bombards on the top of the mighty keep would have a good field of fire. I smiled to myself. I had been a soldier but a short time and yet here was I ready to criticise my betters. We stabled our horses in the outer bailey. The hard journey from the south meant that they were ready for a period of rest and Gerard was probably right. Moving on foot would be easier than riding through what looked like leg-breaking terrain for a horse. After grooming and watering our horses we took all our gear, including my plate. I doubted that I would need it unless there was a battle, we were, after all, seeking one man but after the incident with Tad, I determined that I would take my breastplate. It was not heavy and an enemy who thought I wore just a jack would have a rude shock.

I saw as we entered the inner bailey, why Sir Simon had been in Alnwick seeking aid. I counted but ten knights and whilst there was twice as many archers and men at arms it was still a small force to face the might of a Scottish army and an army of mercenaries. While Sir Edward and William were taken to the keep, we were led by Gerard to the warrior hall. We had arrived early in the afternoon and had plenty of time to seek a place to lay down our gear. It was clear, as we soon entered the warrior hall, that Gerard was a well-respected warrior and that made me more comfortable about leaving our belongings there while we scouted. My money purse had almost been emptied after my visit to my family at Ecclestone, but I had more than enough with me, and we would all be well rewarded after we had found the enemy.

That evening we ate fish stew. We were so close to the sea and the river teemed with salmon that Gerard said they ate fish four days out of seven and only ate meat on one. I had rarely eaten salmon and I enjoyed it. Gerard promised that before we left, he would procure for us, some provisions. The wink he had from the comely cook left us in no doubt that he was bedding her and enjoyed better fodder as a result.

The lords who run castles seem to think that they are all-seeing and that they know everything that there is to know. It is not true and as we ate we learned much. Gerard's approval of us meant men were open and we spoke with two hunters who had been across the river to kill some Scottish deer; venison that we would be eating once it had been hung. They told us that they had seen the trails of horses and scouts heading along the river to the Twesilhaugh crossing. They were astute men and as the tracks were fresh, they guessed that they had been sent by the Scots to ascertain the depth of our defences.

I said to Gerard, "Will the constable not know this?"

He laughed, "Unless he asked them then no. Men like Alan of the Woods do not speak to the constable unless spoken to." He lowered his voice, "If you would have my advice, I would stay this side of the river. We keep a good watch for a mile up and downstream. That leaves you with a two-and-a-half-mile section to watch."

Sam asked, "Will the garrison of Twesilhaugh not have men watching?"

Gerard shook his head, "With but twenty men in the garrison they will hunker down behind their walls. If the enemy comes, then the folk who live in the village will flee to the castle with all that they can carry. That way the walls will be manned but if the Scots have bombards, then the castle will fall in hours not days."

I used my eating knife to slice some ham to go with the salmon, "Then it all depends upon Sir Ralph Neville and when he can get here."

"Do not expect them here as quickly as we made the journey. When we left Alnwick, the muster was not yet complete and it could take them a week to reach us. They will be afoot."

Despite the confidence of, seemingly, everyone around us about our ability to find Warbeck, I was not sure. I knew that we could alert the castles to the danger of the attack but penetrating the iron collar they would have around Warbeck was a different matter. Lord Lovell and, if he still lived, Sir John Bardolph would have Robert and Giuseppe with their men, four deep around the would-be king.

Surprisingly we were not summoned that night and we retired with full bellies and, in Sam and Gerard's case, the unsteady gait of men who have satiated their need for drink. The next morning we all rose early but that was a call of nature and the need to make water. As we did, we could smell the bread and pies being prepared. If there was a siege, then there would be no hot food and men would make the most of hot food whilst they could. The garrison would have to be on cold rations and so we would eat well until we left. The comely wench flirted outrageously with Sam and a tryst was made for that night. It was not meant to be for even as we finished the first of the pies we were summoned.

Gerard said, "Fear not, I will save you some pies."

The servant said, "You are summoned too, Captain Gerard."

The comely wench, Katie, laughed, "Do not worry, I will watch your food, Sam Sharp Tongue." Sam gave her a kiss and then hurried after us as we headed to the imposing entrance to the donjon. We passed the guardhouse and then climbed, not the main staircase but a smaller one that twisted around the walls. Sir Edward, Sir Simon and the constable were awaiting us. I saw that Sir Edward wore his breast and backplate. Their squires had jugs of ale at the ready.

It was Sir Edward who spoke. Sir Simon and the constable were spectators, "We leave this morning to spend the next days, perhaps weeks, in the woods watching for the enemy. Gerard of Etal, Sir Simon has given us permission to ask if you would accompany us. We need a man with local knowledge and..."

Grinning he nodded, "I would be offended, my lord, if I was left behind."

"Good. Our numbers mean that we can send messengers back here and yet still watch for Warbeck. Go and prepare but keep your tongues still."

Sir Simon nodded, "Aye, for while we trust everyone within Norham, some live in the village and what they deem to be petty gossip may well be valuable intelligence to an enemy."

We hurried back to the warrior hall. I took out my breastplate and had Stephen fasten it on me. I noticed that Gerard used his breast and backplate. It made me feel less of a fool for arming myself thus. I slipped a plain tunic over the top and, after fastening my sword slipped Tad's dagger in my boot and my other two in my belt. I hung my costrel from my belt.

I looked to Gerard, "Should we take helmets?"

He shook his head, "Had we open ones then I would say aye, but a closed and visored sallet will get us killed a lot quicker."

Katie with a disappointed look on her face, followed by another servant girl, brought in some loaves, pies, a cheese and some ham. "The steward told us to fetch this to you." She looked at Sam, "Does this mean I will sleep alone this night?"

He took her chin in his hands and kissed her full on the lips, "Aye, but when we return, you shall need neither blanket nor cover. It is like the smell of a good pie, Katie, my sweet, the wait enhances the appetite. We will not be long."

"And where do you go?"

Sam tapped his nose, "We hunt for special delicacies."

I smiled. My friend knew how to be enigmatic. After dividing up our supplies between us we packed them in hessian sacks we carried upon our backs, and each took an ale skin. We would either make hovels or convert our cloaks into tents. We headed across the bridge towards the west gate that led through the village. I saw the gunners already preparing their cannons. They were falcons and falconets. A useful gun and, firing through the embrasures, would be well protected but they were not the weapon that could destroy large bombards. Once the Scottish bombards started to fire then the walls above the embrasures would begin to fall. Of course, if we did our job and if Sir Ralph Neville arrived in time, then the walls of Norham might be safe.

Once we reached the village, Gerard pointed to our right and led us between two mean buildings down a muddy well-trodden path to the river. Sir Edward's eyes widened but he said nothing. We had Gerard as our guide, and it was as well to heed his advice. We were, of course, seen but that could not be helped. Once we reached the river, we saw stones just below the surface of the water and I deduced that this was where the locals crossed into Scotland for whatever purposes. One, of course, would be to take wood for their fires and to hunt for rabbits and other small animals. Our purpose was more sinister. The water came up to our knees. The fine boots I had been given in Mechelen were well made but icy river water pouring over the top would do neither them nor my feet any good. Once on the other side, we had the difficult task of ascending the bank. My breastplate made it harder for me than Sam, Stephen, and William.

Halfway up Gerard stopped. I thought it was to gather his breath, but he knelt down and examined the muddy prints. He stood and said, quietly, "These are not the marks of soldiers but villagers. The enemy, whilst they might have scouted this side of the river did not use the steppingstone causeway."

We climbed the bank and then rearranged our loads. Sam asked, "If the Scots know of the stones will they not use them?"

"They would if they were still there when the Scots come. Sir Simon will bring men down this day and the stones will be moved. It will inconvenience the locals, but they will be safer. The moving of the stones is always a harbinger of danger, and they will prepare too."

We soon found the path that paralleled the river. Gerard knew his business and he pointed to the imprint of a boot. "They headed down to Twesilhaugh and then returned." A few paces later he dived off to the side and grabbed a piece of blue cloth, "And here one went to make water. I could not smell it and that means it is days old. Come, Sir Edward, we can hurry now and recross the river."

Sir Edward said as we followed the man at arms, "How can you be certain?"

"The hunters told me where they had seen the tracks and I gave us a soaking to confirm it."

Sam snorted, "Next time, just inconvenience yourself and I will have dry feet!"

We headed down the path in the formation we had used when crossing the river. Gerard at the fore, followed by Sir Edward and William, then Stephen, me and finally Sam. Sam and I had the unenviable task of constantly turning to see if we were being followed. Just as we were scouting out the enemy it was possible that they might be waiting for us. About half a mile before the island we passed a large clearing to the north. It looked to be a place others had camped before for the trees had been hewn down. I wondered if we might use it, but Gerard pushed us on.

When we reached the island in the middle of the river, closer to
Twesilhaugh, we stopped, and we waited while Gerard ensured
that there were no locals fishing. He returned to the trees and led
us down. Here the water was just as deep on one side of the
island but shallower on the other. As we passed over the island
Gerard pointed to tracks in the mud. Had he not pointed them out
to us then I would have been none the wiser, "They crossed the
river here and then back. This is where the attack will be."

William said as we emerged from the river to climb the
southern bank of the Tweed, "Then we can return to Norham and
tell the constable."

Sir Edward shook his head as we left the path to climb
through the trees, "We shall warn him, of course, but we are here
to ascertain if Warbeck is with them. That is the prize we seek."

William was a pleasant enough man but he was a little dull-
witted. Sir Edward tolerated him, no more. We did not travel far
and Gerard led us to a small clearing on high ground. We could
see, through the trees, the northern bank and, I guessed, the path
we had taken. "Here is as good a place to wait. Sir Edward,
while you and the others make the camp, I will return to advise
the constable and Sir Simon what I have discovered."

William apart, the rest of us knew what we were about. As
Stephen and I began to tie pieces of cord between trees the squire
asked, "What do you do, there?"

"Traps and snares. We cannot enclose ourselves completely
but this way we do not need to have more than one man on
watch at night."

"On watch?"

Sir Edward sighed, "Each of us will have a three-hour watch
at night. That way we will not be surprised."

We would not risk a fire. There is nothing else that gives
away the position of a camp than the smell of woodsmoke. We
were far enough away from Twesilhaugh that the smell of their
fires was faint. We would have to endure cold rations but the
pies we had brought, made with mutton and carrots, would still
be warm when we ate them. Out of courtesy to Gerard, we
waited until he had returned before we ate them. In truth, we did
not have long to wait for it took us time to build the hovels we
would use for sleep. William was bemused. Hitherto he had

enjoyed the comfort of a tent. I saw him looking askance at the leaf and branch covered home he would use to sleep.

I took one of my cloaks and laid it down on the ground, over some grass and weeds I had torn and spread around, "This shall be my bed and with my second cloak above me I shall be snug."

"I only brought one cloak."

I nodded, "Next time you will bring two." I took off my breastplate. I doubted that I would need it any time soon.

By the time Gerard returned we were finished, and we took out the warm pies to share. As we ate he said, "Sir Simon has ridden to Twesilhaugh, and the constable has sent word to Alnwick."

Sir Edward swallowed some of the delicious pie and wiped his mouth with his napkin, "It is one thing for Sir Ralph to know whence the enemy come but if the muster is not complete then he cannot come to our aid."

I nodded. That meant that there were three castles, by Gerard's own admission, that would fall and with them the villages that were close by. They would lose their livestock, their homes and, perhaps, their lives. This part of England was a dangerous place to live.

Chapter 22

For the first two days, we just watched and tried to help Sir Edward train William in the skills he would need. As a squire, he understood his duties around a castle and a court, but the outside world appeared to be a mystery. Gerard showed him on the second morning, the way back to the castle. We had decided that he would be the one to take the news to the constable. I think Sir Edward chose him because he was not confident in his ability to be of use if we had to act quickly. We also had a night of rain and William's hovel was not as well made. It leaked and when we rose, he was wet whilst we were all bone dry.

On the third morning, we spied men across the river. Leaving William at the camp we edged our way to the undergrowth on the south bank and peered through the grass. It soon became clear that these were Scots. They were local men, living north of the Tweed who knew the land; they wore homemade buskins and breeks. They wore no brigandine but instead wore a homespun tunic and they each carried a short, curved sword much like a falchion but with a basket hilt. They had caps upon their heads and were clearly scouts. They halted opposite us and I wondered when they stared if we had been seen but their interest appeared to be on something to the north of them. Then I realised, it was the large open area we had spied days earlier. Seemingly satisfied they continued down the path.

Sir Edward waved Stephen and me to head down the path to spy the ford. We crawled back to the camp and then, after standing, headed down the now familiar path to the ford and the rough road to Twesilhaugh. The scouts were moving cautiously, and we reached our vantage point before they arrived at the ford. The men knew their business. There were six of them and they viewed the island and ford from the safety of the trees. I saw their keen eyes as they looked for footprints. The rain had washed away ours and they seemed content that none had crossed into Scotland. They left two men to examine the path along the Tweed and we spied the other four as they headed back.

We returned to the others and, without saying a word lay down. Soon we heard the noise of men as they came down the narrow path. If this was a large army it would take all day for them to pass us. The first elements, after the scouts, were the horsemen. These were the hobelars, light horsemen who could act as scouts. They halted opposite us and when they brought their horses to drink, Sir Edward tapped us on the shoulders; he began to move back. Leaving Sam on watch we slid backwards and only rose when we were beyond their sight. We hurried to the camp, and he said to Gerard," Well?"

"It is their army or part of it at least."

"That is my conclusion too. William, head back to the castle and tell the constable that we have spied the vanguard of the enemy army. We will remain here."

"And when I have delivered my news, what then, my lord?"

"If it is deemed safe then you return here. Otherwise, you obey Sir Simon."

He looked crestfallen, "Yes, my lord."

When he had scurried off Sir Edward smiled, "He should be safer there than here."

Gerard shaded his eyes to peer up through the canopy of trees. There were scudding clouds, but we could see a cloudy sun, "It is gone noon. I will rejoin Sam. If they make a camp, then that tells us that their target is Twesilhaugh."

"And if not?"

"Then we will have to find a new place to hide for it will mean that they intend to attack Norham, and this is their best route to do so."

"We will prepare food and I will relieve you soon."

With William gone we had more food to share. We had supplies for another two days and we prepared the food for all five of us. We ate, drank and made water. All of us knew that lying and waiting just encouraged a bladder to demand relief. We knew not how long we might have to watch."

Leaving Stephen to watch the camp Sir Edward led me back to relieve the others. We had heard noise from the north while we had eaten and now, I could see why. The hobelars had moved off and a dozen horsemen, they looked like the mounts of knights, were being watered by squires. We could hear the noise of tents being erected. I wondered at this for they were not being secretive. True, they had not crossed the river but the noise they made might be heard from the castle.

It was when I recognised Robert of Guisborough that I stiffened and tapped Sir Edward on the shoulder. He looked at me and I mouthed, silently, 'he is one of Warbeck's bodyguards.' He raised his thumb to show he had understood me.

It became clear, when we smelled smoke, that they intended to camp opposite us. What were their intentions? I felt very vulnerable. The plan had seemed vague at best when it had been discussed in Alnwick and now, as we lay, peering through nettles and bramble bushes it seemed almost suicidal. When darkness fell we headed back to the camp. They had shown no signs of wanting to investigate the south bank and so we returned to hold a council of war.

"You are certain that Warbeck will be there?"

"If he is not, my lord, then he is still in Edinburgh and safe behind the thick walls of that fortress. He would not be on the road without his bodyguards."

"Stephen, you and Sam go to the ford and keep watch. I doubt that they will cross this night, but it pays to be careful. Take your cloaks and take it in turns to sleep. We will do the same here."

I knew not the hour, save that the Scottish and rebel camp was quiet, but I had been woken by Gerard to take my turn at watching. I saw movement across the river and spied once more Robert but this time he was with Giuseppe, and they looked not only across the river but up and downstream. They appeared to look directly at me, but I knew it was an illusion. Robert said something but I did not catch the words. However, when I saw Perkin Warbeck approach the river, I knew that Robert had said it was safe.

It had been some time since I had seen him. If anything he was even more grandly dressed. He had a fine tunic and when he turned and lowered his breeks I knew why he had come. The three men chatted while he emptied his bowels. I had done the same when we had gone hunting and too much fruit had necessitated a bowel movement. Perkin made some poor choices when it came to food. When they had done and Perkin had used the cloth brought by Giuseppe, they returned to the camp. During my watch, I saw more men come to the river to do the same. An hour or two later, not long before dawn, I was about to return to wake Sir Edward for his duty when a horn sounded. In the night it sounded alarmingly loud and even had we not sent words to Norham then they would have known there were Scots about. The camp was coming to life and the enemy, Scots and Yorkists were moving. I slid back to the camp and woke the others although, they were both stirring having heard the sound of the horn.

"They are waking, and I have seen Warbeck. He is here."

"Prepare to leave."

I donned my plate and grabbed some food. If we were going to move, then who knew when I would get the chance to eat again. Just as I had taken a swallow from my ale skin, Stephen ran in, "They are crossing the river. There are hobelars, men at arms and the scouts. They are heading for Twesilhaugh."

Dawn was breaking and that meant the castle at Twesilhaugh would begin its day. Men on the walls would scan the ground before the castle to ascertain if there was danger and when there was none would open the gates. I knew that the constable would have warned the castle at Twesilhaugh, but I also knew that the army that was coming had at least five hundred mercenaries. This was not a band of roving border reivers, this was a professional army who knew how to take a castle. Stephen grabbed his gear and I Sam's. We hurried to the ford and the islands where we could hear the army as they splashed through the water. That they were confident was clear for they did not bother to send men into the woods but headed immediately down the road. It was not a big road nor even a well made one, but it was cobbled in places and much wider than the path they had taken along the river. It meant that they could spread out and move faster.

We watched the mercenaries as they approached. Our task was to identify Warbeck and when Sir Ralph arrived, to somehow take him. I realised that the scouts and hobelars apart, the men I was watching were mercenaries. It was as the thought went through my head that I realised the cleverness of this plan. To the east of us, we heard the unmistakable and regular boom of a bombard. Norham was under attack. Twesilhaugh would relax their vigilance knowing that the larger fortress was the subject of the Scottish attack. When first we had met Gerard, he had said that Twesilhaugh and Norham were always the main points of the attack but that both had never been attacked simultaneously. Our hands were tied, and we could not warn Twesilhaugh. Even as the thought went through my mind, I saw Perkin Warbeck flanked by Robert and Giuseppe. They were followed by Sir John and Lord Lovell.

Perkin was riding a magnificent white horse and his almost white armour seemed to shine. Lord Lovell was a clever man and used all means possible to make the pretender seem real and, more importantly like some sort of white knight coming to rescue England from King Henry. The plate armour, we had been told was a gift from King James, was of the best quality. The pretender would be the safest man on the battlefield. We began to move through the woods paralleling the most important five men in the rebel army. Even without me, Warbeck would have been identified. A youth rode behind him with the royal standard. That would have been my task had I remained. Moving through the woods and remaining hidden meant that we often lost sight of our prey but there was only one road and it followed the River Till.

We heard shouts and cries from ahead; the regular boom of the bombards seemed to mark the regular passing of time. Twesilhaugh was less than a mile from the island and the men at arms, hobelars and scouts had surprised the garrison. A gap in the trees meant we had a clear view of Lord Lovell and Perkin Warbeck as the Yorkist leader pointed with glee ahead and said something. They spurred their horses and we lost sight of them. The villagers had cleared, at some time in the past, the trees that lay to the north of them and we had to move away from the leaders to avoid detection. By the time we saw them again, we viewed them across the village. The gates of the castle gaped wide; the garrison had been surprised. The mercenaries were charging through the village and folk were fleeing. Men and boys used slings and pole weapons to give their families the time to flee but it would be a vain defence. The mercenaries knew their business. Spears were thrust at men and boys without any armour or protection, and they died. Some of the women and

children were trampled as they headed for the road leading to
Norham. I prayed that they would make it. I saw the grim looks
on the faces of Sam and Gerard. It galled all of us to have to
watch. Had we intervened then whilst we might have slain some
of the mercenaries, we would have perished, and Warbeck would
escape.

When the slaughter had ended then the looting and the
destruction began. We knew when the poor houses had been
emptied for torches were fetched and the wattle and wood walls
set alight. When flames also appeared from the walls of
Twesilhaugh I knew that Castle Heaton was also in danger. Just
over a mile away they would see the flames and bar their gates,
but the mercenary army had lost, so far as I could tell, not a man
and even with the gates barred they would have to endure a
siege.

We still had a task to perform, and Sir Edward waved us
forward. The bombards' crack and the sound of burning
buildings meant that we could talk. Gerard pointed ahead, "They
will take Twesilhaugh Bridge to get to Heaton. We must ford the
river."

Sam said, "And this time I take off my boots."

The road to the bridge lay due east of us. The road followed
the River Till around a loop so that the enemy would then be
able to cross the river and head south and east. Our problem
would be that we would have to backtrack and risk passing
through the baggage of this army. I do not think we would have
managed it had it not been for Gerard who had grown up in this
area. We headed back west, through the trees until Gerard
stopped us. We heard the creak and groan of wheels and, as we
waited in the trees, we saw guns passing us. There was one
bombard and another four smaller guns. A wagon filled with
foul-smelling gunpowder also passed. Gerard had a good nose
and even better ears. There was a gap between wagons and he
hissed, "Now!"

We scampered down the slight slope and slithered across the
road which was now muddy and slick from the wheels of the
wagons and guns. Gerard had chosen a good place to cross the
road as there was a slight bend and overhanging trees hid us
from the ford. We tumbled down the bank through scrubby

undergrowth to slide to the river. It was not before time as we heard the groan of more wheels as the last of the baggage passed above us. Like Sam, I took off my boots and we waded across the river. There was a danger that we might be spotted by a wagon driver as we climbed up the other banks but there was no shout of alarm and I deduced that they were too busy guiding their wagons along an uneven road. We made for the trees and Sam and I donned our boots.

Sir Edward spoke as we did so, "I had hoped we might be able to, somehow, abduct Warbeck from their camp at Twesilhaugh."

I shook my head, "That will not happen, my lord. The two mercenaries you saw will act as chamberlains and sleep close to him. We need Sir Ralph and his army to come and give them a bloody nose. Perkin is a fearful man and if he thinks he might be taken then he will run. That will be our best chance."

Just then there was a double boom from the north. Sam said, "If Norham can survive."

Gerard nodded as Sam and I stood, ready to walk once more, "Aye, King James and the Scots have ever wanted Norham. I pray that Sir Ralph moves quickly."

Sir Edward asked, "And Castle Heaton?"

Gerard shook his head, "Once the Yorkists have their guns in place then the castle will soon be reduced and its fate will be that of Twesilhaugh."

Stephen said, quietly, "And a village has ceased to exist. They will not rebuild."

Gerard nodded, "Aye, you are right there. While the castle stood then the people had some protection but with their men slain and the walls destroyed, they will seek another home."

I looked at Stephen who said, "Aye, Ancroft was not destroyed but when my mother and I left, it was dying. These men should be punished."

Sir Edward turned, "And they may well be, Stephen, but not by us. We may well have to watch and endure things we should not have to but we serve the king and you need to remember that."

Our crossing of the river and the narrowness of Twesilhaugh Bridge meant that we reached Castle Heaton and the village not long after the hobelars, knights, and mounted men at arms had surrounded it. The black plume of smoke had warned them that there was danger and the garrison had barred their gates. The horsemen ringed the castle but were cautious enough to stay beyond both bow and crossbow range. That showed that they respected the archers who would man the walls. I knew that they would now be choosing a bodkin arrow and looking for the chance to send it in to one of the knights or men at arms. I had not been with the archer, Sean of Flint for long but his words were still in my head. I wondered had he survived the battle of Bramham Moor?

The castle was bordered on one side by the River Till and there was a good ditch that looked to be wet. I say that because I spied a stream meandering its way towards the river and knew that castle builders like to use nature whenever they could. We found a small copse some four hundred paces from the castle. There were horsemen before us but their attention was on the castle. As more men arrived so the mercenaries began to build their siege works. I saw now the cleverness of their plan. By using the Scots to attack Norham they had ensured that Perkin Warbeck could have an easy victory at Twesilhaugh. They would have time to reduce Castle Heaton and then, I guessed, Gerard's home of Etal and its castle. Lord Lovell and Sir John would not be risking Perkin's first combat with Sir Ralph's army. They were giving the pretender confidence.

It was late afternoon by the time the baggage arrived. The tents were erected and the work of placing the cannons ready to pound the walls began. We ignored the guns and looked for the tent of Perkin Warbeck. Fortunately for us, it was on our side of the castle, and we were just two hundred paces from it. I thought that they had taken a risk as a good archer could easily hit any of them. When no arrows were sent at them, I realised the defenders were waiting for the attack. They did not have a plentiful supply of missiles. I saw Sir Edward's head sink to his chest when mercenaries began to make their beds around the outside of Perkin Warbeck's tent. We were good but there would be no chance for us to overcome professional soldiers and abduct Warbeck, especially without horses. This close to the enemy we had to keep a good watch and, as we had rationed our food, smelling the slaughtered animals being cooked in the enemy camp made the watching even harder. They had sentries guarding an approach from the woods but after a cursory inspection, they seemed happy to just use the trees to shelter from the occasional shower. We were too deep in the forest for them to see us but we could not speak and, especially for Sam, that was hard.

The cannons began to pound the walls from first light. They were not as regular as ours had been at Boulogne, but they did not need to be. It was arrows and bolts that came back in their direction and not cannonballs, and by noon we saw cracks appear in the old castle walls. The booming of the guns meant that we could speak, and Sir Edward was quite concerned that we had not seen Sir Ralph and his army yet. We knew that we would know of their approach when the attitude of the attackers changed but they seemed to be in a jolly mood and we saw Perkin, Sir John and Lord Lovell enjoying wine while seated on chairs and cheering each time a piece of masonry flew.

By the early afternoon, it was clear that the castle could not last another day. Once that happened then they could move on to Etal. Sir Edward hated inactivity and he was a man with ideas. He spoke and we knew that he had been planning this while we had watched, "Gerard of Etal, Stephen of Ancroft, you two know this land better than any. Leave now and see if you can make contact with Sir Ralph."

"On foot?"

"I cannot see how you can get horses."

I ventured, "I have a way with horses. The horse lines are close to the river. What say I go with them and try to cut out a couple? So long as they are poor horses then I doubt that any would notice."

I could see that Sir Edward was not convinced but Gerard provided a good argument, "On foot, my lord, we might travel for a week and not see Sir Ralph. On a horse, we can cover the same ground in two days."

"I am not happy about this for I do not wish to risk James."

I smiled, "You forget, my lord, that you have all now seen Warbeck. I am superfluous."

He nodded and we prepared, as darkness fell. We had
observed the sentries enough to know their routine and it was
relatively easy to slip past them and reach the horse lines. Food
was in the process of being cooked and the smell wafted over.
Now that the guns had ceased firing the smell of saltpetre was
less strong. The guard on the horse lines looked furtively around
and appearing to be unobserved left his spear embedded in the
ground and sloped off to have a bowl of food. After all, the
castle was besieged and who would go near to the horses? I had
already decided on my plan. The sumpters were at the far end of
the line. If we took the last two then they would be noticed and
so I headed for a horse four from the end. I held out an apple and
one obligingly turned his head to eat it. Stephen untied him while
I stroked his head. As Stephen led him away, I walked back two
horses for one had been nodding his head up and down. That was
a good sign of a friendly horse. Holding out another apple the
dappled sumpter greedily took it. I handed the reins to Gerard
but never took my eyes from the main camp. By the time I
looked around my two friends had led their horses away. They
would mount when they could and only ride hard when they
were beyond the hearing of the camp.

I know it was a risk but I had been a spy for some years and
knew that sometimes a risk paid off. Instead of going back
whence I had come I headed closer to the tent of Perkin
Warbeck. I did not think I could contact him or abduct him and if
truth be told I am still unsure of my purpose but once the idea
was in my head then I could not shake it and I headed for the
tents. There was a cacophony of noise. The mercenaries were in
good spirits and having lost none and captured supplies from
Twesilhaugh they were eating well. I knew from my
conversations with Robert that was key to keeping hired swords
happy. I picked up Flemish, German and even Swiss. Flemish
and French were more familiar to me but I could make out the
odd word. I had the hood of my cloak up and my face was
covered but as I had allowed my beard to grow since I had left
Mechelen then I hoped I would not be recognised.

I neared the tent of Perkin Warbeck. He was surrounded by
senior knights as well as Lord Lovell and Sir John. I headed
away from the tent as though I was going to another tent further

away and the sentries watching me relaxed. I affected a limp and, spying an old stump sat on it to take off my boot as though I had found a stone. As I shook the boot and examined it, I heard some of the conversation.

"It is going well, King Richard, the messenger from King James said that another week will see Norham fall and Heaton can only last another day or so. We will have three victories." I recognised Lord Lovell's slippery tones.

Sir John's voice sounded cautious as he said, "Do not forget, cousin, that we had a message that the Earl of Westmoreland was heading north."

"And is a week away. We can destroy Etal but if they make it sooner then we join the Scots at Norham and end that siege quicker."

One of the sentries was heading over and so I donned my boot and stamped it on the grass. The man spoke Flemish, "Is everything alright, friend?"

His tone was a little suspicious and I nodded, speaking to him in his own language, "I must have eaten some bad fish yesterday. I should stay away from those bushes unless you are a gong scourer. A fir cone fell in my boot whilst I rid myself of the foul fish."

He relaxed, "Aye, this food takes some getting used to." He moved back to his watch and I rose.

I headed for a tent that looked unoccupied. As soon as I dared, I glanced around and saw the sentry had returned to speak with his friend and was taking no further interest in me. I slipped into the woods and waited behind a tree. My detour had taken me far from our camp. I made sure I was unobserved and then made my way through the trees towards the place I thought we had used. It proved to be further than I had thought. I paused to get my bearings and then heard a Scottish voice.

"I am sure I saw some movement in the woods."

"But who can it be? Come, Angus, the cow we butchered should be well on the way to being cooked."

"Our job was to make sure that this English king and his foreign army were safe. I may not like the task we have been given but if there are spies watching and I do nothing then how shall I look our king in the eye again? It is not for the handful of gold they paid us that we do this. Besides I want to take back these spies' bodies and hurl them before that arrogant Lord Lovell. We spend an hour and find them. The meat will be tenderer later and even fat Ewan cannot devour it all. Come, draw your weapon. You go to the left and I will go to the right. I can smell them!" They pulled their short, curved swords and parted.

They were heading in the direction of our camp and Sam and Sir Edward would think the noise they heard was my return. I pulled a dagger from my belt and slid, silently, my sword out. I had to kill quickly and silently, or all our work would have been in vain.

Chapter 23

I had killed before but this felt like I was going to do murder. I also had two men to follow quietly and to kill. The Scotsman was right, the wind was coming from the camp. I could not smell the camp, but I could smell the two Scotsmen. I had learned since I had left home, that a man's smell is determined by many things, not least what he eats and his bathing habits. I could smell them and it helped me to follow. The noise from the camp faded behind me. There was no sound of an alarm. That in itself was reassuring as it meant Gerard and Stephen had a better than good chance of escaping capture. My eyes were accustomed to the dark and I could make out the shadows of the two men. They were moving more cautiously than I for I knew where our camp was and they were seeking it. I moved carefully ensuring that my feet did not crunch leaves or crack twigs.

Suddenly the two men stopped and one hissed, "Ahead, twenty paces. There are two of them."

I peered through the gloom and felt my heart sink. The clearing was bathed in a shaft of moonlight, and I could see the backs of Sir Edward and Sam. If I shouted a warning, then while I would save them, I would also alert the Yorkist camp and we would be taken. The one on the right appeared to be the more dangerous and I stalked him. The camp was now clearly visible and with their backs to the two Scots, both would be dead in a blow or two. Sir Edward and Sam were eating, that was clear. Sir Edward might survive one blow for he wore his plate but if the Scot aimed at his head, then he would be dead.

It was not me who made the noise but the Scot to my left and when the twig snapped it sounded like the crack of thunder. Sam leapt to his feet and his sword was drawn so quickly that it was a blur. The man I was following cursed and ran at Sir Edward. Had either man called out then the three of us would have failed but the man I pursued was intent on taking the bodies back and the other, I assume, was keen to make up for his error.

Sir Edward began to rise but it was almost in slow motion. The Scot I followed raised his sword and it was clear to me that his blow would connect. I did the only thing I could, I threw my dagger, underhand. It struck the Scot in the side and whilst it did not penetrate far into the tunic he wore, it alerted him to my presence and he stopped mid-stride to face me but by then I had reached him and rammed my sword under his chin and into his skull. I withdrew my sword and whirled around. Sam was pulling his sword from the middle of the careless Scot. Sir Edward stared around him almost in a panic.

I sheathed my sword and retrieved my dagger. I hissed, "They are alone, but they will be missed. We should move." I knelt and took the dead Scot's purse. From his boot, I took the thin dagger favoured by such men. A warrior can never have too many such weapons.

Sam had also taken from his Scot and went to pick up his gear. Sir Edward said, "You are right but where do we go?"

Sam said as he wrapped his spare cloak around his body, "The one place they will not seek us, north of the Tweed." Sir Edward looked at him as though he had lost his mind and Sam asked, patiently, "James, did our friends get away?" I nodded. "Then they will bring the Earl and his army here. From what James says that will necessitate a flight by this Perkin Warbeck and when he crosses the ford we will have our best chance of taking him."

It was a convincing argument and Sir Edward nodded. We moved through the woods and away from the Yorkist camp. The sloping ground and the intermittent moonlight also helped us to pick our way back to the junction of the Till and the Tweed. This time we were on the deeper side, and we had first to ford the Till. All three of us carried our boots this time and then we waded across the River Tweed to the island and thence the north bank. After donning our boots we hurried to the place the Scots had camped when we had first spied them. We collapsed there. I worked out that we were at least two miles from Norham and the same from Heaton Castle. As the Twesilhaugh Bridge had the main road to Norham and avoided wet feet then any communication between the two sieges would use that route.

As we ate and drank a little of our precious ale I told them what I had heard. Sir Edward said, "Then if they join King James at Norham, they will not come this way. We need to watch the other road too."

Sam laughed and wiped the ale from his mouth, "And with three of us, how do we do that, my lord?"

I saw the knight's dilemma and I offered a suggestion, "My lord, Sir Ralph cannot be here until tomorrow at the earliest."

He frowned, "How do you make that out?"

I sighed, "The rebels know that he is on his way and that means he has left Alnwick, but Lord Lovell thought that Heaton would fall first. Gerard and Stephen, if they are lucky, might reach the earl after the sun's zenith." I saw Sam smile at my use of the word zenith. He was always improving my vocabulary. "Even if the earl hurries with his mounted men he will not reach Heaton until after dark and I do not think that the earl will risk a night attack. One or two of us could leave this vantage point tomorrow night and get to Twesilhaugh Bridge. It will be the day after that the prey is started and the hunt begins."

Sir Edward shook his head and smiled, "James, I know not where you found this mind but it is as sharp as Sam's tongue. Sleep the two of you and I will watch here and consider your words but you are quite right."

The Scots had left some hovels when they had decamped and Sam and I took them. As we did, he said, "Was the purse you took as heavy as mine?"

I nodded, "They were well paid by Lord Lovell but they like him not."

"If we take more purses like this then I may come to like this rebel for we grow richer by the day."

Sam was a practical man and I smiled at his attitude as I rolled in my cloak and knowing that Sir Edward watched I slept soundly.

There was no sun when I woke for the wind that had brought the smell of the camp in the night had freshened and brought clouds that threatened rain. I made water and Sir Edward yawned, "I will sleep until dark. Sam has gone to check the ford and I have decided that I will be the one to head to Twesilhaugh Bridge and watch there. You and Sam can stay here."

"Is that wise, my lord, to go alone?"

He gave a wry smile, "I think that the fates have intervened, and wisdom is no longer a factor. We have to do what we must do."

"But you, alone, cannot take Warbeck."

"I know but I hope that if they flee then the vanguard of the Earl's army may be close on their tail." He shrugged, "It is all that we can do."

As he lay down, I knew that as soon as the earl was seen then the frightened rabbit that was Perkin Warbeck would ride his fast horse as far away from danger as he could get. He would not head for Norham but for Edinburgh. His mercenaries would ensure that none could get close to him. The fantastical plan for us to take him was just that, a fantasy.

The rain soon began to fall and it was almost biblical. The guns ceased firing as the rain doused linstocks. The two attacks would falter for the day although Heaton might fall in any case. The cracks I had seen in the walls would grow as the rain weakened the foundations. It also meant that the relieving army would struggle to reach us any time soon.

Sir Edward was adamant about his plan and when he awoke, he took his share of our dwindling rations and headed back across a river that was swelling by the minute. The ford might cease to exist within a day if the rains continued.

Left alone but secure in the knowledge that none would approach us Sam and I spoke not of Perkin Warbeck but what we would do back in Hedingham. "That wench in Alnwick set me to thinking, James. I am ready for a family and for that I need a wife. There are women back in Essex who would be glad to have me as their husband and I have coins in my purse. Serving alongside you is profitable."

"And then what?"

"I will ask Sir Edward if I can live in the village. I can still serve but I want my own four walls."

"And if he says no?"

"Then I will hang up my bill as your father did." He snuggled a little deeper into his hovel, "I like not this sneaking around and while I do not mind fighting for my king to defend his land this does not feel right. I would rather be snug in my own home with a roaring fire and a plump wife to cuddle with."

I knew not what I would do when this was over. I knew that Mechelen and Paris had changed me. Had I stayed in England I might have become like my father, but I had tasted from a gilded cup, and I wondered if I would be happy with my leather-covered costrel. In Flanders I had been desperate to return home and see my family but did I have warrior's blood in my veins? Was I destined to be a warrior?

The rain relented towards evening, but the bombards did not resume their battering; the gunners would want dry powder. The river, which we saw when we went to make water, was in full spate and roared towards the sea. The stones, which may well have been moved by Norham's garrison would be of no help to any trying to ford the river and we realised that, without horses, we were trapped on the wrong side of the river. Sam's whimsical reflections on his future seemed a desirable dream to me now.

When we woke the next morning the rain had gone, and the river subsided but a little. About the hour of terces, by my estimation, we heard the bombards sound from Norham. They had kept their powder dry and the siege continued. Ominously there was no noise from Heaton.

"We have but one day of food left, James. We cannot stay here on an empty stomach."

I pointed to the river. "And how, without horses do we cross that?"

"Then let us make rations for two days and hope that the river has gone down enough for us to cross."

We foraged and found some berries and roots to augment our meagre rations, but the fruit would have an undesirable effect and the roots would, uncooked, be hard to digest. The foraging filled the time. We seemed to be alone in the world and that was not a surprise. The two sieges would have everyone's attention. We spent the rest of the time sharpening our weapons. I had the Scottish dagger to hone too and when I had finished, I slipped that into the top of my other boot.

It was late afternoon when we heard the crack of the harquebus. It came not from the direction of Norham but Heaton. As we had heard no noise from there all day it seemed ominous. I had expected that, if Heaton had fallen, then Lord Lovell would have headed to Etal. The noise came from close by.

"I know not what that portends but it cannot do us good. Let us prepare to move and move quickly."

We had eaten most of our rations and it was simplicity itself to fasten our spare cloaks diagonally across our bodies with our supplies and almost empty ale skins the other way and then head to the bank close to the diminishing islands where we would hide. Our time watching the islands meant we knew the best places to hide and hide we did. The clash of steel and the crack of harquebuses grew closer, and we knew that there was some sort of battle coming our way. We both drew our swords in anticipation.

We heard the horses approach while the combat seemed some way off. They whinnied and complained as their riders forced them into the swirling waters by the islands. The island was almost completely submerged at this point. The first to try it were the Scottish hobelars or border horse. Without armour, they could move faster but one was obviously not in control of his horse and we saw horse and rider swept from their feet as a rogue log struck them. We were on the river side of the narrow path and saw them as they were driven towards Norham, Berwick and the sea. The horse might survive but I doubted that the Scot would. Three of the hobelars made the north bank and they galloped past us. That they did not see us proved we had chosen an effective hiding place.

"Watch for the bodyguards and Perkin. They will be next." I knew the mind of Warbeck. He would seek safety.

"We are two men, what can we do?"

I said nothing but I knew I had taken this commission and I would have to try. I saw them as they appeared at the riverbank. They had seen the hobelars make the crossing and the one who had been swept away. I saw the mercenaries and recognised some of them. Perkin Warbeck was flanked by Giuseppe and Robert who held his reins. Robert was ensuring that Warbeck did not suffer the same fate as the hobelar. Before them were another six of the mercenaries. I recognised most of them. Robert waited until the six had negotiated the ford before he risked moving. As they waited, I saw another six mercenaries and then the familiar figures of Lord Lovell and his cousin Sir John Bardolph. Both had lost their helmets.

Robert shouted, in Flemish, "You six ride ahead and make sure that the road to Berwick is clear." The six advance riders galloped up the slope and then thundered past us. With our brown cloaks, we were invisible. I knew that if we chose we could stay there and they would pass us but I had given my word. Robert turned to the other six and said something. They rode towards us on the opposite side of the river. It was clear what they intended. If Perkin fell, they had a chance to rescue him as he was swept downstream. One dismounted and went to stand in the shallows as Robert and Giuseppe led a terrified horse and an even more terrified Perkin Warbeck, across the river. The water came up above the legs of the riders and the horses were forced to swim. Robert and Giuseppe, I knew from experience, were consummate riders and they controlled and calmed all three horses. They had just reached the other bank and the dismounted rider had just remounted when I saw knights appear. They bore the livery of Northumberland. They were Percy men. Lord Lovell and his cousin shouted something to the mercenaries and then they began to cross. As Robert and Giuseppe led Perkin up towards the path the mercenaries raced to buy time for their leaders to cross. The rescue plan for Warbeck was abandoned as Lord Lovell sought to sacrifice his mercenaries and save his own life.

I looked at Sam and shrugged as much as to say with the odds now lower, we had no choice. As Robert galloped up towards us, the three of them filling the path, I stepped out and raised my sword to slash across the leg of Robert. I should have known better for even without a sword he was my superior and he flicked his leg from his stirrup and kicked at me. I had the satisfaction of knowing I had struck his leg and, no doubt, hurt him, but I was left sprawling in the bramble bush as the two mercenaries took their charge to Berwick and safety. Then our prey was gone, and I looked up at the figure of Sir John Bardolph.

As I rose to my feet he shouted, "You! Traitor!" He rode at me and Sam was forced to act for I had yet to raise my weapon. He blocked the blow with his sword.

Lord Lovell rode his horse directly at me, "You shall die at my hand." Behind me, I heard Sir John and Sam as they exchanged blows and I prepared to face a charging horse and a deadly knight who had murderous intent. When I had been at

Mechelen I had observed how horses moved and knights fought. A rider normally committed to a move and was forced to stick with it. A man on foot was often pinned to the spot with fear, I raised my sword as he rode at me. He was helped by the fact that his sword hand was on the side where the river lay and behind me I had just the slippery bank to the roaring river. I thought I had timed it perfectly and I jinked to my right when he was half a horse's length from me. He was wily and he wheeled his horse's head as he swung down to his left. My sword was still coming down when his blade struck first my coiled cloak and then the breastplate. He was close enough for me to see the shock on his face. My sword connected where his backplate met his fauld and it found flesh. He spread his arms as his back arched and began to tumble from the saddle, I could not see the horse die and so I grabbed the reins. The result was that I was pulled towards the slippery bank and Lord Lovell fell from the saddle. I watched as his head struck a rock and then, despite his plate armour, he was swept down the river towards the sea.

I turned and was just in time to see Sir John strike down and hit Sam. Sam had just moved and so it was the flat of the blade that hit Sam and not the edge but with blood pouring, he fell to the ground. Sir John pulled on his reins to make his horse trample Sam and leaving go of the reins of Lord Lovell's horse I took my sword and ran recklessly at Sir John. My movement was enough to make his horse turn and when it landed it was on the thorns of a bramble bush. The horse turned and fled down the path towards Norham.

I heard as he fled, Sir John say, "This is not over, traitor, and I shall hunt you to the ends of the earth." The last word was almost indistinct, but I had the gist of it. I was no longer considered dead and with Robert and Sir John aware that I was still alive I could expect retribution.

Putting those thoughts from my mind I ran to Sam. He was breathing but there appeared to be a lot of blood. I took my ale skin and washed the blood away. It was a deep wound, and I could see bone but the bone was whole. I went to the horse which now stood disconsolately on the path. There were saddlebags and I took a piece of cloth from one. I took it to be an undershirt. Lord Lovell was always concerned about being clean and I tore it to make a bandage. I ripped a large piece from the shirt and, after wasting more ale, put part of it next to the skull and I held it there. When the bleeding slowed, I fastened the rest as tightly as I could. I waited to see if blood seeped from it, but it did not. I risked leaving him there while I went to see if there was more danger from the ford. I saw the Percy knights debating if they ought to cross. Cupping my hands I shouted, "Your prey has fled!"

One of them raised his hand in acknowledgement and they turned to head towards Norham. This did not help Sam and me. He needed help and we had a river in spate. Of Lord Lovell, I could see nothing. I manhandled Sam so that he was on the saddle of the horse. I led the horse back down the path to the ford. It looked daunting but Sam's life depended upon me. I had staunched the bleeding but who knew what went on beneath a skull. I spoke to the horse as I led it down the slippery bank, "There's a good fellow. Come now and when we have crossed I shall find you a bushel of apples. Come, boy." In this way, I led him so that the water came up to my waist. I knew where the island lay beneath the water and I knew we had no other choice. We just had twenty paces of rough water to cross and I knew we would have to swim. I decided to do it in two parts: to the island and then beyond. The two shorter crossings did not seem so bad. Taking the reins in both hands I urged him towards the hidden island. He walked and then, as my feet left the bottom, he swam. I kicked my legs but, alarmingly, we were being swept downstream. When I felt the island beneath my feet, I breathed a sigh of relief. After checking that Sam had not moved, I walked him upstream knowing that when we swam again, we would risk being swept to the sea. "You have done well and there is not far to go. Let us venture forth once more." This time I walked him upstream and when I lost my footing and he swam, his head was forced around to head downstream. I think the weight of my plate and Sam's body helped for he began to walk and then my feet found the rocks. I walked and led him up the bank.

As I reached the top I heard a familiar voice, "Praise God, Gerard of Etal, we have found our friends!" I looked up and saw Stephen and Gerard. There was help and I was no longer alone.

Chapter 24

We did not leave Norham for a month. There was no further fighting. The Scots and the Yorkists had fled as soon as the earl had brought his army north. Although Heaton and Twesilhaugh had been destroyed Etal was unharmed and Norham had proved too hard a nut to crack. We stayed, long after the earl had headed south because Sam needed attention from the healers. Sir Edward and William headed south too but we three billmen remained. Thanks to Gerard's words we were treated as heroes. I did not feel like a hero for we had just watched while others had fought and died but I accepted the praise as modestly as I could. Sir Edward had left us but not with any sense of disappointment. He told us he would ride to the Earl of Oxford and king and tell them that we had failed. We knew not whence Perkin Warbeck and his mercenaries had fled but they were beyond our reach.

The healer in the castle had done a good job stitching Sam's head and one reason we had stayed a month was to let the hair that had been shaved, grow back. He was now even more determined than ever to wed a comely wench. He had been disappointed that Katie, the one who had stirred his loins, had been evacuated from the castle with the other serving women not long after we left. They had been sent, for their own safety, to Alnwick.

When we did ride south, I rode Lord Lovell's horse. I know not what his real name was but I called him Fate for my life had been ruled by fate since I had met Mistress Gurton and I still wondered if she was some sort of witch. Our farewell from Gerard was one of warriors who had shared danger. Even if we never saw each other again there would be a bond. We stayed at Alnwick on the way south for the Percy family knew what we had done and they were grateful. There, fate took a hand again and Katie, the woman who had caught Sam's eye wasted no time and did not hide behind feminine wiles. Even as we were stabling our horses, she entered the stables and stood with her hands on her hips.

"Sam Sharp Tongue, why the delay in returning to me? The battle was a month since. If you have tarried with loose women of the camp…"

"Kate, sweet Kate, I have been wounded and I hurried back as soon as I could."

She was slightly mollified and came to his side, "I did not know." She cast a venomous glance at the grinning man at arms who stood nearby, and he quailed. "Well, now that you are back do you stay or leave?"

I could see that Stephen was confused by Sam's answer, but I was not, "Kate, when I left it was with a lover's tryst in mind. My encounter with a rebel sword has made me think again." I saw the disappointment on her face. He held up his hand, "This is sudden, but I would have you as my wife. You are comely and I..."

He got no further for she threw her arms around him and kissed him so hard I thought she might burst his wound.

Stephen turned to me and said, "What have I missed, James?"

I laughed and patted the neck of my new horse, "Fate. Sometimes there are people who are meant for each other and these two must be two such. If she is willing to leave the north and travel south to Hedingham then this must be love. For my part, I am happy for our friend."

We stayed a week and that was so that Sam could buy a cart to carry his bride's belongings. They were wed in the castle chapel and I think that all were happy for the couple. Katie was no longer in the first flush of youth but still of childbearing age. I never saw a couple better suited. It slowed our journey south and it took us three weeks to reach Hedingham but none of us cared. The earl's potential disapproval seemed a minor thing.

On the way south, Stephen and I allowed Sam and his bride to spend as long alone as possible although she was such a lovely woman that she chatted with all on the way south. She was entertaining and perceptive. She saw into the hearts of both Stephen and me. Of course, she wished us also to be wed but I knew that I was not ready and I suspected that Stephen never would be. I know not why, it was just a feeling. Stephen and I listened as they made their plans. She wanted a house and some land, and she did not want it to be close to the castle.

Stephen had said, "What if the Earl wishes you to remain in the castle, Sam?"

I knew Sam's answer from our day in the rain, "I am my own man and I can serve any master. While I would like to be a billman and serve the earl, if I cannot be then I shall turn my hand to something else. Whatever else we shall have there will be a stable. The three of us have been lucky with horses and if times became hard we could sell them." He looked wistful, "Perhaps I could be a schoolmaster."

That surprised even Katie, "A schoolmaster? Can you read?"

He affected an outraged look, "Of course I can and whence do you think I earned my name?"

Katie nodded, "There is money to be made from teaching. Many who cannot read themselves wish their children to have that skill and I think you would be a good schoolmaster."

That was typical of the two of them. They got on so well that I knew that they had been meant for each other.

It was almost winter when we reached the castle. The Earl of Oxford was at Windsor with the king and his sons. The discontent in Cornwall had almost reached boiling point. The king's taxes to pay for the war against Warbeck had made them ready to rebel. The news that the Earl was not present pleased us. We met with Sir Edward while Katie arranged for rooms in the local inn. She was a force of nature, and I knew that by the time we returned she would know of the properties that were for sale.

Sir Edward was in good spirits and that surprised me. I was sure he would have been chastised. He smiled at us, "Our trip north did me some good and I am grateful to you. I have been made constable of Hedingham and I thank you. You were right at the battle of Norham, and I was wrong. Had I stayed with you then the three of us might have taken Warbeck."

I shook my head, "We were lucky and those mercenaries would have made short work of us. Sam here barely escaped with his life as it was."

He did not look convinced. He had waited close to the bridge and saw nothing until the bulk of the army decamped to join the Scots at Norham. He had just watched as they had fled over the bridge thence to join the fleeing Scots who abandoned their siege.

"The earl was just happy that Lord Lovell is finally dead. There were rumours that he died at Bosworth but now that it is confirmed even the king is happy. He does not like mysteries. None shall ever speak again of Lord Lovell. You, James, have enhanced your reputation and the king wishes you to be ready when Warbeck lands again."

"Will he?"

"You know him better than any; what do you say?"

"He likes the life but not the danger. Where is he now, my lord?"

"He is still in Scotland but there are rumours that he intends to go to Ireland again. There he has many supporters."

"He may just stay there, or in Scotland and enjoy the life of an exiled king which is how he sees himself. I think that it will be highly unlikely that he lands again in England."

Sam ventured, "Unless, of course, he is no longer welcome in either Scotland or Ireland."

Silence fell until the knight said, "You will all resume your duties. Geoffrey of Wednesbury has done his best with the billmen, but they are not as good as when you led them, Captain Sam."

Sam shifted uncomfortably, "You should know, my lord, that I have taken a wife and I intend to buy a home close by." He waited for a response but Sir Edward merely nodded. "It means I will not live in the warrior hall."

"And that is not a problem for you have two able deputies. Indeed James here has such a reputation that we have had many men trying to join our company just to serve with him."

Poor Sam looked like a pig's bladder emptied of air. He had expected an argument and there was none.

We returned to the life of billmen. Michael, whom we had wished to be left in command of the billmen, was now with the earl and served as a man at arms. I was pleased for I liked him. Stephen and I stayed in the warrior hall and I had been proved correct, Katie had found somewhere and by the time she and Sam had spoken to the landowner and beaten him down they paid a reasonable price. It had stables and that showed that Katie listened to what we had all said. My three horses were stabled there and that made me happy. Sam even paid a young boy from the village to be a stable boy. Others used his stable and he began to earn coins for Stephen and I paid for our own feed and contributed to the boy's wages. All was equitable.

When Stephen and I helped Sam to train men for war it was with the knowledge we had gained in what might be termed unconventional warfare. The three of us knew that the strength of the billman lay in the fact that he could abandon rigid lines and use his weapon in a melee. A longer pike could not. It made our task harder but the three of us were determined to make our company the best in England. Over the winter we drilled the men in all weathers and used seemingly bizarre tactics with them such as using a broom shank instead of a billhook. When they asked why Sam patiently explained, "As we have seen a man can have his weapon severed in two. You can still use the stump effectively. The jagged end can take out an eye and a blow to the side of a sallet can render a man unconscious. It buys you time to draw your sword."

You could see that one day, Sam would make a good schoolmaster for he was patient although still sharp-tongued. When, in April, Katie told us she was with child a change came over Sam. He was overjoyed, of course, but as we celebrated in the warrior hall, as was the custom, he drank less than one might have expected and spoke seriously to Stephen and to me, "I think that when the child is born I shall ask Sir Edward for permission to leave his service. I am a man of my word, and I would not leave my wife and child because I had promised to follow a banner. There is no honour in that."

"You could leave now, Sam. There is no war and no need for you to risk a fight."

He smiled, "The coin I earn between now and October will give us more comfort. I am still committed to teaching children, but I know not how it pays."

"Sam, if you are ever short of money…I have more than I need and I know I owe you much."

"And I am touched but they say that a man who borrows loses friends, and you are two good friends I do not wish to lose."

A little more than a month later when the Cornish rose in rebellion against King Henry and began their march towards London, I wondered if Sam might regret not resigning sooner for we were called upon to prepare to march to London and to defend it. We would be serving not under the Earl of Oxford but the king who with Lord Daubeney would meet the rebels. Our goodbyes were, perforce, briefer than one would have wished but Katie was a strong woman. As we marched south and west, I said, "I am sure Sir Edward would let you stay with the garrison, Sam. You need not risk your life."

"But I do, for the first time, James of Ecclestone, I do not fight just for others but myself. If the rebels take London, then my wife is at risk. I am fighting for my family."

Stephen had been his usual silent self and he mused, "And for the first time in a long time, we do not seek a pretender. These Cornishmen just want to pay less tax."

We marched behind William and Sir Edward and when one of our older billmen said, "No one likes paying taxes."

Sir Edward said, without turning around, "And those words are dangerous ones, Giles Shepton so curb your tongue."

Sam smacked the billman on the back of his head with his gloved hand.

It was good to be marching to a just war and the familiarity of a sallet hanging from my billhook along with the rest of the company was comforting. The main difference now was that both Sam and I wore a breast and backplate. The rest of the armour I had taken from Sir Quentin constricted me but the two pieces of armour gave us an advantage. The sudden war had surprised Stephen who had asked the local weaponsmith to make him a breastplate. It was not yet ready. The army gathered to the southwest of the city. The rebels had meandered through Devon, Somerset, Dorset, and Hampshire. Their numbers were reported to have been swollen by other malcontents and it was said that there was an army of ten thousand men approaching. Some of the newer men were a little fearful of the numbers but as we camped on Hounslow Heath Sam patiently explained why numbers were not important.

"The men who come are led by a knight, Lord Audley, a smith, Michael Joseph, and a merchant, Thomas Flamank. Now you tell me, does that sound like a trio of generals who should make us quake in our buskins?" He made some of them laugh which was his intent. "We have trained together for so long that our company and Lord de Vere's archers could hold the enemy until judgement day if we had to. Do not worry about numbers. All you need to worry about is that you heed my voice when I shout commands and obey Sergeant James and Sergeant Stephen."

They seemed satisfied.

Sir Edward had been to a council of war and he and William returned. The siege of Norham had changed William. When he had been trapped inside the walls and had to endure the pounding of the bombards, he had seen that there was more to being a knight than posturing and tourneys. From the moment he was reunited with Sir Edward he seemed determined to become the best knight that he could be. He no longer looked bored when Sir Edward spoke to us and he had far more respect for the three of us than he had before Norham. Much of that was down to our reception in the castle after the siege was lifted.

"The rebels now have fifteen thousand men. We have a similar number, but we will be reinforced by the companies who are now marching from the City of London."

Sam asked, "And where do we meet them, my lord?"

He shrugged, "The rebels, it seems are heading for Kent to try to raise support there, but it will not materialise. If you were to ask me, then I think it will be southwest of here. The king plans to attack as soon as they are within striking distance of us. We will be fighting in the largest battalion under Lord Daubeney and will initiate the attack." We nodded for that was a place of honour.

"And what of the Scots?" Some of the younger men looked askance at Sam who shook his head, "Whenever there is trouble in England then the Scots cross the border for mischief."

Sir Edward said, "The Earl of Surrey has taken men to march north and join the Earl of Westmoreland. Our friends at Norham will not be abandoned."

I knew that in the time since the siege, Gerard and the rest of the garrison would have been hard at work repairing the damage, but it would still be in a weakened state.

Two days later we heard the trumpets sound the command to move. Sir Edward sent William for news and when he returned, we discovered that the rebels were at Blackheath, and we were heading for the bridge at Deptford. He also brought the news that

Sir Edward would be riding to war not with us, but he and William would be attached to King Henry's knights and men at arms.

"I know that you will command as though I was there, Captain Sam, and you have two able lieutenants."

"Aye, Sir Edward but you and Master William watch out for yourselves. The Cornish may have billmen too!"

As we headed towards Blackheath I worried about Sam. It seemed to me that there were powers at work conspiring to shape our futures. What if, just when Sam was about to find a family and happiness he should fall in battle? If Stephen or I died then whilst people would be sad, lives could go on. For Katie and her unborn child, it would be devastating.

We did not have far to go and we camped, facing an ever-increasing number of rebels. They were spread out along the road even further than we were and as Sam had said, there would be men in the rebel army who were not rebels but those who sought to make a profit from war and they would be off plundering. King Henry seemed still to be waiting for our own reinforcements but, once again Sam said we had the professional army and we should attack whilst they were not ready. We arrived at the camp on Friday afternoon and we set about making our hovels.

This time the three of us supervised our own men so that we had an orderly camp and one that would keep us, should it rain, dry. Satisfied that it was and while Sam went to receive orders, Stephen and I organised the fire and placed the pot with water on the tripod. We threw in the bits of food that would give it taste: a ham bone sliced clean of meat, some salted horsemeat, some wizened mushrooms and then the substance; the dried beans and greens. Precious salt and herbs finished it and we left it to bubble. We took out our whetstones and cloths. We sharpened and cleaned our billhooks. I liked a point to the spike that was almost as narrow as a needle at the end. I knew I could ram it through the eye hole of a visored sallet and kill. Then I sharpened my blades. As I sharpened the sword I thought back to Mechelen. It was as though that was a different life and I was a different person. I realised that Perkin Warbeck and I had both been playing a part. Had Warbeck decided to abandon his life and return to Tournai? Somehow, I doubted it. Whereas I had enjoyed the life of a noble I was much more comfortable with the life I now had. I knew that part of it was that I had been reconciled with my family and there was no longer a void that ached. Warbeck had been bitten by some invisible insect and infected with the illusion that he could become king.

The beans had begun to become mush and the men were waiting with their wooden platters when Sam returned, "We attack tomorrow. King Henry has decided that Saturday is his lucky day and he does not wait for more men. There was a skirmish just south of here this morning and the king took it as a sign. We are to be with Sir Humphrey Stanley and his spearmen. They will force the bridge at Deptford, and we will support them."

Giles Shepton was the one who could not simply listen. He always had to make some sort of comment and he did not disappoint, "Spearmen? What good are they?"

Sam shook his head, "You have yet to fight in a battle, Giles and you have not seen that a battle is not won by one arm but by a combination. The spearmen have shields and whilst their spears are not as long as pikes, they are longer than our bills. They can clear the bridge and then our deadly bills will exploit their success. You just make sure that when we march you are as close to me as a priest to his cross and when the guns crack and the arrows fall, pray that God smiles on you."

Another younger billman, Arthur, asked nervously, "Do they have guns? I heard they had only pole weapons, horse and sword."

"They will have guns, aye, not as many as we faced at Boulogne and Norham but enough to fill the air with the foul stench of the devil and send their deadly missiles to randomly strike us."

"Randomly?"

Grinning, Sam the schoolteacher, explained, "Aye, Arthur, it means that they rarely go where they are aimed but can still kill and maim. Make your confession before we fight and pray that God judges you to be a good man."

After we had eaten the three of us sat close and spoke. "They are good lads, Sam, and they will not let us down."

"I know, James, and God knows that if we cannot beat a mob of tin farmers armed with ancient weapons then we ought to turn our billhooks into ploughshares." He tossed another piece of dead wood onto the fire, "If anything happens to me, James, you know where I keep my coins. Look after Katie, eh?"

"None of that! You shall return to your home and watch your bairn be born."

He shook his head, "I was lucky at Norham, and you know it, James. Had that been the edge of the sword I would be dead. If you had not staunched the bleeding then I would be dead."

I laughed, "But you are not and you found Katie. The costrel is half full, Sam Sharp Tongue and not half empty."

"But even so, I would have you swear an oath to care for my wife and child."

We could see he was serious and I drew my sword with the cross hilt whilst Stephen drew his long dagger. We kissed the crosses and both said, "I so swear."

Sam seemed inordinately relieved, "I go to battle tomorrow now with a lighter heart for you are true friends and you shall not let me down."

We were woken at terces and within a short time were marching to join Sir Humphrey and his spearmen. This was June and the night had been barely five hours long. All around us, the camp was roused, and the jingling of horse furniture and metal would tell the Cornish that we were going to attack. We might be attacking a couple of days earlier than the king had originally said but there would be no surprise. There was but one bridge and we had to take it before the army could cross the bridge over the Ravensbourne River. The river was neither wide nor deep but an army that tried to cross it would be disordered and even tin miners could wreak havoc. We would take the bridge and hold the crossing until the army passed across.

We reached it before dawn and Sir Humphrey organised us. He was a brave man and plated from head to toe, he would lead us. We were arranged so that his spearmen formed a block eight men wide and ten men deep. We would be behind them, and Captain John and our archers would be as close to us as they could to try to keep the bridge clear. I felt sorry for Stephen. He was the one who had no plate armour. He had acquired, after

Norham, a short mail hauberk that he wore over his jack but it was not the same. At least he had a sallet as good as mine and Sam's. Some of the men we led had open-faced pot helmets and bascinets. They would offer protection from above but a spear or sword jabbed at the face could kill.

We stopped just forty paces from the bridge and waited for the sound of the horn that would begin the attack. I saw the smoke rising from the linstocks. They had cannons and I felt my guts rumble. Whilst wild, noisy, and inaccurate they could still kill and maim. Horsemen began to form up on our flanks but far enough from the bridge so that their horses would not be afeard of the guns.

Sir Humphrey ranged along the front of his men extolling them to deeds of valour for the king. Sam just spoke quietly, "We stay together and fight as one. We watch for our brothers, and you heed the voices of your officers. When you strike then strike to kill for a wounded or dying man can exact his revenge upon you."

As more of our battle arrived the sense of anticipation grew so that when the horn sounded Sir Humphrey's men took off like greyhounds from the slip. Sam shouted, "Steady and keep the pace!"

Captain John shouted, "Loose!" and the forty arrows soared overhead. The men we faced were not on the bridge but just on the other side. Most were protected by plate and mail and the arrows would be more of an annoyance except for the gunners who wore little protection. The first guns roared but after the bombards at Norham, they sounded weak and almost ineffectual. Spearmen fell but not as many as one would have expected. We stepped onto the bridge as smoke billowed from ahead and we heard more cracks as harquebuses fired. Arrows fell but the spearmen had shields and were unharmed. An arrow hit my helmet and I heard others as they pinged off metal. There was a cry from behind.

Sam shouted, "Who is hurt?"

One of the older men, Edgar, shouted. "Bastard hit my left shoulder, but I can carry on, Captain!"

As we coughed our way through the smoke, across a bridge with bodies and wounded men, we had to watch our footing.

Thanks to our training none slipped and I was grateful when we stepped onto the solid ground once more. That relief ended when the Cornish charged at us. Sir Humphrey's battered men formed a double line before us. Thanks to our training we had emerged unscathed, and we formed the third line. Sir Humphrey had moved fifty paces from the bridge despite the fact that the move took him closer to the guns. He had lost twenty or more men. More were wounded but they were hardy men and they closed ranks and raised their shields.

The Cornish were not in any particular formation and knights, men at arms as well as men without armour and wielding pole weapons ran at us. The secret was to remain calm and strike at the greatest threat. The spearmen duelled with the Cornish. The knights and men at arms made progress and soon I found myself not in the third rank but the second and as the spearman before me was hacked to the ground by a man at arms swinging a poleaxe, I prepared myself to fight. I stepped into the breach, and he swung his poleaxe. My move had upset his aim and instead of blocking the blow with my billhook, I rammed the spike up under his chin. He was not wearing a gorget and relied on a sallet helmet with a visor. I felt the tip crunch into flesh and the bone of his jaw, and I drove it up into his skull. He died silently. A knight with a broad axe smashed his weapon into the side of the skull of a spearman and then prepared to swing at me. I had been preparing to block the blow of a billhook in the hands of a Cornishman and I was unable to do anything. Sam must have seen my dilemma and he pushed his way to be at my side and caught the axe on his hook. Deftly twisting it he forced the axe down. I blocked the billhook and then did the unexpected. I allowed him to push the head back, towards me and then brought the haft up between his legs. The wood drove up into his groin and I saw his eyes roll. With that sort of pain a man cannot hold on to a billhook tightly and when his grip weakened, I brought the blade into the side of his head.

As I looked around, I saw that while Sam had enjoyed the better of the encounter up to now a Cornish spearman had stabbed at his side. The weakness with our plate was that where the back and breastplate met there was a slight gap and the spear found it. Sam was hurt and the knight saw his chance. He raised his sword, and I rammed my spike at his chest with all the force I could muster. I was lucky and he was unbalanced. As he teetered, I pulled back and, stepping forward, rammed again. I knew that I was in danger of becoming isolated but if I relented then a weakened Sam might be hit again. I had not hurt the knight. His plate was too good for that but he was unbalanced and once I was free from my comrades I was able to swing the blade, not at his side but at his knee. He had a poleyn for protection but I caught it behind the knee and the limb buckled. His head was now at the perfect height for the spike which I drove through the visor of his helmet. It was a mortal strike. I stepped back as a swordsman swung his sword at me. The edge ripped through my tunic and grated on my breastplate. As I pulled back with the billhook, I pulled his sword around and Sam, who had disposed of his spearman, had an easy kill.

I saw that Sam was bleeding, "Get behind the last rank, Sam."

He shook his head, "I am the captain."

"And now you have a wife and unborn child. You can direct the men from there and Stephen and I will lead." Just then a farmer with a billhook lunged at me and the spike hit my plate. "Go now for you are a distraction!" I hacked half of the farmer's face away with the blade and Sam did as I asked. "Hold firm! They weaken!"

My words must have angered them for they rushed at us, but they came as individuals whilst Giles stepped up into Sam's place and a solid line of billhooks were waiting for them. It was like a rainstorm that you think will never stop but our training paid off. We swung our billhooks in unison and beat down the array of weapons used and then when the opportunity arose, we stabbed and hacked at men who, in the main were unprotected. Even so, men still fell but as the king and Lord Daubeney fed more men across the bridge so our ranks became more solid and when I heard the trumpets from the left and right I knew that the horsemen had arrived. That was always going to be our secret weapon. The Cornish rebels were an army of foot soldiers and knights and men at arms, armed with lances charging into the flanks of disorganised men would always have but one outcome. Suddenly those before us broke and fled. The last four men I had disposed of had been peasants with a curved billhook attached to a pole. They died unnecessarily. We were exhausted and just halted to catch our breath and tend to the wounded.

I saw Stephen had survived and he grinned, I said, "Sam is hurt, tend to him while I see who else is hurt."

We had lost six men and two had wounds. Neither wound was serious. I had the six dead placed close together. We would bury them when all was done. Then my men and I began to strip the dead. The knight I had slain had a good sword that I could sell as well as his armour and helmet. He had a purse that was full. I allowed the others to share the treasure from the other dead I had slain. I knew that the knight would have ridden a horse but that would now have been taken. When all was done, I had the men pick up the dead and we headed back across the river to where the healers were tending to the wounded. Sam's wound had needed stitches and he was pale enough to tell me he had lost a lot of blood.

I shouted, "Dig the graves beneath that stand of willows and when Captain Sam is able we will say goodbye to our friends."

Giles Shepton had changed during the battle. I think that a close encounter with death will do that, "Come, you heard the sergeant, let us do as he commands."

Sam smiled, "I think, James, that you should be the one who commands." He winced as the healer finished his work by wiping the wound with vinegar. He glowered at the man and then said to me, "I owe you a life and you were right. Had I stayed in my weakened state I might have died." I said nothing for I knew more words were coming. "This is my last battle. I shall sell my plate and become the schoolmaster I said I would. If we are poor, then so be it."

"You have your share of the spoils from today, my friend, and Stephen and I will make sure that you never want. If this is what you wish."

"Your words hit home, my friend, and you were right. Katie and my unborn child are more important than this."

We did not leave Deptford for a few days. The king rewarded the men who had charged the bridge with a crown each. Many men were knighted. One was William, Sir Edward's squire who had changed after Norham. Some wondered why none of the billmen was honoured. Sir Edward had no answer, but I did. We were too lowly. My time at Mechelen had shown me the attitude of nobles. They felt that their blood made them somehow different. William had noble blood and could be knighted. I was from peasant stock. There might have been a time when I would have resented that but no longer. I would remain a billman for the present but it would not be my future. Sam had shown me a way out.

We made our way back to Hedingham and as the Earl was in residence Sam asked permission to leave his service. When he told him his intent it delighted the Earl who said that he would pay Sam a monthly stipend. Not only would Sam not struggle to make ends meet, but he would also be comfortable for the rest of his life. As a reward for my services, I was made Captain of billmen with Stephen as my sergeant. We were both paid more and I was a happy man for with the Cornish rebellion over, we had peace. The two leaders were hanged, drawn and quartered. The king showed mercy for the other leaders. They were just hanged until dead. Of course, their bodies were quartered but they did not have to endure the pain. The dead men were not replaced for the Earl and Sir Edward saw no war looming on the horizon. We settled into a routine of training and practice. Life was good.

Chapter 25

October 1497

Katie was within a few days of giving birth when the news came that Perkin Warbeck was back. He had landed in Cornwall and whipped up the defeated rebels into supporting him. The good news was that he had landed with just one hundred and twenty men. The bad news was that the Cornish had welcomed him. I knew that Sir John Bardolph would have had a hand in the landing. He knew that he could appeal to the Cornishmen and offer a kinder king than Henry. We were ordered to march west. We had much to do and I confess that Sam and his family were the last things on our minds but, as Sir Edward led us on the road west and we passed Sam's house, he and Katie came to bid us farewell.

Katie looked radiant and as I neared her she stepped forward to kiss me, "You come back safe, James of Ecclestone. When this bairn is born my appointed task is to find a bride for you."

She stepped back and Sam grasped my arm. His wound had hurt for a while and he was now a little thinner, but I could see the guilt on his face that Stephen and I were leaving for war and he was not, "Never mind her, you two make your own choices but be careful. This Warbeck is a slippery eel and I do not want you hunting him all over this land."

"Fear not. I hope the birthing goes well."

He smiled, "Aye, well the prospect of that fills me with fear as well. We shall see."

When we reached London, it was with the alarming news that many of the Cornish nobility had joined Warbeck and that Exeter had fallen. The king had sent Lord Daubeney with his army to face the Cornish but when the news reached him of the fall of Exeter, he joined us at our camp to the west of London. I was surprised when I was summoned to his side along with Sir Edward. His two sons, the princes Arthur and Henry were there along with the Earl of Oxford.

"This Warbeck has caused us enough trouble, Sir Edward, I would have him caught. De Vere thinks you were unlucky at Norham. I hope this time you are luckier. I have men procuring horses so that you can mount your small number of archers and billmen. I need you to join Lord Daubeney but you," he turned to me, "are charged with capturing or killing Warbeck. I care not which it is for I have wasted enough time on this pretender. To that end, I have procured two good horses for you and that other fellow who was so useful. You understand your quest?"

I nodded, "Yes, sire and I will do my best."

He waved an irritated hand, "You will succeed for that is my command."

Sir Edward now had a new squire, Wilfred, and as we left the house the king had commandeered, he asked, "Billmen and archers riding, my lord?"

Sir Edward laughed, "You can thank James of Ecclestone for that. Once it was discovered that he could ride it made the king assume that all men could ride."

For the most part, the men were both bemused and yet pleased that they would ride and not walk. We had but twenty archers and twenty billmen. Captain John could ride, and he helped us to mount the men. Like me, on my ride from Bramham, they would learn how to ride in the saddle. We reached Lord Daubeney four days later as he neared Glastonbury. I smiled sympathetically at the new riders for I knew they had chafed buttocks and thighs. Mistress Gurton's salve was long gone. The rebels had decided to make a stand, when they heard that we were approaching, at the tor. The high ground would give an advantage to their handful of cannons. Mindful of the king's orders which had been passed on to Lord Daubeney, our mounted contingent was placed close to him.

"Keep your horses handy in case the slippery Dutchman decides to flee."

That suited me as the thought of attacking up Glastonbury tor did not appeal in the least. We grazed our horses as Lord Daubeney arrayed his army to surround the tor. Although equal in numbers his lordship had far better troops. The Cornish guns, when they fired, sounded thin and I guessed that they were falconets that fired just a one-pound ball. While it could do damage to a man it was not as devastating as a bombard. By the time his lordship's guns were set up and began firing we could see some of the weaker elements fleeing.

I had spied the royal standard used by Perkin Warbeck. It was not on the top of the tor but lower down the slope and he was amongst a group of horsemen. I recognised him by the shining armour he had worn at Norham and the magnificent grey. I deduced that Sir John must be with him, but I did not recognise his livery.

"They are going to flee, Sir Gilbert, order the attack!"

His subordinate waved to the trumpeter who sounded three blasts and the whole of our army, our unit excepted, began to move towards the Cornish. They did not stand, and they fled west, back to their homes. I spied the shining armour and it fled not west but north and east.

I had not taken my eye from the standard and I shouted, "Sir Edward, our prey has started."

I pointed and Lord Daubeney shouted, "After him, Sir Edward."

I looked at the archers and billmen. Most would not be able to keep up, "Sir Edward, we should just take the best riders and horses."

Sir Edward was decisive. He pointed, "Captain Jack, take the best six riders and give them the best six horses. Giles, Paul, and Geraint, you are the best riders of the billmen. You come with us. The rest take your orders from Lord Daubeney."

By the time the fourteen of us had readied ourselves the shining armour was a good two miles away and in danger of disappearing. Some of the archers tried to urge their horses ahead of Sir Edward who snapped, "Keep it steady. We need not keep them in sight for a knight in shining armour accompanied by, how many was it twenty riders, cannot vanish?"

I urged my horse next to the knight, "They are heading north and east, my lord, why?"

He shrugged, "That is the main road, and we were attacking from the south and east. Who knows?"

One of the archers who had slowed down after being chastised said, "It is Pilton and then Shepton Mallet, my lord. He could be heading for Bristol." He smiled, "I was born here in the west."

"Thank you for that information. Then we must stop them from reaching Bristol where he may have a ship waiting." We spurred our horses down the road now that we had a better idea of the roads. "Captain John, your archers are lighter. Send the best two down the next road to the left and try to get ahead of them. Have them meet us at Shepton Mallet."

The archer shouted out his orders and two men peeled off to the left. We slowed in Pilton to confirm both the direction and numbers of those we sought. We learned that there were eighteen men and they were all plated. They had headed for Shepton Mallet.

As we rode that way I said, "From the description we heard, the men with Warbeck are the mercenaries. I wonder if Sir John has abandoned them?"

"It would be good to catch the last of the traitors, but Warbeck is the prize we seek. I am surprised that the mercenaries have stayed with him for his cause is obviously lost."

"They are paid for by the duchess and the emperor. Each day means more gold for them, and I think they are honourable men who would fulfil their contract." Despite their reputation, I still liked the mercenaries.

Both our archers and the men of Shepton Mallet told us that the riders had headed southeast and not north towards Bristol. One of the archers said, "We almost caught them, my lord, and they were still watering their horses when we rode into the village."

"Then they know we are after them and that will make the hunt harder as they will try to stop us following. "Captain John you and your archers lead. If they see you, they may think we only use archers. The less knowledge they have the more chance we have of finding them."

I wondered how far any of us could go and that occupied my mind as our mounts ate up the miles. It had been ten miles from the tor to Shepton Mallet and I knew not where their ultimate destination lay. As we neared the village of Bruton and the crossing of the River Brue, Sir John smacked his saddle, "They are heading for Southampton. It is a busy port and if they have any sense they will enter in ones and twos. That is where they head."

"Can they reach it today?"

We reined up in the village and let our horses join Captain John's archers to drink at the river.

Sir Edward looked up at the sky and shook his head, "All our horses are exhausted and there are more than fifty or sixty miles. They and we shall have to stop. It will be dark soon."

Captain John came over, "The villager said they left the village not long before we arrived. We can catch them before dark, my lord."

"Perhaps, let us mount!"

Each time we had stopped I had let my horse graze a little and I had taken some food from my meagre supplies. I had learned to eat when I could. I mounted and we trotted across the bridge and then began the steady canter we had adopted. The archers were just twenty paces ahead of us and I rode next to Sir Edward while Stephen was next to Wilfred. The dusk was preceded by threatening rain clouds and that added to the gloom. When the archers rode through the small wood it looked as though they were entering a tunnel. There were cries and the sudden squeals of horses and we spurred our mounts. Had there been an ambush? What we found was almost as bad. The clever Robert and Giuseppe had cunningly laid caltrops on the road. They had told me about these deadly weapons when in Mechelen. They were an easily constructed piece of metal with spikes protruding from three sides. Whichever way they landed a spike was sticking up and they had caught four of the archers. We reined in and saw the devastation. The horses could not be ridden, and three of the four archers had fallen and were lying injured. Even as we dismounted to assess the damage, I knew that the lead of the enemy was increasing.

Sir Edward was calmer than a very angry Captain John, "You four make your way back to Bruton. There was a smith there and he should be able to tend to your horses. Mayhap there is a gammer that can tend to your wounds."

"But my lord that means we are down to ten men and they will outnumber us by nine."

Sir Edward shrugged as he mounted, "Captain John, if there was just James and me left we would follow for Warbeck has been our prey since," he smiled, sadly "forever, it seems."

We headed through the dusk and did not stop for almost an hour until we came to the hamlet of Barrow. The enemy, it seemed, had thundered through without stopping an hour since. "We have to stop but I am heartened by the news."

A farmer offered us his barn and his wife sold us some potage. It could have been water to wash dishes and we would have been happy for we were famished. While we had waited for the food we had fed, watered and then brushed our weary horses.

The ten of us sat in a circle and spoke while we ate. There was a depressing air amongst most of the men and I could understand why. The enemy had outwitted us. Despite being in an enemy land they were moving with impunity and I knew why. The men of this land were with Lord Daubeney. There was no one to stop them and they had always known where they were going. The ride to Shepton Mallet had been to throw us off the scent. Had we not sent the archers ahead then we might have continued to Bristol.

Sir Edward put down his empty platter and drank the farmer's wife's ale from his costrel, "They have been lucky, and they will be more confident now. I know, Captain John, that you and your archers think they will escape but they will not. I cannot see them being afforded the shelter of a barn and the fodder for their horses. They will have to ride more slowly than we, and we now know where they are going. We rise at terces and ride while it is dark. It is fifty miles to Southampton, and they will struggle to reach that in one day."

"But they outnumber us."

"Captain John, I know we have only three archers but you are good archers?"

He bristled, "The best."

"Then when we close with them you loose your arrows and aim for the horses. A man cannot ride a dead animal. All we have to do is to get ahead of them and that is what I plan to do." We all leaned forward as we could see that he had thought this out. "Oxford is not far to the north and while I did not know Cornwall or Devon, I know the land twixt Oxford and Southampton. The road from Ringwood to Southampton passes through the New Forest. We do not follow the main road but take the road to Verwood and wait beyond Ringwood."

"We risk losing them."

"The road is smaller but quicker. We shall not lose them but if we do then it will be my task to tell the king that I have failed." He stood, "Now I go to make water and then to sleep. We need no guards here this night for there are farm dogs. I shall pray to God that he delivers our prey and then I shall sleep."

We all did as he said. He was right but I also had a reason to find Perkin Warbeck and end his reign. I could not get on with my life while he lived. He would always be the wraith haunting me. I prayed and then rolling into my cloak fell asleep.

It was dark when we rose and our moving woke the farm dogs and they, in turn, woke the farm. We would not be popular. We headed down a deserted road until, as dawn broke, we passed through Shaftesbury and Sir Edward, now leading, pointed us down the signed road to Verwood. He was right and this was a local road. We were lucky that it was not a market day and there were few carts and wagons on the road. Had there been then the hedgerows and walls would have slowed us down. We reached Ringwood in the middle of the afternoon and as our weary horses drank, discovered that no party of plated men had passed through the large village. We headed down the main road to Southampton and stopped when we reached the trees.

Leading our horses deep within it we returned to the borders of the forest. We had but a handful of men. Only three of my billmen and their billhooks were with us but that would have to do. Sir Edward had thought it out well. "Captain John, you and your archers go to the north side of the wood. That way the riders will be silhouetted by the setting sun, and you will be hidden. James, have your three billmen kneel before the archers with their billhooks braced against the ground to protect them. You and Stephen shall be with Wilfred and me. Our swords and daggers will draw their attention. As soon as they are in range, then slay their horses. Keep loosing until they are upon you." The six men nodded, "And God be with you. What we do is for the king and that means we serve God too."

We separated and I looked for a place of concealment. The bole of a large beech seemed appropriate, and I drew my sword and Tad's dagger. This might be bloody and might be my last fight. I turned and saw that Stephen had chosen the tree next to me, "You are my dearest friend Stephen and if I die then my purse and plate are yours."

He smiled, "James, you are my only friend, and I would give my life for you. It has been an honour to fight alongside you."

I felt better having said those words and we waited. We did not have long to wait for we heard the clattering hooves long before we saw the riders. When they did appear there were just seventeen of them. They must have had injured horses too. The odds were still in their favour, but we had a slight chance of winning. The sun behind them made them hard to see but its reflection on his shining armour told me where Perkin Warbeck rode, he was in the middle. There were eight men before him and I recognised Robert and Giuseppe who flanked him. There were six riders behind. It was when they were just one hundred paces from me that I saw it was Sir John Bardolf who led them. He wore an anonymous livery to remain hidden. At that moment Captain John's archers released their arrows. The horses that lumbered along the road to Southampton were weary and the range at which the arrows were loosed meant that the missiles went deep into weary horseflesh. They did not bring down the mounts immediately and the archers switched targets, mindful of Sir Edward's advice.

I heard Sir John shout, "A trap! Back!" He wheeled his horse which had an arrow in its chest and now had a second one in its rump.

These were professional soldiers, and they would not die easily. I saw the ones behind Perkin Warbeck overtake the pretender and ride at the archers. Screaming horses made the giving of any further orders impossible. One mercenary had been thrown from his horse and smashed his skull into a tree. Another had risen from the ground only to be decapitated by Geraint. One horse and rider had miraculously avoided a missile and he rode at Captain John who barely managed to send an arrow into his face at a range of ten feet. The mercenary fell from his saddle.

Sir Edward roared, "At them!" and the four of us leapt from cover swinging our weapons. A mercenary I recognised as Rolf, a Swabian, rode his dying horse at me. I knew he was a good horseman and that he should win the encounter but his dying horse stumbled and allowed me to swing my sword at Rolf's leg.

He had no plate there and I sliced through to the saddle. The spurting blood showered me as he fell from the saddle. We were among them and as Sir John, Robert, Perkin Warbeck and Giuseppe had turned and fled down the road we now outnumbered the survivors. Captain John and his two archers sent arrows into the backs of the last two mercenaries who tried to follow the other four. We had won but our prey eluded us still.

"Wilfred, Stephen, fetch the horses. Captain John, you and the archers, along with the other billmen stay with the mercenaries and horses. Take the wounded back to Ringwood and have them held at the king's pleasure. We four shall follow them."

"But there are four of them."

I shook my head, "Sir John's horse is wounded, and Warbeck will not fight."

We headed towards Ringwood, and I saw Sir John's dead horse, it had managed to get more than five hundred paces down the road before expiring. Of the knight, there was no sign although there was blood on the saddle. We reined in to examine it. Stephen provided the answer. His sharp eyes had spied the unharmed riderless horse following the other horses, "He has mounted a spare horse."

Sir Edward nodded, "We can ask at Ringwood."

When we reached Ringwood, the villagers were outside. One wounded mercenary and his dying horse had made it to the village. He lay bleeding his life away and when he saw me, he frowned and then gave a wry laugh, "So the spy has undone us. You always were clever."

Sir Edward asked, "How many riders were there and which direction did they take?"

The headman pointed, "There were four of them and they headed for Beaulieu Abbey. Perhaps they seek sanctuary there."

Sir Edward nodded and said, "My men will be coming and they have more dead and wounded with them."

As we turned to follow them down the road Wilfred said, "Sanctuary?"

"It will not be granted. The Abbot knows that it would displease the king."

The blood we passed told us that either men or horses were wounded.

Sir Edward said, "I will give them the chance to surrender."

"And Perkin Warbeck will take that offer for he has no wish to die."

"Then I hope that the mercenaries and Sir John also take a practical view of it although I doubt that the king will be willing to show leniency."

It was early afternoon and the men we pursued were weary. Most importantly their horses would be exhausted. We had just our four horses left from all those we had taken when the chase began. During the attack in the forest, only Sir John's horse had been a warhorse and that was now dead. Sir Edward was of the same mind and he urged us to be vigilant so that we did not suffer an attack such as we had inflicted on them. There was no attack and the three warriors waited for us in the road while a disconsolate Perkin Warbeck sat astride his horse thirty paces down the road. As we neared them Sir Edward said out of the side of his mouth, "Wilfred you are to support Stephen. James here knows these warriors better than anyone. Let us try words although from their stance they are here to fight."

He was right, their weapons were drawn. I saw that Sir John was hurt and he was not sitting as straight as the other two. Blood was on the flanks of all the horses, and I could see that the charge and arrows had taken the last of the fight from them.

Sir Edward reined in ten paces from them. None of us was wearing a helmet. I knew that to don mine now might precipitate a fight and I left it hanging from my cantle. Sir John spat and I saw blood in the spit, "Are your archers even now surrounding us to send arrows into backs?"

Sir Edward shook his head and said, evenly, "There are just the four of us and you have all fought bravely enough but this is over. Your cousin died on the Tweed and there is now no support for this pretender. Surrender to us and live."

He laughed, "To be taken to the tower and tortured to find out where others who share the same ideals as we live? I think not. We will take our chances. One knight, an ill-trained squire and two billmen will not delay us long and your horses will take us to safety."

I shook my head, "Perkin Warbeck will bever be king."

"Perhaps but I shall have the pleasure of slaying a foul spy and traitor! At them!"

That they had prearranged their charge while they awaited us was clear for he came directly for me. Giuseppe rode at Sir Edward and Robert, ignoring Wilfred, rode at Stephen. I barely had time to whip my mount's head around from the furious charge, and I had no weapon in my hand. Had I been fighting a fully fit Sir John then I should have died for he swung his sword at my chest. The blow was not as powerful as when I had sparred with him at Mechelen, but it was still well struck. It hit the folds of my cloak, the tunic and then the plate. I reeled but kept my saddle and I drew my sword. As much as I wanted to see how my friend fared, I was under no illusions. I was fighting for my life. It was my horse that saved me. He was a trained mount and responded to both reins and knees to enable me, as I regained my seat and pulled my sword from its scabbard to smash it into Sir John's back. He wore a backplate and the strike would have taken some of the edge from the blade, but I took satisfaction that he grunted in pain. I saw blood still trickling down the plates that covered his legs and I saw that his right gauntlet was bloody. He turned his weary horse to face me. His face was a mask of anger and pain. He knew he had failed and the smiling friend I had made in Mechelen now wanted one thing and one thing only; he would kill me before he died. I could hear steel clashing as the other five fought to the death. I was almost distracted by the thought that Warbeck might flee but, just in time, I knew we would catch him, and I brought my sword up to block the strike from the Yorkist knight.

Our blades rang together but it was Sir John's that was pushed back towards his face and I saw the shadow of doubt creep across his face. He had expected to win quickly. I had to use the two advantages I held. I was quicker and I was fitter than he was. No wound impaired my strikes and I used three quick blows, rained upon him to make him move backwards and to weaken his already weak right arm. Suddenly his left arm whipped up. I had not seen him drop his reins. His weary horse would go nowhere and he whipped up his left hand that held a mace. A well-struck blow from that would end the combat and my life quicker than anything else. I did the only thing I could I jerked my horse's head around to pirouette the animal. He still managed to make contact with me but it was my backplate he hit. It hurt but that merely encouraged me to finish the fight as soon as I could.

Turning around to face him I saw that was easier said than done and then I remembered a trick I had seen Robert use in the tourney at Mechelen. I let go of the reins and stood in the saddle. I brought my blade down. His sword arm was weak, and I knew he could not block the blow in time while the mace was too short to cause me a problem. Sir John Bardolph, the last of the Yorkist rebels died when the sword I had been given in Mechelen split his skull in twain.

It was not before time. Wilfred lay in a heap on the ground and Stephen was struggling to fight Robert. My friend was all that was important, and I rode at Robert's back and slid my sword into the gap in the plates at his back. It coincided with a blow from Stephen and the mercenary's head was almost severed. As Robert's body slid to join Wilfred on the ground, we both turned our horses. Giuseppe and Sir Edward were evenly matched.

I said, in Flemish so that there could be no misunderstanding, "Put up your sword Giuseppe. I do not wish to, but I will slip my sword into your back and save the life of my knight. This is over."

He nodded and dropped his sword, "I surrender although I know that I will die. At least the block is a more honourable death than a sword in the back. Robert deserved better from you James!" He shook his head, "I wish you had chosen our side, James. We might have had a chance. The boy was lost without you." I knew he meant Perkin Warbeck.

Sir Edward said, "We will see to Wilfred. I think it is your appointed duty to be the one to apprehend Perkin Warbeck."

Nodding I sheathed my sword and walked my horse to the disconsolate Dutchman who awaited his fate. As I neared him, I saw his hand go to his sword briefly and his eyes told me that he considered flight. Shaking my head I said, "It is over Pierrekin Wezebeque."

He looked at me in surprise, "You knew?"

I laughed, "Of course I knew. Your trouble is that you began to delude yourself and believe that you were truly King Richard IVth. I saw that when the emperor crowned you."

"And what happens now, James?" He stopped, "Is that your real name or is that another lie?"

"No, I am James of Ecclestone and as for what happens to you then that depends upon the King." I took his reins and began to lead the pretender back to the others. "If you would have the advice of one who, despite events, is still your friend, I would throw yourself upon the mercy of King Henry. Tell him all that he needs to know and perhaps, like Lambert Simnel, you will be allowed to live. Who knows, the life may be like the life at Mechelen."

He brightened at that. He was a simple soul in many ways. He wanted the lifestyle of a lord. Perhaps King Henry would grant him that.

To my relief, Wilfred was now standing and Stephen was bandaging his head. Sir Edward said, "Finally, it is over. Let us return to the king. Our work is done."

Epilogue

London 1499

We left Perkin Warbeck and Giuseppe at Taunton with the king. That he was grateful to us was clear and he promised great rewards. On the way west, Perkin acted as though I had saved him rather than captured him. I think he was a lonely man and he and I had enjoyed some sort of connection. Stephen was also a very gentle and kind man and Perkin took to him too. It made the journey easier. Giuseppe, for his part, was resigned to his fate. I had heard him speaking to Sir Edward and Wilfred during the lulls in our conversation.

"You have the right idea, Sir Edward. Find a lord who will pay you well and fight for him. When I die, I shall be a rich man but who will reap the benefit? Robert and I shared everything, and it should have gone to him." He had shrugged, "You make plans and then life happens. Still, I do not regret my life. I am forty summers old, and I have had a good life. Had there not been three of you then I would have won." He had smiled at Sir Edward's expression, "You are good, Sir Edward, but not as good as me."

When the king had slipped us five crowns each I ventured, "Sire, there is not an ounce of malice in Perkin Warbeck and Giuseppe was loyal to his lord. They do not deserve death."

The king had smiled at me, "For a billman, you have some noble qualities. I will reflect upon your words. For now, I have no further need of your services. England and I thank you for what you have done, all of you."

By the time we reached Hedingham, it was almost Christmas once more and soon we would be bidding farewell to 1497. There was joy for Katie had borne Sam a healthy son that they had named James but, for some reason, he was always Jamie. I was touched that they had named their first after me but I was happy that he was called Jamie.

When the Earl of Oxford arrived in February, he gave us the welcome news that Perkin Warbeck had been given a partial pardon and lived at court. His wife, however, Lady Catherine, was ordered to stay with King Henry's queen and so lived apart from the pretender. I was also delighted to hear that the king had pardoned Giuseppe with the warning that if he ever set foot in England he would be hanged. I was happy for him but sad that Robert had not enjoyed the same fate and I had ended his life. The last news I had was that Giuseppe had bought a large manor in Northern Italy. From what I knew Italy was a hotbed of intrigue and I could not see the mercenary enjoying a peaceful life.

For Stephen and me, life was good and we enjoyed the coins we had earned. Stephen and I were given permission to visit my family where, once again, I shared my largesse with all of them. I had to endure my mother's carping about the lack of a bride and grandchildren. My father joined in too and I knew that the next time I visited I would need to be married.

It was autumn when we returned to Hedingham. I had thought he would have enjoyed the life in a gilded cage but we learned the foolish Perkin Warbeck had tried to escape. His recapture saw him with Edward, the Earl of Warwick in the tower. The last man with a claim to the throne and one of those who had impersonated a prince were put together and I knew it was not good. So it proved. I know not if the king planned it this way but Perkin turned the head of Edward Plantagenet, Earl of Warwick, and in November they tried to escape. The Earl of Warwick had spent most of his life in the tower and Perkin Warbeck was ill-equipped for any sort of adventure. They were captured and Perkin Warbeck, no doubt under the duress of torture confessed to all that was put before him. The two were tried and convicted. Warbeck was led from the Tower to Tyburn, London on 23rd November 1499, where he read out a confession and was hanged. John de Vere, 13th Earl of Oxford presided over the trial of Edward Plantagenet, and he was found guilty of treason. Warwick was beheaded for treason on Tower Hill.

So as the century ended King Henry had disposed of all his enemies and England was safe. When we celebrated Christmas that year, in Sam's house, I was sad for neither of the men who had been executed posed a real threat to King Henry. But King Henry had struggled to get his hands on the crown, and he would not relinquish it easily. As the year of our lord, 1500 began I put my thoughts to my future. I had my whole life before me and I was already rich. Did I wish to do as Giuseppe and Sam had done? Did I want to hang up my billhook and follow a peaceful path? I confess that the death of Perkin Warbeck confused me and so I put off any decision I might make. Fate had put me here and I was sure that Fate would decide my future.

The End

Glossary

Carole- a song sung at Christmas and normally accompanied by a dance or a procession

Costrel- A wooden beaker with a hook to hang from a belt; used on a campaign to drink

Falchion- a short sword with a curved end. A one bladed weapon

Gardyvyan- a sheet containing all the equipment that an archer needed

Gong scourer- a man hired to empty human dung and dispose of it.

Goose/geese- slang for whores

Goose bite- a euphemism for Venereal Disease

Hackney- a good riding horse, superior to a rouncy

Jack- a padded vest sometimes made of leather and strengthened by metal. Often called a brigandine

Marchpane- marzipan

Mesne- an old-fashioned word for the men who serve a knight

Reiver-men on both sides of the Anglo-Scottish border who raid

Rondel dagger- the most common type of dagger with a short crosspiece and two blades

Rouncy- a good riding horse

Sallet- the most popular type of helmet at the time having a flared back to protect the neck

Terces- the third hour of the day

Twesilhaugh- Twizell Castle in Northumberland

Historical Background

The real characters I have used all did, largely, what I said. Lambert Simnel became employed by King Henry and ended his life as a hawker for the king saw that he had been used. It was a treacherous time and King Henry was ruthless just as his son, King Henry VIII would be.

The battles and actions I describe all happened. As usual my hero's involvement is fictional. I used James as a spy so that I could give an insight into Warbeck's life. Henry Tudor, however, did use both spies and what we might term agent provocateur. He had fought hard to get the crown and he was not going to let it slip away easily.

The jokes I have Sam recount all came from a Tudor book. Although published a few years after Sam tells them I am guessing that they must have been around. The book was called The Book of Riddles and was produced by the man who took over from William Caxton. He is called the first typographer and with the support of Margaret Beaufort, the King's mother, made books more accessible to the masses. His name and I love this, was Wynkyn de Worde! He was the kindle of the sixteenth century introducing books to a wider audience.

The improbability of two unlikely pretenders in such a short time is hard to swallow yet the followers of the White Rose were so desperate for the removal of Henry Tudor that they supported the two young men. If I have portrayed them as victims, it is because it is how I think they should be viewed. At best they were gullible and sought the life of a celebrity. Are they any different from the contestants on a TV show?

The almost Monty Pythonesque life of Perkin Warbeck beggars belief and I would have been hard put to make it up myself. James and Stephen's involvement is purely fictional and, as far as I know, there was no Sir John Bardolph. Lord Lovell disappeared after the Battle of Bosworth Field. A skeleton was discovered in a priest hole in his home but there was no proof it was him. Such material is grist to a writer's mill.

King Henry was accused of deliberately putting Perkin Warbeck in the same cell as Edward Plantagenet just to encourage the two to flee. That way he could finally, and legally, end the Plantagenet line and ensure that all dissension in his land was ended. To be truthful I can believe it. When you research a man you come to know him. While I think I would have enjoyed the company of King Henry V[th], I think a night in the company of King Henry VIIth, would have been a different matter!

James of Ecclestone will return. I was inspired to write this book by a visit in 2021 to Flodden Field. That took place in 1515 and so there is another novel to come.

Other books by Griff Hosker

If you enjoyed reading this book, then why not read another one by the author?

Ancient History

The Sword of Cartimandua Series
(Germania and Britannia 50 A.D. – 128 A.D.)
Ulpius Felix- Roman Warrior (prequel)
The Sword of Cartimandua
The Horse Warriors
Invasion Caledonia
Roman Retreat
Revolt of the Red Witch
Druid's Gold
Trajan's Hunters
The Last Frontier
Hero of Rome
Roman Hawk
Roman Treachery
Roman Wall
Roman Courage

The Wolf Warrior series
(Britain in the late 6th Century)
Saxon Dawn
Saxon Revenge
Saxon England
Saxon Blood
Saxon Slayer
Saxon Slaughter
Saxon Bane
Saxon Fall: Rise of the Warlord
Saxon Throne
Saxon Sword

Medieval History

The Dragon Heart Series
Viking Slave
Viking Warrior
Viking Jarl
Viking Kingdom
Viking Wolf
Viking War
Viking Sword
Viking Wrath
Viking Raid
Viking Legend
Viking Vengeance
Viking Dragon
Viking Treasure
Viking Enemy
Viking Witch
Viking Blood
Viking Weregeld
Viking Storm
Viking Warband
Viking Shadow
Viking Legacy
Viking Clan
Viking Bravery

The Norman Genesis Series
Hrolf the Viking
Horseman
The Battle for a Home
Revenge of the Franks
The Land of the Northmen
Ragnvald Hrolfsson
Brothers in Blood
Lord of Rouen
Drekar in the Seine
Duke of Normandy
The Duke and the King

Tudor Warrior

Danelaw
(England and Denmark in the 11th Century)
Dragon Sword
Oathsword

New World Series
Blood on the Blade
Across the Seas
The Savage Wilderness
The Bear and the Wolf
Erik The Navigator

The Vengeance Trail

The Reconquista Chronicles
Castilian Knight
El Campeador
The Lord of Valencia

The Aelfraed Series
(Britain and Byzantium 1050 A.D. - 1085 A.D.)
Housecarl
Outlaw
Varangian

**The Anarchy Series England
1120-1180**
English Knight
Knight of the Empress
Northern Knight
Baron of the North
Earl
King Henry's Champion
The King is Dead
Warlord of the North
Enemy at the Gate
The Fallen Crown
Warlord's War

Tudor Warrior

To Murder A King
The Throne
King Henry IV
The Road to Agincourt
St Crispin's Day
The Battle For France
The Last Knight

Tales from the Sword I
(Short stories from the Medieval period)

Tudor Warrior series
England and Scotland in the late 145th and Early 15th
century
Tudor Warrior

Conquistador
England and America in the 16th Century
Conquistador

Modern History

The Napoleonic Horseman Series
Chasseur à Cheval
Napoleon's Guard
British Light Dragoon
Soldier Spy
1808: The Road to Coruña
Talavera
The Lines of Torres Vedras
Bloody Badajoz
The Road to France
Waterloo

The Lucky Jack American Civil War series
Rebel Raiders
Confederate Rangers
The Road to Gettysburg

Tudor Warrior

The British Ace Series
1914
1915 Fokker Scourge
1916 Angels over the Somme
1917 Eagles Fall
1918 We will remember them
From Arctic Snow to Desert Sand
Wings over Persia

Combined Operations series
1940-1945
Commando
Raider
Behind Enemy Lines
Dieppe
Toehold in Europe
Sword Beach
Breakout
The Battle for Antwerp
King Tiger
Beyond the Rhine
Korea
Korean Winter

Tales from the Sword II
(Short stories from the Modern period)

Other Books
Great Granny's Ghost (Aimed at 9-14-year-old young people)

For more information on all of the books then please visit the author's website at www.griffhosker.com where there is a link to contact him or visit his Facebook page: GriffHosker at Sword Books